Cover Design and layout by Manta Publishing
Photo By Richard Bennett
Cover Photo is a single frame of HI8 video tape shot
at one-hundred and ten feet in natural light, off Cayman
Brac in the Cayman Islands BWI.

Deep Quest
The Entry

An Adventurous Lifelong
Challenge Underwater

by

Richard Thomas Bennett

Manta Publishing Company

Deep Quest
The Entry

Copyright © 2003
First printing 2004
By Richard Thomas Bennett
Printed in the United States of America
First printing 2004

All rights reserved. No part of this book may be reproduced or transmitted in any form or by any means, electronic or mechanical, including photocopying, recording or by any information storage and retrieval system without written permission from the author, except for the inclusion of brief quotations in a review.

Library of Congress Cataloging in Publication Data
Bennett, Richard Thomas 1939-
Deep Quest: the entry
Includes index
ISBN 0-9740816-5-5
1. Divers (scuba, hard hat) United States. 2. Diving (Deep Diving, Exploration) 3. Wreck Diving 4. Rescue & Recovery
PS3602 E6645 D44 2003

Manufactured in the United States of America

Deep Quest / by Richard Thomas Bennett - First edition

Published by:

Manta Publishing Company
11609 W. Vliet Street
Wauwatosa Wisconsin 53226

Quotes

"All of us who have actually been in the sea and witnessed its value, must unite to save it for our children"

"We divers are witnessing the demise of the precious wilderness we discovered."

"Divers are the natural crusaders"

Jacques-Yves Cousteau Undersea explorer
(1919-1997)

"Interest in the sea is not a matter of mere curiosity our very survival may depend on it."

John F. Kennedy
35th President of the United States of America
(1917-1963)   (1961-1963)

To the reader

Attempting to write a book about oneself is difficult at best. Telling the true story while reliving each time frame with accurate depiction is also a daunting task. Remembering dates, times and names was by far the single most mind-numbing chore in the preparation of this book. The fact that I changed the names of all the people I brought to this story, didn't relieve me of the accuracy I wanted to portray.

Deep Quest The Entry is based on a true story. For the segments that take place in Andrew Boyd's office in the present time are fictional. It is based on my forty-eight years of sport and commercial diving. I have changed the names of the characters and some places including my own (Andrew Boyd in the story).

Deep Quest The Entry is written as a collection of short stories in chronological order. It was my hope that in these days of truncated periods of relaxation the reader could read a chapter, put the book down and not feel they were left hanging.

I personally interviewed many of the main characters to insure an accurate portrayal of the events. The richness of the narratives could only be reveled by the original participants. After forty or more years they were far more interesting than any novelist could concoct. Many of the terms from the early days used in this book are from the period. Many are seldom used today, such as skin diver for scuba diver or tanks for scuba cylinders and dive shop for training center.

Richard T. Bennett

Contents

Quotes	....	VII
To The Reader	....	VIII
Contents	....	IX
Contents Cont.	....	X
Acknowledgments	....	XI
Acknowledgements Cont.	....	XII
Chapter One	Deep Water Marine Salvage Co.	13
Chapter Two	Blood Bath	22
Chapter Three	The Wreck of the Jenny Bell	28
Chapter Four	Andrew Battles the Darkness	38
Chapter Five	Helmet Memories	46
Chapter Six	Adventures End-Ultimate Dive Center	51
Chapter Seven	An Angel Lost	65
Chapter Eight	The Army Way	78
Chapter Nine	The 2500 Foot Fall	91
Chapter Ten	Raising the Shrouded Wreck	101

Contents

Chapter Eleven   Collision of the Freighter Endeavor 122

Chapter Twelve   Taibbi Chemical first Meeting 146

Chapter Thirteen   Record Deep Dive 159

Chapter Fourteen   Modeling and Montgomery Ward 183

Chapter Fifteen   Missing in Canada 191

Chapter Sixteen   The Old School Yard 216

Chapter Seventeen   Canada Outback 230

Chapter Eighteen   Royal Mounted Police 242

Acknowledgment

I couldn't have finished a chapter without the generosity of the people who contributed to the making of this book. I would like to express my appreciation to everyone by giving credit to them for their enormous contributions.

The idea of the Deep Quest trilogy was born out a love for water. As simple as that might seem it's the truth. My life has been devoted to being in it, around it and under it for more than 48 years. Throughout that time I have worked in it, played in it and found love because of it. None of these things could have been accomplished without the support of and help of the people I will mention here.

Roberta Ricco was the first person to review Deep Quest. She is a Milwaukee educator of the highest quality, with a sympathetic and untiring heart. A woman of superior talents and understanding she took me by the hand and moved me to write the bulk of this first book. It was her patient coaching that guided me through half of this book.
She was also kind enough to edit my first draft and not fall out of her easy chair laughing. She bought me a New Roget's Thesaurus and Webster's Dictionary for Christmas that first year. I wondered what she was trying to say?

Barbara Mackowey, a certified Dive master in her own right, who with the help of an interpreter managed to untangle my pages and find some kind of flow to the remaining chapters. She also made footnotes that guided me through the rambling I sometimes found myself caught up in.

Carolina Garcia, an assistant managing editor for the Milwaukee Journal was gracious enough to take time out of her busy schedule to read my book and write a valuable critique. Her very positive approach to the review gave me the encouragement to press on. One of the biggest problems with writing is the nagging self-doubt in the quiet hours of the morning. "Is my book good enough to publish?" Carolina helped ease that anxiety and helped me press forward.

XII

Marilyn Kindwall used all the resources of her three masters degrees to move me away from the "writers block excuse" while I wrote the last three charters of this book. I am indebted to her for her primary edit of my book and her candid review.

Lynn Mattson, who quietly and consistently pushed the book to completion. Always there, always saying the right things to soothe the delicate sensitivity of a first time writer.

And last but not least a thank you for two nuns from the Sisters of St. Francis Assisi. Sister Lanor and Sister Lucilda who worked for weeks correcting spelling and grammar. Their dedication to correctness is a tribute to the many years they gave to educating school children.

And last but not least one of my oldest friends, Warren McMahon (Ward McNair in the book) who has made hundreds of dives and had gotten me into most of my boy hood troubles. Always there, always ready to back me up. Thanks pal.

Chapter 1

Deep Water Marine Salvage Company

It is almost dawn. The morning sun has etched a hazy, yellow glow on the horizon of Lake Michigan. The Milwaukee skyline has not broken through the phantom shadow images of the night. Traffic along the lake drive is sparse, but it will build into a winding hypnotic snake moving headlong into the heart of the city. Headlights cut into the blackness and taillights blink in the absorbing rhythm of the undulating metaphor below.

Andrew Boyd, Chairman of the Board and President of Hydro-Tec International, has had another long, sleepless night, a night filled with pressure from meeting deadlines. Daily schedules that could eventually mean the success or failure of ocean freight companies large or small. He ponders, "All over the world, at this very moment at least one marine disaster is playing out its final death knell. Millions of dollars in cargo and dozens of lives could descend into watery graves. In a few hours, I will begin another day in the life and death struggle with the dynamics of the sea. Will I make the right choices? Will I give the right directions?"

He stands; staring out the floor to ceiling bronze tinted windows, slightly stooped with hands perched supportive on his hips. His six-foot, two hundred forty pound frame isn't rotund, but he could use a few months of hard core diving to reduce his mid-Atlantic ridge. Andrew is close to retirement. In the forty-eight years that have passed since his first dive in a Wisconsin stone quarry, the daily work load of meetings and decision making have exacted a toll. For one, he has little time to return to the pure joy of diving. Trips to the Caribbean are all business and he is too bogged down with meetings to steal time for a relaxing dive. Years ago, Andrew taught stressed-out business students that scuba diving is a way to relieve that stress. Ironically, now he doesn't listen to his own voice.

At sixty-four, he enjoys perfect health and has more stamina than many of his employees. But something is missing. Lately he finds himself reliving the past, forcing himself to remember the smallest details, his newly found source of escapism from the pressures of grave responsibilities.

Hydro-Tec's Headquarters are located on the thirty-first floor looking east over Lake Michigan. His staff will react in their usual way when they arrive for work in a few hours and find the boss has again spent the night.

"Hello boss, long night."

"Morning Mr. Boyd. In early or up late?"

Andrew stands more erect pressing his hands into the small of his back and stretches backward. He looks out at the empty offices, smiles and turns to his desk. He shuffles a stack of papers aggressively and taps their edges on his desk. The documents are a presentation he will give to his contemporaries the night of his retirement. He lays them in the same order as before. Staring at the stack momentarily he forces himself to reread the first few pages one more time. He will speak tonight about the marine salvage business and how brisk it has been over the last few years with the surge of international ocean freight traffic; the increasing United States demand for oil, electronics, food and automobiles, and how that market will help support economies of developing countries. He will calculate the effects of the accelerating maritime shipping business.

He reads, "Yes, decade after decade, new third world countries will prosper and reach out for democracy. Many will achieve their goals. But their limited natural resources are put at risk in the global market. For guaranteed independence, their resource exports must exceed their imports. The long-term effect of this balancing act may prove disastrous to their nonrenewable resources.

Each time a new trader in the global market succeeds, the ripple effect breeds a new contender. Like the land, the oceans and lakes of our planet have a growing traffic problem."

Andrew pauses and lays the writing down, he then opens the top left drawer of his desk and plucks a navy blue folder from it.

"Let's see, maybe I can use part of this old speech."
He begins. "Now that the superpowers have developed a mutual long-range trust, new satellites will be used for traffic control instead of people control. But until that system is in place, accidents will happen at an alarming rate, and the seas will claim the careless and unwary. Oil spills will continue, and nature will pay the ransom.
Island economies will be devastated when their shorelines and wildlife are covered with thick tar-like goo. Small countries will lose years of tourism, and lawsuits will bring companies to the brink of bankruptcy. Every hour of every day, somewhere in the world, a marine tragedy takes place and ten more are narrowly averted". He flattens the papers on the desk. "God help us", he says.

Andrew's anguish over his roll in the tug-of-war with the sea is at the core of his sleepless nights. Many nights, Andrew simply sleeps on his office sofa. His private office looks more like an apartment than a business domain. It is complete with a shower, dressing area and kitchenette hidden behind decorative partitions. Soon his outer office elevator will deliver its talented and energetic crew. His staff, recruited from all over southeastern Wisconsin, share a passionate enthusiasm for the job. A few even travel the ninety miles up from Chicago just to work for him. The Hydro-Tec nerve center has an office manager, five secretaries, two computer gurus and a satellite communications specialist to handle the work assignments there. In the field are deep-water specialists, a field manager, and one structural engineer to handle the heavy equipment.

Andrew Boyd anchors the team. The office staff grows by six or eight people several times a month when selected field personnel arrive and stay from two to seven days, depending on the training or update programs scheduled. Staff and close friends call Andrew "AB." No one knows why, not even Andrew. Just seemed easier to say than Andrew, and it stuck. Andrew was never one to let formality stand in the way of friendship or business. Although he felt comfortable in a suit or a tuxedo, he likes being barefoot in a tee-shirt better.

Andrew shuffles again through the retirement presentation notes pressing his knuckles into the desktop.

"In our business, nothing is taken for granted. No two marine salvage assignments are the same. No two people respond the same way under the unusual stress each job presents.

Hydro-Tec International is a global marine salvage company that has offices in thirteen countries. Each of these satellite operations is strategically placed so that Hydro-Tec can respond instantly to any disaster call worldwide.

A special marine salvage unit is deployed immediately to execute the rescue of personnel. At HTI, "Went Missing" may represent not only a lost or submerged vessel, but any marine tragedy.

Today Defense Department budget cuts have put pressure on the Navy to reduce costs in all non-defense departments. Emergency response and safety departments are one of the first to suffer when budgets are cut. The search and recovery units of the Navy are just such a group. There is never enough money for the task at hand.

Hydro-Tec staff fills in the void when the government occasionally needs to come to a full complement of salvage hardware. Our expertise in ocean and deep-water recovery has made our global hardware and us almost indispensable to many recoveries.

Our mission is to never let nature win the heart-wrenching game of "went missing".

With an increase in ocean traffic since the early 1970s, we have had little trouble reaching a status in the fortune 500 companies by rectifying the mistakes and misfortune of others.

Andrew backs away from the desk and sits gingerly into his executive chair safeguarding an old back injury. He stares out his office window wondering about turning over control of his company when the time comes. "Will they be ready to take over?" he asks himself.

"Did he instill the lessons about trusting in your partner and the trust from believing in your top-side support crew?" He thinks about his staff. "They all have talent and experience. But did they also learn that in this business it is about loyalty, about believing in each other?" These are the things that made my company. It isn't about steel, cables, water, and buoyancy, its about people."

Andrew swivels the chair back to face his desk, with its massive oak top made from a cargo hatch cover and coated with a thick layer of clear polyurethane. Wormholes and scars from misplaced hammers are visible through the clear surface. He pulls another stack of papers from the filing trays and takes a dolphin-headed pen from his shirt pocket and begins marking the pages.

The papers are the second half of his presentation to the people who will succeed him: a brief primer he hopes will give them the essences of the business he built.

Andrew begins again to read aloud his rough first draft.

"Hydro-Tec's global operations employ 169 people worldwide; sixty of which are the best-trained deep ocean divers available. The remaining staff comprises the engineering department, office personal media and sales. Our underwater team is the best 'in situation' divers in the world. They are trained and gifted, with a natural instinct to resolve any unforeseen event or danger that may hinder their escape to the surface. Our Med Staff is skilled in deep water malaise should our divers be placed at risk. With their assistance, divers will receive immediate attention upon surfacing. Most often, medical surface treatment would consist of first aid and-or hyperbaric compression.

Women and men share mutual responsibility underwater at HTI. If the assignment is within the physical ability of a woman, she gets the underwater work assignment. If not, her role is no less important when assigned as a topside dive master. Topside dive masters usually have served an apprenticeship as divers, trained in underwater operations and how to extricate from an 'in situation.' This firsthand experience prepares them for the 'someday' they hope will never arrive. In a like manner, astronauts commanding a spacecraft don't operate independently. When the pucky hits the fan and astronauts have used up all available resources, they call on ground mission control for help. The best person to have on the control console is another astronaut.

Similarly, with diving missions, topside dive masters make life support adjustments and decisions, while the diver concentrates on solving the underwater task at hand. Taking a diving console that resembles a small television studio underwater is not practical.

Air and gas mixtures, communications, heat sources, and constant diver medical updates need to be interpreted by the dive master and staff to monitor the working diver's safety. Our dive masters are divers first and gauge grunts (affectionate term for someone who monitors the divers below) second. A gauge grunt needs to be there as part of the team to help resolve diver problems.

Watching a monitor for a diver's pulse rate to escalate, or trying to interpret a radio communication that's garbled is all part of the job. A diver using lighter-than-air gases to breathe is difficult to understand. Someone who has experienced that predicament first hand, can better appreciate the situation.

Our professional divers are a breed apart. But in many ways they are like law enforcement personnel and firefighters. They knowingly go to work when there is a high degree of risk or injury, maiming or death. Most of their training is devoted to getting out of an "in situation."

Daily, these situations may be trivial, but in every long-term career, there is a time when their self-resolve is tested. Yet each day their main objectives are to relieve someone's misery or distress. Their mentality encompasses trust and an almost covetous relationship between partners and team members. Once you're into this mentality, your partner becomes almost a bloodline. Life is always a treasured and precious entity. To risk it for another, whether on the street or in a deep ocean environment, requires unconditional partner devotion. Partner devotion transcends survival, which courses deeply through the soul. If survival is not given up voluntarily, the inner self will fight like hell to preserve it. It is not uncommon in these careers for a professional to risk eminent danger to save his or her partner.

Rather placid periods are interspersed with hectic, adrenaline-surged encounters with threats that require expert resolve and ingrained training. Those who strive to 'protect and serve' soon realize they don't walk in isolation. Eventually, a partner will be needed to cover their tail feathers. The forged bonds are secure and rarely need discussion, but are always felt subliminally.

Divers and topside dive masters also develop this same bond, which is so steady they think alike and react alike. No persons outside the team can aspire to this level, because no one outside this underwater world could share the same degree of intensity and skill.

At Hydro-Tec, this attitude is no accident but rather a planned evolution of keen, instinctive unification between partners. No one would put their own hide on the line unless they believed it would be done for them. This is the code that defies explanation. It is this code that provides the mental mastery to override the adrenaline rush that interferes with sound decision-making. It is a code that is necessary when a diver advances down a sunken ship's hallway 450 feet below the Atlantic surface. If the ceiling collapses behind a diver, he needs to know that top-side support is right there beside him; that they are on the same frequency. No doubt can exist that our topside personal will not hold things together, think clearly, and make crucial life and death decisions, particularly if a diver is too weak or injured to make those decisions.

It is a voice that instills confidence at a critical moment. It booms down into the headset when the diver may be trapped face down in a swirl of turbulent sediment. When diffused particles dance and shimmer in front of the helmet window, they distort the light and shape of the normal. This is when it pays to have a partner top-side that instinctively understands this dilemma.

Here at HTI divers and topsides can switch their roles repeatedly during the same underwater operation. Sooner or later, in the whole of one's diving career, he or she will have to rely totally on someone else. To be dependent and then dependable is a succession of roles that builds stamina, character and emotional resolve. It is a natural evolution that an experienced diver will become an expert top-side support technician."

Andrew lays part two of his brief down and pauses, looking out into the space of his office. He thinks, "How did we get here? What is it that I can teach the new staff and the old timers to insure they will carry on a safe business? We are the sum of all the things I've tried." He swivels his chair to look out the window again.

Andrew recalls the many careers he has had in his sixty-four years of life.

At thirteen, he had tarred the roofs of office buildings: a miserable smelly job that his mother said "drove her to distraction".

He would stand in his underwear on the screened-in back porch, not allowed to enter the house with his tar-splattered clothing. Summer or winter, off came the work boots, shirt and pants. They were rolled into a ball and placed on the doormat. He would slip on a bathrobe and head straight for the basement and the washing machine then on to the tub. Andrew's mother had a nose that could smell cigarette smoke two houses away, down wind. As a teenager Andrew had tested the theory a number of times. He always got caught.

The roofing job only lasted until he turned fifteen when his aunt recruited him to set bowling pins. Andrew's short-lived career as a pin-setter ended abruptly, when a fellow pin-setter accused of stealing money from the locker room, was confronted by Andrew. They exchanged words that exploded into a fistfight and ended up in the pin pit. Bowlers were oblivious to the brawl and kept on bowling. It was hard to tell which did more damage, the pins and balls or the wildly swinging pugilists. The pin racks came down several times, pressing Andrew's shoulder close to the floor. The bowling alley manager hurried to the pit and lifted both boys out by their hair. He tongue lashed the boys for several minutes before he fired them. Andrew knew that was nothing compared to what would happen when he got home. His aunt had invited Andrew and his mother to live with her shortly after Andrew's grandmother died. His mother had been struggling for years to make a home for her two boys. She accepted the invitation to live with her sister long enough for her to save enough money for a new apartment.

When Andrew arrived home his mother would be working her night shift and his aunt would serve as the welcoming committee.

"What happened to you?...Wait, let me guess, you had another fight. How many is that?...Wait, that's four since you moved in here. Is that all you think about, fighting and that dangerous water business? All you do is talk about going underwater. I can't see how you think you can make a living out of such foolishness". Aunt Mary would later recant her opinion about the dive business, especially when Andrew's dive company celebrated 25 years in business and had raised a million dollars for charities.

Chapter 2

Blood Bath

Andrew Boyd rolled over on his side, dropping his left shoulder as he looked at the sheer face of the limestone wall in front of him. The exhaust from his scuba regulator bubbled freely toward the surface. A menacing rock outcropping loomed ten feet above his head and shattered the stream of shimmering mushroom-like bubbles into a thousand tiny globes. They danced along the quarry wall until reaching their destination forty-five feet above. Andrew looked down at Ward McNair, his buddy since grade school. He was right where he should be in darkened water, within visual distance. Ward and Andrew already had called in sick to their employer, American Motors, for the tenth time that summer of 1957. Scuba diving had become their obsession. They had logged more than forty dives since the first of January.

Today, just for relaxation, they had completed a circumnavigation of the Racine Quarry at fifty feet and were about to come to the surface. Andrew pointed to his dive watch and held up four fingers, indicating to Ward that they would travel for four more minutes and then ascend. Andrew and Ward, always safety conscious, carefully logged their underwater time and pre-planned to ascend slowly to help relieve the buildup of nitrogen gas in their bodies. Andrew led the way along the wall, checking every crevice and crack for something of interest. He rotated ninety degrees again, looking up the face of the wall. In the distorted backlight of the surface, Andrew saw a twisting, contorting blob coming down straight at him. He shifted and came to an upright position, watching as the blob pulsated past his head on its way to the bottom. Andrew tried to make out the object. Green smoke trailed out behind it in long jade whiffs, looking like lazy cigarette smoke hovering near a lamp.

The object did an almost hypnotic dance, and became level with his eyes. For the first time, he could see it surface-lit on the topside.

Blood Bath 23

"Oh my God, that green stuff is blood. The water this deep must have filtered out the red wavelength. Oh Jesus, and there's lots of it," he thought as the object, now identified as a towel, drifted past his waist.

Before Andrew could fully digest what he had just seen, Ward yanked on his fin from below, scaring Andrew out of his trance. Ward was holding a large rock in his hand and pointed his gloved finger to the top of his head. He pointed up frantically several times. Andrew recognized the gesture, but shrugged with an air of indecision.

Suddenly, a shower of rocks plummeted down upon the divers. Ward, impulsive would not let anyone get away with that kind of act and he pushed off with a powerful fin stroke and headed for the surface. Andrew managed to restrain his muscular friend now fueled with adrenaline, but Ward still dragged Andrew 10 feet higher before he calmed down. That wasn't an easy task, when he couldn't talk. Having spent fifty minutes at depth, they were required to ascend slowly and make a safety stop. They rested on a ledge just fifteen feet from the surface to take their off-gassing requirement. Comfortable with their safety stop, they inched their way up the wall to the surface. Ward was shoulder to shoulder with Andrew as they broke surface.

Abruptly, Andrew's head was squeezed and pulled upward! His thick neoprene rubber hood slid over his mouth, forcing his regulator into his upper lip. He could hear someone yelling instructions, but the commands were muffled and distorted by the rubber hood.

Andrew pulled down on his hood collar with one hand, reached up with his other hand, and grabbed his assailant's wrist. The yelling suddenly stopped but Andrew's feet had only a fragile hold on a waist-deep underwater ledge.

He twisted the aggressor's wrist a little more and pulled it down until he was face to face with his antagonist. Andrew yanked his diving mask and hood off and threw them on a grassy patch of ground.
His attacker was now whimpering, "Wait, Wait" And began to explain in a pleading voice.

As Andrew released his wrist-numbing grip, the man blurted out, "We need your oxygen! There's a guy up there bleeding bad! We need it because his neck is cut real deep! We need to force oxygen into him!"

Andrew, not realizing how serious things were, snapped back.

"We don't carry oxygen. Its only compressed air. Same as you breathe!" Ward was already out of his equipment and stomping up the short knoll eager to find someone to engage.

Ward noticed there was a cluster of young people in their early and late teens lingering in a huddle at the top of the knoll. He forcefully spread two people apart and demanded loudly, "Who the hell else was dropping rocks on us?" He had dismissed the guy near the water's edge because Andrew already had a piece of him. He was looking for more challenging prey anyway. Size or numbers didn't matter. He knew that by the time things started getting messy, Andrew would be there to back him up. There wasn't time for a reply from anyone before a spray of blood hit Ward's legs.

The young man attending the injured victim had lifted another blood soaked towel away from his neck checking to see if the bleeding had stopped. It hadn't. Andrew, still standing on the ledge, commanded the boy who had grabbed his head, "Back off, pal and let me out of here!" He dropped his attacker's throbbing hand and climbed out of the water. Andrew hadn't noticed that his own hand was covered in blood until he started to remove his wet suit gloves. He looked down, staring in disbelief at the amount of blood dripping from his glove. His eyes refocused between his feet. "The ground man, the ground is covered with blood." Andrew, dumbfounded, brought his gaze back up to the boy standing before him. The frail boy mumbled, "That's what I've been trying to tell you. The guy up there is bleeding God awful."

Andrew cast his eyes again at the ground. He precisely moved his feet, stepping out of the small river of blood that was now dripping into the quarry. The blood spread out on the surface of the water like an oil slick.

Eventually, it began to sink in the form of long, stringy stalactites. Andrew was stunned at the sight of all that blood. His eyes never left the trail of blood as he followed the red river back up the knoll to its source. Andrew could only see the lower half of the victim's legs among the numerous people bent over him. The victim's feet were twitching and his legs were bare and ashen.

By the time Andrew joined Ward it was nearly over. The boy trembled at every limb and suddenly he was still. They had witnessed bloody scenes before in their short eighteen years of life, but this was the worst. There was no heartbeat and no breath. The young man had bled to death. The entire event had taken only a few minutes to unfold.

Now it was quiet; no one spoke as the boy lay as if asleep. His face no longer has the anguish of pain, the terror of knowing he is dieing. Behind the group, a rescue team could be seen racing around the rim of the quarry. They carried a stretcher and a dangling first aid kit, but they were too late. The cut was so deep it would have been impossible to stop the bleeding.

The two rescue men knelt down next to the victim and checked for vital signs. Finding none, they pronounced him dead. The young man's face was still visible, but it had a waxen pallid appearance and appeared unreal. The rescuers reverently placed him on a stretcher and covered him with a white sheet. The accumulation of blood beneath the sheet began to seep through and create gruesome, Rorschach-like designs on the surface. The Racine police arrived seconds later. The police restrained the culpable young man. Then they began to interrogate the group. Each witness in turn gave his or her version of what had happened. Both sides pointed fingers and exclaimed, "They started it!"

The perpetrator remained silent until he was confronted by one of the witnesses. The accuser again pointed a finger and charged the boy who threw the bottle with murder.

The police took the arrogant tough kid aside and questioned him. Then they interviewed several witnesses again.

The story began to take form. Six teenagers playing on a knotted rope attached to a huge limb hanging over the quarry, about 10 feet above the water. Another group of four young gang members from Racine were drinking beer out of quart bottles. The leader of the gang, a Napoleon-type character, warned the teenagers to leave the area. The teens ignored the threat and continued to swing out into the quarry.

Obscenities were exchanged and the gang leader threw an empty beer bottle. It exploded on the shoulder bone of one of the teens and peeled back a flap of skin from the top. Shards of glass sprayed in every direction. Tragically, another unlucky teen standing directly behind the first injured teen was hit in the throat. It was slit from front to back producing a three-inch gash. The carotid artery was not only cut, but a portion had been torn away.

The mortally wounded teen stood transfixed, bent slightly at the waist, while holding the lacerated tissue with his left hand. A four-inch arc of blood spurted out from between his fingers. The observers were stunned. They stand paralyzed, knowing what had happened, but not knowing what action to take.

The witnesses reported the young man's upper body began to sag more until his knees buckled and he fell over backward. He did not react to the impact. He apparently was near death, before he hit the ground. The youth lay there for several seconds before one observer grabbed a towel to slow the bleeding. There was no movement or response by the victim to the aid provided.

The last witness interviewed said, "That's when we dropped rocks in the quarry hoping to call the divers to the surface. We wanted to use their oxygen. That's when that big moose of a diver over there pushed his way in and gave us a hard time. The other diver, that other big one, almost broke my arm…I was just trying to help."

Andrew and Ward had little to contribute to the stories already presented.

They faded into the background as the ambulance team carried the dead boy around the quarry. The police escorted the accused tough to a waiting patrol wagon and drove off.

Andrew and Ward later learned that the young man, age fifteen, who threw the bottle, would be tried in children's court. He would be sentenced to a reformatory until he reached the age of twenty-one. Afterward, he would be transferred to state prison where he would serve an additional sentence.

As the crowd began to disperse, a small contingent of people continued to discuss of the events.

Andrew and Ward returned to the water's edge and again donned their scuba equipment. The water was clear now with no trace of violence.
On the limestone knoll, only dark maroon ribbons of dried blood remained. These would soon fade with the cleansing action of the sun and first rain. The divers lowered themselves onto the submerged ledge a few feet beneath the surface. Each diver engaged in his own thoughts about the drama that had taken place. From their horizontal position, they slowly sank to the bottom of the limestone quarry. At twenty feet, Andrew turned slightly and checked Ward's proximity. He was close, as always. Ward pointed down. There, thirty feet below, was the crumpled towel. The blood had been rinsed away on it's descent to the bottom. Only the gray-green hue of the water had left its mark. Andrew rolled slightly to one side and stared deep into Ward's hazel eyes through his facemask. They both felt sorrow but they didn't display any emotion, except to shake their heads and ponder, "What a waste."

Chapter 3

The Wreck Of The Jenny Bell

Thirty-six years ago, Andrew learned how important the scuba buddy system is. By 1966, he had been diving for ten years. He was one of the original twenty-nine diving instructor board members of the newly formed organization, Professional Association of Diving Instructors (PADI). Teamwork and the buddy system were bywords of PADI, and absolute safety their ultimate goal. That year he would be one of three PADI members who would use those skills.

A local television station ran a story on the rediscovery of a wreck off the Door County Peninsula of Wisconsin. The wreck of the Jenny Bell had a history of salvage attempts, but were unsuccessful. The last attempt in the early 1930's broke her in half. She lay upright in two equal halves in 130 feet of frigid, murky water. The news story generated so much interest, that the station decided to do a follow up with a half-hour documentary. An enthusiastic station reporter retrieved a dozen pictures of the wreck from the Milwaukee Public Library's Marine Historical Room. The Marine Room has documents covering 150 years and thousands of shipwrecks in the Great Lakes. But the faded, vertical file pictures were insufficient. The program producer wanted at least six minutes of current underwater movie footage of the seasoned wreck.

Andrew had been building custom underwater camera housings for several years and selling them throughout the Midwest. So when the station called about renting a pressure proof camera housing, Andrew volunteered to do the shoot. The production manager agreed to cover the expenses and give him recognition in the documentary credits. A union cameraman on staff was also a scuba diver, but the 130 feet depth greatly exceeded his skill level.

The affable station cameraman was more than happy to stay on deck and monitor the beer cooler and pack movie film. Andrew felt he needed additional support. He called several Milwaukee divers who had experience in deep water.

David Brownie, a professional colleague and PADI scuba instructor, agreed to act as topside support, log dive times, and monitor the decompression tables. Dave and Andrew were not drinking pals, but each had a deep-seated respect for the other's ability. They had taught scuba for several years at the same YMCA pool. Like Andrew, Dave ran his own class and had friendly and competitive feelings with Andrew about their lesson plans. Andrew recruited two additional divers, Peter Bismeter to assist with the lighting and Thomas Terry to act as backup diver with Dave. The backup divers would be used only if Andrew's bottom time ran short, before the filming was completed. Dave, as part of the second team, would take over the filming if Andrew needed a long surface interval after his first dive.

The day was clear when they arrived at the wreck sight, with a southwest wind, blowing at four knots. Waves lapped gently on the side of the salvage vessel, *Sea Walk*. Dave fitted the lamp heads to the newly converted lighting device. He said, "If the winds don't shift and the seas stay calm Peter, you won't be busting your behind hauling this old lighting system around on the bottom for Andrew."

Dave looked up again from his project and began to explain to Peter how the gadget he was working on was invented. The lighting system was an evolution of ideas from Andrew's and his diving buddies. It was made out of an old steel pressure cooker, the kind his grandmother used in her kitchen to steam the family dinners. It can hold two motorcycle batteries inside mounted side by side. On the top cover are brackets that allow two car headlights to be positioned on a plexi-glass shield.

Andrew designed it primarily to be used with electric power cables from the surface. Dragging cables through a wreck provides a line guide out of the wreck. A second or third diver is always required just to handle the cable. That can be a hassle sometimes so he designed a disconnect for the cables."

Peter steps off the dive platform, enters the water and bobbed back to the surface next to the platform.

Dave never missed a beat in the history of the pressure cooker.

"That way he could switch to the batteries if he entered a wreck. And this...this is real important...this steam gauge on top vents off hydrogen gas from the discharging batteries and keeps the vessel from exploding. It's also strong, inexpensive and the perfect portable lighting source for any entry-level underwater filmmaker."

Dave finished testing the lamps. He switched from low beam then high. "Looks good,... Ready to go," Dave said, as he handed the lights down to Peter, who had entered the water.

Breaking the mirrored surface and gliding past the spare emergency scuba tanks attached at the ten-foot level, Andrew and Peter paused. They appeared suspended on light beams from above. The divers stroked slowly with their fins to maintain their depth.

Andrew decided to test the spare regulators and make sure the air is on. Depressing the small black buttons in the center of each regulator sends a burst of glistening bubbles dancing in the reflected light as they move toward the surface. Slowly the black silhouettes restart their descent. They continued clearing their ears every few feet on the way down. Andrew wedged the camera between his legs to free up his fingers for equalizing his ears. He struggled a bit, because his dive mittens only had one finger and a thumb. Jamming a finger into each side of his mask nose cups, he blew gently against his index finger to equalize. They descended 60 feet, 70 feet. Down, down, they fall into the blackness of the deep. The wet suit compressed to fit tightly against his skin.

The sound of the regulators was heightened with every dry breath. The air thickened, making each sound reverberate within his compressed ear canals. At 90 feet, all surface light disappears. The thin narrow shaft of light from Peter's movie lamp penetrated into the darkness, but revealed nothing. He turned his toggle switch from low to high beam. Andrew looked over at Peter, less than six feet away. The stainless steel rim of his dive mask was the only thing visible. Andrew looked down between his fins from the one hundred-foot level and still saw no sign of the wreck.

The 80 year-old history on this wreck indicated the masts were removed on the second salvage attempt, otherwise they could ride them down. Andrew thought.... "Damn, it's cold." He bent over slightly and searched in long arching downward sweeps. A tingling chill ran down his spine from drops of water that entered the nape of his neck. From out of the murky gray looms the awkward shape of the wreck loomed. Andrew cautiously checked his wrist depth gauge: 125 feet. Before he could look up, his fin tips bent under the weight of his body as he jarringly came to a stop. The downward momentum of his negative weight pressed him to his knees on the deck of the Jenny Bell. Peter landed a second later in an explosive puff of sediment near by. Andrew had only been at this depth three times before, and he had miscalculated how much his wet suit will compress at this depth. His weight was negative, especially with the burden of his heavy camera housing. Andrew instinctively checked his descent time.

He knew he had no time to dump his weight belt and pick it up on the way back. He had to dance on his fin tips against this negative weight. That's what he figured as he pushed off for the long dive ahead.

The pre-dive plan called for a filming sequence around either port or starboard deck rails depending on which side they land.
Then, the plan called for moving forward to the bow and returning to the stern on the opposite side.

Peter was to dive just parallel to Andrew on the outboard side providing the necessary light to film the wreck. An experienced lighting person sees the composed image in the same perspective as the cameraperson does. Because of the limited bottom time and dark water, the cameraperson often shoots what the lighting person sees, not the other way around. At their current depth, there was barely time for the cameraperson to set up the shot. That's why Andrew chose Peter for lighting, since their thinking was in accord.
Andrew followed Peter's light up the starboard side past a deck bilge pump. The handles were still at the ready as if they were used in a feeble attempt to rescue the ship in its last dying moments.

Block and tackle lay in clusters everywhere. On the oaken rail, rigging lines lay draped. Half on deck, some had fallen haphazardly over the side, and some lay in coils on the bottom. Peter followed the

line down to the lake floor and saw the potential for a great shot. Andrew trailed down the wooden, textured walls of the vessel, hoping Peter will just stay with him for this next shot and follow the anchor and chain.
Peter moved up over the rail once again, lighting the deck and the opening to the chain locker.
Andrew almost imagined that Peter had read his thoughts. He hadn't realized how good Peter was at setting up a continuous flow shot, especially under such demanding conditions.
Peter was so good Andrew considered asking him to form a small movie company when they were done with this project.

 Andrew, with Peter right behind, made their turn on the bow, moving outward to better show the bowsprit. Shooting the only remaining torn and tattered sails and dangling lines from 20 feet away, would give the effect that she was still under sail. As they swam past the bowsprit back to the port side, it looked like the ship was approaching them. Andrew shivered at the haunting image of a ghost ship set adrift on a silent voyage.

 Halfway down the port side, Andrew straightened up and settled gently to the deck. Laying the camera down he checked his pressure gauge, 1500 pounds left, plenty of air.
Peter moved in close to look at Andrew's gauge, and compared it to his own. "Close enough", he thinks.

 Andrew pulled back the cuff of his mitten and felt the blistering sting of the frigid water. Uncomfortable at first he adjusted his thoughts to check his watch for total bottom time.

 "Only four minutes left. I sure as hell don't want to take a decompression stop at ten feet in this cold water. We had better make it quick!"

 Andrew writes, "four minutes and up," on his wrist slate. He showed it to Peter and gave him the Okay sign. Peter returned the sign, and they headed to the stern.

 Passing over the jagged break in the hull, Andrew and Peter drop to the lake bottom to give some definition to how far apart the two sections are resting.

 "Eight fin strokes... that's about twenty-five feet. Just ahead are several antique relics and personal effects from inside the wreck." Andrew speculates they have spilled out when she broke in half after the second lift. The gray-brown wall appears suddenly from the gloom. "It must have fallen off center, as well as apart," Andrew reasoned to himself, as he points over Peter's shoulder to where he thinks the port outside wall should begin.

Peter turned to his left and forcefully pushed off the bottom. A billowing dust cloud kicked up and Andrew had lost sight of Peter's light. He swam forward in hopes of running into Peter. "No luck. I better go up a few feet and get into clearer water. Maybe then I can see his light."

Andrew started his ascent, "Damn this housing is heavy... I must be running out of steam."

Andrew's head thumped into something overhead. In pain he anxiously reached up with his free hand to feel solid wooden beams. "Holy balls, I'm inside the wreck, he thought... his mind racing. "Oh God, no light. No safety line. I'm going to drown sure as hell...now, calm down, calm down. You've got plenty of air; you'll find your way out." Andrew's panic is only held in check by his scope of experience as a scuba instructor and some commercial work. He takes in three huge breaths.

"That's the rule: If you start to lose it, think first; react later."

"Oh Jesus! Oh, Mom, Help me! Help..." Andrew starts to lose it again. His panicky thoughts are randomly spinning from logical to nonsensical, from childish fears to adult images. Each time the wave of panic surges, the beat in his chest thunders out of control. "Stop... now stop you dumb jerk, get a hold of yourself. You have enough air to make a swim around this whole stern section."

He turned 180 degrees very slowly measuring each degree in his mind. He had to drop this camera. He was burning too much air trying to stay off the bottom. Andrew bent at the waist. Before he can put the camera down he banged the faceplate of his mask on something.

"Oh Jesus, Jesus... shit, I'm behind a wall... I'm in a room... no a hall...no, Oh Damn. Calm down...calm down." Andrew gropes into the darkness to feel the obstruction in his path. It must be a stand or divider of some kind. His mind raced. "I can't think anymore, I'm getting cold, which way did I come in? Did I make a full turn? No, I couldn't have or I would have run into this thing. Oh shit, I can't think. Yeah, I'm thinking about what I'm thinking about...I'll just rest a minute. Maybe the sediment will settle and Peter will come in looking for me."

Andrew stared into the indigo blackness. The darkness is so dense he feels it. He listened to his own breathing and then held his breath in hopes of hearing Peter. For agonizingly long minutes, tense moments, Andrew knelt in the ghostly reaches of a dead ship.

His mind wandered with visions of drowned sailors in corners of the hold. He envisions the life and death struggle as the ship went down.

"God damn it," he screams in his mind. "You're not getting me!... Besides, I have to piss like a racehorse. Oh, man, I am cracking up." Andrew straightens up and moves forward leaving his camera behind.

"If I just sit here I'll sure as hell drown. I won't go that way. I won't. I have to try, I have to."

Leaning forward with his hands rigid in front of him, Andrew strains his eyes to penetrate the veil of light-less space. Ahead he sees the suggestion of a light in the distance and questions,

"Is that really a light or am I just seeing what I need to see?"

The light disappears, then appears, and then disappears, "Oh damn, its Peter.' Andrew paused again to make sure that he really saw a light. The bleary glow of a light beam appeared again, this time there is a shape edge to the left side of the glow.

"Its the opening, there must be a wall on my left. He reached out cautiously testing his resolve to fight the fear that has made him immobile. He stretched to the point of loosing his balance. "I can't loose direction, must remember how much I moved my foot. Was it a ninety degree turn toward the light? God I don't know. Maybe a little more. Got to find the hull." His hand touches something firm, its the hull. Andrew lays out horizontal and then lowers his right shoulder to better follow the hull. He moves slowly hand over hand for the last place he saw a glint of light. Just outside the broken hull frame Dave, not Peter, was tying off a guideline and preparing to enter the wreck. Andrew gave him a big hug from the side. Dave never saw him coming, almost scared him to death. They calmed down, regrouped and started their ascent.

At 20 feet from the surface they took a decompression stop. Dave has kept a close watch on Andrew's bottom time. He made a fast calculation and then built in a small safety margin.

After a few minutes they ascend to ten feet for a longer decompression stop.

Seven minutes into the stop Andrew's triple forty cubic foot tanks go on reserve. He reached back and pulled down the long stainless steel rod that activates his reserve air supply. He has approximately five minutes left at this depth.

"Balls, that was close," he thought. Face to face, he stared dead into David's face and shook his head...as if to say. "Whatever you're think'n, you're right, dumb ass all the way...I'll wait for a few hours and go back down and recover my camera." Both divers stay at the ten-foot level a few extra minutes, just in case. At the surface and back on board, they discussed the chain of events that almost cost a life. When Peter broke the surface yelling he had lost Andrew, Dave was geared up, ready to start a rescue attempt. If he had delayed even a few minutes, Andrew would have been out of air inside the wreck. A combination of luck, topside support, and diving experience saved his life.

The station cameraman was impressed with the chain of events that had taken place. He felt it important to interview Andrew on camera as a side bar to the story. He started his interview by asking Andrew questions about a phrase he used often. "What is an, 'in situation'?"

Andrew thought for a minute and began, "Control is the key. A racing heart, an accelerated pulse, blood pressure pulsating in the ears... seemingly expanding the head...can all be controlled. Either by the diver themselves or by an encouraging topside person. Either must deliver in a monotone, confident voice a message to ease the "in situation" tensions.

Topside personnel become one with their charges. They place themselves mentally and physically shoulder to shoulder with the diver on the bottom "in situation".

"Give me a sign John, Come on babe, get your head back; get control; we'll get out of there." These or words similar have been heard many time in the diving business. The loneliness and vulnerability of the predicament immediately begins to fade. Without top-side dive masters, it might take more 'right stuff ' than the diver's stamina.

The top-side's added ability to envision the problem helps because they may have been there themselves."

The station cameraman found the subject intriguing and felt Andrew should keep expressing his view of the buddy system or topside support. He would use this portion as a voice over when the underwater scenes are running. He urged, "Andrew please continue with your explanation and give us a feel for what is going on in the commercial field."

"Divers in the future will be wearing helmet mounted television cameras that help to evaluate their work. On more than one occasion they will be used to show the divers dilemma. A remote operated camera will sent down to view the problem from a different angle to help evaluate conditions also. Often, this is outside the range of the diver's field of view. A mini-submarine, about the size of a child's coaster wagon, with a wide-angle television camera, propeller thrusters, and an umbilical cord to reach the surface and connect to the diving console is also possible.

Heart rate and inhalation and exhalation monitors at a surface console will also give their own view of the diver's mental and physical state.

As for the crew, a unique underwater bond has evolved out of necessity. Divers and all their support crew live, eat, and sleep in close quarters, many times without thought of gender because it is not practical. Living aboard a salvage ship or oil-rig platform in the North Atlantic usually mean divers share cabins as spacious as the average bathroom. The rooms are big enough for a bunk bed, washbowl and commode. Few, if any, have deep-seated problems that cannot be discussed with other crewmembers. Everyone has some superstition; most are good luck beliefs, a pair of socks, a special knit cap or diver's knife that must be worn on every dive. Most are harmless. There is no room for excesses.

Feelings of inadequacy, insecurity, claustrophobia, fear of the unknown are dealt with in the early development of the diver's training. If one of those peculiarities manifests itself while working below, someone could die.

Long before a diver reaches the ultra deep or saturation stage of diving, they are in control of their fears. They put all emotions aside, think clearly and get it done."

The reporter turned off the camera and thanked Andrew for his insight. He packed away his camera and microphone and joined the other members of the crew. Andrew remained on the bow, alone.

It will be a long ride back to the shore plenty of time for thought.

Eventually each member of the small craft found a little quite nook to contemplate the day. They stare out at the Lake and relive the roles played. The rescuer, the unfortunate, the observer, and the unscathed.

Chapter 4

Andrew Battles The Darkness

In the corner of his office, majestically displayed on its own pedestal, is an old Navy standard, Mark V hard-hat helmet plated in gold leaf. Installed in the faceplate opening is a finely tuned Swiss clock. It chimes four times and echoes against the gray plaster walls.

Andrew often thinks of his childhood and early days in diving, whenever quiet pervades his office. Unfortunately, that doesn't happen often. The vibrant chimes seem now to conjure up buried memories. He carefully pours a cup of steaming coffee...one of the five or more he will have before the pressure of the challenging workday begins. He walks back to the window line and settles into a glove-soft Corinthian leather chair. A smile crosses his face as he puts his feet up on the window ledge and stares at the sheen on his new Allen Edmonds shoes. The smile was brought on by the memory that carried him back to the Governors Conference on Small Business in Madison in 1986. The Chairman of the Board of Allen Edmonds Shoe Company, a Wisconsin based firm, had just completed a very dynamic speech. He had pleaded his case for import tariffs to be placed on foreign leather goods. The audience of two hundred fifty high-powered businessmen were in full accord with the chairman's views. As he finished his presentation they gave him a thunderous three-minute ovation.

Now it was Andrew's turn to step to the podium to express his views on the issues surrounding his congressional candidacy. As he approached the speaker's stand, he inadvertently kicked the base of the podium. A deafening boom startled the attendees. A few seconds later another boom filled the room as the microphone loosened by the vibration fell to the podium top. Andrew embarrassed, stood motionless until the echoes subsided. Then, without hesitation, he raised his left foot knee high, pulled up his pant displaying his Allen Edmond shoes and

said, "These Allen Edmond shoes are certainly more aggressive than I am. They are always way out in front."
The audience applauded and Andrew settled into the rhythm of his speech. Andrew's smile faded as he thought to himself. "That was a while ago but for right now I want to go way back in time." Pensively he gazed out the window and recalled when he was a baby. "No, not a baby, a child of...what was I, seven, maybe eight? We lived in a dump of a building, a third floor walk-up on the near north side of Milwaukee." Andrew whispered to himself. "Someday I'm going to buy that dump and burn it down."

He grew up among fast living adolescents in one of the city's poorer neighborhoods. His home was an old two-story building that had the attic refinished to house five families. Three of those dubious apartments shared a common bathroom. Each apartment was comprised of a single room with a partition that separated the kitchen from the bedroom. It was more a cubicle than an apartment. The walls were single sheets of wallboard with ageing cracks and peeling layers of paint.

Andrew's mother, Irene, worked two jobs to keep their little family unit together. It included Andrew, age eight, his brother, age eleven and herself. She had divorced Andrew's father a few years earlier and without much support, she had to take whatever apartment she could afford.

Andrew muttered to himself, "Brown Street and 28th; what an emotionally debilitating neighborhood. Bullies and pimps even back then." His brows furrowed as the thought crossed his mind of the fifty plus years earlier when he was about eight years old. No matter what your size or age, self-defense was a primary concern. Fear was very hard to deal with when he was young, when his mother had taught him not to be aggressive. The conflict only added to his anxiety

"Don't ever hit anyone in the face, you might poke someone's eye out," she would always say with her hands on her hips and leaning forward at the waist. A stern mask only when needed, her face seldom reflected anything but kindness. Irene was Irish, German, and French on her mother's side and German and English on her father's side. She had many of the personality traits as Andrew's grandmother. Irene could become angry as hell for five minutes, make her point and then move on. Having lost a protected social position with the divorce, she was under great personal stress to secure a living for her children. A Catholic divorce in the 1940's rendered a woman an outcast, not only from the church which excommunicated her, but her family shunned her as well. Andrew's mother never held a grudge. Once a rule was broken and punishment issued, it was forgotten. She would never allow anyone to go to bed angry. She had a fear they might not wake up the next morning.

Living across the hall was a recluse thirty-two-year-old man. His door was rarely opened and his privacy assured by a fully shaded window. The man would come home drunk almost every night. He would stumble up the stairs, fumble with his keys, curse the landlord for the poor lighting, and then shuffle into his apartment. A few minutes later he would exit his room, cross the hall, and go to the bathroom.

He repeated the same haunting routine every night. There was a common wall between Andrew's tiny three-person bedroom and the shared bathroom. When the man thumped on the wall in an effort to get closer to the bowl, Andrew would cower under his blanket in fear. He knew that someday that wall would come crashing down and the man would get him.

One evening, while Andrew was playing in the hall, the man came home early from work. It was late in the year and already dark outside. The single light bulb hanging in the hall was only bright enough to create shadows and demons. As the man came up the spiraling staircase, Andrew could see only an outline of a figure with dangling arms and rounded drooping shoulders. The man scuffed his feet with each step. His overweight body made the bare, wooden stairs creak liberating an avalanche of sinister monsters. Andrew was terrified. He could not make it to his own door without being seen. The man made the last turn and paused just ten steps from the top. Andrew had to hide somewhere, but where? Down the hall in the dark shadows, that would be the only safe place, Andrew scurried ever so quietly, crouching on hands and knees. He sat back trembling in the corner with his knees up to his face and his arms wrapped around his knees. Peering just over his forearms, he saw the man stop in front of his apartment door, turn, and then looked hard into the shadows at the end of the hallway.

"Oh no', he can see me. He's going to kill me. Oh, please, please, don't let him see me. I'll be good, honest, honest, Oh Gees."

Andrew waited five terror filled minutes after the man went inside his apartment before he moved. When he did start down the hall, all he could think was, "To get to my house, I have to pass his door. He will reach out and grab me and kill me, and no one will ever see me again." He began to cry, quietly, so he would not wake up the sleeping monster. Only steps from the man's door now, he could hear the man's snoring get louder and then recede into a muffled drunken gush of air. He felt safer and took broader steps until he was finally in front of his own door. He turned the knob ever so slowly not to allow the rusty mechanism to squeak. Safe inside his apartment, he breathlessly told his older brother, Steven, what had happened. Bemused and unaffected, Steven just shrugged away his little brother's exaggerated fears.

Andrew and Steven fought like rival bear cubs, as brothers do. It drove their mother crazy. Irene was constantly separating them, banishing one or the other to a friend's house for a cooling off period. No one else dare harm either boy, or there would be hell to pay. Each member of this tiny family protected the other members from outside threats in their own way.

When Andrew told Steven about his ordeal in the hallway, Steven gave him some advice. He said, "All we have to fear is fear itself. I heard that from our former President on the radio. He was talking about the Japanese and bombing this little island." Andrew didn't understand. It took a long time for Steven to explain, but Andrew finally made sense of the story. "It's me that's afraid. I'm making it worse than it is. I can take care of myself. I'll never be afraid again."

Later that night, Andrew decided to test himself, to take the ultimate challenge, and go down into the dragon's den... the basement, dark and spooky; with spiders, rats, and trash in every corner. Even the old people disliked going into the basement. When the women did their laundry in the winter, their husbands would accompany them.

Andrew prepared his mind and thought, "This is the perfect scare test. I'll go downstairs, sit in the old bathroom that hasn't any door and wait in the dark. How long should I wait? ... no fair to come up as soon as I'm scared. I'll stay there until someone looks for me or someone comes down to wash clothes."

Andrew descended the stairs to the basement. The handrail felt wobbly and insecure. The covering of brown paint had long ago been worn away. What was left were long black patches of human deposits. Years of sweaty, dirty hands had left their layer of oily debris behind. Andrews mother would say, "I can't bring myself to hold that rail. I'd rather fall down the stairs." The buildings absentee landlord never made repairs and only appeared on the scene when the rent was due.

The stairs from the first floor were maintained in some repair and cleaned by the tenants. The usual quote from all tenants was " I'll clean my own space but I'll be damned if I'm going to do Kent's work for him." Kent, the landlord, was a small weasel like man. He only lacked a handle bar mustache and damsel tied to a railroad track to make his image complete. He took financial advantage of everyone he could, including Andrew's mother. He never repainted the ugly beige walls or repaired the cracked plaster.

Andrew slid his fingers down the wall, as he took one cautious step after another. It was already dark outside. Only the single 25-watt light that hung from a frayed cloth-covered cord lit the entrance to hell. He peered down into the darkness and the last bend in the stairs that led to the basement. After the bend at the bottom of the stairs was a pitch-black hall. There was another thirty-foot walk until you reached the large door into the main basement. From there it was fifteen feet to another 10-watt bulb. Fifteen more feet and you could turn on a light in the laundry room. A sign taped to the basement window said, "Do Not Use Any Bulb Larger Than 25 Watts…signed Kent."

There was no light source, once you turned the corner from the stairs, until you turned the corner into the laundry room. The damp smelly hallway was completely black. Tenants stumbled blindly straight ahead after they turned out of the laundry room, until they bumped into the wall. Then they turned left and could see the dim glow half way up the stairs.

Andrew stopped again at the base of the stairs. He turned and looked back up. He kept his fingertips on the wall and cautiously turned the corner. Careful step in front of careful step, he made his way deeper into the darkness. "God, I'm really, really afraid. This is more scared than I have ever been." His fingertips barely touched the walls now for fear of touching something that might move as he closed in on his target.

The bathroom was on his left side two-thirds of the way down the hall. Andrew's fingers hit the frame of the door. He stopped and paused. He turned ever so slowly, keeping his left-hand fingers on the frame and swinging his right hand out to find the right door-frame. When he found it, he jumped back slightly and lost contact with it. He stepped forward in tiny baby steps, with his arms outstretched. When he made contact again, he tried to see inside. "There could be a monster in there just waiting for me," he thought. He stepped inside the doorway and inched his way forward until he kicked the toilet bowl with his boots.

He reached down to feel the toilet seat. He knew the women always kept the seat clean and down just in case of an emergency. It was a long way up to the third floor. And it was so dark at night that even with the candle lit you couldn't see anything, door or no door. He settled down on the edge of the seat and breathed a quiet sigh of relief.

He waited for what seemed a lifetime. Occasionally, he would hold his breath to make sure that any monster lurking out there wouldn't hear him. He felt what he thought was something crawling on his hands. He brushed it away quickly and tucked his hands tightly into his sweaty armpits. His nose began to itch and without removing his hands from his armpits, he scratched it with his wrist. More time passed and he began to feel the pressure of the darkness. He could feel the walls, without touching them. He thought about all the features he saw in the bathroom during the daylight hours. There was a broken toilet paper roller on his left side and crumpled papers lay behind the toilet bowl. A small stump of a candle melted onto a chipped diner dish lay precariously on the dank water tank behind him. Young Andrew felt the beads of sweat forming on his forehead and perspiration running down his face and back. He sat there on the old toilet seat, keeping only the very toes of his 'high tops' touching the floor. He thought. "Nothing could get through this tough leather of my favorite high top boots." How intense the sounds of darkness were. He could hear in the distance the rats scurry across the old rumpled newspapers. Again, he felt the spiders, or what he thought were hairy arachnids, run over his bare arms. The invisible dirty webs that festooned the room and lay over beams brushed against his face and tickled his forehead. Tiresome minutes dragged like loathsome hours.

"Maybe this wasn't such a good test. Maybe if no one comes down the test won't work anyway; so if I stay just a little longer, it will mean the same thing. Besides, nobody knows I'm here, and so I can't prove it: that I... I wasn't chicken. Even my dopey brother won't believe I was here."

Feeling he had measured up to what was his gauge of manliness, Andrew stepped out from the bathroom. "Holy Cow, I did it! Now a second test would be to walk to the back of the basement and touch the wall".

Andrew Battles The Darkness   45

Chapter 5

Helmet Memories

The helmet clock chimes once again and brings Andrew back from his memories. A clock in a diving helmet is nothing new, but gold leaf... that was impressive. The seasoned helmet was Andrew's first hard-hat rig. It sported well-earned dings and dents from his early days in commercial diving. It was reinstated with him as a 50th birthday present from the entire Hydro-Tec staff ten years ago. It was found in an old dive store along the Louisiana coast. Andrew had worked for a deepwater contractor near the Avondale Ship Yards in Gretna, Louisiana, some thirty years earlier. It was there that he had gotten his first taste of deep water hard-hat diving. A year before Andrew's birthday, a Hydro-Tec subcontractor was working the coast and used the same dive store as his base of operations.

There is often a close commercial tie between sport divers and professional hard-hat divers. It is difficult sometimes to tell where sport diving leaves off and commercial shallow water diving begins. Many of the sport diving advanced training programs create an introduction to the semi-commercial field.

Because the subcontractor's assignment was rather straightforward and the equipment requirements were few, he decided to use the rental equipment and charter boat available at the dive store. An old hard-hat helmet was one piece of equipment he rented. Its previous owner was now the most recognizable figure in marine salvage today.

The helmet was purchased from the store's rental department by the subcontractor and sent Federal Express to Hydro-Tec's home office manager, Chris Avery. She is a petite, fiery, 5'2" redhead. Her size and beauty were a bit deceiving, with so much business sense and loyalty packed into so small a frame.

She carried herself well in boardroom discussions and knew more about high-pressure fittings and twelve-ton cranes than anyone at Hydro-Tec. and had earned the total confidence and abiding friendship of Andrew. If he were not on-site to resolve a problem, his capable female associate would be. The subcontractor was wise to send her the boss's old diving helmet. He knew the emotional impact it would have on Andrew and the staff. In Boyd's home are many of the early models of diving equipment. He has dozens of sport diving regulators. A few were built from old U.S. Air Force, oxygen respirators. In his boathouse, he has a mini-submarine, full dress diving equipment from the early forties and numerous hand pumps from as far back as 1880. Most of these collectibles have some monetary value, but are treasured because they remind him of his roots.

The subcontractor knew of Andrew's collection, as did most of the people who worked or socialized with him. At one time or another, everyone who came in contact with Andrew, ended up at his home for a dinner or lively conversation and a beer.

Of course, the subcontractor's next contract with Hydro-Tec would have less red tape and more profitability. It was no secret how Andrew's staff was trained. He would say, "We work hard and we play hard, but we never work so hard that we can't play the next day."

There inside the helmet, next to the spit valve, are the names Andrew Boyd and Lisa Deu Rae enclosed in a heart with an arrow through the middle. This battered old helmet represented much of AB's past hard work. The dented and etched heart reminded AB of a gentler side of himself. A side few would see in those early days. Feminine companionship and their social input was always important aspects of his life. Thirty years ago, Lisa became Andrew's wife and later his reason for changing his often times hazardous way of life. She complemented his personality with her passion for life. A man who lived and struggled with the power of the sea on a daily basis, needed someone with a potent spirit to balance that life. The unrelenting fear that he could one day lose someone to the sea, permeated his subconscious. She helped to distract him from his obsession with her independence.

Before Lisa, he believed his daily work routine was not much different than any other job. Instead of putting on a business suit, climbing into a car and fighting traffic on his way to work, Andrew put on a commercial diving outfit, adjusted his equipment and went to work underwater. Lisa taught him to appreciate the uniqueness of his chosen career and taught him to appreciate companionship, flexibility and the need for relaxation. He became content then to make a comfortable living, possibly raise a family and plan for the future.

They had met while Andrew was working at an upscale ski and scuba store in Milwaukee. Lisa was hired by the store to model for their new winter television ski show.

Adventure's End was the Midwest's most modern and innovative specialty store. Lisa, at five foot nine and one hundred twenty eight pounds, made a statuesque model for the show. She was athletic and moved with the grace only the modeling runways of California could produce. Born in Milwaukee, Lisa moved to California to attend modeling school and hoped to be discovered by an agent who could appreciate her stunning beauty. Three years and a thousand disappointments later, she was hired by a department store chain for fashion shows running several times a week. She made an income that was above average. The work was demanding, but tolerable. Her recent visit to Milwaukee included seeing a high school girlfriend and interviewing for a modeling job. Her girlfriend's husband wanted to hire her to model for a series of winter shows at Adventure's End. Her captivating smile, athletic body and subtle sophistication were a great combination for a model. She was perfect for the job.

As head of the dive operation, Andrew's position at Adventure's End didn't require him to write dialogue for the ski show. But the individual departments at the store often overlapped. In that case, Andrew made a point of being especially helpful. From their first meeting, he couldn't take his eyes off Lisa. She responded in kind but with more subtlety. Each paid increasingly more attention to details of the show, spending more time in each others company under the guise of helping the project along. They played the courtship dance until the end of the program's third taping session.

Lisa had returned to the store from the studio and was waiting for the owner to give her a small remuneration for her modeling. It was after the store had closed at 9:30 PM. Andrew couldn't make that videotape session because he was teaching a scuba class. He finished the class at central YMCA in downtown Milwaukee about 9:00 PM. and headed back to the store. The class took a little longer to complete because this group was scheduled for a certification dive the next morning. All the class equipment including the dive cylinders, had to be loaded in the truck of his car and taken to the store. The cylinders needed to be topped off and regulators checked.

When Andrew entered the rear of the store with an arm full of regulators, he saw Lisa waiting in one of the boot fitting chairs. She was sitting perfectly upright with her legs crossed in a model-like stance. She gave Andrew a slight wave, continued to read her book and finished her cigarette. "Not much interest there." Andrew thought as he hung the wet scuba regulators on their assigned hooks. He started out the rear door to bring in the dive cylinders when Mr. Hyland Stark stepped out of his office with the check for Lisa. "Need some help?" He questioned.

"No there are only 10 cylinders." Andrew replied.

Hyland said, "Then I'm going to give Lisa this check and split for home. I'll see you in the morning."

"See you about 8:00 o'clock, boss."

Andrew finished lugging in the remaining cylinders, locked the back door, and set the alarm. To his surprise, Lisa was still sitting in her chair and Hyland had already started for the front door. She didn't make any motion to catch up. Andrew walked toward her and hesitated a few feet away. She casually looked up and said. "I suppose that means its time to go home?"

Andrew, never a loss for words, blurted out. "How about a drink?" Lisa, now showing interest replied. "Fine. Where should we go?"

"How about the Court Yard Inn. It's only about a block and a half from here. Leave your car in the parking lot and we can take my car."

"That's even better," said Lisa. "My car is so loud. I have a broken muffler and I'm embarrassed to drive in public."

The Court Yard was one of Andrew's favorite watering holes in the neighborhood, so it wasn't long before there was a small group of people talking and swapping philosophies. The lively exchange continued for nearly two hours at the bar. Andrew checked his watch at 12:00 midnight. He put his hand on Lisa's arm to get her attention. She leaned back to hear what he had to say. "Lisa, remember? I have to pull the hook in a few minutes because I have a scuba class tomorrow morning." Lisa nodded agreement, but continued her lively conversation. Andrew went back to his little group thinking she would turn to him as soon as she finished her thought. That was a bad guess on his part. At 12:30 AM., he swiveled on his stool to get her attention. "I really have to go now Lisa." She said hurriedly. "OK, OK, a few more minutes."

Andrew was annoyed now, but tried not to show it. He put on his best 'I don't give a damn face' and engaged in the conversation. He knew he had already broken a steadfast rule he had made the day he became a dive instructor. He would never have more then three drinks the night before he took students on a training dive. He would not go without sleep, because that might affect his ability to think clearly in an emergency. And after any dive, when it came to celebrate the graduation, he was never the last one to leave the bar. In addition, he was aggravated by the way she waved off his professional concerns. Like he was to wait until she was ready leave. He did wait for another half-hour and got her attention. She said. "I just want one more drink, then we'll go." Andrew, with minimal control, said calmly. "Then you can walk the block and a half back to the store!" He spun off his stool, bid a farewell and left. The evening set the stage for their future together.

Chapter 6

Adventures End-Ultimate Dive Center

The Adventure's End owner, Hyland Stark, was a former truck driver, a man of two hundred ninety, hard-packed pounds.
He caught the 'skin diving bug', as it was called then, now called Scuba, when he was in California on a buying trip. The U.S. Divers Corporation, owned by Jacques Cousteau was a subsidiary of the French company Sperio Technique, which had opened in the early nineteen fifties. Hyland visited the plant and became the Midwest distributor of Aqua Lung, the brand name for the scuba equipment at U.S. Divers.

Diving had hit the United States with a flurry of excitement. Many would-be frogmen with homemade or converted Air Force surplus regulators could now buy the real thing. No more converted carbon dioxide gas cylinders for air tanks. Now there were 71.2 cubic foot tanks with reserve air valves and harnesses that held the tank in a somewhat upright position on the diver's back. Hyland, a strong swimmer and former high school, middle linebacker, decided a specialty shop for scuba was how to market this new adventure. He gathered together eight buddies as investors. His usual charm and persuasive nature maneuvered each man out of five hundred, hard earned dollars. They formed a partnership and opened a shop on Fourteenth and State Street in Milwaukee.

The eight investors were not involved in the day-to-day operation of the business. Their main concern was to buy personal diving equipment at cost and get their investment back some time in the near future. The total shop inventory consisted of twelve masks, twelve fins and twelve snorkels. Miscellaneous tanks, regulators, weight belts and the like, lay in clusters around the shop. The numbers were counted in the one's and two's instead of dozens.

A sense of enterprise and risk was apparent in the shop's decor. Hyland's creative talent for making something from nothing was abundantly clear. Discarded telephone company wire spools were drilled out to hold scuba tanks. Large plastic water pipes, six inches in diameter and eight inches long, with faces painted on each, served as displays for scuba masks. Big round eyes beamed out at the customers from inside the masks. Coat racks made from household water pipe were constructed for hanging wet suits, dry suits and swimwear. Pegboard screwed onto the roughly patched walls served to hold the variety of accessory items. Two glass showcases, slightly chipped and mismatched in color, displayed pieces of fragile coral, corroded bottles and well-worn coins behind glass. These intriguing specimens from antiquated shipwrecks were always a point of interest. An old US Navy Mark V dive helmet, and full dress canvas suit stood in the corner. They kept watch like some oceanic knight from the Kingdom of Atlantis. No talisman showed that this rudimentary, basic operation would burgeon into a multimillion-dollar chain of stores fifteen years later. The smallest store would be thousands of square feet and employ a dozen people.

Adventure's End opened in 1953 and three years later, Andrew met Hyland for the first time. Andrew became interested in scuba during that period. He and a friend skipped a high school class and headed for a stone quarry just off Highway 16 near Pewaukee. Two events that day would change Andrew's life forever: a near death experience and the exciting discovery of scuba. He and his friend had been snorkeling. They had only one pair of fins, which belonged to Andrew. The shared fins were used for several hours. Each boy would snorkel for a time and then he would relinquish the fins to his friend. As the afternoon progressed, they became fatigued and decided to rest and get a sun tan. They laid out their blanket on the barren pristine beach and rested.

Andrews' friend, Joey Webster, rested only a few minutes before he jumped up and announced that he was going to swim across the quarry. Not inspired by Joey's burst of energy, Andrew mumbled into the blanket. "You can go, I'm beat."

Joey chided, "Come on it's not that far."

Andrew's cheek was pressed hard into the blanket, as he said. "I got an idea. You go and I'll wait here. When you come back I'll applaud you."

"OK, I'm going." Joey ambled into the water without any equipment and started to swim.

Andrew, with his cheek now turned toward the water, watched out of his right eye. The sun felt good on his back and he had finally stopped shaking. He squinted against the glare of the sun, watching Joey as he swam further away. Suddenly, Joey turned upright in the water and splashed a little. He looked back toward Andrew on shore and yelled,

"I can't make it. I need the fins." At first, Andrew thought Joey was doing one of his 'help save me' routines. But there was no female audience to be amused. Could he really be drowning? "Oh God he is." Andrew said out loud, and yanked on the fins. He sprang to his feet and took four giant steps to the water. His big fins flopped and slapped the beach, as he belly flopped into the water. His fins were churning air before he was fully in the water, which seemed really icy now. He forced himself to swim hard, kicking up a water rooster tail that billowed out behind him. He reached Joey in less than two agonizing minutes. Andrew was panting and drooling saliva when he arrived. Joey was gasping for air and appeared shaken, but not in a state of panic. He directed Andrew, "Give me the fins, I'm still going to the far side." Andrew was incensed. He thought. "All that effort and worry. Now you're going to swim even further?" Then he shouted harshly, right in Joey's face. "Are you nuts man? I have to swim all that way back, because you want to impress someone you haven't met yet." Andrew started to realize that he was now the one who was in trouble.

The adrenaline rush felt by thrusting his stiff Navy Frog Feet at full speed to supposedly rescue his friend receded now. It left him gasping for air. The need to tread water during the hurried exchange of fins further added to his air deficit. It was a long way back to the starting shoreline. Now thoroughly fatigued, a new wave of cold was attacking Andrew, and his teeth chattered as he started to shake. Panic set in. Joey knowingly had already turned and was swimming away with the fins. Andrew wanted to yell for help, but he suddenly realized that Joey wouldn't be able to save him. He had to save himself. He instantly sensed the distance to the shoreline, and determined that his starting point appeared closer. It was hard to tell from that low in the water, however.

He thought, "Go, go.., get going. Go to your shoreline." Andrew started to swim with slow, determined strokes, knowing that he needed to conserve his strength. Stroke after punishing stroke, he pushed himself. His arms felt anchor-like and his breathing became painful and more labored. "Keep going, keep going," he chanted to himself.
Half way back to the shore, he thought he couldn't make it. His arms were flailing in the air, slapping into the water, and losing effectiveness. His legs still had some strength. He pressed down harder, until his legs were screaming for oxygen. Andrew was now on automatic pilot. He could have been going around in a circle for all he knew. His face slammed down into the water and came up again, gasping for air. Still, he kept moving forward. Down and up, down and up until he swam right up onto the shore. His face lay buried half in the sand. Water and sand trickled in and out of his gaping and gasping mouth. Andrew didn't move, he felt paralyzed. For a time, he thought he might be dead. It took long minutes until he recovered enough muscle control to spit out the sand and close his mouth. Then he comprehended that Joey had been yelling for some time from across the lake that he had made it.

Finally Joey realized that Andrew might be in real trouble. He sat down on the beach and just stared across the water at the body on the beach. He had little strength left to swim back right away for he needed time to recover. He could see Andrew was out of the water and realized that he had survived.

Ten or fifteen minutes had passed before Andrew felt the cold water rippling across his lower body. Exerting great effort, he rolled onto his back. With little muscle control, he dragged his limp forearm over his eyes. "The sun is out again. Was it ever gone? I don't remember anything."

Joey was close to total exhaustion, as he painstakingly pulled himself and his fins across the waters edge. He fell to his knees a few feet from Andrew's head. He bent down and lifted Andrew's arm.

"Are you all right?"

"No, you jerk, I'm dead." Andrew struggled to sit up and regain some clear thinking. They moved back onto the blanket and lay there soaking up the sun. Young boys recover from these exertions quickly and Andrew and Joey were no exception.

An hour later they heard a gurgling sound coming from the water. They both sat up and saw a stream of bubbles coming up from the lake bottom. They moved closer to see what caused the gas stream. Suddenly, a manlike sea creature emerged and scared both boys nearly to death. It was the first time either one had seen a scuba diver. Living near the lannon-stone quarry, the man dived there often, using a scuba system fashioned out of an old US Air Force surplus oxygen regulator. With strands of lake weed and dripping water, he mumbled an apology for scaring the boys. Soon they all relaxed and talked excitedly for a long time. Andrew was entranced with this new marvelous diving machine. These adventurous and eager young aquanauts persuaded their newfound mentor to allow them a test dive. He was very generous with his time and offered each boy a chance to dive.

The earlier near fatal accident was soon forgotten, at least for the moment. Images from that day would make a lasting, positive impression on Andrew. In the distant future, with sentimental appreciation, he would buy that very same, homemade scuba system from the man. He has it today.

Four years later in the spring of 1957, a long time friend and grade school pal, Ward McNair, brought a book to work, called "Diving with Safety" by E.R. Cross. Andrew eagerly read the twenty-five plus pages with riveted attention. That triggered a spark of creative energy and passion for diving. Intrigue and challenge became the call words of the day. They fit Ward and Andrew like carefully measured wet suits. Their passion for diving began to grow at a most opportune time, a time when Andrew believed his brain was becoming stagnant. His assembly line routine at American Motors was beginning to wear on him. He knew that all systems, even his brain, needed to be exercised, or it would atrophy. Scuba allowed his imagination to embark on an intellectual and physical voyage. A conveyor filled with automobile parts could not compete. Andrew's mind and soul were withering amid the crashing and clanging of steel.

A television series staring Lloyd Bridges as Mike Nelson in Sea Hunt, fed his imagination with the mysteries, travels, and challenges offered by the sea. Scuba diving was his pathway to the underwater world. Few people at that time were privileged to explore the vastness of the sea.

Over the next forty-eight years, Andrew would recall the irony of a man, a book, and a TV series leading him to become possessed by the ocean's relentless call. He would become an inventor of safer diving equipment, a world record holder, and a medical researcher. He designed a method to challenge the blackout border for high altitude pilots and pushed the edge of the envelope a little further. His life from that day forward would be dominated by the sea's influence.

Andrew and Ward saved their weekly paychecks for two solid months. In those days, with overtime and working second shift, it wasn't hard to accumulate a thousand to fifteen hundred dollars to spend on a fool thing like scuba diving equipment.

They visited five of the dive shops in the area before deciding to buy from Adventure's End, which also sold downhill snow ski equipment. They were not impressed with the treatment they received on their first visit. However, the selection and the prices were competitive. The clerk, new to them, was one of the partners filling in for Hyland Stark. Stark was the only real active partner that worked the store. The clerk was sullen and short on conversation, not the sort of person you would expect in a specialty store. They didn't discover until their third visit that the other storeowner was in the Atlantic, off Florida, diving for lobster. When Hyland Stark returned a week later he made an instant impression on both Andrew and Ward. His size seemed to fit the sport: big and bulky. His bulk was not conspicuous in the water because the water it displaced would buoy up his weight. This buoyancy allowed him to transfer his strength to movement only, instead of balance and movement. Quick and agile on a downhill ski run, he moved with some grace even for a 'Beefy Burger' as he often called himself. Maintaining a center of balance with that big body consumed a lot of energy. He would say, "I come out of the water exhilarated, not exhausted like I do on a downhill ski run."

Scuba and skiing, as main shop activities, are known as 'specialty sports.' There doesn't appear to be any valid reason to call skin-diving, or scuba (self-contained underwater breathing apparatus), a sport. There are no spectators in scuba diving. Once the mirrored glass surface is broken and descent is initiated, it is for participants only, often just you and a diving buddy. Participants often assume a horizontal position during much of a dive. Diving enhances every sensation. The sense of hearing for instance changes, because the whole skull becomes an acoustical sounding board. Vision is magnified by twenty-five percent with dramatic light changes as depths increase. The rich, dark hues of blue and green that appear beyond 25 feet of depth often evoke a sense of peace in divers.

There is no competition between buddies, since the pace of the dive is always set by the skill of the lesser diver. High stress situations caused by novices, who are diving beyond their skill level, can lead to severe shortness of breath and panting.

Andrew, before he became a certified Scuba instructor told his buddies, "The feeling of the stress to 'catch up' can be a hazard in this sport. It leads to panic. Never get behind in your breathing. Dive at your pace and always be aware. These are the rules. Ankle banging, wrist snapping and body twisting are all elements of other sports; not a part of scuba or snorkeling. A seasoned diver generally evolves into a competent underwater explorer with graceful control. For me and Ward it is an exploratory adventure, not a sport."

After their first meeting, Hyland probably celebrated all night after the huge equipment sale he made to the boys. They had spent more than two month's pay and still weren't set up with all the "I gotta' a haves."

Hyland became their mentor, explaining equipment needs and colorfully describing the best dive sites. He would become their guide, who pooled and provided new directions for the boys' earlier experiences together. Of course, they bought the very best equipment of that time with name brands like U.S. Divers Royal Aqua Master a two hose regulator and the new molly-chrome steel cylinders. Ironically, the cylinders were made in Milwaukee at Pressed Steel Corporation and shipped to Santa Ana, California where valves were installed and shipped back to Milwaukee.

As a regional distributor, Adventure's End dispersed them to the thirty-six dive shops around the Midwest.

Air monitoring pressure gauges weren't that popular in the 1950's. (They became an accessory in the '60s and a requirement in the '70s). The air supply was breathed down to where the inhalation became difficult. That meant you had about three hundred pounds per square inch left in your cylinder. A reserve lever attached to the left side of the cylinder was pulled down to release the remaining five or more minutes of air depending on your depth. Then a diver had to start immediately for the surface.

Colors of wet suits in the early years never captured the excitement of scuba. Basic black or navy blue was the order of the day. It wasn't until the early '60s that Parkway Fabricators came out with a colored suit. One of its designs was a 'kelp or seaweed' look that resembled a military camouflage uniform. Not a big retail seller for that time.

Now that they were fully equipped they were left to their own devises. Andrew and Ward strapped on their new toys and went diving in Racine Quarry. These would-be macho adventurers wanted to learn how to dive by trial and error. There were only a few formal training classes in the Midwest during the fifties. Most courses cost about $25.00 for thirteen-weeks of training. Even a nine week course was way too long to wait and far too expensive for something as simple as going underwater, and $25.00 fee was a bit high to have someone tell you how to inhale and exhale. Andrew had done that for seventeen years.

The courses in the area consisted of classroom and pool sessions, but no open water training. So the young men decided to take their dive manual and experience the open water on their own. Each step was based on trial and error, with mistakes repeated more than once. A series of errors however, did spoil entire days of diving on more than one occasion. One careless day almost cost Andrew his hearing.

Two months into their new pastime, Andrew and Ward gave sick day notices to their bosses at American Motors. The sick days were beginning to mount up. Their absentee record had already forced their foreman to issue three day suspensions to both boys. They used the 'time off without pay' to go diving.

Andrew and Ward car-pooled to work each day. A sudden impulse to play laid waste to any kind of work ethic. Ward would drive miles out of his way to pick up Andrew. Often before arriving at Andrew's house he would have made up his mind to call in sick. All he had to do was set the gaff and Andrew would be hooked. Of course on alternate weeks Andrew would pick up Ward and he would set the hook. It had gotten so bad that all they had to do was look at each other and in synchronized voices, would say. "Screw it. Let's go diving." They had little responsibility, living at home with their parents, which allowed them more time to go diving. They also had well paying jobs that were now tenuous at best.

That early summer, before mid July, the boys had more than 60 dives to their credit. And they were just getting started. Still with no formal training they dived deeper and deeper until they hit the bottom of the Racine Quarry. At ninety-four feet they hit a long trench with frigid water. Andrew and Ward stood flatfooted and congratulated each other. It was bone chilling cold because their wet suits were only three sixteenths of an inch thick. A little more training or formal knowledge would have helped.

The 'ice-cream' headaches were to be expected on every deep dive. They had missed that class, too.

As mid July turned into August, the daring duo grew tired of the three-block walk around the quarry rim to the point of a possible water entry. Only the most determined divers reached the small beach area. One of the boys decided it would be easier to make a forward entry from the cliff side and save all their energy for the actual dive. The challenging problem was at it lowest point the cliff side was thirty or more feet above the water.

Ward would herald each new diving adventure with an inspirational proclamation. His latest call to arms was, "You don't have a hair on your ass if you don't try it."

After assembling his hundred plus pounds of equipment and standing with his fin tips quivering over the wall's edge, Ward prepared to launch himself into space. He stepped off and hit the surface with a smack. This created a burgeoning cascade of water that took a full five seconds to shower back to the surface. He popped back up smiling.

"Cover your balls man, it's a long way down, "he said.

Andrew was fully dressed and waited until Ward tested the landing zone. He leaned over the edge and said. "You OK or is your voice always that high?"

Ward yelled back. "Come on in the waters fine."

Andrew shuffled closer to the edge and looked through his fin tips, framing Ward who was thirty feet below.

"It sure looks higher than it did before I put on this fogged up mask," he thought to himself.

Checking his weight belt to make sure it was secure, he yelled,

"Get out of the way bozo, before I plant my butt on your head."

"Come on sweetheart. Just say Air Born on the way down."

Andrew sucked in a deep breath and took a huge giant stride off the ledge, forming an upside down 'Y' as he raced towards the water. He hit with a concussion that momentarily dazed his senses. He kicked downward with increasing effort. "Hey, I'm not going up, what the hell." He stroked a few more times and nothing happened. He looked down at his fins. They had been jammed up his leg to his knee by the impact with the water. He couldn't believe it. These were solid gum rubber Duck feet. The heel strap was solid, molded as part of the fin. There were no adjustment buckles to slip. "How the hell did that happen?" he thought. He dog paddled his way to the surface and waddled to an outcropping from the wall. Ward joined him and they stared with amazement at the position of his fins.

Ward's smirk was revealed as his facemask bobbed up and down half underwater, and then above.

"Now you can play Toulouse Lautrec." Ward said.

"Funny, now help me get them down."

Ward pulled on the fins as if he were pulling off riding boots. Finally they were back in place. Andrew questioned. "Do you know how far my foot had to bend up for that fin to get up there? I can't believe it's not broken."

Ward, still smiling joked. "Next time carry your fins in your pocket."

"That was my next and last time. You jump, I'll hump it down the old bunny trail," said Andrew.

"Honest to God. You are turning into such a wimp. Hey, next time, how about out of a plane?"

Andrew didn't reply for he knew Ward wasn't kidding. He had that "I dare your ass" look in his eye.

Andrew sank below the surface and headed slowly across the quarry to the opposite side.

He checked back and Ward was right next to him, just as expected. They quickly reached the other side, just south of where they aimed. The trip across would take them to a depth of sixty feet and they used less then a third of their air supply. As they broke the surface, there was something strange about his dive buddy, but Andrew couldn't place it. Then it dawned on him. Ward wasn't wearing a facemask.

"Where the hell is your facemask?"

"I dropped it when I pulled your fins down."

"Why the hell didn't you say something?"

"You were so damn hyper; I didn't dare say anything."

"What the hell are you going to do now."?

"You sure swear a lot..; I'll just go back and pick it up."

"You mean scuba dive all the way back without a mask?"

"We can stay shallow; maybe fifteen feet, then we won't burn much air… see."

Andrew rolled his eyes, broke a smile and put his face down in the water. He led the parade back to the original outcropping.

Once there, he dove down and recovered the mask. It was right where Ward said he lost it. That would be the last time Andrew would ever find anything so quickly that someone had lost.

Andrew didn't realize it at the time, but he had stretched his eardrum when he was kicking to come up after his giant stride entry. He had a slight twinge in his right ear but nothing he couldn't shake off. Unknown to him he had broken his right eardrum, a bad case of barotrauma. The disorientation he felt, after the concussion, was the cold water entering through the break and numbing his middle and inner ear. Not to mention the damage to his ear canals and cochlea. He did notice an acrid taste of blood, but with the excitement of the dive, he shook it off. The eustachian cushion prevented nasal contaminants from migrating to the middle ear, but allowed some blood to run out. Spitting up a little blood was no big thing when you compared it to having your nose broken three times, which had happened before Andrew was thirteen years old.

This minor ear problem, however, was only the beginning. The next day Ward and Andrew had a unexpected opportunity to dive in the big one, Lake Michigan.

Early that next morning they arrived at Bradford Beach. They had to set up their blankets outside the swimming area, because neither knew if it was against park rules to let divers enter from the sandy area. Scuba was still new and a crowd gathered before they had the regulators mounted on the cylinders. Both Andrew and Ward loved the attention and milked it for all that it was worth. They did lots of prancing and gave slow thoughtful answers to the very basic questions. It never failed to take twice as long to get dressed when there were attractive women around. You would have thought these two novices were Navy trained and tested, the way they manhandled their equipment.

Andrew loved to place his upright cylinder on his bent right knee and inspect the harness. He would reach through the nylon webbing with his right hand and place the cylinder on his back. He had large enough hands to position and hold the cylinder. He could then reach down and back for the left strap.

Once all the straps were tightened the real show stopper would take place. Andrew would bend slightly at the waist and knees.
There was a quick snap upward at the waist and a straightening of the knees. Then the two hose regulator would flip over his head, perfectly set in place, and come to rest squarely, just below the breastbone. Meanwhile, Ward would drop his own cylinder onto his back, by lifting it over his head, then sliding his hands inside the harness and letting it drop. What a show it was, well worth the admission.

They gracefully entered the water backwards, walked straight out

Adventures End-Ultimate Dive Center 63

over two hundred feet, and stood only chest deep. Andrew turned to Ward. "Maybe it's this deep all the way to Michigan," he said.

"If it doesn't get much deeper soon, I'm going to sit down on the bottom for ten minutes and go back into shore."

The two pushed on until the water finally was up to their chins. They settled to the bottom and started to kick. The bottom was beige and barren with nothing but an occasional rock. After a boring half-hour they decided to head for the beach.

Two days after the dive, Andrew noticed a disturbing itch under his right ear. He pressed his right index finger hard into the spot and wiggled it for all it was worth. "There, that's better" he thought.

From time to time over the next four days, he found relief with the same practice. The sixth morning the right side of his face was numb. He thought it was from lying on it all night. A quick and horrifying reflection from a mirror, however, revealed a grotesque, inflamed glob of human flesh. The right side was apple red and shiny. His nose was no longer in the center of his face but nearly under his right eye, which was almost closed from the swelling. His mouth was pulled to one side and stretched upward at a corner. He had seen his face swollen many times from fights, but nothing like this. The grotesque image really scared him. Good thing his mother was at work, or she would have had a coronary.

Andrew called every ear nose and throat specialist in the book, and settled on Dr. Dieaway. That was a pretty spooky name by itself, but Andrew was in real pain now. He raced to the doctor's office and had to wait for an hour before the nurse called him in. The doctor took one look and said. "Take off your shirt. Lay down, this is going to hurt like hell."

Andrew grimaced as he laid his head back into the padded headrest. Even the soft cushions hurt when he put the full weight of his head down. The doctor forced a long yellow tube up Andrew's right nostril. Andrew winced with pain. His right eye began to water. Finally, the doctor stopped pushing and Andrew relaxed his body. "Wow Doc that hurt like hell."

"Wait" The doctor, said, "It's going to get better."

It was apparent to Andrew that the doctor had little sympathy for anyone dumb enough to let an ear infection fester so long. No sooner did he think how sadistic this doctor was when the doctor confirmed it. The doctor flipped on a machine that sounded like a vacuum cleaner and said. "Now this is the part I really enjoy; when you can hear all that ugly repulsive green stuff being pulled out of there." Andrew stiffened in the chair gripping the arm rests until his knuckles were bleach white. The doctor leaned over the chair and came close to Andrew's face and pointed at a jar sitting on a porcelain pedestal. "You must like it too, if you let that infection go this long. I'll be back before this thing sucks all of you, into there." Andrew rolled his eyes to one side. He had to lift his head slightly to see the small jar on the machine table filling with the vilest green and yellowish-white glop he had ever seen.

The doctor grinned, and with a wink left the room. It took weeks of treatments and shots for Andrew to get his face back. It took another five years before the ringing in his right ear stopped. An otoscopic examination revealed a tiny permanent scar remaining on the eardrum.

Andrew had an audiologist test his hearing many times since then, with no detectable difference in hearing in either ear. He was very fortunate indeed.

Chapter 7

An Angel Lost

By the late 1950s, Andrew and Ward had a solid grasp on diving procedures and an extended base of experience. They had completed several demanding auto salvage operations and made a number of thrilling excursions under the ice to recover fishing shanties, snowmobiles, and assorted flotsam and jetsam. They also eagerly volunteered to recover drowning victims for the police department. To date, the department had not set up a formal dive team. Andrew and Ward added fifty to sixty dives per year to their agenda. This helped tone their bodies, gave them stamina, a lifetime of self-confidence and a reputation for competence in the community.

It was late 1958, the first week in September, when Andrew got a frantic phone call:

"Andrew, is that you? We've got a girl who drowned in Michigan off the break wall. Can you scrounge up a few guys to help me do a search?", pleaded the baritone, gravelly voice. It was Sergeant Bill Delaine, a mountainous, barrel-chested Irishman with fifteen years on the Milwaukee Police Department. His job was to efficiently coordinate the underwater recovery group of volunteers in the metro Milwaukee area. Andrew, recovering from an early Saturday afternoon marathon of card playing and beer guzzling, mumbled into the receiver, "What the hell time is it?"

The voice on the phone bellowed out again, "You in bed already? It's only 11:00 P.M., for Christ sake. I got a twelve-year-old girl drowned ... my ass is grass if we don't find her soon. She's been missing since the report came in at 9:00 P.M."

"Wait up, Bill. I've got to get my coordinates. Damn, can't you find anyone else?"

"Hell no. Everyone's gone or they aren't home yet"

"How about Ward? Did you try Ward?"

"I called his home three times and let the phone ring for far longer than I can hold my breath. No answer."

"He was with me until I stumbled out of Wyler's about 4:30P.M.. He's probably shit-faced in some babe's apartment. Haven't you got anybody but me? I'm really hurting!"

"Hey, dip-shit, you owe me one for bailing your ass out of that Wisconsin Avenue brawl, remember?"

"Remember...? Who the hell could forget? You remind me every time you need something."

Andrew gathered his wits and felt pressure to act. "OK, you big, heartless, mean person in a blue, too-tight uniform. Where should I meet you...? At 5th district or at the lake?"

"Meet me at the lake. The Red Cross will be there with the coffee and doughnut van set up."

"How much time do I have? I haven't even started my makeup yet."

"Hey jag off, you want to shoot the bull all night or get it done? I want you here an hour ago."

Always in meticulous showroom condition, Andrew's 1951 Mercury convertible surged to life and zipped the forty city blocks to the lakefront in record time. He jerked to a stop just north of the old government pier and concrete break-wall. There, he surveyed a disturbing scene of several hundred anxious onlookers, milling around in tight knots, their faces cast with anguish and concern. The group appeared tense, but ready to respond to directives. Several were holding flashlights, one had an almost spent, rose-colored flare and one carried an olive-drab military blanket. At the south end of the crowd were two police vans, a squad car, and the Red Cross van, all with lights flashing. People were converging on the scene from every direction. The crowd control for this late in the accident scene was a challenge for the police they had to practice restraint as the crowd grew to several hundred. Everyone pressed forward vying for a better view. Bill was pressing people back behind the makeshift barrier.

The custom-painted, candy-apple red Mercury glistened even in the moonlight, as it came to a stop one hundred yards from the crowd. Andrew left the car and walked up behind Bill.

"Hell of a party you're throwing Bill. Save me a dance."

The officer turned straining his neck to reply.

"They better get me some warm bodies from downtown or this crowd will push us right into the water. How am I supposed to run a recovery and handle crowd control, too? Get suited up. I'll give you the breakdown as soon as I get a handle on things."

Andrew returned to his Mercury and backed down the narrow service road leading to the entrance of the government pier. The two-mile ribbon of faded concrete, ran east-southeast for a half-mile and turned almost straight south for another mile and a half into the darkness of the night. This break wall had a turbulent history with a number of accidents. Fishermen, hikers, and even strollers, many of them preoccupied, had fallen or been washed off its seven-foot wide surface in storms. If a person were to drown anywhere along Bradford Beach, known as the northern swimming area, they would drift into the wall. The almost imperceptible current along Lake Michigan shoreline appeared trivial, but had a relentless pursuit toward Chicago. It carried many objects into the wall first before sending its cargo on a southerly route.

Andrew mumbled, "Damn good thing that mob doesn't know the search will start here, or I'd be up to my can in people."

Sitting on the edge of his open car trunk, Andrew felt the cold wet sand between his toes as he took off his shoes and socks. His car trunk was filled with a complete array of scuba search equipment, including an extra set of dry clothes. He kept the equipment handy, because he never knew when he would get a call for a commercial underwater job or an emergency like this.

Treading clumps of sand, Bill quickly wound his way past the crowd past the barriers and climbed on to the pier. The barriers made a huge crescent shape to the path. He walked to the start of the concrete path.

Andrew had already donned his wet suit and spread out his equipment. " You going in alone?"

"No, I'm going in with the memory of you."

"I don't want you in alone. Shit, I don't want another stiff on my hands."

"Unless these bloodshot eyes deceive me, you and I are the only one's here, sweet cakes."

" Why don't you hang on for a little bit, see if someone else shows?"

"By that time she'll be half way to Chicago."

"God damn it, I want you to hang loose for a minute." Bill's face stiffens and grew more intense. His concern was very noticeable even in the dim light of the Coleman lantern that Andrew had set up.

"All I need is a hot-shot hot-dog, like you going out and getting drowned."

"OK, big guy settle down before you dump in your Levi's. Tell me what you know, and if no one shows by then, I'll let you tie a rope around my neck, so I won't get lost."

Delaine began, "The 'vic' was swimming with her family, about twenty of them. She and her cousin were going back into the water for the third time, both had been drinking. He wanted one more beer and went back to the group, so she went in without him. Five minutes later, several family members heard someone screaming. The cousin and two brothers ran into the water. The cousin disappeared swimming down along the beach. A few minutes passed and the brothers came out; now the cousin was gone too. The crowd had swelled to a hundred. Twenty or thirty people went in looking for the girl and her cousin. Meanwhile the distraught cousin came out down the beach, and went home to get the father and mother who left earlier. The cousin came back, but half the family thought he was the one that drowned. The whole family is Mexican and can't speak much English. Squad 45 got the call about 9:30 P.M. and was on site ten minutes later. By the time they found someone to interpret all the stories, it was 10:00 P.M., and they still weren't sure if the girl was the one that screamed. The night-watch commander said it might be too late to start a search especially for someone who may or may not be drowned. I got here fifteen minutes later. That's it. You feeling better?"

Andrew looked up and shrugged his shoulders.

Lake Michigan off shore is for the most part clean and free of debris. It has a hard packed bottom of clay and sand, with water of an emerald green tint. The thin, half inch of bottom sediment is easily disturbed. Movement must be slow and deliberate without bottom contact. Visibility on that day was less than four feet. The water surged hypnotically into the rocks and then swelled high against the pier.

Andrew stood in three feet of water, pulling on his wet suit glove. He looked up at the pier and watched it disappear into the night along its length. Shuffling forward a few feet, he laid horizontally in the water and sank to the bottom. He expertly adjusted his weight belt and snuggled it up tight against his stomach. He thought, "The water is cold but not uncomfortable yet. I have a feeling this is going to be a long night." Moving slowly forward and surging gently from side to side as each wave rolled over him, he pulls himself along the rocks. His dive plan was to swim parallel to the pier on the bottom and close against the rocks on the way out. Coming back, he would ascend a few feet higher on the rocks, which would put him closer to the pier and in the stronger surge of shallower water. Andrew thought to himself, "If she drowned two and a half hours ago, she will probably be dancing off the bottom where the sand meets the rocks."

He swam nearly a half-mile, starting at a depth of three feet and followed the bottom out and down to a depth of fifteen feet. He saw loads of fishing gear and trash dropped or thrown by the people on the pier.

Disappointed in the way people held the lake with so little regard he thought, "Out of sight out of mind. Don't those dumb bastards know what impact they're having down here? They should have to come down here and look at this junkyard"

Andrew's train of thought was broken, when he strained to see what looked like long black hair sticking out of the rocks. The surging water made the image ebb and flow. Within arms reach, he realized his mask was a little too fogged up to see clearly. Before making contact, he flooded his mask and cleared it by holding the high point and exhaling out of his nose, forcing the water out the bottom of the mask. As the water exited the mask, his view became focused. He blinked water from his eyelashes and recoiled, grunting and biting hard on his regulator mouthpiece.

There in front of him in the shallow beam of his light is the corpse of a dead cat. Its teeth were exposed, and it was frozen in terror with glazed eyes that seemed to penetrate even in death. Andrew gulped and thought,

"That little fur-ball must have slid down the slant side of the pier, drown, and lodged in the rocks. Man, I almost shit a brick. My heart is really pounding."

Hours passed, and more volunteer divers appeared on the scene. Some were there only to get recognition as a diver. They had little intention of searching for a body.

Andrew had been on more than one accident scene where the local hero showed up in all his diving finery, strutted around giving interviews and left without ever getting wet.

Within a few hours, the morning sun was due to arrive. A three-man dive team that arrived during the night was now tired and chilled to the bone. They had made grid patterns on the bottom, starting just out from the pier and extending one hundred yards into the lake, and nearly a half-mile along the pier.

"No girl has drowned here," said one of the veteran divers. "I've covered the bottom here better in four hours than I've covered my wife's bottom in four years...she isn't here, man. Maybe out there, but not here."

The diver turned and stared out into the lake as if he might see something that would give him a clue to the little girl's final resting place.

Andrew was short on gas both in his cylinder and in energy. He dragged himself out of the water; his fins over one arm and shoulders hunched with both fatigue and cold. The weight of the cylinder, the cold of the water, and lack of sleep were taking their toll. He dropped down on his knees in the sand in front of Bill, looked up and said, "I'm cooked." He slumped sideways onto the sand as if shot by a silent bullet. He groaned as he bumped his head on the valve head of the scuba cylinder, but even that flash of pain didn't supersede his complete exit of strength.

Bill smiled knowingly. He saw the price Andrew was paying just to show how he could take it.

"If you're going to soar with the eagles you can't hoot with the owls. Get your sorry ass up here, I've got an idea."

Bill walked over to the command truck that was set up, while Andrew was gaining some strength. He rolled up a chart and returned to where Andrew was resting. Andrew rolled over to his right side, pulled his left knee up almost chest high, and with an effort-filled grunt, pushed himself off the sand with his right hand. Feeling the pinch in his wrist from the extra weight, his hand sank into the sand. He sat on his heels for just a moment, with his hands in his lap, as if in meditation. He groaned once more before lifting himself into a standing position. Sand cascaded down his wet suit and onto his feet, refilling the body form pressed into the sand. Bill held a flashlight under his chin as he sketched an outline of the shore.

"Here's what you've covered, and here's the coverage for the second team. That doesn't leave us a hell-le-va lot of area left to search. I think you should dive at the swimming area markers. It's about seven feet there, maybe a little more. If she tried to make it there, she may not have drifted with the current like we thought."

Andrew tiredly paused for a second, not wanting to disagree with Bill. They both knew these waters and both were acting on judgment based on years of past experience. Andrew decided to put ego aside on this one.

"You're the boss," he said, "Only make my run a short one, or you'll be looking for my sorry ass too."

"Take a hundred foot search line, tie off at the base of the float anchor, and sweep about a foot off the bottom. If she's lying flat on the bottom, you might snag her. Run out the full hundred feet of line before you start the sweep."

"OK, man. Have the coffee hot and the buns in the oven. I'll be back in half an hour. I've still got enough air to make this run."

Andrew smiled a diminishing grin at Bill, knowing that this extra effort without aggravation was appreciated. "Find her for me on this one. Her parents have just about had it."

Andrew nodded and stared at the distraught parents, who were halfway down the beach, vacantly looking out at the predawn fog on the lake. They stood holding each other, thinking their own thoughts, rejecting, then accepting the fact that their daughter had drowned.

Walking into the water with his fins hooked over his left wrist, the search line in his right hand and a light dangling at his waist, Andrew stopped to put on his fins in knee-deep water. Before he could turn around the mother rushed over to him with tears streaming down her flushed cheeks.

"Please.... Please", she said in broken English. "If you find her, you be gentle with my baby." She placed her hands on either side of Andrew's face. He could feel the warmth of her heart, even through his thick neoprene hood.

"Find her Señor… please. My baby should not be left out there." Tears streamed down her tired face as she turned and walked back to the shoreline. Not noticing that the hemline of her dress was soaked with lake water, she returned to the consoling arms of her husband.

"Balls, this is tough. The one flaw that nature does not forgive, is carelessness." Andrew thought as he positioned himself in the water for the hundred yard or more swim to the marker. Lying on his back and looking toward the shoreline, he kicked with a slow, rhythmic stroke out into the lake. Back on the shore, he could see several patrol cars, a rescue van, two motorcycle cops, and a half dozen patrolmen.

The crowd had really thinned out with only about fifty sight-seekers left. Many family members had gone home to rest, so that they might return in a few hours to continue the vigil.

"That's better anyway," Andrew thought "A smaller crowd would be easier to manage when we bring her in."

Two-thirds of the way out, Andrew's muscles were starting to get very tired. A small amount of icy water trickled down his back, as he questioned, "Why do I always get myself into these kinds of predicaments?"

He looked over his shoulder to the swimming marker. "Damn, did someone move that thing out further?" Kicking with slower strokes, he laid out flatter on the surface to reduce his resistance in the water. Parallel with the water and looking straight into the dark black sky, he watched the mist from his warm breath billow out of his mouth. The combination of exertion and the early morning chill were starting to take effect

An Angel Lost   73

as he felt ripples of cold water wash against his hood.

Minutes later, he looked over his shoulder once more. He was only a few feet away from the float. He was careful not to kick downward with his fins. He knew that the thrust from his fins would radiate downward at least eight feet, stirring up the silt-filled bottom and reduce what little visibility there was.

In this shallow water, it looked like a bomb blast messing up the water for twenty feet in all directions.

Andrew took the search line off his arm and turned on his light. With his safety vest air-inflation valve held high, he released air and started his descent. Flat out in the water like a skydiver, his descent was very slow. He touched bottom and moved forward. Visibility was less than two feet. His light was floating chest high connected to his vest by a short lanyard. He knew that even if it wasn't pointing directly at its target, there would be enough light for him to snap clip his search line to the anchor. He tried to snap the line onto the float cable, but it was too thick. He took a few turns around the cable and snapped the clip to the search line. His fingers were getting numb.

"I must be really cooling down. My fingers have no feeling left."

Andrew laid out ten feet of line and starts his circular search pattern.

Suddenly, out of the powdery fog, he saw the death mask of the drowned girl appear. It looked peaceful and serene, anemic and unblemished. His light swung freely, with its flashes falling on the face and then away. Andrew jolted back, gasping a restricted, unrecognizable sound of fright into his regulator. He paused for a moment trying to regain his composure. He reached for his light, almost afraid to point it at the ghostly image before him. He brought the light-beam up, slowly at first, to the base of the anchor, then nervously to where the little face was.

He remembered the number one rule of victim recovery *"never look them in the face if possible."* That makes it too personal. Detachment from human emotion is paramount in such a situation especially underwater.

The lifeless girl came into focus. Her hair flowed gently in the water movement. Her hand was tightly gripped around the anchor cable. Her body, almost buoyant, danced near the bottom as if she were playing a game of May pole. Her eyes were closed. Jet-black hair covered, and then uncovered a trace of fear on her face.

"She's so young to die all alone like this. She sure doesn't look like it was such a bad way to go," Andrew thought to himself, as he tenderly released the little girl's hand from its death grip. "Oh man, how am I going to tow her all the way back in without her parents racing out to meet us."

Andrew wrapped the search line around her waist and started to tow, with her back close to him. Staying underwater just off the bottom, he didn't have to fight the surface waves that would be against him on the way in. However, after a short fifty feet, the struggle was too awkward. "This isn't working, he thought. "I'll take her up and hope no one sees us from shore until the last minute."

At the surface, Andrew rolled on his back and put three puffs of air into his safety vest. He then placed the girl between his legs, towing her with the search line. In the distance he saw a faint light coming toward him. He dropped the regulator from his mouth onto his chest.

"Oh, God damn it, I bet those bastards don't know we're here. Sure.. wouldn't you know? I can see both port and starboard lights; that means the dumb jerks are coming right at us," he said out loud, as if he were having a conversation with his new charge.

"I'll signal them with my light... great. Now where the hell's my light...? Damn, I must have dropped it when we were wrestling to get to the surface...We better get our asses below before they run us over."

Andrew vented his safety vest, and they descended to the bottom. The young girl glided down next to him 8 feet below. Her hair billowed on either side of her face as she settled softly to the bottom. Like a tree falling in slow motion, she fell off to her left side. Straining to peer upward, Andrew listened intently for the sound of the boat motors. Within two minutes, the churning propeller passed less than ten feet from where Andrew and his delicate, young victim had been resting.

"Way to keep up on the latest information boys. I guess no one told those bozo's that there are divers down here. "Andrew grumbled to himself. Seconds later, a grappling bar with four six-inch hooks dangling and skipping along the bottom passed a few feet away. The boat motor sound faded and Andrew figured they made one pass and were on their way to the break-wall hundreds of yards away. He pauses for a moment to make sure this evaluation was correct.

"This time I'll just do a hip carry," he decided. He started to untie the line but his gloves were too thick. He took off his right glove and stuffed it up under his wet suit jacket.

He brought the body close to him by wrapping his right arm around her waist. He made sure that she faced away from him. The progress underwater was far easier now, but fatigue was taking its toll. After twenty yards, Andrew's breathing rate had increased, and he knew he must settle down to the bottom again to rest a moment. He stopped kicking and the two drift gently downward, eight feet to the bottom. As their forward movement stopped, the girl's right hand stroked his. He recoiled by instinct, but then realized she was dead and placed his arm around her again.

"Maybe her spirit is telling me thanks," he thought. He started up again with two powerful thrusts from his fins. His grip weakened slightly and his hand slid up from her waist, clutching her right breast.

"Sorry sweetheart... what the hell, did I do that on purpose? No, don't be stupid. Of course I didn't." Andrew found he was arguing with himself. "Shit, I must be going. Now I'm talking to dead people."

He felt the wave action of the surface and knew he must be getting close to shore. He peered down at his compass. The glow of the dial was just about gone. "Still on target," he thought, as he prepared to come into an upright stance. Lifting himself out of the water, his head just broke the surface.

"Man, there are the parents." Looking through his fogged mask, he could barely see their silhouettes backlit by the streetlights. In front of him, less than a hundred feet away, was more heartbreak than he may be able to handle.

His thoughts vacillated between the reality of dealing with a dead person and protective detachment. In the future, rescue and recovery dive experiences would broaden his detachment.

Andrew shuffled his feet forward to gain better balance and to find an even bottom. Grasping the girl's hand with his hand, he bent over slightly until his head was below the surface. Making a figure four with his left foot against his right knee, he removed one fin, then reversed the position for the other fin.

The parents felt that Andrew had found her, because they had watched him perform his water exit ritual many times that night and he had never stood up in water so deep. Each time before, he had surfaced close to the shore and stood up backwards facing the lake, taking off his fins and walked out. This time he was walking forward, first mask deep, then neck deep, and finally chest deep.

Andrew advanced another fifty feet before lifting the girl's weight from the water. He was waist deep in the water as the parents rushed to their little girl. The mother was silent. Her hands covered her mouth. An occasional hum, from deep inside expressed the pain only a parent can feel. She stroked her baby's hair as she must have done so many times in the past. As they walked out of the surf line and onto the beach, the father reached under her tenderly and looked into Andrew's eyes for long seconds,

"Gracias, amigo...I will take her now," he said. Andrew blinked with both eyes and nodded, trying to cap his emotions.

The comforted parents and supportive friends silently surrounded the girl, sharing the sorrow and anguish. Tearfully the women buried their faces in the chests of their men. The father began to carry his daughter to the rescue van. The medical personnel walked alongside, feeling that after six hours under water, there was little hope of recovery, but they stopped the father, checked her vital signs anyway, and placed her on a stretcher.

Andrew went to the funeral three days later. He stood in the rear of the church until it was time to pass by the casket. As he gazed down into the little angel face, he wondered, "Why such a penalty for such a small error?" He was startled out of his hollow stance by a gentle tug on his coat sleeve and a trembling fragile voice at his side.

"Sen~or...I thank you for finding my baby." Andrew bowed to return a polite comment, but his voice choked up, and he smiled appreciation instead. He never saw or heard from the family again. Over the years, he would think of the "little angel" often. He would never dive Lake Michigan, again without wondering if her spirit was at his side watching over him.

Chapter 8

The Army Way

Rescue and recovery diving became almost commonplace at the dive store. The response time and successful finds increased. Hyland Stark spent many hours discussing diving techniques with Andrew. Hyland would see a special quality in Andrew's diving maturity. The last four years only added to Andrew's thirst for knowledge about this wondrous world beneath the waves. He avidly read volumes of sea books. Many were on the oceans and on marine salvage operations that took place in Scapa Flow after World War I. The German High Sea Fleet surrendered to Admiral Beatty of Great Britain on November 21st, 1918. A year later, the German crew still aboard, scuttled half of the more than 70 war ships which included 10 Battleships, 6 Battle Cruisers, 8 Light Cruisers and almost 50 Destroyers. The twenty-year salvage operation ended in 1938 with the raising of the battleship *Deflinger*. Ironically, one year later the Germans were at it again when they invaded Poland. He read detailed stories about the ships sunk in World War II that slowed the flow of American war material. His studies were diverse and included; sea life and the delicate balance between humans and nature.

Nevertheless, Andrew's marine education would be put on hold for a while. In 1960 the Soviet Union and Nikita Khrushchev would challenge President John F. Kennedy to a face-off in Berlin. Andrew would be drafted, along with all of his other National Guard buddies from Wisconsin. The proud 32nd Division was called on again to bear arms as it did twenty years earlier in World War II. Andrew had joined the National Guard the summer of 1956 when he was sixteen and a half years old. Impatient to become a soldier, he cajoled his mother to drive him to the recruiter, and sign the induction papers. The combination of the 'right attitude', a sense of esprit de corps, and hard work gave him early recognition in the Army as a probable lifer; a thirty-year man.

In a few years, he would proudly become a sergeant who was eager to defend his country. However, making buck sergeant wasn't easy for Andrew. At age seventeen he had not forgotten the streets, and he was quick of temper. His first training-free evening, after weeks of boot camp, almost ended his military career.

As a new recruit, Andrew wasn't aware yet of the class distinction between the military grades.

The general rule was: men of rank lower than sergeant, often referred to as enlisted men, were not allowed to fraternize with the non-commissioned officers. The company sergeants were having their 'back from the field' party in the mess hall. Andrew and several of the other privates thought they would be welcomed. After all, they were in the same training outfit. As Andrew approached the mess hall, a group of sergeants leisurely rocked on the back legs of their chairs. Their black-laced combat boots acted as pivot points on the porch rail. From that position they could easily block the only entrance into the hall, where the party was in full swing.

Many of these sergeants were veterans of the Korean conflict. A short seven years earlier, these professionals were at war in a far away land. Now they were preparing themselves once again for combat across the sea. Andrew scanned the faces of men with keen interest and judged who may have been exposed to combat. "Perhaps they had killed in hand-to-hand combat," he thought. Those that had, are easy to identify. Their eyes are more hollow and dark as if the frame of life has been diminished; as if the soul that gives joy has been replaced by some spiritually void substitute, a substitute that only keeps them upright and moving. Deep lines etched in the forehead and around the mouth bespeak of pain, memory pain, a numbing aftermath only the soul can feel. Some store it in a hidden place in their mind and control it. Others will carry it closer to the surface, ready to lash out at intrusions. Only luck of association with extremely tolerant people will keep them in check. Many become "Lifers" in the military service, because only another mental casualty of war will be tolerant of their volatile emotions.

Years from now, Andrew would learn from his Army buddies a term for the look. His Vietnam buddies would call it "The thousand yard stare."

As the recruits approached the porch, one sergeant stood up and said, "Off limits, girls. Why don't you go back to your barracks and play with yourselves?"

"Funny, you asshole," Andrew thought. The privates pushed forward to the base of the steps.

"Hey, dip-shit, I said no party time for you, comprende?"
Andrew moved up one step to balance himself just inside his center of gravity.

"It's obvious your brain is no bigger than your dick. We have as much right here as you", Andrew said, spitting directly into his opponent's face.

"That cracked it", said one sergeant. The biggest, ugliest one, of course, sprang off the top step like a leopard lunging at a gazelle. Andrew's street-wise background taught him long ago, "Never let 'em get the first punch." That first punch could be decisive. Squarely placed, it could render the opponent defenseless, with a bleeding nose and teary eyes. Hell, he had his nose broken three times before he was fourteen. After that he learned not to get into the game of chest pounding. If war was eminent, "strike first."
The neighborhood where he grew up had its own code: it was either fight or disappear; there was no place to hide.

All within the space of a millisecond, Andrew's steel blue eyes registered unyielding defiance. They were cold, alert and menacing. His anger escalated. The pupils focused and grew smaller, exposing even more blue danger. His heart surged in his larger than average chest. The primal instinct of fight or flight was at war within him. Images of bullies and warriors flashed through his mind, and he became poised for conflict. The primitive scent of imminent battle was apparent. Andrew's posture and aura left little doubt that if confrontation did not de-escalate now, there would be no prisoners taken on either side.
For Andrew, this was another territorial imperative, no different than when he was younger and defending his life from roving neighborhood street gangs. He sidestepped, and the sergeant landed painfully on the side of his own foot. As he straightened up, Andrew drove his fist in a downward slam into the sergeant's jaw. The sergeant hit the deck like a

mattress being flipped on a bed. The sergeant lay face down, with no movement except the slight puff of air, as he exhaled in gasping pain. Like an old bearskin rug, arms and feet spread out, he lay flattened on the ground. The other sergeants must have sensed the explosive potential in this "upstart of a recruit" and decided to back off. No show of superior rank privilege was worth taking on this 210-pound, six-foot bear in olive drab pants and dog tags.

A path was cleared and the victors went in. One sergeant allowed Andrew to brush past his chest. He leaned into Andrew and whispered,

"You are dead meat pal"...you screwed up boy. Your ass is grass and we're going to be the lawn mowers."

All the privates, including Andrew, thought that was the end of the incident. They were wrong. In the service a severe penalty is levied if a sergeant is struck, either on duty or off. A court-martial was probably out of the question, 'but hard time' was certainly on the table. Now it was just an issue of when the sentence would be carried out.

From that day forward, Andrew was on the 'shit list' for long, hard laborious weeks. Nothing could be worse. He got every dirty detail imaginable in the service: from cleaning grease traps under the mess hall to cleaning the commodes with a toothbrush. Near the end of his private rating, things began to turn around. The company was in the field, and Andrew was in his usual location cleaning immersion burners used on a portable field stoves where water is boiled. The troops dipped their mess kits into boiling water after they were washed with soap. This last step in field dishwashing prevented a soldier from getting the 'G.I runs', caused from left over soap residue.

A private from A company had been assigned to Andrew's detail. Andrew's job consisted of lighting all six of the burners. He plunged a three-foot steel rod into the first gas can.

This soaked the wick, and he then shook off the excess. Igniting the wick, he ran it down the long throat of the immersion burner. After igniting the first burner, he transferred the near invisible flame to the second burner.

The glare of the sweltering noonday sun prevented the private from noticing that gasoline had dripped onto the tinder dry grass. Soon the area had small fire trails everywhere. Ankle high flames and embers engulfed all the standing gas cans. Billowing orange flames shot out of three open nozzles. It was only a matter of time before the half dozen gas cans would explode.

Andrew, unaware of the accident, was standing with his back to the burners. Suddenly, he felt a flash of shimmering heat radiate up his neck. He spun around, pivoting sideways to avoid the intense combustion. "Wrong place, wrong time," he thought. He hesitated for just a moment, then decisively, locked down each can lid, putting out multiple explosive threats. A real fear flashed through his mind "what if the two and a half ton mess truck caught fire?" The truck was backed into the only opening in this side of the mess tent. If the truck were to ignite, a fireball would explode into the squad mess tent where the unaware soldiers were preparing to eat. With the tent sidewalls down on the opposite side the troops could be trapped.

The scalding hot lids seared Andrew's bare hands and wrists. He yanked a loose, wrinkled canvas tarpaulin from the nearby truck, and cast it over the burning ankle-high grass, netting the flames. The heavy cloth reached a lofty height, and then fell to the ground, smothering the spreading flames. An acrid smell of singed, charred hair and charred flesh nauseated Andrew. He felt a harsh sting of flames as they leapt up his arms, incinerating the hair on their way to his face and head. Everything happened so fast that most of the troops, who were eating nearby, never knew there was an emergency until after the fire squad arrived. If it had not been for Andrew's instinctive response, more than a half dozen troops may have been seriously injured in the accident.

Andrew was housed in a military hospital for several days with painful burns from wrist to shoulder. His face and neck escaped with only a loss of facial hair. Clad lightly in a T-shirt for KP duty, his arms were totally exposed. Although, the flash flame surged up his T-shirt sleeves and burned his shoulders, it didn't start the shirt body on fire, and his helmet prevented damage to the top of his head.

"Very painful but superficial. There won't be any marks after the first layer of skin peels off," said the military doctor. The Captain's review took only a few days, and Andrew came out the "soldier who took appropriate action, but not a hero." The first sergeant would say later, when the subject came up,

"Heroes are made on the battle field, not by putting out little fires started by some dumb ass that has dung for brains."

It didn't matter anyway. He was off the 'list' at last and given a cushy job while his arms healed.

Rank came faster after that, and Andrew became more 'Army' than ever. He volunteered for everything. After all, he had tasted the worst of it.. He thought, "Volunteering is a hell of a lot easier than some of the things they made me do. Besides think of all the friends I'm making."

From a bad beginning he rose to sergeant classification, in the absolute shortest possible time. "Balls the size of grapefruits", Captain Danielson would say. Andrew had become the youngest buck sergeant in the Division, which gave him the youngest title through two subsequent ranks.

No wonder the commanding officer wanted him to apply for helicopter candidate school. He insisted that Andrew take the entrance exam. "If you should fail, that will be the end of it," the captain advised more than once.

The flight school exam was not as difficult as Andrew had anticipated. However, a torn retina in his right eye washed him out, based on the Army's preflight physical examination. His flying career ended as quickly as it had began.

The torn retina came from a bell ringing, teeth crunching and hammering left cross during Andrew's sixth and last scheduled amateur fight.

An intensive two-week field-training program had just been completed. The long awaited end of the week had arrived. Andrew and six of his friends were having a few beers at their favorite weekend watering hole, the Club Playboy in Tacoma, Washington.

This club didn't belong to Hugh Heftner, but it might as well have. It came complete with bunnies, costumes and dice tables and all the fan fare of the more famous clubs.

That evening two Army buddies, sitting at another table, got into a verbal tiff with three other patrons. At first Andrew and his two table companions paid little attention. This sort of thing happens in nightclubs frequented by aggressive military types. After glancing at the commotion, Andrew turned his attention back to his table.

Suddenly, a huge glass ashtray came flying across the room. It sailed past Andrew's left ear and hit Dick Benter, a fellow Sergeant, in the face above his right eye. The blood splattered upward and left puddles of red across the table. Dick was flung backwards off his chair and onto the floor. Andrew and another buddy attended Dick until they were sure he was all right. The raucous verbal battle was still going on in the background, when Andrew gingerly helped Dick back into his seat. The bleeding had slowed, but there was a one-inch laceration just above his eye. It would need stitches. Andrew resolutely turned his attention to the argument raging across the room. Sliding out of the booth he crossed the dance floor in huge strides knowing that this wasn't his fight, but Dick was in no shape to avenge the attack. He wanted a piece of the loudmouth leader anyway. Even with Andrew helping, the bullies had superior numbers.

He also knew the bad guys couldn't resist making some physical contact. That was the only excuse he needed. The big lug with the mouth was flanked by two of his buddies. They had an Army specialist fourth class, corralled, who was about to be unfairly pummeled.
When the tough guy in the center pushed the specialist back on his heels, he fell into Andrew's arms.

"You all right kid?" Andrew asked the soldier. He set the soldier aside not waiting for an answer as he lunged forward. Andrew knew better than to throw a right-handed punch off his right heel, but he was so rushed to get at this guy, he broke the rules. The punch was well placed, but did little damage. The big mouth spun away with the punch rolling and ducking low. That was time enough for Andrew to set his feet for the next engagement. It didn't take long. Out of his right peripheral vision he saw a vague shadow coming at him. As a deflective move he swung his right arm up and out to the right. To his surprise his fist caught the man square in the throat, flipping him backward onto a booth table. The braggart fell into the seat choking and gurgling. The guy on Andrew's left seemed poised for a fight but stood frozen in a defensive posture. In the time compression of a fight, milliseconds seem like minutes. Andrew's right arm was already cocked. He lunged for ward, bringing his full body weight into play. With one sweeping movement he nailed the third player, whose body skidded onto the dance floor. Meanwhile, the big mouth didn't make any threatening gestures. The posturing braggart had his once mighty stance reduced to bending at the waist, clutching a napkin to his dripping nose. With some effort he finally stood up straight and peered over his gloved nose. Andrew closed the space between them and stared into bloodshot eyes. They were nose to nose for long seconds. Andrew defiantly turned his back on his opponent, deliberately making himself vulnerable and casually strutted back to his friends. "Just a little showing off." he thought, and a cool thing to do.

Two weeks later, while visiting the Club, Andrew met a fight promoter who offered him a chance to have a sparring match in a local athletic match.

"If you look as good in the ring as you did in the Club a few weeks ago, we both might make some money", said Keith Chappell. Moonlighting from the Army Andrew spent months working out and sparring with the locale boxers. Six knockouts and one draw later, Andrew looked good.
Maybe, just maybe, if he would get serious, he could be a contender in a heavy weight class. A big purse fight was no more than ten to fifteen bouts away. There were many heavyweight fighters in the 1960's that had the attention of the fans; like the one special boxer some called Cassius Clay, a boisterous Olympic medal winner. "He won't go anywhere. His mouth is too big," Keith said at least once a week. "Clay's got great movement and strong legs, and he may 'float like a butterfly and sting like a bee', but he has no discipline. Boyd could be dancing on his grave in 10." Keith felt Andrew Boyd's unusual stamina was unique in the fight game. Maybe it was his oxygen capacity, power of concentration, or complete disregard for fear that gave him this remarkable stamina. He could stay away from his opponent and wear him down. Boyd's boxing style was good, but alone it wasn't good enough to take any title.

His feet were quick. "A blur from the waist down," one reporter would write. Said another, "I know he touches down some time during the match. I just don't know when." Chappell had watched Andrew dance hard, very hard rock and roll for hours at the Club. "Without a break, that's something," he thought. That convinced him of Boyd's unusual edge.

If his opponent runs out of gas in the eighth or ninth round, as many heavyweights do, then Boyd could cruise ahead in points.

Scoring the end of a match is always based on how the boxer's technique survives the hazardous exhaustion of the early rounds. Chappell watched weekly as Andrew's skill improved and his attitude focused on winning. It was never to be. An ill-fated, scheduled twelve-rounder would give him yet another direction in his life. During the remaining minutes of the late rounds, Andrew was getting punched around the ring. His opponent, a Brooklyn boy, was beating his brains out. Mismatched by an impatient Chappell, Boyd was hurt in the eighth round by a fighter who should not have come into his life for at least another year, maybe two. This was not going to be a great Hollywood ending, where the good guy comes to life in the last round and knocks out the bad guy. This seasoned opponent knew the game and played hard for keeps. In the early rounds three consecutive low blows drew a warning on Andrew's opponent. It would take its toll in later rounds. During a clinch in the sixth round he bit Andrew in the neck.

Three rounds later in the ninth, he jammed his thumb into Andrew's right eye until it was almost closed. He constantly moved to his left, pounding Andrew's right eye with left hooks.

Andrew's legs twenty-nine inches at the thigh were big for a guy who never intentionally worked on them, but even his strength, great sense of balance, and sixteen-inch arms couldn't help. This street bum that outweighed him and had a reach four inches longer than Boyd's, simply out-gunned him. The only thing that kept the fight going after the tenth round was the size of the bets placed on the twelfth round.

The two fighters never dropped to the mat, but danced, holding on to each other and throwing one uncontrolled volley after another. The audience was getting riotous. Rhythmic boos and jeers rocked the building. Andrew lost the focus of the fight, which was to defeat the enemy, not to defend himself.

His concentration was on the number of hits he was receiving, not on how many he was handing out. This was an uncommon position for him to be in, and it totally zapped his strength.

At the end of the ninth round, the pugilists were all but spent. Clinging to each other with clenched hands encased in leather, each supported the other temporarily, as if they were old friends. Boyd could smell the pungent sweat on his opponent; no, not smell, taste it. He lay with his cheek pressed hard into his opponent's shoulder. He was gasping for air so hard the vaporized sweat from his rival sprayed the back of his throat. His lips tasted the beaded, salty sweat from his opponent's neck. He had nothing left. He was burned and punched out. Every starved muscle was screaming for oxygen.

It would have been merciful to stop the fight. But, in those days and in an obscure little operation like this, the rules are stretched to the limit. Andrew had believed up to this point, he might become a true professional fighter given some hard work and good management. In reality he was just another kid who could brawl and bring in a good gate. It was all about money and Andrew didn't get it. This fight, unknown to him would be his last paid contest.

He thought. "If this son of a bitch hits me now, I can't even see it coming." The fear of not knowing where or when was more intense than the impact itself. Then it came from nowhere with all the power his opponent could deliver. The punch was placed perfectly, not that this Brooklyn brawler was good, but he had a nearly blind target and plenty of time.

He planted both feet, and then shifted his weight, so the full force of his upper body would carry through until impact. Andrew's head snapped to one side until his left ear was touching his shoulder. There was a blinding flash of lightning, a cracking of bone and ripped tendons, then a full rush of pain. As one throbbing flash left, another followed. Andrew's blood-clotted mouthpiece flew across the ring. Spittle splattered out the side of his mouth and onto his shoulder. The once piercing blue eyes were glazed over like an opaque shower curtain.

He felt himself going down, but he couldn't bring his arms up to stop his descent. Down, down he went, buckling at the knees.

He wasn't falling anymore. "What was happening?"

"The ropes, Christ. The ropes. I'm on the ropes." He tried to think.

"What do I do now? Am I standing? Kneeling? What? Oh man, the pain." He heard a hollow and authoritative voice in the distance.

"Get up, Get up." The roar of the crowd was overpowering and deafening. Through the bloody drool of his bruised mouth, Andrew mumbled, "I can't move. Where is that bastard? If I could only get up." The pain surged again and again." Oh, man, I'm done... that's it...I've got nothing left." Everyone was going out of focus, sounds were far away. Then there was silence, a long hollow silence coming from the cavernous, empty tunnel inside his brain.

Andrew slowly rolled off the ropes. On the way down his head arched back as his chin hooked the second rope. His left arm crumbled under his body and rolled him onto his back. Bent at the elbow his right hand painfully swollen inside the glove, inched slowly down to his side. It was the last sign of defiance. He lay there on the canvas, motionless, a mere lifeless pulp and was out cold for five minutes.

He was treated at the local hospital and released a day later. Fortunately, at the time, he was off the post on a four-day weekend pass that he had traded out with his office assistant. Andrew always planned his fights for Friday night giving him at least two days for the swelling to go down. He returned to his regular duties with only a patch over his right eye, which was prescribed because the eye was photosensitive and had blurred vision. Little treatment was available in those days, other than rest. No treatment could be had on the base because this type of activity would have had serious consequences. Andrew had to keep his secret from his fellow soldiers for fear of a careless slip.

After the service, no other doctor caught his eye problems, not even during pre-deep diving examinations. Commercial deep divers cannot have broken bones because the nitrogen, in compressed air dives can act adversely on those areas. No one at the time thought what could happen to torn retinas under pressure? Andrew would later make more than two hundred dives at more than two hundred feet with no apparent reactions.

Unknown to hospital doctors, Andrew had also suffered a tear in his left retina. There were no broken facial bones, a positive note that would pay off later, when he would become a commercial diver.

The detached retina would create yet another path for him to follow. In the closing days of his regular Army service his commanding officer would say, "Too bad about your blurred vision son. In a few months you could have finished flight school. Think how proud you would have been with your officer's bars and a brand new helicopter." That was at the end of 1962. The war in Vietnam was just starting to escalate. Helicopter pilot casualties would be a staggering one in three.

Chapter 9

The 2500 Foot Fall

Andrew crossed the room, his bare feet sank into the plush carpet. A few hours from now, the outer office will be filled with employees. His massive computer network and video satellite uplink will come on line, and reports from his global system will soon be arriving. Each of the thirteen district stations has a time slot. The entire system is run with the help of video teleconferencing.

Stations report in every morning for a given period and must request additional time, if the need arises. Each station has a field unit that may be at a dive site within its district. Field units have portable satellite dishes that can be taken to sea, if needed. Tele-Conference connects the home office with station and field personnel at the moment the operation is taking place. Satellite usage during regular business hours is limited and extremely expensive. There is little time to chitchat or show pictures of the kids. Between now and "show and tell," there is still time for one more cup of coffee. Time to relax and to lose himself in thought, while he stares out again at nature's most precious gift to mankind and the world... water.

It seems, lately, that Andrew is spending more time reflecting back to his early years. Maybe now, at age sixty-four, he can take time to catch up with his past.

In earlier days, there never seemed to be sufficient time to reflect on happy moments or ruminate about personal feelings. World events always got in the way. "The pressure of deadlines," he often thought was the reason, but down deep he felt the loss of many, deep emotional attachments. It made him wonder whether these opportunities would ever present themselves again. It was easier to constantly bury the feeling than to make himself vulnerable to the sorrow of losing another person he loved. Maybe now enough time had passed and reflection helped him to deal with the present.

Standing at the counter of his office kitchenette, Andrew poured another cup of coffee. Even this worn, chipped mug brings back memories of his youth. The words: "Divers do, do it deeper...Sally" are printed on the cup. Sally and Andrew never engaged in an evening of passion, but they came close many times. She would say to him, "I love men in rubber suits, and you sure give me pause for thought."
One of his dearest friends from the early days of the sixties, she was on many of his adventures and always there to catch a beer after a dive. Sally now lives in Ireland with her devoted husband and their seven children. She writes children books; he is a grade school teacher. Andrew shakes his head, and ponders about lost opportunities.
   "I guess you never know what is in a person's heart, until they meet the right person."
Sally has been wed to the same man for twenty-one years and wants one more child "before it falls off" she would say. Andrew talks to her by phone at least once a year, always on her anniversary.
   "I'm going to see more of her in the future," he thinks, as he stares at the mug. Sally gave him the cup the day he set the freshwater deep diving record in Big Green Lake.
   It was 1967 and Andrew had been back from the military service for almost five years. His diving occupation had taken him from sport diving to commercial diving, and then back to sport diving. Milwaukee never did lend itself to a full time opportunity in commercial diving, but he did manage to get twelve to fifteen high paying assignments each year. It was not enough money to live on, but enough to supplement his scuba teaching salary.
   Andrew had a penchant for getting into the local newspaper or on television. He tried any number of things to keep his name out in front of the media. While most of his competitors waited for business to come knocking at their door, Andrew went out searching for it.
   Scuba diving records were starting to be set around the country. Male and female records were being broken in deep diving and duration diving. First, it was hard-hat helmet diving; then scuba started to catch on. Every month, someone was pushing for the Guiness Book of

World Records. The time was right. Andrew was in the best physical shape he had ever been in, better than when he was in high school, playing football.

His skill level was high in both deep diving and free ascent escapes. Most importantly, he was motivated.

No one at this point had made compressed air dives deeper than two hundred feet in fresh water. At least no one had come forward to claim it. Andrew decided to test the record in the deepest inland lake in the Midwest, Big Green Lake near Ripon, Wisconsin.

To make it official, he needed to have witnesses with some stature or credibility. The Milwaukee Journal had stature, and the Conservation Department had credibility. He enlisted staff reporters from the Journal and researchers from the Conservation Department.

Both groups felt that the way Andrew had structured the event; it would be a safe and newsworthy challenge. He made the dive a huge promotion. Sixty volunteer divers would participate in a field study of aquatic growth for the Conservation Department. If the deep dive didn't take place for any reason, the Journal could still shoot a great story about people caring for their environment. Andrew always liked plans that had second and third level benefits for everyone.

The plan was set. The dive would take place in the summer of 1968.

Winter was almost over and the lakes were starting to thaw. Andrew chose six of his most trusted and talented diving friends. All were advanced scuba divers and had worked on one or more of Andrew's commercial assignments.

Big Jake Faller got the duties as the hundred-foot safetyman. He was chosen for this important position, because of his skill, sense of humor and size. One had to have a sense of humor to be involved in some of Andrew's schemes. Jake was well over six four and weighed two hundred forty pounds.

On the day he was selected, he said "Andrew, in case you come screaming past me on your way to the surface... because... a... you ran out of air... don't worry, I'll just jam the spare tank with the valve open in your butt as you go by."

Andrew always loved the sensitivity and compassion of the big guy.

Otto Gehrung was a local artist who resembled a World War II U-boat commander; with his short brush haircut, blue eyes and German accent. He was a character among characters. He sarcastically defended Hitler by saying, "He built the Autobahn and the Volkswagen, didn't he? He also made moustaches popular."

Otto took diving lessons from Andrew the year before and developed a high level of efficiency in just thirty-five dives. Andrew would never forget their first meeting. It was in the pool area of the downtown Milwaukee YMCA.

Otto arrived early for his first class, and as he approached his new scuba instructor, he casually flopped his foot down on the bleacher-type seats while he waited to talk to Andrew. On the other end of the six-foot long board was Andrew's high pressure gauge for testing the student's dive cylinders. The pressure gauge flew into the air seven feet, and then came crashing down at Andrew's feet. Andrew stared for long moments at the broken and shattered gauge. Then without looking up, he put out his hand and said, "I'm Andrew Boyd. I have a feeling that this is going to be an interesting relationship."

Andrew had no idea how true that statement would become. Over the next two years, he and Otto would share numerous, exciting adventures together, including the raising of the 'Alvin Davis, a hundred and five year old, two-masted brigantine. Otto was a lovable clown. 'Clumsy' was a kind word for his lack of grace and skill on two feet. Under water it was a different story. For the 'deep dive', Otto would be stationed at the thirty-foot level with a spare tank and a second regulator attached to it. Andrew should have enough air left after the deep dive for the long decompression stops. If he didn't, Otto would help him change cylinders under water and then follow him through each ten-foot ascent stop on their way to the surface.

Decompression stops were at thirty feet for five minutes, twenty feet for eleven minutes, and finally twenty-three minutes at ten feet. Andrew's good friend, Dr. Edgar Send meticulously calculated each stop. Andrew also threw in a little fudge factor of additional time at each stop. In 1967 there were few, if any, deep diving tables that could be referenced. The U.S Navy's compressed air tables were the commercial 'bible' of deep diving around the world. Unfortunately, the tables had a limit of one hundred ninety feet. Andrew would be diving more than one atmosphere deeper than that.

Dr. Edgar Send would work up the extended tables. He was a general practitioner, but had years of research in the field of high altitude flight and deep tunnel decompression sickness.

Send worked with the first recompression chamber built in Wisconsin. The chamber was in the Milwaukee County Emergency Hospital's lower level on Wisconsin Avenue. Most Milwaukeeans never knew of the important work done in this chamber. Heart patients, burn victims, gas gangrene patients and many others were treated in the chamber.

The Navy often called upon Dr. Send as a consultant for dive tables. In the early sixties, he worked on the " Man in the Sea" project with the Navy.

At the time, the U.S. Navy was duplicating the living under the sea experiments that had been initiated by Cousteau in the late fifties. During their years of association, Dr. Send had scheduled Andrew for a number of deep diving tests. Andrew had an unusual tolerance for nitrogen narcosis, the dreaded 'rapture of the deep.' Narcosis is similar to being under the influence of some mind-altering substance. The diver has the feeling of euphoria; a sense of well being, even when in extreme danger. Dr. Send was surprised at the ability of Andrew to withstand such high degrees of nitrogen saturation.

The day of the 'deep dive' was drawing close; only a few weeks away. Andrew needed to have a meeting with Dr. Send. He hated to ask the 'Doc' to work up the tables, because he knew that Edgar would be resistant. The doctor welcomed a challenge to set records but felt that there should be a rigorous training schedule, a formal research regimen and an appropriate safety plan. He didn't believe a hazardous dive should be attempted without a valid reason. The goal of a record dive alone wasn't going to convince him to participate. Nevertheless, Andrew went purposefully to the doctor's office that late spring day, and approached him with confidence. He explained to him that this wasn't just a whim. He had trained for five months and there was a safety plan in place. He described the seven buoyant ascents from one hundred sixty feet that he and his team had completed.

Dr. Send softened his objection to Andrew's deep dive and began his pre-dive lecture. "Nitrogen won't be your problem at two hundred forty feet," he said, "but the cold and the darkness will be tearing at your mind. You have to believe you can do it. Belief in yourself and your abilities will relieve the stress of possible failure. Second, you need equipment, and divers you can trust with your life. Third, get into even better physical shape... in case something goes wrong. The extra surge of energy, because of pure muscle may bring you through. Fourth, don't get laid for two months, to conserve your strength."

There was a long pause. Then Dr. Send said, "Just kidding. Don't look so frantic."

Andrew's mouth hung open for a moment, then closed to a smile. Dr. Send asked, "What about your back problem? Does it still bother you? What are you going to do if it starts to act up again?"

"I haven't had an attack in six months. If I just watch it, I won't have another one."

"Andrew, don't be ridiculous. Those kinds of things don't just go away. You need to stop putting so much pressure on yourself with these damn foolish things you do. If your back is inflamed when you make the dive, you could be in serious trouble."

"Doc, you worry too much."

Andrew knew the doctor was right. If he had what he called an "attack" within a week of the dive, he wouldn't be able to get out of bed, let alone make a water entry.

Andrew's back injury was the result of a parachute jump he had made two years earlier. Under the always-present peer pressure of his good friend Ward McNair, they signed up for jump lessons at Rainbow Airport near West Allis, Wisconsin.

Parachute jumping in the early sixties was hard on the feet, legs, spine, and nervous system. Most of the chutes were of the old military style, designed for people up to one hundred seventy pounds. Ward and Andrew each weighed in at over two hundred pounds.

Jumping in the late fall or early spring, when the air was thick, made the landing softer. Any other time, these heavyweights would hit the ground with a body-jarring impact; the same powerful impact as jumping from a second story porch.

After spending weeks hanging out at the aviation school, they were primed and ready to go. Andrew was a little less enthusiastic. He dearly loved adventure, but jumping out of a perfectly good airplane, seemed somehow just 'too macho' for him. Ward did every damn fool thing Andrew asked of him. The least Andrew could do was to die crashing into the earth for one of his oldest friends.

Their first jump was to be from a single engine Cessna 172 with the passenger seat and door removed. Ward and Andrew sat on the uncomfortable floor with their backs positioned against the rear bulkhead wall during take off. They were cramped and claustrophobic with a bulky main chute backside, and the tightly folded reserve chute clamped to their bellies. Knees were pulled up as tight as possible. There was no place to stretch out. Breathing was difficult, because their reserve chute pressed into their diaphragms. When the pilot neared the jump zone, he yelled back to the two skydivers "Stand by, get in the door."

Andrew was the first to jump, as he had lost a coin toss with Ward, just before takeoff. Sliding across the floor, while pulling with his left hand on the back of the pilot's seat, he dropped one leg out the open door. His leg snapped back under the plane.

The pilot yelled impatiently, "Wait till I throttle back." Andrew pulled his right leg into the plane. One pant leg pulled out of his jump boot and flapped wildly in the wind.

"It's going to be a little drafty in the crotch," Ward yelled in Andrew's ear. With determined effort, Andrew strained to see Ward, beyond the edge of the helmet and said, "How do I let you talk me into this stuff?"

"OK, I'm cutting her back...get ready", the pilot commanded. The wind outside the door thrashed at ninety to one hundred miles per hour. It blasted Andrew in the face. He could feel the wind vibrate his goggles. They dislodged at the top, causing the rubber seal to flutter against his forehead. He must reach out, grab the wing strut with his left hand, and simultaneously pivot on his left foot to balance himself. A small steel pad six inches square was welded to the underbody of the plane for the jumpers left foot. The right foot rested on the locked right wheel.

"Let go of the God damn wing," shrieked the pilot to the stricken novice, whose position was frozen. "I can't hold this stall speed forever."

Andrew didn't think he had been there that long, but Ward was already inching out the door.

"Make the ground soft for me" was the last thing Andrew heard as he pushed off by kicking backwards in a belly flop position. He was tied to the plane with a static line that deployed the chute after he cleared the plane. Within a hundred feet of the plane, the chute billowed out and jarred Andrew into conscious thought. The wind gently whirled in his helmet as he smoothly descended to earth.

"How like diving this is; the excitement of the entry... the quietness... the self reliance... the visual impact. Man... the houses and people look so small. Damn, where's the airport?" he thought.

Andrew pulled the small toggle line attached to his left riser. He spilled air from the chute and turned slowly in that direction. He stopped his turn on a straight line with the airport. He thought, "Now all I need to do is ride her in."

Ward left the plane only seconds after Andrew and was closing the gap between the two. "Ge-ron-i-mo, Re-con." Ward screamed with a chuckle as he sailed past Andrew on the downwind leg toward the airport. They both landed, not more than twenty feet from the target mat next to the airstrip. With renewed energy and enthusiastic applause from the other jumpers on the ground, Ward and Andrew signed up for a second jump.

The pilot grumbled less this time, maybe because his charges weren't doing everything wrong. The new chute Andrew was wearing felt tighter, and more emotionally uncomfortable than his first one.

"We should have waited for our old chute to be repacked", Andrew muttered as he tugged at his crotch strap walking to the plane.

At twenty-five hundred feet, the pilot cut the engine and both adventurers exited the small plane. Andrew felt the chute deploy. This time he was conscious of the sound and sight of the chute opening and looked up as he was instructed to do. "Just to make sure the chute was in the bag," the instructor had mused before they took off.

98   Richard Bennett

Andrew looked up again, checking to make sure the chute was fully deployed. "Man, that baby is big. Looks good to me this time. Right on target. Where the hell's Ward? Oh, way over there. He'll have to start running if he is going to land in the same neighborhood."

Andrew pulled heavily on his right toggle. "Now what the hell's wrong?" He felt the chute lurch downward. Beneath his nylon jump suit he feels beads of perspiration trickle down his sides.

His feet started to slowly swing out to the side. He was spinning out of control, corkscrewing toward the ground. The toggle line has locked the chute in a hard right turn, dumping air and descending rapidly at four times the normal speed. Andrew struggled with the line to free it, but the centrifugal force pressed him outward into the harness. The spinning pulled the blood to his feet and made him light-headed.

The raiser straps cut deep into his left biceps, while he tugged desperately to release the main chute and deploy the reserve chute mounted at his stomach. 'Twang, Twang', the main chute released. Andrew pulled the D-ring and the reserve chute was free.

He threw the chute out as if he were making a bed. Air was captured in the billowing nylon in front of him. Dropping backward at one hundred thirty miles per hour, the chute puffed out, snapping Andrew solidly backward against the waist harness. His taut stomach muscles stretched and his spine compressed, increasing the adrenaline rush. His mind displays thoughts unrelated, disconnected, and finally, there was a narrowing of his peripheral vision.

He hung stunned for a second, trying to catch his breath. The downward speed hadn't slowed. The ground rushed up to meet the plummeting, out of control parachutist.

Andrew had but a second to get his feet up and protect his face, as he tore through a tree covering the airplane hanger. Screeching sounds of scraping twigs crashed against his helmet. Jagged branches shattered against his body, snapping and popping. The horrific noise seemed to go on forever. As he descended through the tree at an angle the branches became larger and more forbidding. Andrew kept his tuck position tight and knees bent arms in tight. The ball of his left foot bounced off a large limb and clipped his left knee tearing his jump suit.

Then, with an abrupt halt, he crashed against the side of the hangar with a loud 'boom.' The storage shed outer wall collapsed inward, snapping its two-by-four inch braces inside.

Andrew, hung like a marionette, dangled almost lifeless, as if stashed away after a performance. Blood oozed from his contorted nose and lacerated face, where the tree gave full resistance to his intrusion.

Ward, meanwhile, was unaware of Andrew's mishap. During the last few minutes of his jump he was in a state of total focus. The only thing in his mind was the ground target and how much closer he was going to hit than Andrew. He rolled into the ground in perfect form and only inches away from the target mat. He unbuckled his chute and laid back the goggles on his helmet. After gathering his chute in his arms he began looking for Andrew. He turned in a full circle searching the horizon. Then cupped his hand on his forehead and scanned the skis for the red and white-stripped chute of his friend, "I really beat his ass this time, he's not even in sight."
Unable to make any visible contact Ward figured he missed the drop zone completely. "Andrew must have dropped behind the building in the field. How could he have missed the drop zone by such a huge margin? He was right on track, all he had to do was sit back and ride her home." Ward couldn't imagine why people weren't gathered around the target mat. Usually a few instructors and a helper or two would congratulate each jumper as they came down. On the last jump they yelled instructions up to the trainees to; "keep your feet together and bend your knees, roll." Just before they hit the ground.

One of the jump school instructors was running toward him yelling that Andrew had a chute malfunction and hit the shed next to the hanger. Ward dropped his chute on the ground and ran full force toward the crewman. Ward and the panicked ground crew raced across the tarmac toward the building.

"Jesus, did you hear that crash?" the instructor yelled at Ward as they turned the corner of the building. Ward stopped in his tracks. He seemed almost paralyzed by the thought that his grade school pal might really be injured.

"Holy balls, is he dead?" asked one of the helpers, with hysterical concern."

"Easy now, his neck or back may be broken," said one of the machinists who had cradled Andrew's head gently in his hands. Ward and the others unsnapped his chute and gingerly lowered him to the ground, while Andrew slowly regained control of his body. He groaned, "Oh man...I hurt all over. Get me up, up." Ward asked with real concern,

"Are you all right?"

Andrew didn't reply. Not one to show how worried he was, he quipped.

"If you are, then I want to take a picture of your chute hanging in the tree and that broken beam. No one is going to believe this."

The attendants removed Andrew's helmet and loosened his jump suit. Andrew regained his senses and began to mumble, "I told you we should have used our old chutes." Ward had taken the photos he wanted, returned to Andrew's side, and knelt. He leaned into Andrew closing in to hear the gasping comments Andrew muttered while still in pain.

"I must still be alive, there isn't anyone that damn ugly in heaven." They stood Andrew upright after a few minutes, at his insistence. Andrew paused before straightening up completely because of a numb feeling in his legs. Ward helped him out of the jump suit and half walked; half carried him to his car.

He sensed he was seriously hurt. Months of extended rehabilitation and labored pain lay ahead, but Andrew recovered sufficiently to consider parachuting again by April.

Chapter 10

Raising The Shrouded Wreck

Frank Mariman, a slightly built, boat captain, called Andrew in early November 1967. Frustrated as an apartment manager in Illinois, Frank moved his family to Wisconsin and started a small fishing charter boat business in the Door County area. His two-year-old business was doing well. It was just natural that he began to take scuba divers out when he had an open weekend.

Andrew had been using Frank's charter service from its inception. He was very pleased with Frank's personal style of detailed attention to his customers. Andrew would put groups together three or four times per year for long weekends in Door County. Their business relationship grew to a trusting, personal friendship. The emotional phone call would show how close these two men had become.

"Andrew? This is Frank. We got the best damn perfect wreck you ever saw. Holy jumper, it's in the best shape. You 'gotta come up and help me raise this damn thing." Frank was panting out of breath and almost out of control, rattling away as he spoke. "I just docked the Sea Hawk ten minutes ago and charged in to phone you. You 'gotta see her. She's as pretty as they come."

"Slow down Frank, before you have a heart attack."

"Hell son, how am I supposed to slow down? This is bigger than anything we've ever found, and it's whole. Not a break in her."

"What's the name of the ship?"

"Hells Bells, boy, how would I know? I just found her an hour ago; we weren't even looking."

"Well, how did you find it, if you weren't looking?"

"One of the local fishermen caught his trawl net on her mast and anchor windlass. The net costs $1,400 to replace. He wants me to untangle it and bring it up."

"Are you working on it now?"

"Not yet."

"When are you going to do that?"

"Soon as you get your fur down here."

"Frank, it's up there, and I have to work until 6:00 P.M. Friday night."

"Sorry, keep on think'n I'm still in Chicago. I'll get some guys together and pull that net free. Then, when you get down here; oops, up here; you and I can run her for a look-see. Sound good?"

"Sounds good. I'll see you no later than 9:30 Friday night."

Frank called back the next day and said, "Better hold tight. Our dive boat, the Sea Hawk, broke loose her moorings and ran aground. Hell-la-va blow here. Better wear your snuggies if you come up yet this year."

Andrew never kept his appointment The delay and conflict of scheduling in diving classes and the start of ski season made it impossible.

By the time Frank had re-floated his boat and repaired some minor damage, it was the middle of November. Frank and two husky buddies from Chicago cleared most of the nets on a frigid Thanksgiving Day. After that bone-numbing weekend, diving would be put on hold until the spring thaw.

April of 1968 brought several early disappointments to Frank and his band of stouthearted men. Storms were as relentless as they had been in November. On two arduous attempts, Frank could not locate the ship. The forlorn divers had to reluctantly return to their daily jobs. Only weekends afforded an opportunity for further searching.

The month of May would bring better luck. They fortunately relocated the ship and systematically finished removing the nets. The real salvage work would begin. The laborious work on removing the eight-foot deep silt from the holds and crew's quarters had begun. The small pumps and limited size of their salvage boat made the task enormous.

James Dysart of Maine Marine Corporation called Frank for a meeting. Frank thought they were to meet at the boat yard, but instead James designated the Country Club for lunch. Not prepared for stylish social affair. He went scrambling to borrow dressy clothes from friends and was just able to make the meeting. He brought along 16-millimeter movies of the "Alvin Davis," that his friend, Joe Blair, had shot the week before.

Although his pants didn't fit, Frank's colorful presentation and amazing footage won him celebrity status. James Dysart was impressed. He offered Frank the unlimited use of a sixty-foot military landing craft, an LCM6. The craft was named "MV Eden's Barge," and would serve as the secure, surface-support vessel for the entire two-year operation.

Fortunately, September brought good dive weather, and MV Eden was ready and fully outfitted for her run to Chambers Island. One crisp fall afternoon, Andrew was late arriving. Frank and the boys were already well into their second bottle of brandy. Andrew greeted everyone and wearily hobbled off to bed.

He often thought what a tough old man Frank was. He looked every part the old sea dog. His black hair was speckled with gray. Time and weather had etched his sea story upon his face. Deep lines told the story of many hours on deck watch. A shaggy beard and mutton chop sideburns bordered his face. A cigarette-stained mustache only added to the look. Frank's hands were thick at the fingers and yellowed from his two-pack-a-day habit. Hard, toughened hands validated a vigorous working man of five foot nine and one hundred sixty pounds. Several fingernails were blackened from recent, ill-placed, hammer blows.

Most men in their mid-forties think about slowing up a little, but not Frank. He would drink with the best of them late into the evening. The twenty-year-olds would struggle to keep up and finally relent. He was always the last soldier standing and always the first diver up the next morning.

He started work at sunup and continued until the bar closed. In those days, heavy drinking was a sign of masculinity, almost a requirement. Not as the diving community views it today. In the last two years, Frank's small motel and bar were the only revenue sources for his charter business and support for his salvage attempt. It was a quaint bar on the main street with a real wood burning fieldstone fireplace and beamed ceiling. In the winter, most of the clientele were local people. In the summer, most of the clientele were tourists. Frank's wife, May, was a princess among barbarians. She would patiently cook meals and manage the motel-part of the business. Tirelessly, Frank would fish, take out divers, run the bar, and tell war stories late into the night. It was hard work and long hours, but they worked well together. He was a crusty man with the sea in his blood, and she, a petite, hard workingwoman. When pushed too far, she appeared to stand ten feet tall. Andrew enjoyed the company of people of this ilk. They were gracious and considerate of everyone with whom they came in contact.

Locals and tourists gathered nightly in the bar. In the beginning they never felt threatened by the ragtag unshaven divers, and felt comfortable in the presence of these colorful, newfound celebrities. But after the first season, the pirate image began to wear a little thin.

Word of the shipwreck find and possible recovery of the old lake shipper spread to the newspapers and television. More and more sightseers poured into the bar taking the favorite bar stools of the locals. Life would not be the same for the quaint little community.

This night, Andrew was exhausted and needed some sack time, so he kissed May good night, got the usual round of razing and went to bed.

The next morning May woke him, cutting into his vivid diving dreams.

"You were wise." she said. "That damn fool, Frank, sat up most of the night telling 'fish stories' again." Andrew nodded clearing his head.

"Can't you talk to him about his drinking?" he asked. May's frustration with Frank was held in check most of the time, but late nights and early mornings were taking their toll. His novel celebrity status kept him afloat in customers until the wee morning hours.

Recently, she had become short-tempered and lost her sense of humor.

"He won't listen to me. You know how pigheaded he is," she said.

"He wasn't bad before, but since he found that damn wreck, he's been talking to everyone about raising it."

"OK, OK, May, I'll talk to him about slowing down, said Andrew, "but he will only call me a candy-ass, slap me on the back, squeeze my cheek, and tell me not to worry so much."

"He respects your opinion, so..." May never finished her sentence. Frank burst into the room, half-dazed and bleary-eyed. He said, "Son, half the day's gone. If we're going to get to Chambers Island before 10:00 A.M., you better get the beef out of the fart-sack and get on the deck."

Andrew and Frank left Egg Harbor and headed almost straight north, past Fish Creek to Chambers Island, which is an eight to ten mile run.

In midsummer, the Green Bay side of Lake Michigan could be as calm as a mill pond, but in the late fall to winter, old-timers would say, "keep a weather-watch or the lake will get' ya."

The raising of this ship could be fodder for a full-length feature film. She is a two-masted brigantine of 110 feet, sitting twelve degrees off vertical in 105 feet of frigid, dark water. According to the Door County Advocate, the "Shrouded Ship" went down in a heavy blow in June of 1864, with all hands aboard. One hundred and four years later, Frank, Andrew, and two Chicago divers would begin their descent to the ship's deck. It had been silent and hidden from view since the Civil War. Now and for the last few months she has been poked and prodded by dozens of humans. Andrew's uneventful descent was filled with the usual excitement of seeing the well-preserved, haunted image of a virgin wreck.

Frank had removed the entangling fish net months ago. All that remained were the tattered remnants of other nets, long since forgotten. As they slowly dived over the crow's nest; a platform, mounted two-thirds of the way up, the mast came into view. Andrew checked his depth gauge. "Thirty-five feet and still good light. I love Door County. It's so clear down here."

Andrew looked up to see the silhouette of the mast against the surface. Frank and the two divers were slightly below, falling through space like skydivers with unopened canopies. Their frothy bubbles raced to the surface and hit Andrew in the chest, bursting into thousands of tiny shimmering pellets. Andrew stopped for a second to examine the broken line that held the sail and cross-arm in place. The line in this upper warm water was soft to the touch.

A slight pressure between Andrew's forefinger and thumb crushed the material, as if he were pressing his thumb into the ash of a cigar. The line fragments fell away into the voluminous blackness of the depths. Much of the line had fallen away and was lying coiled, like abstract art, on the deck below.

Frank leveled off ten feet above the deck and waited for Andrew to reach him. The two Chicago divers Frank had enlisted were given an assignment to survey the entire outer hull of the ship. At this point no diver had seen more than two or three feet of the ship at any time. Visibility was often reduced to a sense of touch only. Rough water held up work for several weeks, and now the hull might be clear enough to inspect. Their job was to see if there were any breaks or damage caused when she hit bottom. The two divers moved forward about amidships and rolled over the starboard side, as if they were two combat pilots with a target in sight.

Frank and Andrew cautiously moved to the stern of the ship to inspect the crew's quarters and steering gear. They completed their hull inspection and returned to the surface.

Frank called the group together and asked each diver to review in detail what they had seen. The hull appeared to be sound not a plank out of place. It became clear that additional planning was needed to develop the next phase. There was a dive plan and a schedule, but it was always in flux. Frank postponed his second dive, took his notes and retired to the helm. A summary of everything that had been accomplished this far was long overdue and Frank knew it. They had made hundreds of working dives to this point, but there always was some new task that demanded immediate attention.

Several weeks earlier the crew quarters had finally been pumped clear of silt, after months of harrowing, backbreaking labor. Because of the possibility of decompression sickness, divers were limited to only minutes at this depth. The cold and stress added to the restrictions on their actual underwater time. Water temperature was a bone numbing 38 degrees F. and reduced dive time to less than 15 minutes.

A six-inch suction pipe, connected to an old firehouse pump was the main tool used to clear the ship of over eight feet of silt. One diver descended the pipe straddling it into the interior of the ship. With a small hand-held rake, he pulled down walls of silt that had the consistency of coffee grounds. A sturdy catch screen at the inlet nozzle stopped any small items that might be blown upward to the surface.

At 110 feet, the wet suits of the day compressed to the thickness of a kitchen rubber glove and divers lost their thermal protection. Rugged, heavy-duty dry suits were still a few years off. Some suits were lightweight and cost less then $150.00, a first choice for the underpaid diver. Andrew tried gum rubber suits on several jobs, but one snagged and it flooded in seconds. Some had grooved rubber rings that rolled into the jacket and pants at the waist. They were a hassle to put on and most leaked water after a few minutes underwater.

Andrew loved to tell new divers about the super-suit he designed and which he called the "Challenger." Today he had two new prospects for it so he began his sales pitch.

"I use a wet suit of my own design, cut more for comfort than for extreme cold-water diving. I sell this unique design to customers at Adventures End. He lifted the suit legs displaying them to the divers.

"See the ankle-to-throat, two-way zippers that allow ease of suiting up. I fit each suit to the customer, using sixty-five measurements. These large patch pockets on each front thigh are perfect storehouses for gloves, slates, and other things." Andrew turned the suit inside out.

"This suit also has nylon on both sides and has matching zippered gloves and boots. You know, wet suits a few years ago did not have nylon linings. That made them hard to pull on. We had to apply baby powder all over ourselves to ease the tug of pure neoprene rubber against the skin. I call my suit the 'Challenger.' It sells for about $260.00."

The two possible buyers listened intently, but they were on a salvage boat anchored on Lake Michigan. On this dive and during the next two years, Andrew wished he had given a little more thought to warmth and less to innovation and style.

The wreck that was resting below their keel was called the "Shrouded Ship", because the christened name of the ship would elude researchers for almost a year. It caused many an investigator a sleepless night before her name was revealed.

Andrew and more than one hundred divers volunteered their courage and brawn to raise the Shrouded Ship. Andrew's job at Adventure's End, plus his monthly commercial jobs, limited his project commitment. Yesterday, like many other Fridays, he tirelessly drove to Door County. During the 1968-69 summer and fall season he was committed to dive every available three-day weekend.

Andrew has already made his first dive and finished sitting through an "off gassing" period. An overcast sky greeted him and the team as they wiggled back into their damp wet suits. The sun was shining brightly when they surfaced. Now the cloud-veiled sun left a chill in the air. The sun had been elusive like this for more than a week.

Today would be one of the days Andrew would make three salvage dives: the inspection dive he had just completed and two additional working dives. Boyd said to one of the equipment handlers:

"I don't suppose you feel like taking my turn at the pump?" He was speaking about his turn at suction-dredging one of the forward cargo holds.

"Are you kidding? I wouldn't go down there and bury my ass in silt for love nor money."

"Too bad. I'm feeling so toasty in my new pretty blue suit."

Andrew made a giant stride into the water from the lowered front ramp of the MV Eden's Barge. "Pa doosh" the water impacted around his muscular body on entry sending a small cascade of water onto the deck. He surged back to the surface with a few hard fin strokes and gracefully floated on his back. His safetyman said, "We'll miss you, Boo Boo. Don't get lonely."

He handed Andrew the well-used hand rakes he would use to pull the sediment to the mouth of the gulping suction dredge. Andrew grinned just before he started his descent and said, "You're next, sweetheart. Keep the fire in the boiler going."

Frank always insisted that a safetyman be suited and geared up, ready to dive in case of an emergency. There was only one suction pump, and visibility would fall to zero two seconds after the pump started, so extra precautions were taken. Frank would lecture, "If you have a cave-in, hang tight and stay calm. The safety-diver will be down in a few minutes to save your little pink butts." He meant every word. The diver tunneling into the walls of silt caused cave-ins. This method sped up the removal but would sometimes bury the diver up to his hips. Frank made a steadfast rule of "No more tunneling on purpose, or I'll tell May." "On purpose" was the secret phrase. In the dust storm of silt, tunneling just happened.

Andrew followed the pipe down: ten feet, fifteen feet. At twenty feet, he checked the first pipe connection. A thirty-foot surface pipe section was disconnected here and taken on board after each weekend for safekeeping. If a sudden lake storm hit, it might tear loose from the main mast and would be lost.

"This section's OK.", he thought. Andrew slipped off the struts holding up the crow's nest and continues his journey into the inky, inner-space of the lake.

"Damn this water is cold." he thought, as he passed through the thermocline of warm water above and cold water below. "Shit, why do I let myself get talked into these things?" He danced on pavements of black as he dropped twenty more feet into what seemed like the center of the earth. "Why am I so jumpy?" he thought, as he increased his fin-stroke to slow his descent. "I'm just tired I guess. Too little sleep, too much party for this boy... When I get top-side, I'm going to crash until my next dive."

Andrew's suit tightly compressed, and his negative weight pulled down on his body. Downward he dropped; but no sign of the deck. The homemade helmet light is of little use, other than at the start of the dive. Turning to face the mast, he slid his hands and fins down the sides of the eighteen-inch in diameter post to slow his rapid fall through space. The dim glow of his light was bright enough to see the golden brown finish of the mast. It was weathered with small cracks and crevices from the eighteen years of surface storms. Pounded by sea and sun before it sailed the Great Lakes on its final voyage. Andrew senses his depth from the increased hollowness of his exhaled breath. The sound deepened from the more than atmospheres of air compressed in his ear canals and lungs. He knew the deck would soon come into focus out of the gloom. He pointed his fins downward to act as shock absorbers.

"Crunch." His fin-tips almost bent in half and sprang him upward to their full length.

"OK, I'm here...now a little left turn to the rail...down the starboard side about twenty feet...a tight left...and...I should be right...about...there...hey, not bad... dead center." Andrew could have followed the pipe right into the hold, but decides to study the deck layout. Sitting on the rim of the cargo hold, Andrew removed one fin then the other and weighted them down with a tackle block. In one smooth motion, he swung his feet over the hold edge and slid down the pipe as if it were a banister in an old mansion. The broad beam of his helmet light temporarily illuminated the scene.

Near the bottom he paused to inspect the funnel-shaped hole that had been started. "Nice job, Doug", he thought as he settled over the pipe and reached out into the darkness to find where the last diver had finished digging. He gripped a three-foot long rake in each hand and clamped the suction pipe between his legs. He was now ready to start. Turning on the powerful suction, he reached forward to a seven-foot mound of grayish-black sediment. He created a mental image of the crater's inside diameter, which had been dug by a previous diver. Then, he gingerly lowered himself into it. Tiny particles of decayed matter floated past, then clung to every part of Andrew's body. Each movement generated an eddy of swirling fragments. Visibility dropped to less than two feet. Andrew moved cautiously forward being careful not to kick up any more sediment than necessary. Reaching out into the still undisturbed water, he carefully pitched his rakes at head level: first the left rake, then the right, found their mark.

A mountain slide of silt encompassed Andrew's legs up to his knees. There was the disturbing sound of slurping and gurgling, as the suction hose devoured its favorite meal. The vibrations penetrated his suit. He heard the tiny, crystalline fragments race to the surface, rattling against the containment of the metal tube. Steady nerves and a forced sense of calm were required for efficiency.

There was little need for alarm. This process would hypnotically repeat itself every few minutes for the next fifteen-minute work period.

"Pull down the wall, don't tunnel. Check the sides and overhead with your rakes. Feel the wall, feel the wall. Know where you are." Frank's words reverberated and echoed within Andrew's skull. The dim beam from his helmet light exhibited a dull orange glow only inches in front of his mask. It was exhausting to look without really seeing. His strained eyes attempted to focus on the dust storm that danced in kaleidoscopic patterns in front of his mask. His mind accepted, and then rejected, the images created by the vortex of decaying matter. Andrew closed his eyes and allowed his mind to compose a diorama of his work place. For more than ten years, without realizing it, he had trained his mind to compute information gained solely from his sense of touch. He built a three-dimensional mosaic model in total darkness and translated those images into motor skills. Tapping the flat end of each rake in a half-circle in front of him, he defined the outline of the archway he has furrowed. The sediment slowly receded around his legs, lower and lower until he was able to move one foot forward. Releasing the suction with each step, he repositioned himself within three feet of the wall.

Four minutes before the end of his shift, the dredge operator would shut off the water pump then turn it back on. That signaled Andrew to start to clear his legs again and prepare for his ascent. If, after six minutes, he was not holding on near the safety tank at ten feet, his safety diving buddy would descend to help him. Their shifts were timed so that each working diver would pass each other on the guideline. Andrew waited as the safety-diver changed his role to salvage diver. The diver slowly sank until he was parallel with Andrew.

Andrew gave the "OK" sign and pointed down. The sign told the diver that everything was ready to go. There wasn't anything else to report, so he continued down to the ship. Unceasingly, hour after hour, day after day, until 60 tons of black, gritty gunk was removed.

Late in September 1968, the attention was placed on the actual raising of the "Shrouded Ship." A lifting device had to be designed, measurements of the ship had to be taken, and somehow the ship had to inherit a name. Earlier in the summer, a crewmember had found a clue to her identity. The Green Bay Advocate, dated June 1864, hinted that the "Shrouded Ship" might be the Alvin Davis. The ship was lost in the area of Chambers Island, Door County, Wisconsin, in an unexpected storm. It was sailing without cargo for Oconto, Wisconsin. A summer squall rolled her to port side. She capsized and blew her hatch covers. Three men were reported missing. The captain, first mate, and a passenger working for passage were all presumed drowned. A passing freighter rescued two crewmen.

Months of suction dredging and hard labor had fatigued the crew. Frank wrote in his journal: "I am exhausted. I must keep up with the crew. They are great friends: loyal; and they work hard with little in personal gain. I have great fear when anyone is a few seconds late coming up. My stomach is in knots all day."

In addition to the diving Frank spent most of late September building the lifting harness for the ship. The high-pressure pump system used to suction the wreck was refitted to punch six holes under the ship for lift cables. The holes were to be located at the areas of least stress on the ship.

The lake bottom consistency was hard packed clay and not easily penetrated with the high-pressure water stream. Divers worked in teams, one on the deck and one at the lake floor. They worked in unison to drive a sixteen-foot long curved pipe under the ship. The water pressure blew the clay out of the hole and upward. It was an inch-by-inch process. Each time there was a downward surge by both divers, a huge cloud of clay dust billowed out of the hole like a massive explosion.

The first hole beneath the ship was completed on September 25, 1968 the second hole, just forward of the cabin was about to start. Frank called for a pre-dive meeting. His major concern was that the divers were working a lot harder on this assignment than on the suction detail.

At 110 feet and 38 degree water that extra workload saturates one with nitrogen faster, Frank started his lecture. "I don't want any dead butts around here with us, so close to the end." He points at Steel-man, a name given to a diver who had shown an unusual amount of stamina.

"And you take it easy. This bullshit of pushing to get it done has got to stop. From now on everyone will stop working after fifteen minutes, and take an extra few minutes at ten feet." He scanned the group for questions to make sure they understood. He nodded his head yes, staring lovingly at May and said, "Well, lady and gentlemen... shall we make history?"

Andrew suited up for the dive. His triple 40 cubic foot cylinders gave him all the air needed to make the dive and he used almost every pound of pressure. That weekend would be especially hard because of the heavy workweek he had just completed. It started with two basic scuba courses in the middle of the week. On Thursday morning, before working an eleven-hour day, he recovered a motorcycle belonging to the "Hells Angels" from Pewaukee Lake.

Friday morning he had driven to Door County, early enough to catch the MV Eden before she left for Chambers Island. Now two days into the weekend, the overwork was starting to show in his concentration. He bolted a battery pack to the back of his tank assembly and ran the wire for the lamp down his left arm within inches of his wrist.

"Give me a hand taping these wires down", he requested of his dive buddy.

"You got it. Need anything else?"

"Yeah. You can tape my head up so it won't get in the way. Man, my ass is really dragging"

"Listen, Andrew, after ten minutes in that cold water, you'll come to life. I checked the temperature; it's a brisk 39 degrees."

" Brisk, Oh now, I feel a lot better. Where the hell's my regulator?"

"Try the thing that's hanging in front of you."

Fully suited and loaded down with equipment, Andrew's bare weight of 205 pounds jumped to 365 pounds. He was fatigued, as were most other crewmembers. With hunched shoulders and a slight stoop, Andrew slowly made his way to the entry ramp. Standing poised at the water's edge, he took a deep breath of the cool fresh air. He was very aware of the heavy equipment load on his back. Leaning on the ramp cable, he adjusted a fin on one foot, and then shifted his weight to the other.

"Give me a hand", he said to his partner on this dive. Andrew reached out, placed one hand on his buddy's arm, and lifted his foot high, and slipped on the second fin. He entered the water and descended down to the Alvin Davis; trailing 200 feet of half-inch nylon line behind him. The line would be tied to the leading end of the long aluminum pipe.

The pipe end and line were then forced under the ship and out the other side; the line was fastened to the rail on both sides. A one and a half inch thick stranded steel cable was then lowered over the side of MV Eden and tied to the line on the rail. When all was secured the surface crew pulled the cable under the ship and back up to the rail, tying it off on both rails until the day of the big lift.

On lifting day, the cables were shackled to longer cables dangling from a hundred by forty-foot barge anchored over the Alvin Davis. With hand cranks, they hoped to raise the Alvin Davis under the barge and set her down under the shadow of the railroad cranes at Main Marine Corporation.

Andrew touched down at the base of the main mast. He moved to the port side where the aluminum pipe was lying against the rail.
A slipknot around the pipe and rail placed there by the previous diver was easily undone. Leaning over the rail, he slowly lifted the pipe up so he could attach the line to it. The second diver arrived just in time to help hold the pipe while Andrew tied off the nylon line. Andrew pointed to himself and then down to the lake bottom.
The hand gestures indicated that he was going to be working the bottom of the pipe. The other diver returned the "OK" sign.

Andrew slid over the rail and glided down to the bottom. The second hole was already started and extended three feet under the hull. Bracing himself against the hull, he moved to a kneeling position ever so gently so he won't kick the bottom up. He bent down and inspected the two-foot diameter hole.

"Shit, it looks like a boulder in there." He stuck his arm in as far as it will go. "Damn it, I can't reach it." Rolling slowly over to the left side, almost on his back, his two-hose regulator started to free flow. Bubbling out of control, it made his mask dance about on his face.

"That was double dumb," he thought as he straightened up a little to get the free flow under control. "I can't screw around much longer. I'm burning bottom time."

Andrew gave two tugs on the line; a signal to the diver located fifteen feet above him to turn on the water pressure.
The two divers began a pounding motion, like a derrick pumping oil.

Without seeing each other, they felt the rhythm each imposed on the pipe. First, a downward plunge, then, an upward surge, each diver giving the other the full strokes of his reach.
Suddenly the pipe bounced off the corner of the boulder. It dug in and couldn't be retrieved. Andrew wriggled the pipe from side to side, but with no luck. He crawled up the pipe hand over hand until he was face to face with his partner.
He showed with hand gestures that the pipe was locked up against the hull and the boulder. His partner silently gained full understanding.
Each diver placed a shoulder against the pipe to break it loose.
Bracing against the hull rail, they pushed outward, then side-to-side. It wouldn't break free. Over the side they dropped. At the bottom, it was one giant dust storm. Andrew reached out into the cloud of sediment to feel if his partner was up against the pipe. He was shouldered against it. They began to push back and forth harder and harder; their bodies straining.

Andrew was so caught up in the output of energy that he forgot one of the first rules of diving: never get behind in breathing, never pant for air. Breathing becomes inefficient during panting and the lungs never receive the oxygen they need to ventilate. Andrew was out of air, panting out of control, and gasping for air that couldn't be delivered. Escape. Escape to the surface, raced through his mind. Tremendous bursts of bubbles echoed in his ears. The intensity of sound only adds to the anxiety to escape.

"I'm going to die...I can't get enough air...Escape...Run...Go...Go...hold on...Stop...Get a grip...Run...."

Commands sprint through his mind. Experience and instinctive reaction take over. He holds tight to the pipe. Bending at the waist he forces himself to breathe deeply.

"Deeper. Breathe deeper." He visualizes "Suck it in slow, slow." The anguish and burn of deep breaths pain him to his soul.

"I got it...I got it. Damn that was close." Andrew's thoughts come together. The nervous response starts to take effect. His hands tremble, his legs tremble and his temples throb.

In the billowing clouds of bottom sediment, his dive buddy, only inches away, was unaware of the close call that had just taken place.

Andrew completed his shift, and headed slowly to the surface. He was still suffering from the emotional drain of his near panic event.

Back on the deck of M V Eden, he related his experience to the other divers. This was not true confessions. It was not something he wished to admit, but if this salvage operation was going to remain accident-free, every diver needed to detail his or her close calls. That way everyone learns. In the world of commercial diving, close calls are part of the game. Sometimes a half dozen tension-filled occurrences take place on the same job. Under water, a small thoughtless act may become a full-blown accident. How a diver reacts in the first instant of a panic state is crucial. A diver must stop, think first, and then react. A diver must be aware of the environment and himself in that environment.

A mishandled close call can be changed into an overcharged deadly scenario, if the diver can't regain control. In almost every case, the diver must be self-reliant.

On July 22, 1969, MV Eden left Main Marine Corporation with the lifting barge in tow. It was several weeks behind schedule because of bad weather and the final pumping of silt from the holds.

The crew needed an additional few days to do a wide sweep around the Alvin Davis for any artifacts. Once the Alvin Davis was raised, it would be very difficult to relocate the same spot.

MV Eden lumbered. Her twin diesel Gray Marine engines produced almost eight hundred horsepower, but the big barge buffeted against the shallow swells. Water splashed on the deck, creating tiny pools of water around the hand winches and cables. The ride out took more than four hours. The barge required four large positioning anchors. Fixing the barge over the Alvin Davis took the entire day.

Sunset or sunrise would not matter to a working diver in these waters of eternal night. The crew would do the cable hookups and try for the lift as darkness fell. The lake was running smooth, but Green Bay could blow up a storm in the time it took a diver to put on his gear. Too much was at stake now. If the cable hookup were completed, the entire crew would work without stopping until the lift was accomplished.

Deck crew and divers agreed because they knew the Lake's temperament. She would give no quarter for the unwary or the slacker. The lake controls weather patterns for three states around her life-giving resource. In the winter, if moist winds blew in from the west, she could dump mountains of lake-effect snow anywhere on its shoreline. In the sweltering heat of summer, she could provide relief to surrounding cities.

On this day access would be commonplace. Profound exertion would be ordinary. "labor intensive" would not yet be a buzz-word, but practiced. On this day in the heart of Lake Michigan's bosom, tranquility would be paramount.

More than 2800 feet of steel lifting cable were placed and then attached to the cables under the sleeping giant. At 4 A.M. the slack was taken out of them. The cables became banjo taut and vibrated where they entered the water. Small ripples emanated outward. The big barge creaked and settled nearly a foot deeper in the water. All systems were ready and double-checked. The crew tried to get at least an hour rest before the sun rose.

The smell of stale oil and dry rot wood rose from the stained deck, as the barge tugged at her anchorage over the Alvin Davis. Exhausted divers lay about the deck. They curled up behind anything that would break the gentle chill of the early morning breeze. The sun appeared on the horizon at 5:30 A.M., spreading a carpet of glistening gold foil in its wake.

The crew cleared the deck of equipment they missed the night before. Twelve men lined up and simultaneously began turning the hand cranks. The barge set six inches deeper in the water; then moves up slightly.

"The Alvin Davis has broken free!" One of the crew yelled. The rest of the men turned to each other and shook hands. Frank bellowed,

"Bernie, you and Gary go down and check her."

Fifteen minutes later, the divers returned.

"She's free from the bottom. You can continue the lift", Gary barked out to the crew, as he broke the surface.

Each 100 turns of the winch brought the Alvin Davis five inches closer to the sun, that hadn't washed over its deck in more than 100 years. Blistered hands strained to make each agonizing turn of the crank.

Sightseeing boaters, who wished to tie off at the barge, were required to make 100 hand crank turns at the winch. The sun baked down on the once oil-stained deck, which was now fast becoming sweat-stained. The cranking continued. By 3 P.M. the wreck was 60 feet below the barge. A radio message, warning of an approaching storm, sent shock waves through the spent adventurers and crew alike. The hand cranking rose to a frantic pitch. More than 20,000 revolutions would be required to bring her up. If the storm hit, the Alvin Davis could slip from her sling and the recovery would have to begin again. No one wanted to even think about that, let alone say it.

The storm formed a darkened sky rising from the horizon across the Bay.

"Son of a beach. It's coming this way"; Frank muttered as he cupped his hands above his eyes to scan the horizon. "It'll be on us in an hour."

The storm hit with the customary first cold gust of wind. The rain came down in torrents and the lightning snapped in attention-getting cracks. Thankfully, the storm was the common summer squall and passed with no damage, other than a thorough soaking for the crew.
The Alvin Davis would remain cradled in her slings another day. Meanwhile, the mentally exhausted and physically drained crew got some needed rest. By Friday morning, the painfully stiff and sore divers were barely able to bend over and crank. The Alvin Davis was now within a few feet under the barge.

The bowsprit broke the surface and a feeling of "We have her now, it will be all right" filled the air. "We have done the impossible" runs through the mind of the crew.

The slow, sometimes motionless towing of the Alvin Davis took most of the morning and early afternoon. Check and recheck became the order of the day. "Make sure the cables are not slipping. Check the stress on the ship. Watch over the crew." This close to the end, someone may get careless.

Less than a mile remained before the Alvin Davis would come to rest under the massive cranes of the shipyard. Once there, the "Shrouded Ship" would be laid on the bottom.
The barge cables would be removed, and the crane cables attached for

the final lift. "God, can it be over? Unbelievable!", Frank whispers to himself, with eyes frozen on the shadows of the crane as they embrace the deck of the barge. Frank watched as a crowd of 15,000 spectators lined the shore near Main Marine. People from the township and countryside wanted to be on hand to view history in the making. Viewers cheered and passed along best wishes.

Frank Mariman's chest was visibly expanded and rightly so. He had led his band of assorted divers with varying skill levels, to a remarkable finish. The feeling of "We did it. Sweet Jesus, we sure did it" popped out of his dog-tired lips.

"Nearly 4,000 dives without an accident...a salvage task of this magnitude, with little or no funding was impossible," many professionals said. Only a few short months ago they were crazy, adventurous vagabonds who were amateur divers looking for an accident to happen. Now the "Shrouded Ship" divers are the best there are.

"I'll match my people against any in the world," Frank would say many times, when asked how good his divers were.

After 105 years, history would be brought into the present with all the rich texture and spirit, of that past. Local city fathers donated the inlet where the Alvin Davis was docked. After two years of intensive and laborious effort, she settled into her final resting place in ten feet of standing water.

Frank and a few of the original divers constructed a nineteenth century setting to display the hundreds of items recovered from the wreck site. The other members of the dive team returned to their jobs and families, and took with them the memories of an extraordinary feat.

Andrew would hear regularly from Frank over the years. Sadly, each year the Alvin Davis would deteriorate a little more. The small amount of money Frank raised, in entrance fees to the park was barely enough to pay wages. Little was left to pay the cost of restoring the wood decking.

Wisconsin winters are hard on untreated wood. The oak timbers creaked and groaned with the pressure of expanding ice. Snowfall, thaw, and repeated freezing repeatedly reduce even the mightiest of roadbeds to mere road gravel. Inside the hull, the melting snow found low points and crevices in which to accumulate, turning below deck into an ice cave. The Alvin Davis needed thousands of dollars to completely protect her from the elements.

As the years rolled by, Frank would call on Andrew to do letter-writing campaigns and make phone calls to raise funds. Andrew, mindful of Frank's problem, would often use his personal 8-millimeter movie footage to solicit funds from customers or clients. Every time he would speak at local gatherings, he would use videotape that had been commercially produced and supplied by Frank. The tape produced by a Green Bay television station documented the plight of the Alvin Davis after it was rescued from the bottom of Green Bay.

Frank, under constant pressure for years to raise funds, had to file for bankruptcy. He was about to lose the Alvin Davis to land developers. A local developer wanted the inlet for a new marina. Frank tried to keep the real barbarians at the gates but he was overwhelmed.

A newspaper article in the Milwaukee Journal detailed a story about Frank starting a fire on the Alvin Davis and holding the firefighters at bay with a rifle. Frank called Andrew at home the next day. He said with a quivering voice, "You know I couldn't really burn the Alvin Davis. Not after all we went through to bring her up. You know that, don't you?"

"Of course I don't believe it, but what the hell are you doing?" Andrew queried, with a demanding timbre in his voice.

"I'm up against it, God damn it. They are going to take her away from me. You know, I put everything into her these last twenty years. We called everyone for help...nobody cares...nobody."

"Jesus, you could have gotten killed. What if the damn thing had gotten away from you?" Andrew eased his tone to his long time friend.

"I started the fire because I was desperate for some notice. They can't all be blind out there. I thought that maybe someone might see what was happening to her. I can't do any more."

"Frank, we will try again to raise some interest. Just don't do any more crazy things like this, OK?...OK? Frank, for Christ sake, tell me you won't."

"OK, don't get your sail in a puff. I didn't want anyone to think I was going to shoot someone on the fire department. That's why I'm calling all the old time dive crew. I want you guys to know I'm not off my rocker." Frank's voice was steadier now. He and Andrew reminisced for an hour about the old days.

Andrew heard from Frank from time-to-time over the next five years. Word had it that he and May were divorcing and Frank was in very poor health. Andrew never stopped pressing for the restoration of the Alvin Davis. On one occasion in the 1980's he would take the issue to the lawmakers at the capitol in Madison. His speech was on a related matter, but he was never one to miss a chance to pitch the plight of the Alvin Davis. As happened many times in the past, it fell on deaf ears. The rights to Alvin Davis would be taken over by the land developer who took her in the deal for the inlet. He towed the Alvin Davis onto the shore and crushed the hull with a tractor until only a pile of lumber remained. Her oaken skeleton was then trucked to a landfill and buried.

Andrew and Frank continued their contact periodically over the next fifteen years.
Frank called Andrew for the last time in 1997. He wanted to put together all the old dive team and produce a documentary on the raising of the Alvin Davis. He told Andrew that he had a Hollywood producer who was very interested. Andrew believed him and said he was in. Whatever Frank could put together, he would be there. The meeting never came together. Frank died two weeks later.

Andrew felt Frank had died of a broken heart, as much as he did of poor health. Of all the iron men Andrew had met over the years, none matched the fortitude and determination of Frank Mariman.
The men of the wooden ships would have been proud to serve with him.

Chapter 11

Collision of the Freighter Endeavor

Commercial jobs in 1969 were challenging and always typically unique. Even if the pay wasn't attractive, Andrew would take the job if it proved challenging. This provided hours of invaluable experience. One job that always stood out, in those early years, was the hull inspection of an old British freighter named the "Endeavor."

Late fall in Wisconsin brings biting, blustery winds. The Endeavor was docked in Milwaukee at pier C. She was preparing to get underway. The winds that day were gusting across the pier and exploded broadside against the Endeavor's ageing, steel gray portside. As the lumbering freighter backed out, on its way to Chicago, the winds blew her stern first into the massive structure of Pier B. Out of control, without docking lines attached, the freighter's starboard side collided with the adjacent pier, producing a thunderous thud. Inside the ship's engine room, the hydraulic rams that control the rudder, exploded when the rudder jammed against some underwater obstruction. Two thousand pounds of iron castings sprayed the room. Fortunately, no hands were in that section of the ship when these deadly missiles ricocheted off bulkhead walls and embedded themselves into the metal cabinets. Shock waves radiated outward and lapped against the pillars of Pier C. Finally the Endeavor settled gently against the same pier.

The phone rang at Adventures End. "Mr. Boyd, this is John Berry of the Winthrop and Smith Insurance Company. We are the regional offices for Lloyds of London and have a damaged freighter in the Milwaukee harbor. Are you available for an underwater inspection the day after tomorrow, Thursday the 20th?" Andrew was so stunned by the abrupt request that he stuttered a meek reply, "Of course we can."

"Please call my office later this afternoon for additional details or any on-site support you might need."

"Ah, one question," as Andrew began to recover, thinking, "Lloyds of London, this could be my big break."

Collision Of The Freighter Endeavor 123

Maybe this would be a turning point in his commercial diving career.

"How did you get my name, and wouldn't you like to know how much it's going to cost?" Andrew paused for the answer, thinking to himself, "Oh damn, what the hell did I say that for?"

"Are you the Andrew Boyd who did the insurance inspections on the Prins Willem V?"

"Yes, I am, but that was for a local firm that had aspirations of raising her." Andrew thought, "What the hell are you making such stupid comments for? Shut your face before you blow it."

"Your name came up in conversation with the owner of that very firm. His company is insured with us. He spoke highly of you and said that ships were your specialty. Based on your inspection of this ship, we may or may not be liable for a very substantial damage claim. If your inspection finds more damage underwater than is presently assumed, the claim could escalate several hundred thousand dollars. Phone my office about three this afternoon. Ask for Anthony Chandler. He will have more details for you. As for the fees, we will pay a flat rate plus a ten-percent bonus for the inconvenience of this short notice. Will that be acceptable?"

"You bet, ah, see you on Thursday", Andrew said, displaying more self-confidence.

Andrew eagerly called the insurance office and received some very vague and sketchy details. During the conversation, Andrew had the first insight that he could become a pawn in the insurance game. According to his sources, the insurance company was listing the accident as a collision with an underwater obstruction. Hitting the pier was an aftereffect from the loss of steering control.

He also learned, that if the obstruction were in fact there, he would become a witness against the City of Milwaukee.

Most of his commercial diving assignments in the last few years were from city projects. Now he may be required to give testimony that could cost the city hundreds of thousands of dollars.

A person doesn't have to be a "brain trust" to know the politics of a city. Once you take sides in litigation against the city, you might as well pack it in and find new employment. Lately, it seemed that no matter how hard he tried, he couldn't keep from being politically squeezed.

Andrew pondered the problem, "It could work in my favor. If the claim does go to court, I'm only doing my job; if I tell it like it is, I can't get burned... Ah, bull! They'll probably fry my ass... I can't pass up this job just because of what might happen. No, but if the city loses a suit, I'm not going to be number one on their hit parade. So, what are you going to do?" Andrew, impatient with himself decided to drop the debate raging inside his head.

"Well, I suppose I'll squat in the frying pan like always."

New dive locations inherently have new problems. Andrew often went to a job site a day or two early. A pre-dive inspection of the location made him more comfortable. This job was no exception. He had dived the city piers two years before, so a little reconnoitering to get an update was in order.

Adventures End closed at 6 P.M. that August evening. This proved sufficiently early for Andrew to pack his dive equipment and still make it to the Milwaukee harbor for a quick inspection of the entry and exit points. Arriving at 7:30 P.M., he had a little trouble getting past the relaxed harbor security. They had been notified of the accident, but weren't expecting a diver until Thursday. Andrew had an easy approach when it came to gaining access to restricted areas.

He showed his photo ID card as a diving instructor, with the flare of any FBI agent. Then he would graphically explain his need to check out the dive site.

As Andrew walked onto the pier, the smell of dead alewives and dank water filled his nostrils.

Gray water surged back and forth, pressing a mixed cluster of debris to and from where the pier and bulkhead wall met.

There were two ladders leading to the water, nearly fourteen feet below. An overhang made it difficult to see the opaque liquid directly beneath the concrete structure. Andrew had already decided to make a giant stride entry from the pier. The stricken ship was resting on its dock lines fifteen feet away. There would be more than enough room for entry, eliminating the need to swim two hundred feet after climbing down a skimpy little ladder. The ladders were ten feet apart and attached to the bulkhead wall, not the pier. They were also surrounded by assorted trash that drifted there with the lake surge. Rusted cans, an old ketchup bottle, bits and pieces of paper, bloated fish, a few rotting apples and some unknown objects floated by, half submersed. Lowering one's body into that frigid lake decorated with repulsive refuse was not a pretty sight.

Climbing up would be the easy part. He would drop two lines in the water from the top of the pier. After the dive, he would take off his weight belt and attach it to one of the lines, and his tanks would hang on the other. He worried, as he walked the full length of the pier, "My luck, I'll make the entry right on top of some piece of steel hidden just below the surface. I'll break my leg, have crotch crunch, and spend the rest of my days trying to explain how my balls got lodged in my throat." A large man in a navy blue peacoat approached Andrew, as he took one last reflective look around.

"You need some help?", the man said, with what looked like a smile practically hidden under his walrus mustache.

"No, I'm the diver who will be inspecting the ship tomorrow. Just taking a quick look around, so I have a feel of what I'll need."

The man swaggered forward and closed the gap with Andrew. They faced each other almost nose to nose. The rank smell of tea and cigarettes hung on his breath. Andrew backed up slightly to avoid the next blast of exhaled abuse.

"I've always wanted to try that", the man started. "I mean, I've always wanted to do commercial diving, but never had the time to get official; or ah, what do you call it here in the States, certified?"

He glibly elaborated a personal narration of diving history, current diving status and the future of diving. All these issues were delivered in breathless pants and nonstop lingo. Succinct would not be a word added to his epitaph.

"How the hell can one guy talk so much about a subject he knows nothing about?" Andrew thought, as he drifted into a trance; blocking out all the monotonous banter; seeing but not hearing. Almost as easily as he had drifted out of touch with the present, he began to come back.

Without waiting for a proper pause from his newly found buddy, he blurted out, "Certified as a scuba diver and certified as a commercial diver are two different things. Just because we put on a diving suit the same way doesn't mean the skill requirements are the same. A person could end up in the morgue thinking like that."

"Ah, you Americans have a flair for the dramatic... come on then lad, and meet the rest of our crew. They will be delighted to meet a celebrity such as you."

The man growled and spat over the rail as he stepped up the gangwalk to the deck level. Andrew mused, "Oh yuck, nice shot, ace... he looked over the side into the water where the glub had hit. "And he expects me to jump in there...pal this is going to cost your boss a lot of money. Hell, I've never been on a freighter before, unless it was underwater. This is very impressive" Andrew loved the accents and was thrilled at the prospect of meeting a foreign group comfortable in their own surroundings. He had met many people from different parts of the world, but they were always at hand in the U.S. Now he would be in their environment, even if it were restricted to a country 50 feet by 250 feet. This could prove to be another turning point in his life and he felt it.

Andrew clambered below deck after the man and followed him into several passageways to the crew's quarters. The halls, not quite wide enough for two large men to pass each other, were scratched and stained, with oily dirt hugging the corners. The floor was covered with a rubber mat that fell a bit short at each door jam. Shiny bare spots several feet long greeted men as they entered or left each compartment.

Layers of battered red, green and brown paint had been worn away by foot traffic. They colorfully revealed a feeble attempt to decorate the walls and floor. Wire caged, twenty-five watt bulbs hung over each door entrance, providing just sufficient light for security, but certainly wouldn't impress safety inspectors. The sound of raucous laughter and a cacophony of chatter reverberated off the uncovered steel walls. Enough blue smoke billowed out of the room to season twelve pounds of cod.

Two open portholes on the starboard wall of the quarters helped to ventilate the room heading into the hall. The blue-gray swirling clouds were a portent to hold one's breath.

Lounging inside the room were seven grizzled crewmen, intently playing cards on a makeshift table. The quarters were about the size of a small office, with three compact bunks stacked floor to ceiling on each wall. The head was in the hall with room for one commode, two rust-stained sinks and a shower stall covered in soap scum.

"Must be a lot of laughs in the morning. The Army was bad, but this could get on my nerves," Andrew thought as he made a mental comparison between the military service latrines and the heads on board ship. "At least we had our own hole," picturing in his mind the number of efficient holes expertly cut into a board that lay over a long earthen trench. The army-style bathroom remained riveted in his mind, because in his "bad boy "military days, he had to dig plenty of latrines. Andrew was casually introduced to each of the crew. He earnestly shook hands with each member, but couldn't remember anyone seconds after meeting them. He was still mentally outside the cabin looking in. His body and mind were on separate spatial planes. His present thoughts blended with an old Humphrey Bogart movie, with the hero aboard a wartime freighter, heading for an exotic, foreign port. There was intrigue, romance and excitement.

"Man this is it. I'm here in real life... it's really happening." Easily impressed, with a penchant for daydreaming, Andrew often blended reality and fantasy.

It must have been left over from the countless hours of isolation he had experienced as a child, or more recently, while working the holds of the sunken Alvin Davis. There really didn't seem to be any deterrent to his fantasy world. He would simply mix movie magic with what was reality. It made it easier for him to cope with the many fears he hid so well. As outspoken and gregarious as he appeared to the world, there were deep and impenetrable insecurities that rarely gained entry to his conscious mind.

At age twenty-nine, he kept these fears at bay with an affable mask to the world.

A full ship's tour was proposed by one of the more approachable crew.

"Dullhearty, why don't you show our good friend around the ship?" Dullhearty, an athletic, handsome man that looked the part of a British'er, was playing his best hand and reluctant to quit when his chief sternly barked out the curt request. He stalled for a moment, then slammed down his cards and proclaimed that he was folding. Andrew thought,

"Oh great! First I get Mr. Spooky Spitter and a chronology of diving; now I'm stuck with Mr. Duffy Dimples who is in a bad mood."

After nearly a third of the ship had been explored, Andrew finally found out that he was being lead around by the third engineer's mate. They entered the stern portion of the ship through passageways painted flat forest green and beige. Andrew thought, "No wonder these guys are so ill natured. This place is depressing." Andrew's thoughts are suddenly broken as Dullhearty blurted out in a brash, loud voice, trying to compete with the engine room clangor.

"One of these days, I'm going to paint these depressing walls with some folk art, maybe the Queen sitting in an out-of-house water closet." Andrew broke a grin and thought. "Maybe this guy isn't a putz after all. He turned to Dullhearty and said, "that's outhouse... more appropriately called the throne room."

The conversation became more relaxed as they exchanged idiomatic insults and approached the engine room door.

Andrew stepped through the hatchway first. "Holy smokes. It looks like a bomb went off in here... Was anyone hurt? There must be a couple hundred pounds of iron on the floor."

"Actually, there are more than a thousand pounds, Mr. Boyd. Thankfully, no one was injured. We were very lucky. I was over there in the next compartment oiling that 5-kilowatt generator when the ship hit... whatever it hit. I fell on my buttocks and covered my head. Here, see this." Dullhearty walked up to a panel of gauges and points to one of the gauge faces. Embedded in the upper left quadrant of the gauge is a chunk of iron the size and shape of an ice cube. "That might have taken my life had the good Lord not been watching out for old Readie."

"Readie?... Readie? That's your first name, Readie?... Dullhearty? Man, talk about a tongue-twister."

"Don't be making fun of a good Irish name, mate. I come from a family tree that goes back on one side over 400 hundred years."

"I thought Irish names sounded like O'Brien, O'Connor, or Goldberg." Readie turns and scrunches up his face and repeats

"Goldberg? ...My mother is Irish and my father is British, God save the Queen."

Andrew flashed back "Does she still wear combat boots?" Too late Andrew thought, "Oops, bad, bad thing to say. I suppose only the Englanders can poke fun at the Crown." Readie's eager smile drooped to a narrow half frown.

Andrew wondered, "They're still a little testy with Americans. Haven't forgotten Concord, I guess."

The two men finished their survey and returned to topside and the starboard rail.

Andrew tried to establish a game plan for the morning, "I'm not sure what my role is for tomorrow. It looks like the Captain wants me to check the rudder post for damage, but everyone keeps bringing up this underwater obstacle."

Readie commented. "If you be asking my opinion, the whole thing will require two divers. One to check out the rudder assembly and one to search for the obstruction." Readie's air of confidence began to emerge as he detected a lack of understanding in Andrew's voice. "You need me to show you the place where the rudder damage is most likely to be. I dove before; many times... this would be my chance to show my Captain and the ship's owners what I can do. Maybe even become the company diver."

Andrew didn't want an amateur on this dive or any commercial dive. They never listen to all the instructions and almost always make your job twice as difficult. Readie's enthusiasm and drive to get ahead moved Andrew to bend his hard fast rule this one time. He felt that if Readie would agree to a test dive in his apartment pool, then he might let him dive, but only as an observer. Maybe he could question Readie and search out the true story.

It didn't seem logical to be hired for a job with this much damage and with so little discussion on what his real objectives were. Readie vigorously agreed to the test dive. They arrived at Andrew's apartment a little before ten o'clock. The pair had a sense of humor and their approach to life in general blended very well. As the evening progressed they kidded about everything, making bad jokes about politicians and the economy. The easy banter was interrupted by the pool exercises. Andrew felt a niggling sense of insecurity after observing Readie's skill level in the pool. It was apparent that Readie hadn't been in the water for a while, but he performed each exercise as if he had some formal training. At the end of two hours, Andrew was still concerned about how Readie would perform in open water. Readie's poolside humor disguised some nervousness and a level of inadequacy.

"Pool exercises are one thing; commercial Lake Michigan diving is quite another," Andrew ruminated, as they dried themselves off.

"You know how high that pier is? If you screw up, you could drown right there."

"Andrew, if you will be better for it, I won't dive unless I get permission from my old chief and the captain. That will take you off the fly."

"That's hook, Readie. Hook. And I will feel better for it."

Upstairs in Andrew's apartment they had a few drinks of Scotch and swapped sea stories. It was close to midnight when they decided to do a little pub-crawling.
They felt that Readie's sailor fatigues wouldn't help them score any points with the male set.
However they were torn on the reaction of females. The males won. Andrew lent Readie a pair of pants and a shirt.

It was two o'clock in the morning when Andrew finally dragged his sluggish, overindulged body into bed. They had closed a local bar and taken two females home. He could not remember where they went or whom they were with. He was almost positive he had taken Readie home, but wouldn't have bet on it.

Later that next morning Andrew awoke without much of a hangover and worked until 2:00 PM at Adventures End. He gathered enough equipment for himself and Readie and headed for his 3:00 PM., appointment with the ship owners and insurance company executives.

Collision Of The Freighter Endeavor   131

Andrew strained to look at four figures standing half way down the pier. They were huddled together under the shadow of the vessel. Every so often someone dramatically pointed a finger toward the ship. As Andrew approached, they turned and wholly welcomed him into the group.

"Mr. Boyd. Right on time. We are indeed pleased to see you. I'm John Berry. This is Jeffrey Daisue, our claims adjuster. You know the captain and Mr. Dullhearty."

Andrew shook everyone's hand and winked at Readie with a knowing smile. He knew that Readie drank a gang of booze last night and wasn't all that chipper this afternoon.

"How's it going?" Andrew queries Readie.

Readie fired back as he finished his handshake. "Not bad, old chap...a bit in the grog though." The Captain asked. "Would you care to suit up here or on the ship?"

"Right here is fine, I'll get my equipment."

"Mr. Boyd...before you go, Mr. Dullhearty has expressed an interest in accompanying you on this dive. We have discussed it and agree that one of our own, so to speak, might be helpful in the survey, if you have no objection. What are your feelings?", asked the Captain.

"I have no objection with Readie being there. It's just the high entry that might cause him some problem."

Readie said with assurance. "No problem old man, I can handle it."

Andrew shrugged his shoulders and trudged back to his car for the equipment. He watched Readie closely as they don their wet suits.

"Not bad," he thought. "But wait until he stands at the edge of the pier and looks down between his fin tips. He'll be crapping in his shorts." Readie hid the physical stress well and Andrew continued to watch as he put on his fins with steady hands. Andrew was evaluating Readie's every move.

Andrew is thought, as he shuffled carefully with his fins to the edge of the pier. "I still don't trust this guy. I better go in first. That way I can catch him, if he does something unexpected. Why do I let myself get talked into these things?" "OK...Ready, Readie?" Andrew grinned from ear to ear as he stared at Readie's fogged up mask.

Readie sputtered. "Not new, old chap, heard it before." The mask edge pulled his upper lip back, uncovering his front teeth and giving a slight lisp to his speech. Readie waddled from side to side as he closed the gap between them.

"I'll make the entry first. You wait until I yell up to you; then you drop in. Remember to keep your thighs together. If you do it wrong the first time, you will be dancing on the surface for half an hour. Remember, hold the mask and regulator."

Andrew finished his pre-dive check of Readie's equipment and turned to make his entry. The tips of his fins stuck out in space. He paused only for a moment. The massive freighter pulled tight on its moorings. The harsh sound of twisting lines and creaking bollards resonate between the freighter and the sea wall.

Andrew stepped forward and dropped perfectly vertical into the water. Pa-doush! A ten-foot high geyser of water mushroomed into the air and fell back into the lake. The impact sent lofty waves in every direction. The water crashed into the freighter and rebounded back towards Andrew. A foot-high wave traveled to the underside of the pier, chasing the debris out of its shadowy hiding place. Andrew bobbed to the surface and adjusted his tank harness. He swam out from under the lip of the pier.

"OK, OK, come on in."

Readie stepped forward, half falling; half-jumping into the dark, emerald-green mirror. He hit the surface leaning slightly forward, slapping his face and mask into the water. The concussion broke the seal on his mask. It flooded partially and he panicked. Reaching out, groping for anything that will support him, he dog paddled and made grunting sounds as if someone were jumping on his diaphragm.

Andrew quickly pulled him in close, making sure he is positioned behind and to one side of Readie. Giving him reassuring commands and helping to drain the water from his mask, Andrew managed to calm him down.

Readie suddenly started to back-paddle, pushing water in front of him, making sounds like a baby blowing bubbles. He slammed his back into a pier post: then turned around and tried to climb it. The slime that forms around the base of the post made the climb impossible. The green gobs bunch on his chest. He has lost it completely again. Before Andrew can move, Readie delivered his morning breakfast to the fish. Andrew thought, "Oh God, bad act. This guy has gone bananas again."

Looking over his shoulder as he moved in to repeat his rescue, he saw what caused the look of fear in Readie's fog-obstructed mask. Only inches away from Andrew's left ear was a fuzzy ball... a dead rat, maybe five or six pounds when it was alive. Its true weight was hard to measure. The methane gas from deteriorating food in the digestive tract must have blown it up to twice its normal size.

Even for Andrew, it was a surprise to be face-to-face with a wide-eyed rat the size and shape of a football. Its mouth grimaced from the expanding and stretched skin, and its yellowed teeth struck a defiant grin. Andrew shuddered. A small shiver ran down his spine.

"Get cool Readie, get cool... I've got you," Andrew barked into Readie's ear. Green swatches of moss hung from Readie's chest strap, mask rim, and regulator.

Andrew splashed water gently on all the covered areas, washing them clean. He thrust his right arm, then his left in a wide arching motion on the surface of the water, sweeping the loosened moss away. Pulling Readie away from the post by towing him backwards, they broke out of the shadow of the overhang. Andrew can feel Readie's calm returning.

"I think you're just about done. Maybe you should hang it up for today," Andrew said with more compassion than he has shown in the last ten minutes. "I'll tow you over to the ladder; you go up and be my surface man. It will help a lot if you lift my equipment up when I'm through."

Andrew was waiting for a "yes" from Readie when a voice from the pier deck resonated off the freighter.

"You fellows all right down there?"

Andrew laid his head back into the water and yelled skyward, "Yeah, we're all right. Just an equipment problem."

"Thanks, mate, I guess I made a bit of a shambles of it."

Andrew replied gently, "Just a bit...Now how 'bout haulin' your behind out of here so I can finish the job your boss ordered?"

With a sheepish grimace, that has replaced the look of fear, Readie pleaded his case." If I go up now, they will never give me another go-at-it. This is my only chance."

Andrew pondered his dilemma. "Do I let this guy get nuts again? Or do I force him up right now? He did get control back pretty quick. He looks like he is calm now."

"OK, but if you lose it again, I'm pulling your pin."

Readie stared into Andrew's mask. "What"?

"Old parachuting expression. Means to stop the free fall, to pull the rip cord; to deploy the chute."

"Oh, I get it...right, old man...yes indeed...pin."

Andrew took Readie under one arm and surface swims him around the rudderpost, out of sight of the onlookers above. And in the shadows of the ship he fixed Readie's hands to the propeller blade of the stricken freighter.

"Now stay here, don't move. I'll check out the hull and the propeller housing for cracks. Are you going to be all right?"
Readie sputters, "Without question, I'll stick as close as the fog in Piccadilly Circus."

Andrew shook his head and lowered himself down along the hull. Feeling the curve with his gloved hand, he imagined in his mind's eye the different layers of paint. The bumps from welds that were not fully ground down felt like bands around the hull. His fingers danced over every imperfection on the skin of this giant, conjuring in his mind, then rejecting the data patiently gathered by his sensitive and experienced touch.

At ten feet, darkness is so intense that up or down is often not clear. Andrew's exhaust bubbles rush to the surface past his cheeks, giving him his only sense of direction. He swept his hand gently in front of himself. At chest height, he located the 100-watt light that floated upward from its tether line on his weight belt.
Little can be seen in the light glare. He moved closer to the hulk.
Still nothing, but a persistent orange-green glow is reflected back.
He can almost feel the massive hull coming closer to his mask. He is so

close now that the light illuminated the hull, but his vision is unfocused.

Andrew knew even at this early stage of his diving career that the application of touch is the only information-gathering source he has. Without sight or hearing the sensitivity of touch becomes more acute, and certainly more critical.

After fifteen minutes of persistent search, he found a small ridge in the steel. He paused, feeling every raise, every depression in the scar he has discovered.

"Damn, I think I've got something here."

Kicking slightly with his fins to stay pressed up against the hull, he followed the jagged trail. Gliding over the contour of the rudder housing, his hand passed up and over the frame.

"Oh damn I've lost it. I kicked too hard. Got to maintain contact with the hull." The motion of his fins twisted his body gently from side to side.

"Got to get my fins lined up to thrust me back into the hull."

His right arm tentatively stretches out into the dense blackness.

"Feel it. Feel it with your mind... think, it's there. You can feel the mass without touching it. Find it...that's it." His hand made firm contact again. "Good, now find a spot to anchor your left hand." Andrew pressed his left-hand inward to anchor on the hull, while gently stroking with his charcoal-colored fins again.

"OK, now press and stroke. Not too hard not too soft." Andrew's right hand swept gently to the right, away from his body, then to the left in a slightly smaller arch. Each pass covered a six-inch wide path by the full length of his arm. Ten minutes passed and the concentration and feeling in his fingertips began to fade.

"All right, all right, I found it. Damn, it isn't the same spot." He pondered for a moment trying to collect his thoughts. "Oh, damn it! I can't think. I must be getting cold. Is this the same crack? Or are there two cracks running in the same direction?" Forcing himself to recall every image gathered thus far, he determines that there are two ridges.

"But, are they really cracks or just paint chips?" He struggled to sort out the mental images imprinted on his mind.

"Got to take off a glove and feel it bare handed."
The thin, eighth-inch-thick neoprene glove he usually wears is thin enough to feel small bumps in the steel hull. It also gives an acceptable degree of warmth at this shallow depth. He removed one glove with some difficultly.

"Holy Smokes! That's cold!" Andrew's hand stung from the bone-chilling 50-degree water. "Got to figure this thing out quick, or my hand will fall off. OK, right, it's a crack...deep, too...I'll run my fingernail down the inside wall. That's no paint job. It's too thick. Must be over three-sixteenths of an inch deep. Great, Now I can get the hell out of here."

Andrew backed out away from the hull slowly put one hand over his head to protect himself in case he was to come up under a propeller blade. Suddenly a limp arm draped over Andrew's right shoulder.

"Jesus Christ the son of a bitch drowned." he mumbled, with his teeth pressed deeply into his mouthpiece. The arm came to life and grabbed Andrew diagonally across his chest, pressing hard.

"Your not dead, you dumb shit," Andrew blurted out as the two divers burst to the surface, his mouthpiece spitting out in front of him in its haste to clear a pathway for the verbal tongue-lashing that he is about to level at Readie.

"You dumb shit. Didn't I tell you to stay on the screw? That's way the hell over there. For Christ sake didn't I put your hands on the propeller blade and tell you to stay put?"

"Yes," replied Readie, "But you were gone so long I just came to help."

"Bull shit. I told you to stay put. What if you would have gotten into trouble? How would I have known? Ah, shit... help me? You could have helped me by staying on the pier."

Twice in less than an hour, Andrew had let his emotions get away from him. Fighting the cold, the pressure of the task at hand, and dealing with a novice diver, all took their toll. Andrew, now with a short temper, couldn't let it alone.

"You're out of here. Come on, out of the water. Last time, God damn it! Last time!" Andrew hustled Readie up the ladder and onto the pier. The captain and the insurance agents had left the dock shortly after Andrew and Readie made their water entry.

After a warm shower in the captain's cabin and a light repast laced with Irish coffee, Andrew comfortably waited for the captain and the insurance agents to come back aboard. Andrew didn't make eye contact with Readie for the entire time.

All the parties had agreed earlier to meet and discuss what was found during the inspection. Andrew was asked to do a line drawing of the damaged area. He had just finished the last careful details of his drawing when Readie re-appeared from the companionway with renewed energy, and now escalating arrogance.

"Ah, Mr. Dullhearty...I hope you don't mind if we get an opinion from Mr. Dullhearty, do you Mr. Boyd?" asked the Captain.

Andrew cautiously nodded assent, but had the sense of imminent betrayal. After all, he was the outsider and Readie had proven an unseasoned diver. Suppressing thoughts of mistrust, Andrew began his debriefing.

"Visibility was zero, zero. No way to really tell by sight if a crack does exist. But by feeling the area with my bare hand, I am very confident that the break extends from here." Andrew traced over his original drawing. Dullhearty leaned over the table and studied it. He rubbed the back of his neck, straightened up and said matter of fact," No, no crack in the hull that I can tell. I think Mr. Boyd is incorrect."

Andrew would have been dumbfounded, had he not felt betrayal coming. "What do you say, Mr. Boyd?" asked the captain as he rolled back in his chair pulling on the pleats of his pants to relieve the pull at his knees.

Andrew blatantly gasped, "He's absolutely wrong." The captain interrupted, "Now I'm left with a terrible deliberation to ponder, Mr. Boyd and Mr.Dullhearty." The captain stood up slapping the tops of his upper legs. "You both have to be more convincing than that... Mr. Dullhearty is a third engineer's mate and is a trusted member of this crew. Let me explain the severity of both sides of this discussion. If we take Mr. Boyd's impression of what condition the hull is in, we will be obligated to have our ship towed, without engine power, across Lake Michigan hundreds of miles, all the way to the Mackinaw shipyards.

That will require two tugboats for towing and one for steerage. We are getting late in the season and, barring any rough weather; it will take us almost a week to make the trip. The bad weather is our primary concern. If we are undertow with engines shut down, as your drawing suggests, and weather hits the ship, it may have to be cut loose from its tow. If, however, we agree with Mr. Dullhearty that the crack is nonexistent, and the only hull damage is chipped paint, then we may use our engines and one tug for steerage. Our shipping time will be cut to a quarter of the time, and our exposure to bad weather reduced. To add to this dilemma, we have perishables on board that must be off-loaded here, if the trip were to take the four or more additional days. "

Andrew breaks into the captain's explanation, " Captain, if I may, your only problem is..." He paused for a moment trying to collect his thoughts so that he doesn't appear unsure of himself.

"Your only problem here is ... if you are willing to believe an inexperienced seamen... or the word of a professional who makes a living at interpreting what he can see with his hands. I realize that sighted people don't understand what touch visualization is, but you can't be successful in this business unless you master it.

"Captain take something out of your desk that has some detail or relief on it. I'll turn my back and you place it in my hand."

Dullhearty mutters loud enough for everyone to hear, " Really, this is a bit more serious than a magic trick."

The captain commanded. "Mr. Dullhearty, please restrain your comments,"

After rummaging about in his desk, the captain delicately placed an object from his top drawer in Boyd's hand.

"It's a letter opener, no, a knife. Chrome plated blade, too smooth for stainless steel; curved blade like an Oriental or East Indian, I guess. The handle is made of bone or ivory." Andrew then balances the knife on one finger.

"It is attached to the blade at the hilt. It doesn't run through it. There is an etching on the handle. It's a figure sitting on a pillow with fringe. On top of his head is a crown...four...no, five points on it. It's a he... no... a... she: got bumps on the chest.

In addition, it has six arms; two raised over her head forming an arch...two pointing up at the elbow, and the bottom two lying in her cross-legged lap. Hum, and she needs a shave."

"A remarkable display of your power of tactile sensitivity and concentration," the captain expounds, as he warmly wraps his left arm around Andrew, while shaking his right hand. As the captain escorted Andrew through the companionway, they are interrupted with indignant pleading from Readie..."But captain."

"But, my butt, Mr. Dullhearty, see Mr. Brianworth on the bridge, now please." Readie dejected, scoffs past Andrew and the captain, commenting: "Yes sir...Captain."

"You will forgive Mr. Dullhearty. He is a hard working lad, but sometimes he does have a problem with authority. He can become overzealous. When he doesn't command the floor he does have a snit. I tend to favor your assessment of our problem. However, it is not my decision to make at this point. The company is flying in a marine engineer. He will make the final determination on the condition of the hull. Part of his decision will be based on your observations and my recommendations. I tend to treat these things with ultimate precaution. Maybe my thirty-five years without a serious accident, save yesterday, has something to do with it. Without some kind of x-ray of that area I believe multiple opinons are our only alternative. Metal does quite unusual things, dare I say extraordinary things when it is stressed."

The captain pored himself a tea and continued, "I recently read of a 100 meter ship in the North Sea heading into a storm. She came into a wave on her port bow and peeled back the bow plates for three meters. Peeled it, like an orange. That plate was 'one and a half inches' thick, to use your terms. The plate didn't break at the weld, but several inches behind it. The tear was as clean as a knife cut, and the flap lay so tight against the hull that a newspaper couldn't be placed between it and the hull.

When it comes to Lake Michigan, or the open sea, you must be prepared for the worst possible situation. I am sure I don't have to tell you about how brutal your lake can be even in a mild blow." The captain waited for Andrew to respond as he stepped to the cabin door and motioned for Andrew to follow. They walked along the portside to the stern railing staring out into the lake. Each man deep in his own thoughts, as if the lake would give him the answer he needed. The captain made a half turn facing Boyd.

"So Mr. Boyd, you were going to tell me one of your sea stories, yes?" Andrew paused for a moment. He had been preparing for that question from the time they left the cabin.

"Ah, yes sir, I will. It isn't as dramatic as your story, but it does go to the power of Lake Michigan and how quickly it can turn from a beautiful calm day to, 'I wish I was somewhere else' kind of day.

After months of planning we set up a dive expedition to the Door County area a few years ago. There were four divers, making two dive teams and a 26-foot aluminum cabin cruiser stacked with eight hundred pounds of search and dive gear.

I should have known it would turn into another adventure when things started to go wrong on the drive up. The camper we used to haul the boat broke down one hundred miles from Milwaukee. Three marred and skinned knuckles later we were back on the road. It was evening by the time we arrived in Door County. There weren't any public parking areas for us to overnight and with a 60-foot rig, parking on the street didn't seem like an option. It was dark, very dark, when we finally stopped at what looked like a boat ramp near Gills Rock. All of us were dog tired. It didn't take much to persuade anyone that this was the place to stop for the night. After a restless night in 'mosquito heaven', we awoke to water lapping along shoreline. We had stopped at a makeshift boat landing. It looked like a public ramp in the beam of headlights, but in the morning it was a shoreline with rocks placed haphazardly to create an incline. We spent the next two-hours placing more rocks in the ramp. We loaded our dive equipment and the search gear into the boat and parked the camper out of everyone's way." "Mr. Boyd, are you going to get to the sea story, soon?" The captain asked.

"Yes, I'm sorry. After a two-hour run in four foot swells we arrived at Poverty Island, which is one of the last islands leading out into the lake along the Door County peninsula. It is only a few miles from the Michigan shoreline. The purpose of our little adventure was to find the treasure of Poverty Island."

The captain interrupted, "A treasure you say, in Lake Michigan? I don't believe I have heard of a sunken treasure in the lakes. I assume you are talking about sunken treasure because you went there with a crew of scuba divers."

"Yes, the treasure is within the range of most scuba divers using compressed air. We planned to make about four dives a day with each team. The depth would be swallow enough for us to make multiple dives and stay away from doing depression diving. The captain asked,

"Is this your first attempt at finding the treasure?"

"No, this was the third team of divers I had assembled and the second year. The first year all we did was go to the island, pick a spot and blow bubbles for four days. That trip was to say the least, unorganized. Anyway, would you like to hear how the treasure ended up in Lake Michigan?"

"By all means, I'm very interested. But, we will get to the storm at some point in this story."

"I'm trying captain." Andrew said with a twinkle in his eye.

"The legend says that the treasure was being smuggled into the Midwest by the Confederate Union in 1863. It was shipped overland to Escanaba, Michigan, because the Union Army had a blockade along the entire coast of the United States. Of course, there were blockade-runners who made it through but, many went to the bottom trying. The gold bullion came from somewhere out east to Escanaba and was loaded onto a small lake sailer, so the story went. The gold was sent by Napoleon III to keep the confederates in the war. Cotton in those days was as valuable as oil is today. The French populace was antislavery, but the government wanted the import of cheap cotton. A covert plan was put in place and the gold was sent on its way. At Escanaba there were sympathizers on both sides of the war. Anyone who had the money, had the loyalty. After the gold was loaded on the boat it left leave port in a hurry because the secret had been leaked to French braggarts. They were in pursuit when the captain of the escaping sailer ordered the gold dumped overboard near Poverty Island.

And so the legend began. I believe the gold is real because the legend appeared in many parts of the lake at or about the same time. It has withstood the 'test of a century'. Someone told me that a legend that lasts a hundred years has an eighty percent chance of being true.

Napoleon III did try on several occasions to infuse money into the Confederacy and had his own entanglement with the United States in Mexico. This legend comes to life every ten years. Some new clue prompts a new wave of interest in the story."

The captain turned to Andrew again. "You mean like the story about the power of the sea?"

"Sorry, I get very involved when I talk about the 'Treasure of Poverty Island'. The storm snuck up on us from the northwest. We were into our third dive and were close to calling it a day. The late arrival and the rough boat ride took its toll. Suddenly, a cold blast hit us. It was a good thing both teams were on board. The storm hit, and the wind kicked up blowing the tops off the waves. In less than ten minutes there were five-foot waves and building. We headed for what we thought was the only safe place at Poverty. The only dockage was a broken concrete pier that formed an L'-shaped break-wall. A second concrete finger ran parallel to it with a twelve-foot gap between them. At the head of the finger pier a boat had to be manhandled through the opening and muscled down the sixty-foot L' portion. The steel cleats were stationed eight-feet apart along the pier. Some were pulling out of the concrete while others were twisted and bent over. As we neared the opening, Allen, one of my divers, jumped for the pier just as our boat went into a trough, he hit the pier and skid across it into the water on the opposite side. His wet suit cushioned the impact and saved him from serious injury and possible drowning. He half crawled, half rolled by force of the waves back on the pier. Allen shook off the injury and caught a line we had thrown to him. The lake had become savage on that end of the island. Torrents of water pored over the crumbling pier,

Collision Of The Freighter Endeavor 143

making it nearly impossible for Allen to stand. He struggled with the line trying to assist in docking the boat. He took in the line, then payed it out as the lake tossed our boat around. We were standing off ten-feet from the head of the pier. Each surge of the lake brought us within inches of crashing into the pier. The timing was critical, he had to direct the bow of the boat at just the right moment to turn it into the small opening then pull the bow smartly to starboard and tie the bow off as quickly as possible. We made it into the opening and charged recklessly down the narrow channel. The motor power of the boat was useless at this point and all hands fended off the boat as it came to a jolting halt between the two concrete break walls. We jumped out of the boat on both sides and tied off the spring, bow and stern lines. We used all the fenders coming into the dock and then added whatever cushioning we could invent to protect the hull from damage. Rain pummeled our faces and drove us to gasp for air. It came in at us horizontally and stung when it hit our eyelids. I took a dive mask out of my bag and slipped it on. The other divers did likewise. After we had secured the boat as much as we could I stepped back and took one final mental check of what we might have missed.

Allen said, "Lets get the hell out of here." The boat rose and sank three feet and snapped the docking lines. The lake was still building into a rage. Our thoughts of sending out an SOS never entered our minds because we felt reasonably safe on the island. After all, the light house was a hundred years old and was still standing. We were more worried about the boat. George the owner of the boat took a cavalier approach to the fate of his boat.

"Hay, if she breaks up and sinks, I'll get a bigger one." A few of the dive bags were hurriedly dropped on the pier and then run up to the half destroyed walkway that led to the shore. It was too risky to handle the dive tanks with the boat bobbing and weaving like it was. They were in very secure tank racks bolted to the decking. George had spent many a day on Michigan, and knew how dangerous a rolling tank can be with 2250 pounds of pressure inside. The only fragile part on a steel cylinder is the 1/2' valve. Knock that valve off and you have a steel balloon full of air trying to find a place to lodge. We were very sure that they would stay put even if the boat would be tossed on shore.

"I did screw-up big time by not calling in a 'situation report' to the Coast Guard. We weren't expected back for three or four days and that could mean it might be several additional days before we would be reported missing. By the time we gave it serious consideration the boat was thrusting like a bucking bronco. It was far too dangerous for us to try to get back on board.

All of us were still wearing our full wet suits, hoods and boots from the earlier dives. Our wet suit boots had some traction on the concrete, but we slipped around as if on a pond of ice. After struggling to get the boat in and evenly centered between of the two break walls, we were burned out, beat. We had to get under cover, the driving rain stung as it hit the areas of exposed skin around the mask. The guys headed up the small hill to the lighthouse keepers building. It was barely visible through the pounding rain. As we got closer we could see how deteriorated it was. Roof shingles lay scattered on the ground. All the windows were broken and the door lay inside on the floor. The paint was peeling in long strips of flapping confetti. We stepped inside the abandoned building thinking some shelter is better than none. There were some tough guys with me, but when we stepped through the doorway and looked around, they were stunned. Aside from the hanging plaster and broken glass and water dripping everywhere, there were tens of thousands of flies hanging on the walls and ceiling. 'Deer flies', I think they call them. Five-feet up from the floor it was clear. The rest of the wall was pure black dots. So close together you couldn't tell the wall color. The little dears probably didn't want to get splashed from the dripping ceiling. I would describe them as airplanes, but they didn't have motors. Everyone went to a window in hopes of seeing a break in the weather. Fatigued by the morning dives and the struggle to dock the boat, each of us picked a clear spot on a wall and dropped our dive bag against it. We sat down and leaned back thinking about what it would be like tonight if the wind died down and our little fuzzy-backed friends began to look for food. They, like us, had a long day and missed lunch. Our food was still on board. There wasn't enough time to off load everything. 'Save the gear first' seems to be a motto of some kind.

I asked for a volunteer to stand the first watch and check on the boat

Collision of The Freighter Endeavor   145

every half hour. Everyone would take a turn standing guard. One hour on, three hours off. The rest of us settled in trying to get a little sleep before it got dark and we would be harassed by the creatures. I remember leaning back and thinking, 'I can't believe 'Poverty Island' beat me again'. Well, all I want now is a little rest, we will see what happens in the morning."

There would be none for two more nights and days.

Andrew stopped his story short, without the grand finale of the 'struggle for survival'.

The captain waited for Andrew to finish his thought. He didn't.

They had waited out the storm with nothing more than growling stomachs and sleepy eyes. After returning to Gills Rock, he made plans for one of the dozens of future trips to Poverty Island.

Andrew finally received payment for his services on the Endeavor, after waiting eight weeks. As part of the captain's official log, he put in all of the discussions that took place that afternoon. The comments by Readie were enough to place a question in the engineers mind. The owners and the captain elected to balance the trust between Boyd's opinion 'treat the ship as fractured' and 'the need for speed'. Using the engines at dead slow ahead, and monitoring the ships rudderpost housing and stern hull plates, they cut days off the travel time. Thousands of dollars a day on tug boat rental fees and a valuable cargo that would have perished were saved. The extra caution taken with Boyd's advice reduced the stress on the housing. For the owners, 'The need for greed' had a lucky few days.

Once the massive freighter was in dry dock and the rudderpost was sandblasted clean, the matter was resolved. The elusive crack was nearly four feet long, encircling a third of the rudder hub. Had the engines been used at higher revolutions, the vibration might have broken off the entire rudder hub. A flood of frigid water five to six feet high poring into the engine compartment might have caused an explosion, or the ship could sink from the shear volume of water.

Andrew's form letter, thanking the insurance company for the assignment, contained but one printed line "Thank you. I told you so."

Chapter 12

Taibbi Chemical First Meeting

April in Milwaukee usually ushers in the same type of harsh winds that are common in the fall. All too often they are backed by hard, wet snow. Hardest hit, are power lines, fragile trees and flat-roofed buildings. They feel the wrath of Old Man Winter not wanting to say a final good-bye.

Dive training at Adventures End continued unabated. Andrew had been doggedly teaching five combined classroom and pool sessions weekly and was close to burning out. Students, backlogged from a full winter of training, were impatiently waiting to earn Professional Association of Diving Instructors certificates in their open-water challenge. This strenuous summer schedule would be another killer. Andrew would spend every weekend taking new tadpoles to Racine, Wisconsin.

Nestled comfortably behind an avenue of quaking aspens, the tree line separates the quarry from highway 38. This is a favorite dive spot for both novices and experts. Racine Quarry is an eight-acre, lime stone quarry, with walls one hundred and thirty feet high and ninety-five feet of clear cold water. Visibility in the mid-to-late nineteen sixties, was forty to fifty feet. The Quarry proved a perfect location for the first open-water certification dives. In those early days, the open water certification required a diver to make only three dives. This was easily accomplished on Sundays, which was the only day the store wasn't open for retail business. Halfway through the summer season, Sundays would become a blur of wet and eager faces to a rather tired diving instructor.

Andrew had his students assemble at the store at 7 A.M. sharp. After a safety briefing and assigning of rental dive-gear, he would lead his would-be divers to Racine. The routine was always the same. He had it down to a carefully rehearsed pattern. Ten to twelve students required about four hours of training to complete all the exercises.

In the fall months, Andrew still had sufficient time to charge home and savor the Green Bay Packers attempt to make NFL history, again. This relaxing interval was his only respite from the tension of training countless eager students. Currently, he was in the spring season, and a relentless parade of students was about to begin. He had enough seasons behind him to know how to keep it professional. Now that the Alvin Davis was no longer taking up all his free time, he longed for some other diversion. Had it not been for the commercial jobs, his brain would have been fried months ago.

Suddenly, the persistent ringing of a telephone snapped Andrew back from his youthful reflections. His somewhat numb backside felt damp as he leapt from the chair.

"Woo, wet butt. I've got to stop daydreaming with such intensity," he mused to himself as he leaned over the four-inch thick walnut desk to answer the phone.

"Good morning, Hydro-Tec."

"A.B., is that you? This is Alan. I'm still in Miroshol."

"What the hell? Don't you pay your secretary enough to answer the phone?"

Andrew replied, "She makes more than I do. But I have to let her go home at night. It's four fifty in the morning here, you know. Alan, why the hell are you calling now? Why not wait for the satellite hookup?"

"Big-time problems, Boss... sorry about the early call. I just lost track of time zones. I flew in to Miroshol last night. Ah... Premier Blakansky was assassinated last night at the palace. They blew the hell out of the whole damn place. There was trash from his personal quarters blown blocks away."

" What about the government? Is it still intact?" Andrew asked.

Alan answered, "If it is, you can bet everyone and his mother's uncle will be in there, jockeying for a new job. You had better call in a few favors from the State Department on this one."

Miroshol, a small country of six and a half million people, almost unnoticed in the global scheme of things, was just starting to emerge from the snare of old communist doctrines. The discovery of an aluminum alloy that bonds and increases aluminum tensile strength gave

Miroshol its place in the world market. While quantities were limited, it was enough to promote world corporate interest.

Alan said, "We have three quarters of a million dollars worth of dredge equipment and pipe lying at anchor in the bay. How the hell are we going to get it out of there?"

"Don't get excited Alan. I have the bases covered on this one. That equipment is no longer ours. I sold it to Blakansky's port authority over a month ago. I leased it back from him long enough to finish our installation. It would have cost me a ton of money to move that dredge to another sight anyway. It was cheaper to sell it to Blakansky at a low-ball price. This way we both made out. He was supposed to maintain our installation with it.... I really liked that little guy. The man had a bizarre sense of humor and knew how to play the game. Have you heard anything about his wife and the two kids?"

"Yeah, first thing I asked. They are in France with his mother."

"Good. At least they are safe for the time being. No man had worked more diligently or risked more for his country," Andrew reflected. His voice was noticeably shaken by the loss of a friend and Miroshol's best hope for true democracy.

Andrew spoke softly into the receiver.

"He must have known he was in danger. That's why he farmed his family out to France. That little shit knew he was a target six months ago, when he and I closed Melba's. Man, what an escapade that was. He got so drunk I had to carry him to his room. Funniest damn thing; his bodyguards were frisking me as I hoisted him on my shoulder and stumbled up the stairs."

Andrew reflected silently about the event. "He surely lost a lot of palace decorum that night. Next morning at breakfast he sat on the balcony with a handkerchief over his face. His wife wouldn't give either of us any sympathy".

"Instead, she scolded the hell out of us for being so adolescent. She was only half-serious because she knew the pressure Blakansky was under. An hour later he would revert back into the Presidential role; with the first appointment that morning."

Andrew spoke after a his quiet reflection, "See what else you can do to help his wife from your end. I'll make some calls and make sure she has some protection, just in case...now listen... you and the crew need to finish that job as fast as you can...what have you got, maybe seven-eight days left?"

"No, about nine or...ten at the outside."

"OK. Finish up, and don't take any chances. If things begin to look a little sticky, bail out. Leave tools, plans, whatever, there. Just get your bodies out. Understand?"

"I understand boss. I've got it under control", replied Alan.

"Call me if anything pops. Call me at my private number. I'll be here all the rest of today and early tomorrow. Take care of yourself, and watch your tail-feathers."

Andrew hung up the phone and walked over to the coffeepot, which was nearly empty.

Lifting the slightly stained pot, he thought, "All I need is one more cup. I'll be a nervous wreck by noon." He slumps in his chair again, unsettled and troubled by the news from his field agent.

The sun first peeked, then shone a golden shaft of light across Lake Michigan's aqua blue and green field.

"Damn, I liked that little guy. It seems as though the people who truly love their fellow man get penalized for that love. Sadat bought it, he paid the ultimate price. Funny I would be thinking about the sixties when that call came in. The mid and late sixties, man; that was a time when we lost some very good people, real humanitarians."

After sorting out his thoughts about the phone call, Andrew drifted backward in his thought timetable. He remembered where he was when President Kennedy was shot. Andrew was changing the oil on a 1956 Ford Crown Victoria at his service station.

What an impact the news had on him! He had stayed glued to the radio all day and couldn't believe what he was hearing. The facts became clearer on how Kennedy died as the endless day wore on.

Andrew got very little accomplished that day. He didn't know why Kennedy's death affected him so. Maybe the fact that it was instantly replayed, in such graphic detail. Or, that Kennedy was the President of the United States. Maybe it was just because he was a kind man who had a loving family and cared deeply about people. It wasn't that Andrew voted for him or even followed his campaign. Andrew had been a hard-core Republican since the seventh grade and was twelve at the time of his first real campaign. Dwight D. Eisenhower was running for the Presidency. Ike was Andrew's childhood hero. He thought Eisenhower was the most rugged, fearless and compassionate man alive. Andrew had been elected to draw all the campaign posters for his grade school. Some of the posters were outrageous. His teacher told him he was being a little dramatic and should consider a career as marketing director of war movies.

When John Kennedy ran for office, opposing Richard Nixon and won, Andrew turned away from politics for a while. He hadn't paid much attention to Kennedy until that fatal day. Troubled for months, Andrew began a personal crusade to prove that it was not a lone gunman that shot Kennedy. He absorbed every bit of information he could lay his hands on. He researched the archives and became somewhat of an expert over the next several years. If anyone even hinted that the Warren Report was gospel, Andrew would become argumentative. He donated money for years to groups who kept the debate in the news. Andrew's small campaign stayed alive long after the media and the hierarchy in the White House deliberately obscured the issue of who killed Kennedy.

The old diving helmet-clock chimed 6:30 A.M. resonating its concord in the stillness of the pre-office activity, Andrew rearranged his chair again so the radiant sun would not shine directly into his eyes. Scanning the parade of traffic below as it started to build along lakefront drive, he settled into his chair and propped his feet on the windowsill.

"Now where was I? I think 1969?... or a ...Yes, must have been early '69. I was still working for Adventures End. That was the year I first met Steven Taibbi." Steven was a smooth, black haired, Jewish man in his late fifties. He was the second of three sons born to one of Milwaukee's wealthier families. Steven's father, Allen Taibbi a graduate chemical engineer from Harvard, had an innovative soul. He was a soft-spoken introspective man and the perfect partner for his boyhood attorney friend, Malcolm Judge. Malcolm, a well-to-do corporate attorney, was a hard driving business magician. Contracts and negotiations were his forte. Putting international trade packages together was for him a mere daily exercise in mental magic. It involved more play than work. The chemical business was extremely competitive and a consummate challenge for Malcolm, a role Allen would have failed at miserably. As president of a seven hundred million-dollar multinational company, Allen, holder of twenty-one patents, preferred a lab coat to a blue suit and tie. Steven Taibbi, unlike his father, never found a calling for himself. Now in his 'plan for retirement years' he was still trying to define himself. Steven's wife, Diana Lanc Taibbi, didn't help much. She was the sole heir to Aunt Gladys' candy bar fortune, and was paid four hundred thousand dollars per year as their acting President. Four days per week, Diana, with her broken-handled briefcase, would leave her Pleasant Lake, Wisconsin home and tackle the corporate world. She would jaunt out the door with her briefcase tucked tightly under her arm, yelling back over her shoulder... "Bye sweets, I'm off." On the other hand, Steven would meander down the steps of the foyer, duck walking in his famous wing-tip shoes with white inserts. He would flop haphazardly into his pride and joy... a 1953 Cadillac two door, forest green sedan. Smoke billowed from the tail pipe, as he cruised to Milwaukee at twenty miles over the speed limit. He would arrive there thirty minutes later, only to role-play as a corporate director in the Taibbi Chemical Corporation's mid-west office. His daily routine of pretending he was in charge of the office, included signing checks and handling trust funds for the Taibbi-Lanc family tree. Steven was paid a comfortable living wage, but not compared to that of his better half. The position gave him some status but little personal reward.

Steven's father, Allen, and his friend, Malcolm, died within three months of each other. Malcolm died first, of complications from a stroke. Allen was devastated. He mourned for weeks, missing days of work. This was an unusual occurrence for a man who may have been absent fewer than seven workdays in his lifetime. He was losing his incentive to follow a healthy life-style at age 78, and was lost without his long time protector pal. Losing strength as the weeks wore on, Allen suffered a massive heart attack and died, on what would have been his friend's 79th birthday.

For the last three years, Taibbi Chemical had been operating on automatic pilot. The former marketing manager, now acting as vice president, and a few board members struggled to take up the slack. After his father's sudden death, Steven secured a position on the board, in the hope of making a bid for the presidency. The months of infighting and political jockeying had left the company without a functional president. After the board voted four times and held two general stockholders meetings, the company still had no clear candidate. Steven lost in the first round by an embarrassing vote of eight to two. His effort to garner votes was impaired by his lack of corporate leadership skills. Taibbi Chemical had lost significant profits in five of the last seven quarters.

The old boy network wasn't about to give up the helm of a floundering ship to a seaman first-class. The consensus of opinion was, "If he earns his stripes, he can stand the watch."

Cautious that Steven might do something rash, just when a new president was sworn in, a delegation from the board went to reason with him.

At the time, Steven and his two brothers were substantial stockholders in Taibbi Chemical. That made the conservative board somewhat nervous. They made Steven a tempting offer, which he reluctantly accepted, knowing he had little choice. Steven's token placement as manager in the Midwest office was, to many, an appeasement for the poor confidence vote he received. It was a starting point with a more than generous salary. He was neither especially qualified nor truly interested in the position, but he took the post, which enabled him to remain close to the corporate insiders. This gave him access to the company's computer system and data. It thereby allowed him to keep a finger on the pulse of the company, something he would use to his advantage. In addition to his brothers, Steven's extended family owned the lion share of stock in Taibbi Chemical. When matched with the Malcolm Judge heirs, it could prove a formidable package. He would need to carefully bide his time for any takeover. The remaining outstanding stock and a disenchanted nephew of Malcolm Judge stalled any attempt of a Taibbi take over. Steven resigned himself to waiting it out until things turned around or he could find the chink in the old boy armor.

Steven's job as manger of the Midwest region included check writing and complaint deflecting. His talent for spending money facilitated matters, and his endless charm made him a success in customer service. The public loved his "I'll take care of it attitude." Line foremen and shipping personnel however, hated to see him enter their domain, because he would pull products from the line and request immediate shipping. Steven's actual management role was so limited that he had more than enough time to squander, and was often inconsiderate of working personnel. More than once, he had been reprimanded for disrupting a department's efficiency. Depressed by what seemed like a family possession being violated with intruders, Steven began to seek refuge by escaping to his little afternoon hideaways. A network of buildings in downtown Milwaukee lent itself to just such a past time. A person could leave one cocktail bar and meander along several passageways, finding any one of five favorite watering holes. Steven was no stranger to this type of escapism. The nomadic treks became more and more frequent. Daily wanderings increased, until Steven's wife grew tired of seeing him come home ill-prepared to meet guests or participate in family activities.

Steven and Andrew would cross paths for the first time in July of 1969. Steven, who had been trying to recover from his dependency on alcohol, was under pressure to spend more time with the family. At his wife's suggestion, he had joined a little known social getaway club in the Cayman Islands. After frequent family visits to this charming and remote island, he volunteered his service as president of the island club. Excited about the potential of scuba diving there, Steven looked to Adventures End for instruction. As the largest supplier of dive equipment and scuba instruction in the state, it was the obvious choice.

The morning Steven arrived at the store, the air was redolent with geraniums, and the sun burst through the windows, streaming its radiant shafts of light. He stepped inside the store, and in a challenging General-like pose he surveyed the displays, as if on an inspection tour.

"Young man, come here a minute!" he thundered.

"Andrew was straightening a display, when Steven marched in. He casually turned, looked over his shoulder in response to the command, and thought, "Who is this guy? A drill sergeant or the cape crusader?" Steven jauntily strutted over to the scuba cylinder display near the entrance.

"Tell me, if you were I, which system would you purchase?"

Andrew was amused as he closed the distance between the two. He reflected on the words he loved to hear from his heavy-spending customers, "What would you buy?" Andrew responded in an authoritative voice,

"It would depend on what kind of demand you will place on the equipment."

"We are novices and have little expertise in skin diving."

"Its actually called scuba diving now, not skin diving," Andrew corrected.

"In any event, I am looking for good durability and quality."

"In that case I would recommend one of these two packages. They should cover any of your needs now, and long after you become more proficient."

"Are you a diver yourself?"

"Of course! I'm also a certified scuba instructor."

"Excellent, then you shall be our guiding light. My name is Steven Taibbi," He said as he assertively thrust forth his hand.

Andrew returned the handshake, expecting more of a power grip. As their hands clasped, Andrew noted the self-confidence but had little inkling as to the adventures that lay ahead.

"Nice to meet you. My name is Andrew Boyd."

Steven placed his hands back in his suit jacket pockets. Pockets that had been pulled and stretched many times by the weight of hands longing for a place to safely reside. He shuffled back and forth in and around the cylinder display, almost starting a domino effect by knocking over one cylinder. "My mentor in the islands informs me that the regulator is the most important piece of equipment. Is that true?"

"Certainly one of the key components of the system."

Taibbi Chemical First Meeting   155

"Andrew, define for me what makes one regulator better than another."

"As a category I think breathe-ability. Broken down... Ah, first: how effortlessly does a regulator deliver air at one foot or one hundred feet in a relaxed dive mode? Secondly, will it deliver enough air in a full effort mode; meaning if you make an unusual demand, will you experience a dead spot or drop in line pressure because the regulator cannot deliver the volume you need.

Thirdly will the regulator breathe the same when your steel cylinder is pumped full to 2250 pounds per square inch, as it will when you have 1500 psi or maybe even 500 psi at the end of your dive?

A good regulator should allow you to forget that you are breathing from it.

"You should constantly be aware of the environment around you, not concentrating on the equipment."

An hour had passed and Andrew had explained and demonstrated an entire scuba package, including mask, fins, snorkel and wet suit. Nothing else was needed except to close the sale. Andrew took one final breath and prepared to ask for the order. Before he could make eye contact, Steven said, "An impressive sales delivery, Andrew. Please assemble three scuba units and I will pick them up day after tomorrow if that is convenient with you."

"Very convenient!"

Andrew walked Steven over to the checkout counter. They wove their way through the display with Andrew hoping to avoid a repeat of his earlier footwork.

"Will that be Adventures End, charge or cash?" To Andrew's surprise, Steven presented three new $500.00 bills that were still crisp from lack of use.

"Here is a deposit, I'll pay the balance when I pick up the equipment."

Andrew finished writing up the purchase and thanked Steven for making his afternoon. Steven shook hands, made an almost military about-face and marched out the door. Andrew stood transfixed as he watched his customer leave the building. He couldn't help musing,

"Man, is that guy a strange duck or what? He walks like he's marching into a wind with shoulders sloped forward. Those wing tips with the white inserts, toed out just enough to keep him upright. That is no John Wayne walk."

Andrew did not see or hear from Steven for nearly three months after he picked up his equipment. Then, one afternoon late in September, he received a phone call from Steven requesting a luncheon date, so that they could discuss some diving instruction. Lunch was at the Milwaukee Athletic Club, an upscale meeting place for business people in downtown Milwaukee. Andrew was impressed and felt a little intimidated by the formality of the luncheon.

Several business people graciously stopped at Steven's table, wishing him well on his recent appointment to the board of directors. Others saluted him for his new regional manager position at Taibbi Chemical. It appeared to Andrew that everyone was either a business associate or relative of Steven. When lunch was finally over, it was arranged that Andrew would teach a private scuba class to both Steven and his daughter, Penny. They would take their pool sessions with a long time friend of Steven's, Arthur Selter, who was a self-made millionaire in the electronics field. He offered his 40-foot long swimming pool, which was attached to the main house. Although huge by most standards, it was a bit small according to Arthur. The stunningly beautiful house was situated across the lake from Steven's home and overlooked a pristine setting. There was however, an aura of sadness within the walls. Much of the furniture was gone, with the walls reflecting the hazy outline of where pictures had recently hung.

Arthur was in the throes of a bitter divorce. His soon-to-be former wife had moved out just a few weeks before, and had removed a good quantity of her possessions.

Andrew started the lessons in her pool. It was quite a surprise, when during the third weekend lesson, the recently separated Mrs. Arthur Selter appeared pool-side. Vivian was, to say the least, upset.
Her thoughtless husband had let people use the pool before she had finished removing her furniture and personal items. It was a very embarrassing moment for Steven, his daughter, and for Andrew. Mrs. Selter

appeared to lose complete emotional control.

"How dare that bastard just open my house up for people to do as they please? And how dare you defile my home? I still own half of this house and until the court tells me otherwise, I still have the rights of an owner."

"Calm down Vivian. We are almost finished. We had no intention of upsetting you. As a matter of fact, we came on Sundays because Arthur felt you would not be moving things on Sunday."

"That thoughtless son-of-a-bitch never cared about my feelings when we were married; now he's doing the same thing."

"Vivian, I'm sorry we upset you. That is the last thing I wanted to do to you. I felt we had been friends for so many years you wouldn't mind."

"You thought...I wouldn't mind? You're as thoughtless as that other bastard. Now get the hell out of my house!"

"Vivian, please understand. We meant no harm. I..."

Before Steven could finish his sentence, the low rumble of an outboard motor broke into his pleading. Vivian snapped her head upright. Looking over the heads of the three divers standing in waist deep water, she glared out the floor length pool windows. A hundred feet away and down a gentle slope was the Selter pier. Pulling up to the dock was Arthur Selter in his newly refurbished, 1953 mahogany-clad, Chris Craft runabout. Snuggled along side Arthur, nearly in his lap, was a blond bombshell that would turn most males into jelly.

Vivian dramatically stormed out of the pool door screaming obscenities at her husband. Stomping down the hill, she ranted and raved abuse.

Once she was on the pier, she hovered over the couple while continuing her assault. After a verbal tirade, she worked herself up to a physical assault. She lunged forward, awkwardly placing her right foot on the beautifully varnished boat surface. Her purse swung out wildly, hitting both parties a glancing blow. Arthur, at first, took a number of blows to the head as a seeming penitent, but then he staunchly defended himself by blocking the onslaught. Finally, incensed with the situation, he slammed the throttle forward and the runabout jumped ahead. Vivian was caught off balance as the boat lunged ahead. She fell forward and placed one foot on the smooth stern deck of the runabout. The other foot could do little else but dangle in space for a second. With a one-legged giant stride she stepped off the deck to maintain her balance and plunged into the water behind the boat. It was a miracle that the propeller didn't hit her. A bedraggled Vivian stood up in waist-deep water, too exasperated to speak.

Andrew and his students stood motionless, staring out the steam-covered windows. After hesitating long enough to make sure Vivian was all right, Steven politely announced: "I believe this would be a good time for us to depart this humble abode."

Within days of this explosive encounter, Steven received apologetic phone calls from both Vivian and Arthur. Vivian removed the last of her belongings. Two weeks later, the scuba lessons were completed in the same pool without any melodrama. Andrew arranged the written test and the open-water exercises to complete their triad of requirements. He issued the scuba certification cards to Steven and his daughter, thinking he had seen the last of the Taibbi family. But one year later they would cross paths again, leading to a dangerous international adventure in treasure hunting.

Chapter 13

Record Deep Dive

The scuba season was an unbelievably busy time for Andrew. His retail obligations, training classes and commercial diving occupied most of the daylight hours seven days a week. In the evening he had the demands of the YMCA Scuba Club to fill in any free time. He served two-year stints as president, then vice president and finally divemaster. He was also newsletter writer for all six years, and it was apparent that his life revolved around scuba diving. By the end of this 1969 season, he was happy for the relief of fall and the slowing of scuba classes. It would take quite a stimulus to move Andrew out of his doldrums.

For more than a year, Andrew had worked toward setting a freshwater world record. His plan was to dive to the bottom of Big Green Lake, the deepest inland lake in the mid-west. Located near Ripon, Wisconsin, this lake had a recorded depth of 237 feet, with bottom water temperatures in the upper-thirties.

Andrew's first attempt was in 1968. After considerable preparation, he had organized a large group of YMCA divers and chartered a huge houseboat at Green Lake. The plan was to combine a social dive and a record dive, all in the same morning. Over a period of three years, Adventures End chartered touring buses to move large numbers of divers. They participated in social dives all over southeastern Wisconsin. The dual-dive stage was set. The turnout exceeded seventy divers. Andrew needed witnesses and credible documentation to lay claim in the Guiness Book of World Records; he had an ample supply of witnesses on this trip.
The players were assembled and two bus loads of people headed toward Big Green Lake. Andrew had arranged for the giant houseboat to take all the divers, reporters, and friends out to Sugar Loaf, a shoreline on the other side of the lake.

Thirty miles out of Milwaukee, a valve spring in the engine of the lead bus failed. Both transports pulled off the roadway and called for a backup. After more than two maddening hours, the replacement bus showed up. By the time the group arrived at Big Green Lake, it was noon and everyone was eager to get wet. The scheduled plan for the day was to motor over to the deep end of the lake, and while the other divers were getting ready, Andrew and his deep dive team will begin their dive.

As soon as the team made their entry, the enormous houseboat will move to shallower water. Everyone else left on board would dive, and set up barbecues. The deep divers would be less than fifty yards away, doing their decompression safety stops, while hanging on a buoyed float. The shallow divers will be diving on the sixty or seventy-foot shelf, just a short distance away.

Andrew anxiously gazed across expansive Big Green Lake, as the divers stowed their gear aboard. The whole day is going wrong. Thoughts of doubt lingered in Andrews mind. "Maybe I'm not supposed to make this dive."

Otto read concern on Andrew's face.
Andrew turned to Otto and said, "Man, I don't like the way the wind is blowing. It may be too rough out there to make the dive."

Otto replied, "Early this morning the wind was just right... now it's running right down the alley; some big chop out there I'll bet."

They were both right. The lake had churned up, and four-foot waves broke on the bow. The deep dive would have to be canceled.
The huge houseboat didn't have enough line for both high winds and a deep-water anchorage.

Otto continued, "No one ever anchors in that deep spot, especially in high winds... we would have to lay out three times the depth in anchor line." The captain cautioned firmly, as they neared Sugar Loaf,

"That diving would be hazardous at best."

"That's over seven hundred feet of line," he said. He had agreed to drop the hook in the deep spot, only if the seas were calm. This is bullshit... no one is going to be comfortable with half the divers upchucking over the side...you have to dive somewhere else... how about motoring around that point in sixty feet of water?"

The captain gestured toward an area protected from the wind. Nodding his head slightly in agreement, Andrew stood transfixed and dejected, with his face close to the bridge window. Dense fog appeared and then evaporates on the windowpane each time he exhaled. Deep disappointment registered in the rigid lines of his face, as he reviewed the six months of training that brought him to this moment.

"Damn, all that work and effort down the toilet." Andrew's hands tightened their grip around the brass rail in front of him. This was not the first time nature has handed him a "package of horse-pucky," an expression he used often for a major problem. For wearisome minutes, he didn't take his eyes off the choppy, blackish water. A liquid void that covered the biggest challenge of his young career. Only the chill from the bridge door thrust open interrupted him from his dark thoughts.

"Cap'n, I've got some pretty sick dudes on the aft deck", the concerned crewman announced, as he wiped the frigid lake spray from his face.

"We better head for a lee side somewhere." They're soaking wet, cold and getting ugly. Better park old "Grace" and let the landlubbers ashore."

The huge houseboat lumbered against the wind and built waves for more than an hour until she made a final course correction for the pier. The captain yelled out over the roar of the engines, "Right you are Jack, land fall in a few minutes...tell your shivering little brood...tell them they'll have solid grass underfoot in five minutes."

The remainder of 1968 seemed to accelerate at supersonic speed. Andrew's dive classes, commercial jobs and the international scuba tours filled the remainder of the summer. Packed away in his subconscious, was the forgotten promise that he would try Big Green Lake again, next year. Perhaps the credibility would come from local newspapers, television or radio, to prove he had in fact reached the bottom. His task was simple, he thought. He would take all his divers out on the houseboat again and anchor at a point near the site called Sugar Loaf. Then he and his team of support divers and reporters would board a twenty-foot power-boat that would be used as the actual deep dive platform. They would motor about fifty yards out from the houseboat to the deep spot and drop a one hundred twenty five-pound anchor. The unusually heavy anchor was to assure any skeptics that he could not raise the anchor while underwater and shorten his depth. Tied to the anchor, just three feet off the bottom, would be an inflatable balloon. When Andrew reached the bottom he would detach the balloon, swim it up to a predetermined depth, and pull the carbon dioxide cartridge. He had to swim it up because, at 237 feet the volume of gas that would be released, wouldn't expand enough to lift the weight of the balloon. The pressure at 237 feet was 120 pounds per square inch, which is equivalent to the pressure an elephant exerts on the ground with one foot.

All the plans seemed simple enough, but like the best laid plans of mice and men, they oft times, go astray. The morning of the dive, the two buses arrived at Adventures End before 6:30 A.M. The divers were already excited and eager to meet the challenge. Most had their equipment stored in the undercarriage compartments of the bus. Small groups of divers loitered around the makeshift dining table, munching on carbohydrate rich, sugar donuts and drinking piping hot coffee.

Brightly colored dive jackets and weathered jeans were the order of the day. Ripples of excited laughter broke the stillness of the morning. Divers who hadn't seen each other for a while shook hands, poked, prodded and patted each other on the back. Girlfriends and wives hugged and traded compliments.

"This will be more than just another dive. It will be a comfortable 90 mile ride out to Ripon and a relaxing bus ride back," Andrew promised the crowd. This would especially be true on the way back for the divers, who would be comfortably relaxed from all the diving. The non-divers would have had a very restful place on the upper 40'x 25' sun deck, while the divers made their one-hour dives.

At mid-morning, four barbecue kettles were lit for anyone who wished to utilize them. The weather was predicted to be in the high eighties with only a slight breeze. It was a good sign. If Andrew were to keep his long-awaited challenge with Big Green Lake, the buses would have to leave by 7:30 A.M. That would give them a drive time of just under two hours. If they were to arrive at 9:30, it would take another hour for loading the boat and getting to the dive site. Starting the dive at 11:00 A.M. would give the support divers the maximum amount of light penetration underwater. The sun, if it were out, would be almost straight overhead.

Andrew felt nervous and tense when he climbed aboard the second bus and commented to one of the support divers.

"Man, I'm really wound tight. I can't shake the feeling that something has been forgotten."

One of Andrew's safety divers reasoned. "Hey, don't worry. You've covered it all. Remember last night?" We ran over every detail. Everything's been planned for months."

"I know, I know, but I guess the fight I had with Samantha last night is still bugging me. I'm just a little off center. She really got on me about how insensitive I am. She said that I don't care how she feels about this dive, and how worried she will be.

"Why don't you just marry her and give her something to really worry about."

"Marry her? I hardly even know her. We've only been out together maybe ten times, tops."

"You're banging her brains out, so now she has possession."

"I haven't been banging her brains out, as you so delicately put it. She and I have had a few moments of tender embrace."

"Right."

The conversation shifted to other topics. It was just as well. Andrew didn't care to expand on his relationship with Samantha. He had already apologized to her and she had already acquiesced to his dive. However, it was too late, the threat of dying kept ringing in his ears. Last night, during their argument, she had given him at least ten different visual images of how he was about to die.

Andrew leaned forward and stepped out of his seat, noting the loud ambient chatter in the bus. He needed to review a few security procedures with Erv Washington, the deepest safetyman. Dave would be stationed at the 150-foot level, with a spare cylinder and regulator. In case Andrew had a total equipment malfunction, Erv would be stationed 85 feet above him. There would be two more safety divers: one at 100 feet, another at 30 feet. Each would have an additional spare cylinder and regulator.

For months, Andrew had practiced emergency free ascents. At first, he tried shallow water ascents from 30 feet to the surface. As his confidence grew, he pushed the limit 30 feet at a time until he reached 160 feet. He made the ascent twice, with full scuba equipment and a regulator in his hand with air turned on. Two weeks before his 1968 attempt, Andrew decided that if he were to be totally comfortable with an emergency, he would have to try a 160-foot ascent, without air. His attempt was unsuccessful. At the start of this, his last test dive, Andrew decided to begin the dive with a short air fill less than 1000 pounds per square inch according to his gauge. The object was to run out of air at 160 feet and be forced to ascend without any air left in his cylinder. If he could duplicate a real emergency and contend with the drag of full equipment, he would feel very confident at 237 feet, if anything went awry. He knew that "emotional control" was the deciding element with an out-of-air emergency. Panic was the one predicament he could totally prevent.

Descending feet first, he lowered himself down the anchor line. Finally reaching 165 feet, Andrew primed himself by taking several deep, slow breaths. He released the last air he had in his cylinder, taking one last breath, as the cylinder went dry. He had practiced out-of-air problems at 30 and 60 feet, but at 165 feet, his emotions began to surge a little. He grasped the line and started ascending hand over hand. With methodical slowness at first, he then ascended faster and faster.

"Remember-breathe out continuously and relax, "he repeatedly told himself. His pulse throbbed a little, but he got it under control.

"Oh, man. I think I exhaled too hard to start with. God this seems longer than before."

Andrew pulled harder and harder, feeling the rough texture of the rope through his gloves. "Pull, pull, up, up. Go."
His strength began to falter. Emotions, even controlled emotions, began to misfire. Racing up through a glistening mushroom of exhaust bubbles, Andrew scarcely made it to his thirty-foot safety diver.

He lunged at the spare mouthpiece and jammed it into his mouth, pressing the purge button all the way to its stop position.
A burst of air gushed into his mouth and billowed out the sides. Andrew's face distorted, partially dislodging his mask and making it leak.

Andrew thought, as he started to calm down, "That was too embarrassing, the way I grabbed that spare regulator out of Carl's hand. I guess that was about as dumb a thing as I have ever done."

Moments later both divers broke the surface. Carl removed his facemask and regulator and said, "Damn, Drew. I thought you were going to rocket to the surface, the way you came up at me. I'm surprised you didn't get an air embolism or something."

Andrew felt embarrassed but more confident now, than he was before the dive. Later he said, "I couldn't have made it all the way to the surface even if it were only another thirty feet above me."

Andrew put a lot of stock in biorhythms. His explanation for not making the full 160-foot ascent was that he was in the low end of his physical biorhythm.

One week after his failed practice ascent, he had completely removed the incident from his mind. He labeled it as bad timing, nothing more. Now he was only hours away from his dive, and some self-doubt was eroding his confidence. Doubt, like a shadow, is always lurking and ready to overtake its creator.

He reviewed responsibilities with each diver, hoping to soon realize his ultimate challenge. All the concerted effort, endless planning and the tiresome waiting would soon be recognized. A small pod of detractors and critics would await the outcome like parasitic lampreys.

Andrew was winding his way back to his seat, when the driver pulled over to the shoulder of the road. With a concerned expression, he released the door latch and stepped out. An anxious hush swept over the crew. After what seemed an interminable wait, he pulled down the rear engine hood. Andrew was worried, because the driver clambered back into the bus, shook his sun burnt head and muttered to himself.

"I told those bastards back at the garage that I heard the engine missing this morning. Well, now I think the fuel pump is gone." Then he announced to the entire bus, "We'll have to call for a backup vehicle it may take an hour before another bus will arrive."

Andrew felt a roll of spasms in his stomach muscles.

He thought, "No way, not a second time. Stalled in almost the same spot. They can't get a replacement bus out here in 60 minutes. We're at least an hour from town, and they still have to locate a spare bus and driver." After the first hour of stagnation, each minute began to drag.

Suddenly, the first tour bus pulled up behind the stalled bus. The first bus had dropped off all its passengers at the lake and was radioed that Andrew's bus was disabled.

The driver knew he could unload his passengers at the lake and return to the first bus faster than any vehicle coming from Milwaukee.

He was right. A phone call from a nearby service station determined that the repair truck and third bus had not even left Milwaukee by the time the first bus arrived.

Andrew was relieved that this emergency was resolved, but time was running out. If he didn't hit the water by 1:00 P.M., at the latest, he would have to abort the dive. He didn't want to think about the disappointment and the problems of getting all these divers in the same place at the same time, again.

Andrew arrived at the lake a few minutes before noon.

The houseboat had already left and was anchored near Sugar Loaf.

It made little sense to hold everyone at the dock until the remaining divers showed up. They might take hours to arrive. A twenty-two foot runabout was used to shuttle the remaining twelve people out to the houseboat. It was decided to have Andrew, his divers and the reporters go out last. That way, they could motor right to their deep-dive location.

Divers started unloading their equipment. A mad scramble to get six divers and all their equipment on board began. The fully loaded runabout made slow progress out to the houseboat. A black stripe water line painted on the side of the boat was five inches underwater. Divers were sitting on each other's laps or draped over assorted equipment. Bow surge thoroughly soaked everyone on board. Fortunately, the sun radiated a hint of nurturing warmth. The remaining four divers and reporters could do little else but watch as the dive boat disappeared in the wash of the lake. It would take an agonizing hour for the runabout to make a return trip. The diligent reporters lay against the lumpy dive bags, penciling in their story outlines. They took full advantage of the lull in activity. The divers took the benefit of the suns beaming rays, and removed their shirts for better tanning.

Andrew anxiously paced back and forth, reviewing last minute details of the deep dive. It was twelve o'clock noon and still no sign of the boat. Than suddenly, Carl yelled "Thar she blows" as a small image on the horizon came into view.

Standing at the edge of the pier, Andrew studied the image as it becomes larger. "I sure as hell hope you're right. If you're not, we won't be able to make the dive."

Carl replied. "Think positive. It's coming like a bat out of hell, straight for us."

Andrew shouted with relief, "Damn if you're not right. OK, let's get our tail feathers in gear."

Equipment was loaded with great care, first in, last out! Andrew wanted to avoid having to dig to the bottom of the pile, for the first piece of equipment he would need. The dive site was located more than two-thirds of the way across the lake. Headway was slowed, since the boat was more than fully loaded. Halfway across, Steven Ernst, the boat operator and topside safetyman leaned toward Andrew and cautioned.

"The water is getting choppy. The wind shifted and I think it could get rough. I hope it doesn't kick up any more than this or we will have some sick little puppies on our hands." No sooner did Steven finish his comment, then one of the reporters suddenly leaned over the side and deposited his breakfast into the lake.

"I got to get to shore. I'm sicker than a dog," the reporter sputtered, as he bent over the side one more time.

Andrew empathized, but was running out of time. "Wally, you're looking a little green around the gills. I'll drop you on the houseboat; it will be a lot calmer in the lee of Sugar Loaf. From there you will be able to see everything. The minute my float hits the surface; you'll know I've reached the bottom. Will you guys be all right?"

The second reporter interjected. "Hey, I'm not sick. The Journal's the one that hires the candy-asses. I'll just tag along with you and give this old man here, the news secondhand."

The runabout was buffeted by the waves. Glistening spray from the bow wake wrapped around the boat, until the vacuum created by the windshield pulled it into the boat. Everyone was thoroughly soaked, except for Steven who was in the center of the boat.

After nearly an hour of thumping and bobbing, the seemingly fragile craft pulled alongside the cumbersome houseboat. Climbing up to the deck was a daunting task. The slippery deck gunwales were a towering six feet from the water. Located at the houseboat stern, was a swim platform the size of a cutting board. It was designed to be large enough for a half dozen personal friends of the captain. It wasn't designed for a group of water nut-cakes loaded with diving gear. Stretched to the limit, the platform was loaded with swimmers, inner tube floaters, and divers about to make entries. It looked like an anthill during lunch.

Amid the confusion, a few spent divers, who had completed one of their two planned descents, were now trying to climb aboard. It was more logical to dock away from the mayhem: forty feet rearward.

Andrew rendered assistance to the ill reporter by pushing hard on one cheek of the reporter's butt. Under other circumstances, the reporter may have had some objections: not today and not the way he felt. Desperately weak from seasickness, the reporter sat down hard against the cabin wall and slowly wedged his head between his knees.

"Oh, I'm dying," was all Andrew heard echo from above, as he settled back into the runabout.

"Wait a minute, as long as we have room, let's jump into our wet suits," shouted Andrew. The dive team pulled their dive bags out of the runabout and lifted them overhead onto the wet houseboat deck. Divers eagerly climbed aboard, scaling the six-foot wall. They pulled on their suits, dive boots and hoods, and strapped on the dive knives.

Andrew belted out, "OK everybody, lets go, let's go." He directed his displeasure at two of his safety divers. They had altered their attention away from their given task toward two of Andrew's rather attractive female students.

The three dive team members, Steve Ernst, the Sentinel newspaper reporter, and Andrew, jumped back into the runabout.

Andrew commanded. "Watch for divers. Then step on it, James, and don't spare the horses."

The boat drifted to the stern of the houseboat. Clear of the divers, it sped away from the houseboat and carved a foam-filled S-wave into the lake surface. Turbulent waves rolled and battered against the huge houseboat. Any movement from the wave shock was undetected by people on board. It easily fended off any minor wave action because the houseboat was so massive and sat heavy in the water.

Over the deep trench, the divers prepared the cinder block anchor. Over it went. "Paa-dush." A white nylon, braided line unraveled from the canvas bag. It made a swishing sound as it raced through the boat cleat on its way to the bottom. The charcoal gray bag in which it was stored was now nearly empty. Only a few coils and the 300-foot marker were left. At the two hundred fifty five foot mark, the line suddenly went slack. The extra line length was necessary, because the cinder blocks settled into the soft bottom and the slight scope in the line.

Steve Ernst double-checked his depth recorder. "I got 242 feet... maybe 239, since the boat's riding up and down a little."

Andrew leaned into the chart recorder. "Steve, run a hard copy now and another when I'm under the water. If we get lucky, maybe we will get a record like the Hope Root dive, without the same result."

Mr. Hope Root was a record-breaking diver, who lost his life on an ultra deep dive a number of years earlier. The boat chart recorder displayed his descent and showed his image drifting further and further away from the descent line. That may have been the point where he suffered from nitrogen narcosis. A nitrogen pop" as some call it. It impairs a diver's judgment, making it difficult, if not impossible to get out of a predicament. Nitrogen narcosis may sneak up on a diver without them ever realizing it. Similar to symptoms of intoxication, the diver is prone to take more risks than normal.

The graph had shown Hope leaving the descent line after hundreds of feet and drifting into the depths. His body was never recovered.

Steve glared back at Andrew. He knew the Hope Root story. "That was cute, he said. Any other little visuals you would like to share?" Andrew apologized. "OK, OK. I know it was a stupid thing to say. It just popped out. Now will you hand me my dive bag?"

Steve clawed into the pile of canvas belongings, searching for Andrew's duffel bag. Before their stop at the houseboat, all the bags were arranged in order. Now they were just thrown in a jumble. Space was so tightly restricted that divers were perched on the boat side rails, with feet braced against the assorted dive equipment. Andrew unzipped his bag and systematically pulled out his safety vest, mask, fins, snorkel and dive knife.

Steve shut off the engine. It was now hauntingly still. There was no wind. As suddenly as the breeze shifted and created a chop, it had shifted once again and brought a soothing calm.

Andrew forced his tense muscled index finger into the corner of the dive hood. He pulled it away from his ear so that he could hear better, and said, "Damn, is it quiet, or what"?

Steve answered, turning almost completely around, searching in all directions. "Man, this is spooky. I don't see any storm clouds."

All the divers searched the horizon for any sign of an impending storm. None could be seen.

Steve said. "I have rigged your triple 40's with the Scubapro Mark 2 regulator and the 10 cubic foot pony bottle and spare regulator. Your tanks are topped off at 1800 pounds. You're ready to rock and roll."

"OK, Carl you ready to jump?"

"As ready as I'm going to be."

Both divers inched themselves onto the side rails again. Facing each other from opposite rails of the boat, they placed their gauges and spare regulators in their laps. With meaningful nods, they let themselves plunge backwards into the emerald green surface of Big Green Lake.

The two safety divers followed only minutes later. This gave Andrew and Carl time to reach the thirty-foot level.

At 30 feet, Carl helped Andrew take off one of the two weight belts he was wearing. The heavier of the two, a fifteen-pound belt, was tied off at this level. There were few buoyancy control devices in the 1960's. Andrew's wet suit was compressed enough at this depth and required only the remaining ten pounds to take him to the bottom.

Before the men reached thirty feet, Carl grabbed Andrew and stopped the descent. Grimacing in pain, he pointed frantically to his ear: a sign Andrew knew well. "Carl was having trouble equalizing the pressure in his ears." He struggled, jerking from side to side, forcefully jamming his fingers under his mask into the small nose cups. Andrew motioned by shaking his head 'no' and made a hand movement not to push so hard. It was too late. The inside of Carl's mask was splattered with blood. Even a few drops of blood mixed with the water in the mask looked as if someone got hit in the face with an ax. But this one looked really serious. Carl knew he had pushed too hard and possibly blew a small nose capillary. He paused a moment and filled his mask with water, rinsing it clear of blood. Holding the high point of his mask, he exhaled out through his nose, forcing water to surge out the bottom. It cleared, but only for a moment. Unfortunately, the blood continued to stream out of his nose.

Andrew thought as he peered into Carl's mask, "Man, this is the worst squeeze I have seen in a while. He's done; I better take him to the surface."

He gave the thumb up in front of Carl's face, but the injured diver firmly shook his head no. Andrew motioned again; only this time, he directly confronted Carl.

Carl and Andrew started up, just as the two safety divers descended into them. There was temporary confusion, while the divers tried to figure out what had happened. Andrew finally pointed up with his thumb in a forceful, demanding manner.

A green stream of fluid flowed out the corners of Carl's mask. Red is one of the first colors to disappear during a descent. At thirty feet down, the color darkened to an emerald greenish-black.

As the two divers neared the surface, the color of red returned and Carl's contorted face looked anemic. Blood was seeping out of his hood just above his upper lip. It followed the hood edge and streamed down his chin. This meant one thing; a throbbing and painful ear for days.

At the surface, the divers hung on to the side of the boat. Carl dropped his regulator out of his mouth into the water and it burst into a geyser of spraying water. Andrew reached down and closed his hand over the mouthpiece, restricting the airflow until it stopped. Carl couldn't wait to argue. Spitting water in Andrew's face he said,

"Why the hell did you signal us to surface? I was all right. Just broke a couple of capillaries in my nose."

Through choking gurgles, Carl complained, "Andrew, now we have to start over again."

"Carl, you didn't just break a few blood vessels. I think you broke an eardrum. There's too much blood. It's all over for you. Why don't you help take care of surface support for me?"

"Oh bull, there's nothing for me to do up here. Besides, you won't have a safety man stationed at thirty feet."

"We'll have to go without one. I have to start now. I need to conserve all the strength I can."

Andrew didn't want to delay any longer. His emotions were stressed enough and he could feel a loss of body heat. Carl was reluctant to stay on board but knew that arguing would only make matters worse. Andrew reasoned, that the injured ear would start to throb, just about the time Carl started to relax. Then it would really matter, if he were hanging on the line at thirty feet or sitting in the boat. At some point, Carl would create an unsafe situation, as his mind began to focus on the pain.

Andrew gently helped Carl into the boat and turned his attention to getting the other divers back on track.

They had come up within a few feet of Andrew and were now floating belly-up, resting like basking sea otters. There wasn't any need for them to get into the debate. As project leader, Andrew's decision was compelling, built on experience and pure emotion.

"OK, gentlemen... lets get it together. Erv, you and I will descend together. I'll hang my weight belt on the line at 30 feet. Al, you check the spare cylinder at thirty feet and drop on down to your hundred-foot mark. Keep your eyes open for me when I come up. I may need a basket to put my brains in."

Andrew nodded approval to start the descent. The divers dropped feet first. At the 30 foot level, they halted. Andrew unbuckled the larger

weight belt again and clipped it to the anchor line.
They descended, dropping faster than before, trying to make up for lost time.

Without any warning, Andrew's mask started to fill with water. He cleared it once, then twice, and then a third time. The water still poured in, covering the lower portion of his eyes and blinding him until he exhales into his mask. Erv closed the gap between them. He saw what the problem was and wrote on his underwater slate, "Your mask purge valve is gone."

Andrew blew hard through his nose and took a quick peek into his mask, almost going cross-eyed to try to focus inside his mask. Looking down his nose, he could see water bubbling in through the bottom, where one purge valve diaphragm was missing.

"It must have come loose when I blew the water out," he thought. Andrew placed his thumb over the hole and cleared the mask again. Erv is face to face with Andrew, shaking his head.

"OK. OK to descend" Erv wrote on his slate.

Andrew formed the 'OK' sign with his thumb and index finger.

Their suits compressed tightly around their bodies as they passed the hundred-foot level. Andrew was uneasy, trying to cover the opening in his mask, hold on to the anchor line, and equalize the pressure in his ears, all at the same time. His breathing rate was climbing and he felt it. His thoughts were deeply engaged in how he was going to release the float with only one hand.

At 130 feet, Erv grabbed Andrew's arm and sliced the water horizontally in front of him with his other hand. After giving Andrew, the 'level off here' sign, he changed it to the 'go up' signal.
Andrew thought. "Now what the hells wrong?"
Erv strokes hard with his fins and looked down only a few times, as he passed the one hundred-foot mark.

"Is he going all the way to the surface? Oh, for Christ's sake. He must have had a nitrogen hit."

Erv never stopped kicking. The force of his stroke radiated downward into Andrew's face.

Both divers ascended to the 110-foot level, where Erv stopped and wrote on his slate, 'N2 hit. OK here.' Andrew nodded and gave the 'OK' sign back to Erv. He thought, "Jesus, now I don't have a safetyman at one hundred fifty feet. If I have trouble near the lakebed, I'll have to blow and go 130 feet before I find any emergency air. I can make that."

Andrew's mask flooded again. Pressing it hard against his forehead, he blew with more force than necessary. The mask skirt lifted away from his upper lip and vibrated in a burst of bubbles. The dislodged purge valve, which had been trapped in Andrew's mask, now floated free. Erv swiped his hand in an arc in front of Andrew's face. Confused about this unusual motion, Andrew shrugged his shoulders, as if to ask, "What was that for?" Erv brought his hand back in front of Andrew's face. Slowly, he opened his fist to reveal the missing purge valve from Andrew's mask. Andrew could see Erv's 'I just ate the canary' smirk, even with a mask and regulator obscuring his grin. Gently, not to create a current, Andrew picked up the purge valve with one hand and removed his mask with the other. The cold water strung his face as he firmly pressed the purge valve into place in the mask bottom. After clearing his mask again, he blew Erv a little kiss. Erv's hand signal was equally sarcastic.

Andrew drifted downward; his right hand loosely gripping the anchor line. Free falling like a skydiver with his legs and arms spread, he could slow his descent by gently changing his grip on the line. At 130 feet, he rolled on his right side and looked upward, as Erv's silhouette merged with a white halo of light from above.

"I've done 160-foot free ascents at least five times; I can handle this," Andrew reminded himself, trying hard to keep his emotions in check.

"What else can go wrong: A blown eardrum, a nitrogen hit, a leaking purge valve? How could we have done it perfectly in practice and perform this badly for real. Mom was right... I should have been a doctor. If I had been the safety officer for some other diver, I would have aborted this dive about five mistakes earlier. My emotions shouldn't be the driving force behind this effort. I can't make clear decisions based on emotion."

Andrew checks his wrist-mounted depth gauge. It read 185 feet.

"Man, what are you so nervous about? That's the third time you have checked your gauge in 10 feet... you've been this deep before."

"Yeah, but not alone," he answered himself.

Andrew's 1/4 inch thick wet suit was now compressed to the thickness of a Playtex glove and had about as much warmth. From here on down, his only thermal protection was his body fat. At this depth, with water temperatures in the high thirties, his cylinders cooled to ambient temperature. The volume of inspired air he is breathing has an air temperature less than zero degrees. He was losing body heat from the outside in, because of the cold water. Also, he was losing body heat from the inside out, because of inspired air temperature. Each time he exhaled, he must re-warm the new cycle of inspired air. His large 225-pound body-frame would be tested to the limits before this dive was completed. At 200 feet, the sound of his exhaust bubbles was distracting, breaking into his studied concentration. The compressed air in his ear canals was considerably thicker here than at the surface, with greater magnification of the sound level.

"I have to concentrate on the dive, not on the fear. Where did I put my small back up light?", he thought.

Andrew searched the thigh pockets of his wet suit for a bulge. "All right, I got it." He squeezed the light out from his pocket and turned it on. Sliding his left hand through the lanyard, he pointed it at the descending line in front of him.

"Not very bright, but it will have to do, I guess."

"Andrew brought his depth gauge close to his mask and shined the light across on the dial. He watched the needle push higher, 210, 220, it moved close to its stopping point at 250. At 230 feet he looked down again. I should be somewhere near the bottom now." He thought to himself.

Suddenly, out of the darkness, Andrew saw the cluster of cinder blocks directly below him. It was too late to slow his rate of descent. He folded his body around the tiny mound as if he were hugging a miniature mountain. "Oomph", he blasted into his regulator, as he settled into the soft marrow of the bottom. A filmy cloud of sediment billowed around him, fully engulfing him and the beam of light. "Nice buoyancy control," he said to himself, actually forming the words around his mouthpiece. He paused for a moment, collecting his thoughts.

"OK. I'm on the bottom. Now where the hell is the lantern light we attached three feet above the anchor?" Andrew swept his hand in a broad arch, as a blind person might do if he were unsure of the area in front of him. "It should be floating at least a few feet above the blocks, and the release float should be attached to it." Andrew's hand light was of little use for now, with so much water debris. Almost standing, but bent forward with his knees pressing against the blocks, Andrew widened his sweep. He lowered himself, bracing one hand on top of the blocks.

"Damn it, there isn't any light or float. Maybe they broke loose when we lowered this weight package over the side. I'm going to have to do something pretty quick since I'm running out of bottom time." He leaned over the blocks, touching the bottom on the opposite side of the pile. The bottom felt soft but gritty, almost like coffee grounds. Gently sweeping his hand, as if he were smoothing a bedspread, Andrew covered an area several feet out from the pile. His hand bumped into something that seemed to move on its own. He grasped the object and brought it up to his faceplate. Shining his hand light on the object, he could not focus it close to his eyes. He softly ran his fingers over the object.

"Oh, it's my light. It must have imploded on the way down... the whole lens and the body and bulb are crushed inward. That's why it lost its buoyancy. The release float must be here somewhere too. Yes, here it is. " Andrew untangled the float and unsnapped it from the light.

'Well, this light's done for. No need to tow it to the surface." He dropped the attached light and stuffed the release float into the thigh pocket of his wet suit. He straightened upright as he readied himself to start his ascent to the surface. Pulling up hard with his legs, Andrew realized that his feet had sunk below the soft muck at the bottom. He pulled first the right foot, then the left. Each refused to break free. Andrew wasn't concerned about not being able to free his feet; he knew it was just a matter of working one foot, then the other. What he did not want to do was to pull one of his fins off and then have to dig it out. The situation didn't cause panic, since more than once Andrew had freed his legs from thigh-high debris while working on the Alvin Davis. All the time in the back of his head there was a voice "Time is running out. Get your butt to the surface!"

After five alternating attempts to free each foot, Andrew pulled down on the anchor line and broke the suction that held him to the bottom. He popped out of the billowing cloud that covered the cinder block anchor. His light flailed wildly on its lanyard, casting a short narrow beam in all directions and finally into his own face. He caught the light and shined it at the release float.

"Lets see, how do you activate this thing? God, I can't figure out how to make this work; or, have I even thought about it?
What is it I need to do now? Go up? No, I must prove I was here, but how? Am I thinking straight or is this a dream?"

Perilous seconds ticked by as Andrew struggled to regain his reason. Unaware that he was sinking again, he fell in slow motion to the bottom, doing a surreal dance. His right knee thudded into a corner of the block pile and sent a shock wave through his body. Adrenaline streamed through his system. He reeled back from the tortuous pain, which helped focus his oscillating thoughts. They vacillated between reality and the start of a narcosis.

"If I pull the cord on this float, it will be buoyed to the surface.", he thought. Andrew yanked on the cord, which punctured the carbon dioxide cartridge. There was a small fizz coming from the float. It sounded like popping the top on a flat soda bottle. The balloon inflated to the size of a small thumb. Andrew danced it on the palm of his hand, but it would not float.

"Damn, we are too deep; the pressure is too great. How am I going to prove I hit the bottom?"

"OK pal, time to think." Andrew pulled the top of his glove away from his wrist, bent over, and scooped up a glove full of the bottom sediment.

"Now go up, climb... that's it." He checked his gauge, 220 feet, then 210 feet. Andrew looked up and saw nothing but darkness. He shined the small light up the line, which disappeared again into the haze and then total blackness. He could feel the line sliding past his belly and between his legs. The enveloping darkness had wrapped around him like the folding layers of a cocoon.

"He checked his gauge again 215... 220. Oh damn it; I'm falling backwards again. Oh shit! Kick, stroke, too negative, no buoyancy... long strokes, pull hard." The commands came blustering out, as he yelled at himself. he was moving up, 200 feet, 190 feet, 180. Andrew started to see the bleary glow of light above. "I made it, holy balls, I made it."

For the first time since he hit the bottom, Andrew felt the cold permeating his suit.

The suit was still compressed to a flat thin layer over his body and had little or no warmth. It will stay thin until he reached the surface, where it would slowly come back to its original 1/4-inch thickness. Andrew started to feel painful shivers. The motion gave him temporary relief, but the numbing thought of uncontrollable shaking was still there. His gauge registered 170 feet, then 160 feet, 150 and he began to relax. Andrew looked up and could make out the shadow of a diver against the backlight of the surface. Erv was at the 130-foot level where Andrew left him. Andrew ascended right past Erv, taking only enough time to give the 'OK', and the thumbs up hand signal. Erv responded and followed him up.

At the thirty-foot level, Andrew held for a long decompression stop. He hung on the line, waiting patiently for the bountiful amount of nitrogen gas he had absorbed on his long deep dive.

It needed to be reduced to a smaller and safer amount. "I don't have a clue on how long I have to stay here to decompress. I really blew this one. If I don't screw up my blood, brain or bladder on this misfit of a dive, it will be a miracle," thought Andrew, "Maybe I'll take my triple 40 tanks down to five hundred pounds of pressure and then use up the last five hundred pounds of air at twenty feet." he continued to calculate. "Then what? I guess I'll use the nine cubic feet of air in my pony bottle at ten feet, then the spare safety tank for the last bit of decompression time, if I last that long. Man, I'm cold to the core. I'll be one frozen Popsicle when this dive is done."

Andrew hung onto the anchor line for twelve long minutes at thirty feet. Then he moved up to the twenty-foot level. He was already near the point of hypothermia, but the warmer upper water helped slow his heat loss. Andrew could feel the warm water fill his suit as he stopped at twenty feet. Another twenty minutes passed and he moved up to the ten-foot level. Each of the safety divers had left Andrew to ascend to the surface. They reported that Andrew was all right but taking longer than normal safety stops.

Andrew waited at ten feet using all of his air, including his back up pony bottle. He felt that it would be easier to use up his own air supply, even if there was plenty of air hanging on the anchor line. He thought the spare hanging regulators might make his mouth sore. The curve of the hose and the angle at which they were tied off made him prefer his own. His gums were very sensitive and bled easily after long bouts of irritation from diving. Many times he would exit the water after a long hard dive and spit blood saying, "One too many right hooks I guess." His early boxing career, so he thought, was the origin of most of his aches and pains.

After fifteen minutes at ten feet, Andrew's air was completely exhausted. He began breathing from the spare safety tank. Minutes that seemed like hours crawled by. Andrew dangled like a leaf loosely fastened to a twig. Only his fingertips attach him to the anchor line. He floated face down holding on with one hand, as if fluttering on a current of air.

Finally, when he could not take the cold any longer, he released his fragile grip and broke the surface. To his surprise, there were hundreds of spectators. A number of boaters had heard the captain of the houseboat transmitting Andrew's progress over his marine radio. They gathered in a great floating armada and encircled the area of the dive. All the recreational divers on board the houseboat had completed their first scuba dive. They had now returned to the boat. The captain repositioned his houseboat near the deep hole so everyone on board might get a better view. All the other craft were either tied to his stern or anchored several hundred feet out from his bow.

When Andrew broke the surface, the distance was only one hundred feet to the houseboat. The captain invited him aboard to warm up in his cabin and have some hot soup. Andrew looked back at his surface support boat, not wanting to leave his divers alone on the small runabout. Before he could say anything, three of the divers said almost in unison, "Go ahead. We'll pull the anchor and be right with you."

Andrew rolled over on his back, and with slow, elongated strokes he tiredly made his way to the boarding ladder. The climb up the side of the six-foot high hull of the houseboat took the last remaining burst of his energy. Once on deck, he rested on the railing with both elbows, his equipment still in place. The people on board the boat could not wait to pat him on the back and trumpet congratulations in his ear. Andrew was delighted that there was so much exuberance, but he could not respond in kind. Displaying a broad smile and staying vertical was about all he could manage. He dropped his triple tanks to the deck almost haphazardly. He was that exhausted. His crew finally climbed on board and nudged their way in to help him.

"Funny," he thought. "My guys have to rescue me, now that I'm on board."

The celebration lasted until the houseboat divers started to prepare for their second and last dive of the day. "Fame is fleeting," Andrew thought, as he watched the divers make water entries for the start of their second scheduled dive.

Andrew's sat back in one of the deck chairs and watched divers make water entries and share the wonders of this magnificent lake. The shear lime stonewalls at Sugar Loaf are a perfect stop for new divers. The water depths are within their range and the underwater shelves are shelter for a variety of small fish. A great place for the beginning underwater photographer or cinematographer. After all the divers finished their dives and their equipment was stowed the diners were prepared. The steaks, brats and hamburgers began to cook. Only in Wisconsin could the upper deck of a huge house boat be totally obscured by billows of smoke emanating from barbecue grills.

By seven o'clock in the evening, the houseboat had landed and everyone scurried to their cars or buses to prepare for the long drive home. Andrew took a few extra minutes to thank the Journal newspaper reporter for his 'stick to it' attitude on the boat. He could only imagine how uncomfortable it must have been waiting, hour after hour, for the houseboat to hit the dock.

"Thank you guys, for all the extra effort out there." Andrew said as he patted Wally, the Sentinel reporter, gently on the stomach. Wally back-stepped into Jake's right shoulder and then laughingly said, "Don't worry, Andrew. We'll get even with you in the paper."
Jake added. "The next time you invite us, make it a land based operation...that way old twinkle toes here won't be dumping his cookies in the lake."
Wally, not to be out-quipped by Jake said, "Next time Jake, we're not inviting you, if you're going to be such a schmuck." He pinched Jake's nose with a little bit of hostility.

Jake recoiled and said. "Ouch,...what's the matter, you a little sensitive?"

"No, but I noticed you didn't stay on the small boat either."

Andrew broke into the discussion before it escalated into a real argument. What had started as a little kidding around sounded like "Who took my marbles?"

"Guys, I'm really sincere. It was noble of you to tough it out. If you would have insisted on going back to shore, I wouldn't have had enough time to make the dive."

The two reporters walked away and gave a thumbs-up to him. Both displayed broad smiles, so Andrew felt they were only exercising their competitive spirit.

The next day the deep-diving article appeared in both papers. The Journal surprisingly ran a huge story covering seven columns and 16 inches over most of the front page of the Metro section. Four full-color photographs dominated the feature, with two black and white photos on the follow-up pages. Countless people called the dive store to congratulate Andrew. Former high school classmates, people he had not seen or talked to in years, either stopped in or called him at Adventures End.

Andrew enjoyed his celebrity role immensely. It filled that void evident in most people, to be someone special. This provided a fleeting but inherently important bout with fame. It added a little credibility, which didn't hurt his professional diving business. Andrew had his measure of insecurity, the same as everyone. His humble beginnings and incomplete formal education had left a void in his self-esteem. This dive was more than just setting a record depth, if you consider what it took to arrive at that moment. Like a treasure hunter or mountain climber, it wasn't the treasure or the top, but the journey.
Perhaps that was the reason he was constantly challenging himself. He often thought. "How do I know what I know or can do, unless I test myself?"

Chapter 14

Modeling And Montgomery Ward

More than a month went by and people were still quoting the newspaper article and asking how it felt to dive 237 feet. Andrew tried to answer their questions with a modicum of humility, but every so often a little arrogance would show through. He believed 'if you don't toot your own horn no one else will.' Weeks of publicity generated new interest on several fronts for Andrew. He contracted for a number of small commercial diving jobs and there was a resurgence of offers to do some fashion modeling.

The modeling jobs fitted in nicely; they required little of Andrew's time and paid well for the time invested. After a five-year hiatus, a local modeling studio now showed new celebrity interest in Andrew.

Andrew had been the burglar in the Master Lock posters, the Gusto Man in the Schlitz Beer campaign, the leather clad rider in the Harley Davidson motorcycle catalog, and the accessory-clad man for Gimbel Brothers. Job after job came at him in a frenzy of shoots.

Nearly 24 years of age in 1963, Andrew was slightly bashful and inexperienced. Some even labeled him a freshman in the modeling business after sixty shoots. More often than not, he found himself modestly turning and facing the dressing room wall when women models made quick costume changes.

During one shoot at the studio, Andrew had an experience that truly reflected his mores and values. The dressing room was rectangular-shaped, and held a fifteen-foot long dressing table with an equal sized mirror. It was just wide enough for four persons to sit on, pressed together.

Harley Davidson had ordered a shoot and had scheduled Andrew to wear tight jeans, a tee shirt and a leather jacket. As the first person in the dressing room, he hurried to get into his jeans. Just as he buttoned his pants, two models rushed in. Andrew turned to put his foot on one of the chairs.

He struggled to get his foot down into the motorcycle boot. The footwear he modeled was always too narrow. This pair was no exception; it hurt like hell. His foot was not that big with size ten and a half, but it was a triple E width. Leaning forward over his bent knee, he tugged at his pant cuff to form it over the wide neck of the boot. As he changed position, one of the models patted him on the butt and said,

"Oh, honey, that is one pile driving ass."

Andrew, as usual turned beet-red and stammer some response, trying to ignore the remark. The models loved to watch him blush.

Not that Andrew was all that innocent. He maintained a value system that often contradicted itself. When he was alone with a woman, he was not timid about lovemaking. No holds barred, as long as both agreed. Andrew was a private person. The rules he laid down for himself about sexuality were very individual to him. He felt a man should never come on too strong. 'No,' really meant' no.

"Be a total gentleman at all times; women appreciate that in a man," his mother had instilled in him. He saw beauty was individually perceived, so he was never quick to dismiss someone that others may have seen as less attractive. He made a point of weighting each female on her honesty and vulnerability. He enjoyed the company of women as friends and would never consider taking a friend to bed. By contrast, in a public setting, if he found an attractive single woman, he never felt inhibited to establish contact. She may not have had a date in months because of her beauty. If she rejected him, he would thank her for her time and move on.

These things Andrew believed kept him from being an 'also ran.' He felt fortunate that there were women who filled some of the void in his life. Women who gave him insightful conversation, an evening of fun, or an intimate moment. He learned early on to maintain friendships. "If you do not, he thought, you may regret it. People change. A girlfriend who pushes the wrong buttons today, may not have the same effect on you tomorrow. If there was a strong interest in the past it may reappear in the future."

Andrew assumed, of course, that both persons mature with time. He also believed that when a relationship gets to the point where either party makes all the decisions, or tries to manipulate the other, then it is time to part company. When it's over, it's over. Andrew's bachelor life wasn't all that great; there would be times when he felt quite alone. Companions and one-night stands didn't fill that special space where a soul mate should be. He knew that, but like most people, he plodded along naively in the art of maximizing a relationship.

Andrew was in his mid twenties and still searching for the right woman, whatever that meant. He could not define his 'Miss Right.' Modeling gave him a chance to be exposed to a variety of people at different business levels. Some clients who came to watch the photo sessions would be very pleasant and talk at length between setups. At intervals, Andrew would be invited to lunch or parties with company executives. Some proved to be memorable, others simply boring

It was a very materialistic and ornamental world, but the money and power never overwhelmed Andrew. He just went along and did what was comfortable for him, with one question always there, "What next?"

Several times in his first year of modeling he thought to himself.

"This is it, this is what I'm supposed to do with my life. There's good money, different shooting locations, and the overtime is not too demanding."

The photography studio personnel enjoyed Andrew's work ethic. His patience and willingness to do whatever was required made him a favorite model. Nevertheless, his modeling career was short-lived, lasting just a few years. There was no apparent reason for his career to go on hold. From the beginning he never felt it would be a life long career. The drive wasn't there that successful models have. Andrew didn't have the need to learn the follow-up skills required to sustain a modeling career. He never made contacts with agencies or studios and didn't feel as strong a commitment to modeling as he did to diving. He let it die its own natural death. The industry mantra 'don't call us we'll call you' worked just fine for him. He didn't know what the next adventure in his varied career would be. Maybe the timing for a modeling career was just wrong.

However, shortly after those exciting and sometimes broadening experiences of seeing new faces and new places, he lost interest. The inclination to go back to his old comfort zone, diving, was always there. Perhaps fate prompted him to reflect inwardly on his strengths, when he would question his own ability. However, fate does have a tendency to swing in both directions, given enough time.

The promotional director for Montgomery Ward called Andrew from Chicago shortly after the newspaper story of the nineteen sixty-eight deep dive appeared. He requested a meeting with Andrew at his office for the following Monday. Andrew drove to Chicago bright and early, filled with excitement and with an anxious, unsettled feeling in his stomach.

Arriving at 7:45 A.M. he was plenty early for his 8:30 A.M. meeting. As he walked down the long hallway of the office complex, he spotted a businessman coming out of the executive bathroom. Andrew pushed in behind the businessman as he left, and said, "Thank you" over his shoulder in an authoritative voice, as if he had a right to use the room. He spent long minutes in front of the mirror making sure every hair was in place. He adjusted his suit, stepped back from the basin, buttoned his jacket, and said, "Hi, I'm Andrew Boyd." "No, don't be so casual," he shot back at his reflection.

Andrew grimaced in the mirror, disappointed with his appearance and his voice level. Most of all, he lacked a reason why he was there in the first place. "Am I being interviewed for a job? Why the hell didn't I ask? How artless of me not to get a clear picture of what this is all about." Raising one brow as the word "artless" was accentuated

He looked back into the mirror one last time as he walked out of the door. He shrugged his shoulders and sighed;" Oh, well."

Andrew announced himself to the outer lobby secretary a little after 8:00 A.M. The secretary assigned him a seat in the waiting area where he waited until 8:29 A.M.

A dark-complexioned man, slightly round-shouldered and pot bellied, ambled across the beige-red carpet and introduced himself.

"Hello, I'm Neil Offenstein and you're Andrew... ah?" There was a slight delay as he waited for Andrew to fill in the last name.

Modeling and Montgomery Ward 187

"Boyd", Andrew said as he extended his hand.

"Boyd. Yes of course, the deep-sea diver. It's very nice to meet you. Alexander Palmer is your real contact person. I'm just acting as a crossing guard to direct you to his office."

Andrew thought to himself: "Crossing guard; for some reason I can't see this guy in charge of little children."

Neil's handshake was limp and unimpressive. Sometimes, when Andrew met people for the first time, they seemed genuinely interested in meeting him. They usually made eye contact, smiled and used a firm grip during the handshake. That didn't happen today. Neil looked out past Andrew's left ear and closed his hand before Andrew had fully engaged his. Neil shook four fingers, up to the first two knuckle joints of Andrew's hand.

After quickly releasing his grip on Andrew's fingers, he pivoted around his own and girth plunged his hand into Andrew's armpit to lead him forward. "Come on, it's this way," he directed, and stepped forward.

Andrew shook off Neil's grip as if he had sticky paper on his fingers. Neil released his arm and spearheaded the way down long rows of office cubicles, increasing his lead with each step.

Situated at the end of the building were four glass-enclosed offices. Neil knocked and pushed open the door before anyone could answer.

"This is Andrew Boyd, Alex." Alexander Palmer looked up and replied "Thank you Neil. Hello, Mr. Boyd. Please have a seat."

The two men exchanged personal comments of interest and Alexander laid out the itinerary for the day. The morning meeting would include a tour of the Montgomery Ward catalog department including marketing and layout, and also a discussion with some of the sales people.

For lunch, Alexander had made reservations at one of the downtown restaurants near the office. He also arranged for a meeting with five of the purchasing department executives.

Andrew didn't have a clue as to why they included him in their power lunch. He nodded and made eye contact around the table, as if he were engaged in deep evaluation. No one directed any buying strategy or marketing questions to him and he wasn't going to volunteer any pearls of wisdom. He felt relieved that the lunch was almost over and no one had caught on to his deception. One of the younger men did catch Andrew's eye, leaned forward across the table and asked.

"So Mr. Boyd, where do you think the sporting goods market is headed?"

Andrew gulped down his mouthful of food, wiped his mouth with his napkin and replied. "I believe the water sports market is going to blossom in the next few years. I also believe that snorkeling will be the biggest participation sport in the industry. Most people haven't looked at the accessory market for snorkelers. I'm speaking of water related sports...other than boating, of course."

A senior executive added, "Do you believe, it can generate the kind of money downhill skiing is producing?"

"Yes I do, said Andrew. People go on tropical vacations at the same rate that winter skiers do. I don't have any static's on the total days spent on winter ski travel opposed to tropical vacations, but I would guess tropicals are a little longer. If they snorkel on those trips they need an exposure suit, gloves, booties and a safety vest. That doesn't include the swimsuit, cover up, waterproof lotions, insect repellent and other items designed especially for beach needs. More than one hundred million Americans swim on a regular basis. They are prime candidates to become snorkel divers. At present, there are already twenty to twenty five million of them. That's a hell of a market."

Then a young man sitting next to Alexander posed a question.

"What about the international travel market connected to downhill skiing? Nothing out there compares with that in sporting goods."

Andrew, surprised at the redundancy of the question, replied. "You're absolutely right. At Adventures End, we booked over a thousand skiers who were headed west last year. They spent an average of $500.00 per person. And maybe one hundred traveled overseas at $1100.00. But I think the ski industry will be challenged in the next decade by scuba divers and then by snorkel divers."

Alexander broke into the flurry of questions. "Gentlemen, let's allow Mr. Boyd to finish his lunch. Save your questions for when we return to the office. I have a few things to cover also, so you will have time to ask questions then."

The remainder of the luncheon was filled with chitchat and little that might lead to another heavy discussion. It was clear that Alexander Palmer was the man in charge and the lunch was supposed to be a time of quiet relaxation and small talk. Alexander was ahead of his time. He believed it was easier to recycle an old executive than to train a new one. He also believed there was a time for work and a time to build employer-worker relationships. Selling a client at lunch may be necessary at times because of time constraints. However, taking your everyday job-related problems to lunch only implies you can't get it done during regular working hours. "Lunches are for promoting good relationships and not for selling products," was his thinking.

After lunch, at the follow-up meeting, the round table questions intensified. Had Andrew only taken a moderate position during this Q&A he might have ended his visit with an unblemished record, two and 0. Sadly, he was on a roll and couldn't zip it up. When asked about a new line of water skis that were laid out on the table, Andrew blurted out.

"She looks like a dog to me. I don't think it would do much for your new product line. The colors are way out."

There was dead silence in the room. Andrew knew he had stepped over the line on a subject he knew almost nothing about. He did sell water skis at the store and Adventures End had a few brand names, but no one gave them much importance because the volume was so small.

Andrew had just shot himself in the foot. There was no way to recover from this blunder. It turned out that the ski line was Montgomery Ward's hot new baby. Every stunned man in the room had given it a "thumbs up" for inclusion in the catalog, but Andrew couldn't have known. He stood dumbfounded, looking into the foreheads of all the men. They were looking down at the skis and all found it difficult to make eye contact.

Then an authoritative voice reverberated against the walls:

"Gentlemen, I think that will be enough."

Another cautionary and somewhat sarcastic voice said. "I'll say." The room quickly emptied into the outer office. Only Mr. Palmer remained.

Palmer turned and asked Andrew to return to his office for a few minutes. Andrew thought. "Oh man, I sure as hell blew it. All day went perfect... then bang the giant egg drop."

Andrew walked alongside Mr. Palmer, engrossed in his thoughts.

"How could I have said that?" played over and over in his head.

"Remember what you used to say: Never tell people everything you know and erase all doubt. "Remember your story about the guy at the bar who kept espousing his superior knowledge. The guy next to him had said, "You must be smart. I noticed your class ring when you were picking your nose." Then he calmly finished his beer and left. Remember all those stories? OK, then, why don't you take your own advice?"

Mr. Palmer's door swung open and Andrew stepped in, thinking this would be the 'big kiss off. "Well at least I had a great lunch. I did have them on the ropes for a while.' To his amazement, Andrew was asked to consider a consulting position with Ward.

His assignment would be to select a limited number of products from hundreds of new items they might endorse from leading manufacturers. The chosen products were to appear in the succeeding Ward catalogs.

Andrew was totally surprised that the executive was so forgiving.

"Was he out of the room when I had that total brain crash?"

Most of the products Andrew chose were not based on any research he had done. He relied only on a gut feeling and his limited retail background. Unknown to him at the time, many of the items he favored at the earlier meeting were prime targets for inclusion in the current catalog. This only reinforced his credibility with Alexander, who looked at Andrew and said. "Not bad, 18 and one. But you did trash the one item everyone felt was the hot property. All my employees make mistakes. You learn from them. Just don't do any catastrophic ones." The meeting ended at 4:30 P.M.

On the trip back to Milwaukee, Andrew thought about the remuneration from Ward. It was very generous. Imagine going to Chicago and having high-powered executives to work with. That was really something. Halfway home he started to daydream about having his temporary consulting position changed to a permanent status. He fantasized an office overlooking the city with his own secretary and staff of people. He envisioned a well-appointed Chicago apartment embellished with works of art.

Over the next six months, there would be three more Chicago trips and three more paid ego-building sessions. Prior to each trip, Andrew pored over a huge Ward mailer and evaluated the products thoroughly before each trip. His complete reviews were quite detailed by the time he drove to Chicago. He wondered who got the most from this relationship. His daily 'Wards' salary was equivalent to a week's salary at Adventures End. Each Chicago trip required a four or five-hour conference and then he was free to explore the city.

Ward acted on a high percentage of Andrew's recommendations. However, they had screened out many of the "dogs" before Andrew got his mailer. Then, just as suddenly as it had all started, it ended. The company was one of the first casualties of "retail down-sizing," long before it became popular.

The evaluation mailers stopped coming. Andrew waited for weeks before he followed up, a shortcoming common to him. He finally sent a letter asking if he missed a mailing. There was a rather vague reply. He sent an additional letter directly to Alexander Palmer, but Palmer had left Ward for another manufacturing position. To Andrew, this was another dream of success that just faded into obscurity.

During the next two years, Andrew monitored those infamous waterskis. They failed miserably and were finally pulled from the catalog. The feeling of being right had little effect on Andrew considering the near dissolution of Montgomery Ward in the next few years.

No matter how many moments in the sun, Andrew was still a diver. A diver first and last no matter what deviations swayed him from his inevitable path.

Chapter 15

Missing In Canada

Andrew rolled on his left side to temporarily relieve the numbing back pain. Forty-eight years of overexertion, paired with his old parachute injury were beginning to exact a toll. Only in his youth could he fend off the constant throb of discomfort, a luxury he no longer had. Now it was a distraction that plagued him daily. His custom-fitted executive chair had not been living up to its motto, "If life is giving you a pain in the seat, think about where you sit."

Andrew could never stay motionless for any length of time anyway, but now those intervals seemed shorter. He leaned hard on the leather arm of the chair with his left elbow and pressed his stocking-feet down on the windowsill. He rolled one way, and then the other as the old diving helmet clock struck on the half-hour. Andrew looked at his watch to confirm the time and thought, "Man, this is one long night."

His sleepless night passed quickly to the early morning hours, but now that dawn had arrived, minutes seemed like hours. Sinking deeply into his chair, he rested the warm half-cup of coffee in his lap. Looking at his watch again, he reflected, "Still plenty of time to reminisce," and laid his head back on the cool leather headrest.

"Where the hell was I? Oh, yes, near the end of 1969. It must have been my year for getting in over my head." Andrew let himself drift back in time, as he had so often in the early morning hours.

The summer was nearly at an end. Most outdoor enthusiasts in Wisconsin were clinging to the last of the warm days.

It had been a unique and exciting season: raising the ship in Door County, achieving record deep dives, search and rescue programs and four months yet to go. The scuba students kept coming in and enrolling at a steady pace.

Normally, by the end of August, the dive season would slow to a few advanced students. This year, two more classes were scheduled and nearly full. It looked as if the scuba season would be bumping up against the downhill ski season. Andrew and the other instructors at Adventures End looked forward to the end of one season and the start of another with great enthusiasm. It gave them time to rejuvenate themselves. The newness of skiing dialog and events helped erase the tedium of the past season's routine. The shift from one sport to another was easy because of the multi-talented instructors on staff. Downhill skiing in the late 60's was fashion-driven and there were far more women in skiing than in diving. The thought of a long winter did not seem too bad to the mostly male teaching staff. Adventures End would make a complete seasonal change of decor in the store.

Ski equipment, fixtures and clothing began to replace the summer swimming and diving displays. The ski promotions were exciting and great fun. There would be fashion shows, equipment seminars, ski personalities, and lots of avid skiers milling around in the store. Andrew's position as dive training director always left him with the unfavorable duty of assigning the few remaining scuba pool sessions. They often conflicted with the special ski events at the store, which meant the on-call instructor might miss the store skiing promotion. Most of the time he would teach the classes himself, rather than deprive his employees of the excitement.

An hour before one of the ski promotions in late September, Andrew received a call from his close friend, Otto Gehrung.
He hesitated answering the call because he was on his way to the downtown Milwaukee YMCA pool.

Bruce Highsmith, Andrew's store manager and close friend said, "It's Otto. He sounds really stressed out. You had better take it."

Otto lived in New Berlin, a middle class suburb just outside the Milwaukee city limits.

Otto's subdivision comprised a six block square area on the northwestern section of town. The tiny community had block parties and spent much of their leisure time together. It was not surprising then, that a tragedy suffered by three neighborhood families, became the concern of the entire group.

Otto related the sad story over the phone,

"Andrew, Jesus I'm glad I caught you before you left. I have some close friends who really need your help."

"Sure, what's up?"

"Three of my neighbors are missing in a boating accident."

"What lake was it?"

"Its called La Pas, I think."

"You mean Long Lake in northern Wisconsin? I know where that is. That's quite a haul from here."

"No, it isn't in Wisconsin. It's in Canada, near Winnipeg, I think."

"You must be kidding, you want me to do a search and recovery in Canada? That would be a major expedition."

"I know it's a lot to ask, but these folks are desperate. If they cannot confirm that their husbands are dead, they'll have to wait years to collect any death benefits. Their homes, and maybe their entire financial stability are at risk here. They could be forced to go on welfare."

"That's tough Otto, but Jesus, a search and recovery that far up? I'll need four or five guys to help. They will have to take off work. We're talking about four or five days maybe."

"I know, I know, but won't you at least talk to them about how complicated the search will be?"

"When do they want to meet?"

"How about tonight?"

"Otto, Otto baby I'm teaching tonight."

"I know, how about after you finish class?"

"I don't finish class until 10 P.M. Then I have to get cleaned up, drop off the class dive equipment at the store and drive out to New Berlin."

"They are frenzied about how much time has been lost already. I told them you were working tonight." Otto sighed. "They said if you're willing to come out, they'd wait, even if it takes until midnight."

"All right. Tell them I'll be there as soon as I can."

Andrew hung up the phone and paused for a moment. Smoothing the hair on the back of his head in a worrisome fashion, he pondered what he would tell these people.

"God, I can't believe I let myself get talked into these things. There is no way we can coordinate a search, unless I get enough people. Who is going to take off from work, fly to hell and gone, dive in freezing cold water, and look for a couple of dead bodies? Man, I must be nuts!"

Fortunately, Andrew's scuba class was an exceptional group and nearing the end of their course.

For most of the evening he allowed his assistant instructor to demonstrate all the diving techniques. Andrew stood motionless behind his assistant, who removed and replaced his dive equipment under water. He made fewer than normal additions to the demonstration.

The assistant had worked with Andrew for four dive seasons and knew his boss was now distracted.

The lectures were a little out of sync also. The students at this stage of training were very aware of Andrew's lack of concentration. After eight lectures for nearly eleven and a half hours, the students had learned his rhythm and inflections.

Dive instructors must have consistency and a controlled balanced tone in their voice. If they are to keep the students awake for over an hour, they have to present the lectures with varying degrees of enthusiasm. Tone of voice and inflection can make a lasting impression or can lose a class. Story telling is a great way to recover a dozing class.

The stories were often of real life experiences that related to the session being presented. Andrew never considered story-telling that evening.

Rather, he gave the students a passable presentation, but not up to the standard he had set for himself years ago.

His class would have to wait until the next session for that little extra they had come to expect.

Andrew jumped into his new pride and joy, a refurbished 1961 pure white Cadillac convertible. Three earlier models, including one 1951 Mercury, one 1957 Chevrolet and a gorgeous 1959 Cadillac convertible had all died of 'sudden impact' syndrome.

He affectionately called them his "lead sleds" because of all the bodywork used to restore them. A local hot-rod shop also customized his

Mercury and Chevy Impala after restoration. Add a few crashes and rust out, because of the salt used on the city's icy winter streets and you have a lead sled.

Andrew decided to put the convertible top down, hoping the cool fall air would calm his nerves. He felt uneasy meeting people after his pool sessions, because the odor of pool chlorine was so noticeable. He would take the usual shower after each class, but the acrid scent would still last for hours. The aroma didn't seem to offend most people, but it certainly bothered him.

He wound his way through the city in twenty minutes and arrived at the address Otto had given him. There were only two cars parked in the driveway, Andrew felt a sense of relief. He pondered the best way to present his case, as he approached the front door. He surely was not prepared to meet a large group. The door opened before his finger had pressed the doorbell.

A diminutive, rather attractive woman, clad in sweat-shirt and jeans said in a low, almost sorrowful voice, "Hello, Mr. Boyd; I'm Elaine Kollar. Everyone is here, please come in."

Andrew stepped into a nicely decorated, two-story colonial style home. He felt the sadness in the air. Elaine led the way through the dining area into the living room at the back of the house.
He turned the corner of the dining room and was surprised by the number of people present. He thought, "Of course, they just walked here from their homes."

There were fifteen people sitting in a semicircle around the room. Every chair was taken. When Andrew entered, it was almost as if some mighty force pulled him into the center of the room.

Elaine announced. "Everyone, this is Mr. Boyd."

Andrew smiled and nodded, feeling self conscious about being the focus of attention.

"Mr. Boyd I guess any one of us could tell you what happened, so it might as well be me. Joanna, Christi, our husbands and I have been going on fishing trips together for years. We traveled all over Canada to find just the right fishing places. Over the last several years the girls have not been going with the guys, because we all have small children now. The trips were for the guys, we had our own family vacations.

The boys would pack up our travel camper and go to these extremely remote places. Ten days ago they left to go fishing in Canada. My husband and the two other fellows work together at the same trucking company. We all live here in the subdivision and spend a lot of time together.

We first started getting worried about our husbands when none of them called. They always call. My husband, John, called me every night. That's the way he is." Elaine caught herself saying, "is," then decided not to correct it to past tense.

"John has never, never missed a phone call to me." Elaine paused again.

Shiny ringlets of water began to form in her lower lids. Andrew had a hard time not giving up a few tears himself. Elaine was looking straight into his eyes and his heart started to hurt for her. He reached out, took her hand and said, "Go ahead. You had a phone call."

"Yes, the Royal Mounted Police found the untouched camper and all the food. After a few days, they knew the men were missing and were presumed drown. A talisman of their demise included a favorite hunting jacket washed ashore. It belonged to Joanna's husband.

Andrew curiously scanned the group, looking for Joanna. It was not too difficult to tell who she was, although everyone there looked solemn and in anguish. All the women had been crying during the evening, but the victims' wives had a sorrowful pain, made evident in their hollow stare.

Andrew remarked, turning back to Elaine, "You and the other ladies are holding up remarkably well, considering the uncertainty of the last three days."

He paused and thought, "I guess they didn't have much choice. They have to grieve, but they have to get on with their lives. They had the children to think about and mortgages to pay. Maybe they figured there would be plenty of time to mourn later."

Joanna spoke from across the room in a near whisper. She had a handkerchief pressed under her left eye. She said, "Sam, was a big man, a strong swimmer and in very good shape. If he didn't make it to shore, we don't think anyone else did either."

There was a slight pause in the conversation. Andrew collected his thoughts.

"OK. We have to gather a lot of information in a very short period of time. The location is primary, to see if a search is even possible."

"Does anyone have pictures of this lake? The surrounding area or anything like that?"

"We have some snapshots of our guys fishing there a few years ago, if that will help," said a couple sitting in the corner.

"Great, do you have them here?"

"No, but we're only three houses down the street. I'll be right back."

The husband quickly stepped over a few people sitting on the floor and excused himself.

Andrew decided to start a question and answer period where anyone could speak up, if they had anything to contribute. He picked up a pen and writing pad. "I'll just ask some questions. Anyone can answer. Whatever comes to mind, let it pop out. How far up in Canada is this place?"

Joanna replied, "It's way up there, about 50 miles from where the tundra starts."

"You mean where the tree line stops?", said Andrew as he rolled his eyes up into his head. He raised his voice, "Yes, I would say that's up there."

"What highways did they use to get there?"

"Here's the map the guys made for us," said Joanna.

Joanna laid the map on the table and smoothed it out with both hands.
She continued, "Here is the campsite and here is where they found my husband's jacket on the shore. They were clear across the lake on the other side. The lake is twenty-six miles long and about 70 feet deep, I think. I don't know if they drifted there or their boat sank there."

The neighbor, who went home and retrieved the pictures, came in and slid the photos across the table without saying a word.

Andrew leaned over the table and looked hard at Joanna's profile, as she stared at the last place to which her finger pointed. This close, he could see how puffy her eyes were. He felt again what admirable women they were for making it through this sad time without coming apart. He said with a slightly softer voice, "Is there a building at the campsite, or did they stay in the camper?"

Joanna and Elaine began to take turns answering questions, "There is a small building but the accommodations are very sparse."

"What do you call sparse?"

"The building, or cabin I guess, has one room with four bunk beds and a small potbelly stove."

Elaine spoke up, "You have to bring in your own food and anything else you will need. There are no facilities, once you pass through the little village about forty miles from the campsite."

Andrew was beginning to lose what little enthusiasm he had for this project. He said, "Maybe I should explain to all of you how difficult this search would be. First, we have to find four to six divers who are willing and able to leave their family and jobs for about a week. We are giving them only a few days to get organized and packed.
They have to be people of extraordinary determination and have advanced skills in scuba diving. Water temperatures will be in the forties, with little or no shelter directly after the dive. Exposure protection will be of the utmost importance. They all must own dry suits."

Andrew leaned over the table again, giving him time to think. He straightened up and scanned the room. "I'll have to be up-front and very honest with these people," he thought.

"If I expect them to follow me in a situation like this. It would be disastrous if any of them didn't have a clear picture of what they were getting themselves into. It's one thing to enter an area like that and go out hunting or fishing wearing warm, down-filled jackets and pants. After a little fishing, return to a nice warm potbellied stove. It's quite another situation to undress in ten to twenty-degree temperature, jump into forty-degree water and spend an hour diving. After which, come out of the water and wait another hour or two before you warm up. If the search area requires everyone to dive, each of us may have to dive twice a day."

Andrew paused for a moment and looked around the room again, to make sure that he was still speaking to the whole group. He made eye contact with everyone.

"We will have to assemble an array of cold weather equipment and support gear. There are no dive shops in that part of the country, which I might add, will require us to take our own air compressor. We are looking at two thousand pounds of equipment, hauled into a remote area at the start of winter."

Andrew leaned back on the table again, pressing the knuckles of both hands solidly into the map. He thought hard about what to ask next, but there were too many questions and not enough time. The more he churned over what a daunting task this would be, the more his thoughts became conflicted.

"Where the hell am I going to get the people and the equipment from? Yet, I have to do this, otherwise these families will never know for sure what happened. There will be no final closure, unless we find all the bodies... Jesus, what are the chances of finding someone who has drowned anyway? Hell, we have taken weeks to find victims here in Wisconsin, in the best of conditions. But what other choice do they have? When the kids grow up, will they be asking their mothers why somebody didn't go up there to at least look?"

Andrew broke away from his troubled thoughts. He could strongly sense that the people were waiting for the next crucial question.

"Are there any divers in your little community?"

"Not that we know of," someone said from the group.

"Otto is the only scuba diver we know," said another.

"OK, I think we have to cut to the chase. This is the hard part, but we have to discuss two things. The chances of finding your husbands with so little information in such a limited time is slim to none. Do you understand that?" The ladies nodded yes without comment. Andrew nodded his head. "OK then, two, how is the search going to be funded?"

No one said a word until Elaine responded, "The girls and I have only seven hundred in cash. That's all we have in the world."

Two of the women in the group spoke up next and volunteered their family donations of three hundred each. It was obvious that they had discussed some financial aid before they came to the meeting. Others in the group increased the pot to $2100 dollars.

It was getting late and more than half the group had excused themselves because of early morning work schedules. Andrew did not know how to approach the three women with the question of remuneration for the divers. To this point, the focus had been on raising enough money to get the divers and equipment to Canada. He knew the women were financially strapped, yet did not expect this concerted effort to be for free, especially when the divers had never met the women. Still, it was difficult for Andrew to voice the need for diving wages.

"I'm sorry I have to bring this up again, but I'm sure the divers will need some form of compensation for their efforts."

"Oh, my God. I completely forgot about the salaries," Christi lamented for the first time.

Joanna added. "This seven hundred is part of our mortgage money." She placed a stack of bills of the month in front of Andrew. "The guys weren't going to get paid until the first. They all got paid on the first and the fifteenth. That will be eight days from now. We have to get the tickets and food and all that stuff in the next few days. Isn't that right?" Andrew nodded in agreement. He knew there was going to be a money crunch when he first talked to Otto, but he did not think it was going to be this tight.

"Like many people, they were living from pay check to pay check," Andrew thought as he began to wrap up the meeting.

"Well, before we get crazy about the money, I have to find some crazier people who will do this as a long getaway weekend. I'll call you no later than Friday Elaine, and tell you if we have a 'go' or 'no go' situation. Until that time, see if you can come up with any additional money and keep in contact with the Police in Canada. If anything new comes up, call me at the store. I spend most of my life there, so you won't have a hard time finding me. One last thing: then I'll get out of here so you can get some rest. Find the shortest flight to Winnipeg and about how we will be transported to the campsite with all our gear. Also, you might book flights for six people. We can cancel any extra seats a few days before the flight if I can't find the people. OK?"

Elaine and Joanna both agreed. Andrew folded the map and tucked the scenic pictures inside. Christian excused herself and went into the bedroom just off the living room.

Andrew could see her outline in the light of the door. She was wrapping one of her children in a blanket and gently shaking the other awake for the short walk home. A kid growing up without a father, he knew what that was like and he felt a sinking sensation. He turned his attention back to the remaining people. He said goodnight to everyone, then turned and walked to the door. Elaine and Otto followed close behind. Elaine said good-night and thanked him for coming. Otto took Andrew's hand and shook it as only a full-blooded German could. "Thanks Andrew," he said as he slapped him on the back.

"Don't forget I'm one of your divers, so now you only need four more."

Andrew winced a little from the hammer blow to the back and asked, "How's your ear? Is it healed?"

He had a flashback to the Green Lake dive and Otto's injured ear.

"You bet, like brand new. No problem."

Andrew smiled, waved good-bye to everyone and went to his car. The drive home seemed short because he was so impassioned by the events of the evening. Pulling up to his apartment, he stopped two feet from the curb. He stared out the windshield for ten minutes, replaying in his mind the horrendous details of this assignment.

His thoughts were muddled with the many details he must consider. Every diver would need about fifteen pieces of personal diving equipment and an equal number of personal supplies.

He considered the tonnage of adding dive team support equipment to the growing mountain of personal gear. His vision included a surface support boat with crew, a guide to the dive site and living quarters. High on the list was an ample supply of food stores for four to six ravenous, high calorie burning beasts. All that was needed, plus logistical support like moving divers and equipment from Milwaukee to a snow clad tundra, 50 miles from where the tree line ends and pack ice begins. This was a remote area, where the last 15 miles of their journey could be by snowmobile; a scary thought if they did not beat the snow season, which was due any day. Andrew's worst-case scenario now, was the possibility of becoming snowbound in a shelter that was not even considered to be a cabin. These were simple shelters designed for no more than four fishermen for warm fishing seasons.

"Damn, what if it snows us in and we are there for a month?" Then breaking out of his jumble of thought, he said aloud, "Hey, what the hell. I never even said I would do this job. At least I don't think I did." The vivid memory of Christi and her baby however, flashed into his mind. Andrew lowered his head slowly and pressed his forehead into the steering wheel.

"Oh Christ. Here we go again. How do they always find me?"

Andrew spent the next two nights in restless sleep until he had completed an equipment manifest and the search and recovery plan.
Most of the dive plan details were resolved and he had three of the best divers in Milwaukee, plus himself. Andrew needed two more divers to fill his dive team. Rumor had it there was a diver near one of the outposts in Canada, who had a basic sport diver certification and three years experience. Without a face-to-face meeting with the diver, however, Andrew felt doubtful about bringing him on board.

The divers that he recruited were some of Andrew's most trusted and experienced friends. All the men on this dive team had been part of his quest to the bottom of Big Green Lake in 1968. The team was comprised of Michael Gabon, a dive instructor and close friend; Donald Graham, expert power boater, and, of course, Otto Gehrung, mister lovable clumsy-burger. He was the only person Andrew knew who could throw out an anchor and line and go overboard with it. Every time Otto would do something wrong, his dive buddies would kid him. "Otto let go of the line." He was always a good sport and could laugh at himself.

One evening, when his company had arrived for a barbecue in his beautifully landscaped backyard, Otto decided to start the fire in his Weber grill. Before he lit the coals he sprayed the kettle with lighter fluid and threw a match into the center. The coals burst into flames and so did the overhead canopy of vines. The flames raced up the paper decorations and extinguished themselves as fast as they ignited. The fire did little damage to the structure and luckily no one was hurt. If it had not been so serious, it would have been quite entertaining. Otto did a Charlie Chaplain routine running into the house for a fire extinguisher and then stumbling back out again, spraying the nozzle every which way. Everything within ten feet, except the flame, had a coating of white chemical. The fire burned off some of the vines and singed the latticework a little, but the party continued in style.

Three days had passed since the first meeting and plans were coming together. Andrew was in daily contact with Elaine Kollar. She had become the intermediary between the authorities in Canada, the airlines and Andrew's team. His worry about salaries was unfounded; all three divers volunteered their time for four days. Andrew had to cut two days from his original schedule because of airline conflicts.

This was not the best of news, because he had recently learned that the primary area of search was expanded to ten acres. A secondary search area consisted of one half mile of shallow water near the shoreline, west of the primary site. Local authorities determined the site location after recovering what was advertised as an 'unsinkable' fishing boat.

It had not sunk entirely. Ten inches of its bow were visible, bobbing above the icy waves. It had taken the local authorities two arduous days to locate the vessel. High winds and choppy water hid the gray weather-beaten bow. The boat was found diagonally across from the campsite on the twenty-six mile long lake. The boat locale was of little help, because the boat may have floated for days. It was found a long distance from the probable accident site. There was no other boat entry point into this lake, save the one at their camp.

Dedicated Royal Mounted Police assured Elaine that they would keep up the search for one more week. Their efforts would terminate two days before the divers were to leave Milwaukee.

Secretly, Andrew hoped that the Canadian authorities would find the fishermen.

The drowned fishermen and the boat found earlier were the only leads the police had. The entire accident scene so far was based on where Joanna's husband had washed up on shore. He was found near a small bay, in water five and a half feet deep. One of his arms was draped through a nylon handle of a seat cushion. He must have tried to swim to shore, but the cold water got him first. He was the biggest and strongest of the three, so there was little hope that the others had survived.

The tips of his hunting boots were worn down to expose the tips of his toes. The police said he must have been buffeted against the shoreline for the entire time to wear the toe tips down like that.

During the remaining week nothing showed up on the shoreline. Some had speculated that if the men had made it to shore, they might have tried to walk back to base camp.

The ragged shoreline was awash with fallen trees and tangled roots. Walking the water's edge would prove very difficult, so a minimum of effort had been assigned to it. The local search party had little equipment and only two small outboard boats. Search volunteers included three people from town and one Royal Mounted Police Officer.

Nearing the end of the second week, the group had covered only ten percent of the lake shoreline. From the water, the shoreline merged into one amorphous mass of vegetation. Unfortunately, the search area was the wind-spanked and wave-battered side of the lake. As the shoreline eroded away, scattered trees slowly descended into the water, creating their own little islands. These marshy landings were an open invitation for a floating body to rest in a wooden cave or cluster of branches.

It was not like looking down a shoreline at the water's edge and spotting a clear demarcation between land and water. The inland wooded area was also extremely dense and littered with fallen trees and branches. It was truly the most virgin of forests.

Time was growing short. Only two days left before the Milwaukee dive group had to make a commitment.

Andrew made a concerned call to Elaine. "How are you doing?"

"Just fine thanks. We are all starting to settle down a bit. I hope we can stay that way. The waiting is what's killing us"

"How is Christi doing?"

"Not so good, I'm afraid. She hasn't stopped crying since she found out about David. He really was the light in her life. He took care of everything outside of the house. She was the mother, the housewife and the social director. She can't even balance her checkbook.

David was a dedicated husband, wonderful companion and an exceptionally kind man. I don't think I ever heard her complain about him.

"I'll miss him almost as much as my own sweet man."

Elaine stopped speaking for a moment because her throat began to tighten. Then she began again, this time concentrating on her words and not on her memories.

"Incidentally, did you get a visit from some people with the insurance company or the Interstate Commerce Commission?, asked Andrew. "No, I haven't."

Before Andrew could ask why not, two men dressed in dark suits walked into Adventures End and asked if there was an Andrew Boyd working today, and could they speak with him.

Andrew was within voice range, overheard the request, and turned back to the phone.

"They just walked in the front door. I'll call you back when they leave. Bye, bye."

He hung up the phone and turned his attention to the two men.

"I'm Andrew Boyd, what can I do for you?"

"Mr. Boyd, I'm Special Agent, Jeff Scala."

He presented his FBI photo wallet to Andrew with the same professionalism as they do on television. He held two fingers at the fold point of the wallet, with each of his fingers holding open the wallet without covering the photo or ID. In one well-practiced movement, he introduced the other man.

"And this is John Randolph with the Interstate Commerce Commission. "We're trying to gather information on the three gentlemen who disappeared in northern Canada a few weeks ago. We understand that you have been hired by the families to do an underwater search, is that true?"

"Yes it is."

"Mr. Boyd what makes you believe that the three men were drowned?"

"Because one of them has already been washed up on shore and he was the most athletic of the group. If he bought the farm, everyone else probably did."

"I wasn't aware that a body had been recovered. I spoke to the three ladies several days ago and nothing had been mentioned."

"I don't think they knew until the afternoon of the 12th."

"Mr. Boyd, what can you tell us about these men? Were you friends?"

"No, I never met them. A mutual friend who lives in their community asked me to be a consultant on the case. His name is Gehrung... Otto Gehrung."

"How do you know Mr. Gehrung?"

"He took scuba lessons from me a year ago and we just became friends."

"What kind of work does Mr. Gehrung do?"

"He is a fashion artist for a downtown women's clothing store."

"To get back to the missing persons a moment, why do you believe the other two men haven't been found?"

"Well, that is some very cold water up there. If they were weighted down at all, they would probably stay on the bottom."

The agent looked up from his notes and asked. "Weighted down?"

Andrew felt confident the agent knew the answer already but was evaluating his thinking. He knew, too, that this interview was more of a search for people than for victims. The FBI and Interstate Commerce Commission don't get involved unless there is some heavy-duty skullduggery afoot. Andrew also felt this would not be the last time he would have a visit from government level agencies.

Andrew replied, "You know, sometimes hunters wear their steel tipped work shoes inside boots while they're fishing or hunting. Perhaps even heavy winter boots that are laced up tight are used. And they carry all kinds of junk in their pockets: flashlights, lighters, keys, and tools... you name it. Even heavy clothing will be enough to take you down. It only takes a few pounds. Besides, near freezing water won't let food decompose in the stomach. It's the methane gas that brings the victim to the surface, if they aren't too negatively weighted."

"I remember once I found a fisherman sitting upright on the bottom, still holding a fishing pole. His eyeglasses were on the end of his nose. He looked like he was sleeping. He was wearing a tool belt with all kinds of fishing paraphernalia in it."

"Mr. Boyd, do you feel the chance for survival of the other men would be considered unlikely?" asked John Randolph, who had taken a silent but attentive role to this point.

Andrew reflected as he turned to Randolph, "It is pretty obvious the two agencies aren't working together. These two guys must have just met in the parking lot."

Andrew split his answer between the two men, making solid eye contact with each in rapid succession. "If the nonsmoking, better swimmer didn't take the time or have the time to unlace his boots, I doubt the other two were calm enough to take theirs off. The only reason the searchers found him was because he had one arm caught in a seat cushion strap. He was dragging on the bottom and wore out his boot tips, because his feet were heavy. They weren't heavy enough, however, to pin him to the bottom with the extra flotation of the cushion. He may have been blown onto shore in a matter of hours and hung there, half-submerged and buffeted against the rocks until the search party found him. In water that frigid, he was probably unconscious within five or seven minutes. It is likely that they were totally numb in just minutes with no manual dexterity left. My guess is he hit the water, grabbed the cushion and pressed it to his chest. He swam like hell for the shoreline, knowing he had limited time before the cold water got him. It was shock and then instinct for survival in one millisecond of thought..."

Andrew paused and looked down at the floor. As he related his vision of the traumatic scene, he could feel the panic of that moment. He had been there himself, fatigued and frozen, so cold he couldn't hold the regulator in his mouth: his jaw muscles numb from the searing cold of the water.

Andrew remembered another time not long ago, when he could not climb up a boat-boarding ladder. His core temperature was so low, he couldn't grip the hand rails. The deck crew had to hoist him on deck. He felt the fishermen's exhaustion and put himself at the accident scene for just a moment.

Andrew coughed slightly, tugging at his ear, and returned to the original conversation. "Grabbing that cushion may have been the last rational move David made. He had enough adrenaline to keep him going for a hundred to one hundred fifty feet, but not much more than that. No, I think all three men 'bought it' within one hundred fifty feet of where the boat went under or capsized."

The FBI agent, Scala asked. "What is your professional guess on the chances of finding the other victims?"

Andrew responded, "We have a bunch of things working against us. We have little money, a small group with dive talent, and a very limited time frame in which to do the job."

Scala questioned. "What's your best guess on finding one of them?"

"Zero, zip. This is more of an exercise in effort than in productive reality. If we are supposed to find them, we will. If it is done right, you can almost bet on success. It all comes down to time and talent. If we have enough of both, you can be very confident.

Winter is coming, so even if we have the money to support the search, time is still against us. No one in his or her right mind would extend this program into the snow season. Once you're in that season, you're in for the duration. In addition, if the temperature drops, as it surely will, it will require time diving under the ice.

I told all the wives what the real chances are. All agreed they have no choice but to go ahead."

John Randolph asked. "When are you leaving?"

"In a few days. I have to bring together a couple of loose ends and we are on our way. You guys don't dive, do you?"

Both men nodded their heads 'no'.

Agent Jeff Scala reached into his breast jacket pocket and pulled-out his business card and presented it to Andrew.

"Please call me when you return. I will be grateful if you fill me in on the details of your search, especially if you don't find either of the missing men."

"That's a promise."

Agent Scala shook Andrew's hand, turned to John Randolph, and presented him with one of his cards. "I would appreciate your agency's help on this matter as well."

John nodded agreement, as he handed Jeff his card. "I'll do what I can."

Jeff quickly left the store. John turned to Andrew and said. "Do you know anything about this case, other than what you learned from the families?"

"All I know is what people tell me."

John looked to the rear of the store "Can we move back there? I have some information I can share with you."

John took Andrew gently by the arm and led him to the ski boot fitting department, where privacy seemed assured. They sat down, facing each other. Andrew arranged his chair facing the storefront to enable him to keep watch on the store activities.

"I am surprised that Scala didn't fill you in on why there are several federal agencies keenly interested in the fate of these three men." John said. "I think it is necessary that you are aware of the investigation that is going on. That way, you may be more cognizant of your true involvement."

"What involvement? I'm just volunteering my services to some people who have a terrible tragedy to overcome."

"On the contrary, Mr. Boyd, you are up to your ears in interstate commerce illegalities, including hijacking and possibly international illegal trade. You're in the middle of a million dollar multi-state trucking theft ring."

Andrew slumped against the leather chair back. "Balls, are the guys who drowned part of the ring?"

"At this time they are prime suspects. They were truckers and dispatchers and many of their company loads were shorted.

"Mr. Boyd, as far as we know, the women were not even aware of their husbands' involvement. So at this point, it is only an investigation. We are here to gather facts. It's neither Scala's job nor mine to make judgments. That is for a court to decide. For our part, if we find that the people under consideration are not involved, then they'll be taken out of the reports. We don't make a habit of publicizing the names of people we interview. The ill-advised media are the ones who take names of people we interview and make a story out of it. More times than not, the story is distorted. I don't think that the women should be punished for the crimes of others, unless they were involved. In addition, their husbands should not be punished, if they just happened to be in the wrong place at the wrong time. We know that they are all in the same financial boat: no bodies, no insurance. That leaves the women and kids without any support. You planned to help a few desperate women in trouble and you still can. Nothing has changed. The only difference now is that your movements for the next few weeks will be under surveillance and some scrutiny. The pressure is directed at you to find the bodies and to find out if they did drown in a boating accident. If they didn't drown, how did they manage to fake the accident in such a remote place?"

"Wait a minute, John, I'm not a detective. My only job is to find a couple of guys who tipped over in a boat and are presumed to have drowned. I don't remember anyone telling me I had to extend my search to the land."

"Andrew, that's true, but you will be there on the site, and if you are unable to find the victims in the water, then your obligation to the families and the law is to extend your search to the land,... within the limits of your time constraints, of course. That area has little or no law officers. You will be on site two full days before any outside law enforcement can be brought in. My guess is they will never arrive. You have some investigative background, according to our records. Your last hitch in the service was in the Army Military Police and you had secret status clearance. Is that right?"

Andrew nodded yes and grimaced.

"That means you know the rules of evidence, and if you take this assignment, the evidence you find will be vital to all the agencies involved. It will also have some credibility because of your background. My department does not have the manpower to launch such a specialized underwater search. I am quite sure the other agencies can't pull together a team and deploy them before the heavy snows hit in that part of the world. You are our man in the field. Directly or indirectly, you're our boy, tainted evidence or not."

Andrew sat passively and stared at John Randolph. He couldn't believe the conspiracy theory he had just heard. One minute he was a citizen trying to do a good deed; the next minute he was in center stage of a national theft ring.

Andrew pondered his predicament and then stiffened in his chair.

"Let me get this, you mean I'm supposed to take a team of divers to some God forsaken, place that is... a few days, or a week away at the most, from having its first major snow storm. Go there with a dive team I haven't fully recruited? Dive for only a few days in water with a little wisp of ice around the edges and find a couple of alleged bad guys?"

Andrew stared into space and continued.

"All that, while you and the other interested good guys stay here where it's nice and cozy, just waiting for my not-legally binding report? Does it also mean I can't count on any support from your people, like airline passage, truck rental, etc... an immaculate word on future parking tickets?"

"What it means is, you're on your own and we get all the news when you return. I suggest you take notes."

"Wait a minute, I don't think you get it. I have no formal authority to gather evidence."

"On the contrary, you do Mr. Boyd, because you will be the only expert who will have access to the underwater scene. Whatever you find belongs to the locals and us, whether there are bodies or not. You can be given a subpoena for testimony very easily."

"OK, OK, so how do I communicate the information to you?"

"When you return, call me at the number on my card. I will set up an appointment for you to come in and give a deposition.

"Will I have to have an attorney?"

"Cooperate and you will not be under that kind of pressure. Please make your report complete and detailed. Tell us everything you told the locals"

"What about the FBI and the insurance companies?"

"They have their own agenda, and I can't speak for them. However, we are all after the same thing. This case crosses national and international boundaries. It involves a number of law enforcement agencies. The heads of those agencies have agreed to share information. The same questions concern all of us: did all of the men die, and if not, who survived and where are they now?"

Andrew tried hard to diplomatically end the conversation with some control over his position. He realized that John Randolph and the others were using him as a means to secure information. Either way, it wouldn't be pleasant for the families.

Andrew had three possible outcomes to this investigation.

First, if he were to find the bodies, that would bring grief to the families, but give them the insurance coverage they needed so desperately. Secondly, if he didn't find the bodies, there would always be the question of what transpired and of where the bodies were located?

Finally, if he found evidence of one survivor, then was he the culprit who killed the other men? This was a no-win situation, and Andrew knew it.

Andrew said his good-bye to John Randolph and finished the rest of his day with tangled emotions regarding the unfortunate families. No matter what the future outcome, the news for them could only get worse.

The next day Andrew spent the morning and afternoon making phone calls and agonizing over the details of the Canada search. He spent a great deal of time discussing the matter with his boss and their secretary, Rebecca. After using several of the employees as a sounding board to organize his thoughts, Andrew decided to give his problem a rest. Rebecca suggested that they meet after work for a drink and discuss his dilemma. Rebecca Fleming was an extraordinary secretary and fashion buyer for Adventure End. Both she and Andrew were long time employees. They were 'do everything' people. Whatever the job required, Rebecca would come up to the task.

She was not only drop-dead in your tracks attractive, but she could sell clothes, buy fashions and type, too. There wasn't a male customer who wouldn't have given his left... to date her. She had full lush lips and wore shiny lipstick that made men babble and caused women to make catty remarks. When a man came in to try on ski pants, Rebecca would always test the stretch in the fabric. A little game she made up to see men wilt. The pleats in the front and back of the new ski togs were targets. With her hands about a foot apart, she would pinch the fabric on the crease between each thumb and forefinger. While she was pulling the fabric gently in opposite directions, the guys would just smile and look befuddled.

The male customers never knew the power of suggestive selling until they met Rebecca. She would recommend an extra pair of ski pants to match their eye color.

The next step would be to promote the purchase of a few turtlenecks, two pair of socks and perhaps the latest style ski jacket. Rebecca was a natural salesperson. She was skilled at listening to every word the customer said and using it to make the sale. The deep knee bends and sensual sighs while testing the seams, didn't hurt in closing the finale sale either. However, her innocent flirtation sometime got her in trouble.

One afternoon Rebecca had finished selling an older man four hundred dollars worth of ski wear. She had just finished folding and piling all the items on the pant rack, when the man's wife entered the store. She walked up to the rack and examined the selection her husband had made and then confronted Rebecca. "You must have picked these out." Harold couldn't have matched these colors since he's color blind."

The woman didn't seem bothered by the number of outfits her husband had purchased, but a little annoyed at the attention he was getting. After some small talk with Rebecca, she decided to try on a swimsuit and a cover-up. Rebecca selected an outfit and the women agreed she had chosen just the right fashion look for Aspen. After a few minutes in the dressing room, she poked her head around the corner of the dressing room door. With directed effort, she waved her husband to approach. The lady was a little embarrassed about walking out on the retail display floor and drew her husband into the dressing room.

"Harold, will you please come here. I don't want to come out there, she said. It's too cold."

The lady stood at the corner of the dressing room near the full-length mirror. "What do you think Harold? It looks OK doesn't it?"

"It looks fine."

Rebecca moved in closer and stood in just the right position to juxtapose her image and the customer's image. She said, "That fits you perfectly. The lines are very complimentary to your figure.

The lady excitedly replied, "Oh, I think you're right! Harold, don't you like the style?"

Harold shrugged his shoulders. "Yes, it's great!" Rebecca reached over and adjusted one of the straps on the woman's suit, as she pointed toward the mirror.

"Don't worry about that," she said. "I have a suit just like this and every time I'm at the beach and a cool wind blows, my nipples get hard too."

The woman stood dumbfounded, staring in the mirror. After several seconds, the flustered matron crisscrossed her arms in front of herself and scurried back into the dressing room.

Harold was still gasping for air when Rebecca said. "Well, it's true, and it's only natural."

Rebecca knew it was time to wrap up her sale with the husband. He flashed his credit card and signed his name, without losing eye contact with Rebecca. He looked as if he was hypnotized. The woman came blazing out of the dressing room and dramatically dropped the swimsuit on the clothes rack. She clutched the bag of new ski togs, gestured to Harold to follow, and exited the store in a quick march.

Poor Harold was still inhaling, as he stumbled out the door, lagging several feet behind his wife. He was still trying to formulate an apology, as he made a hurried good-by."

"Ah, thanks for the clothes and all the help... bye," he said.

Aside from that one minuscule gaff, Rebecca had an outstandingly productive sales record. Her line of fashion sports clothing was unmatched in the city. Many of her affluent customers depended on her to mix and match the perfect 'killer outfit.' Men and women alike asked for her specifically when it came to choosing a coordinated outfit for some exotic vacation destination. She had talent and retail savvy all packaged in an adorable fashion guru that exuded a fascinating scent, too!

Chapter 16

The Old School Yard

Andrew closed Adventurers End that evening and went to his favorite watering hole for what he called 'a decompression stop.' The 'Old School Yard' bar was less than one block from Adventures End. Most of the store personnel regularly stopped for a few drinks. Like any good after work hangout, it provided a safe haven to reconsider the pressing issues of the day.

The School Yard bar was beginning to fill with customers as it was nearing happy hour. By 6:30 PM. the place was a mob scene. There were only a few empty stools remaining at the bar. A cluster of admiring associates surrounded Rebecca.

Meanwhile Andrew freely roamed among the crowd, chatting with customers and people from the store. Each time he seemed to migrate back to the crowd around Rebecca. This time, he placed one foot on the rung of Rebecca's stool. He balanced on one foot, sipping on a mug of beer and leaned over Rebecca's shoulder, asking if he could buy her the drink they talked about earlier. She arched one auburn eyebrow, closing the distance between their faces to inches and purred a response.

"I'll have another scotch mist. Thank you very much, sweetheart." She sensuously stroked his right cheek and felt his six o'clock shadow.

"Oh my, rough! ...That's OK., I like it like that." Andrew liked to play word games also. Making a close entry frontal assault, he closed in almost nose-to-nose, looking deeply and passionately in her eyes and responded in a resonate voice "Sorry, I'm the gentle type."

Andrew and Rebecca were not an item in the store, but many people thought they were having a 'thing.' With playful banter and humorous innuendo, they only added fuel to the rumors that were already being circulated. Neither of them allowed the kidding to escalate beyond reasonable bounds. Many times, Andrew practiced great restraint from embracing her, not knowing how she would react. Tonight was no different.

She must have just returned from the ladies room, because the sensuous aroma of freshly applied perfume was most apparent.
She had put on just enough of the French concoction to be noticeable, if you were in her personal space. Andrew couldn't help giving her a compliment. "Whatever you're wearing is good on you...very good."

Rebecca took the drink in one hand and said,

"Its called Red Satin."

Andrew smiled and took another long, deliberate sip of his J&B scotch and water.

"I don't think I've heard of it, but it certainly arouses my male instincts."

Rebecca rotated a quarter of a turn on her stool, bracing herself against Andrew's leg. "You asked what was I wearing and I was trying to be cute."

"It worked."

"I meant underwear."

"I know, that arouses my male instincts too."

"One of these days, Andrew, that male instinct is going to get you in trouble."

"How about tonight...is tonight too soon?"

Rebecca leaned forward slightly. She rested her pert chin on her daintily closed hand and pressed her left elbow into her crossed leg, striking a provocative modeling pose. She purred. "Tonight would be perfect".

Three hours later, the crowd had thinned out considerably. Rebecca, Andrew and two Adventure End employees were the only people left. Andrew was feeling a very strong buzz and Rebecca was showing a slight sway as she leaned against the teakwood bar. During the early evening, they had chatted openly and mingled with everyone in the bar. Now they were face to face on matching stools. Rebecca had both of her feet on the rungs of Andrew's stool and he had one foot on hers. They were oblivious of everyone else. They discussed life and nature with its many complications and found themselves earnestly hanging onto every expressed opinion. Their body language was decidedly clear. She sat on the leading edge of her stool leaning into Andrew.

As she lifted her glass to take a drink, she never lost eye contact. He matched her posture exactly.

As a mirror image of each other, they were much like two toddlers playing in a sandlot. The first child starts to kick a little loose dirt, and then the second child mimics the action. If they are both comfortable with each other, then one will motivate the other's actions. Movements are not consciously intentional; they stem from being in harmony. Neither party dominates the other and they move in synchrony.

The last store employees said their final good night and waved good-bye to Rebecca and Andrew. They in turn broke out of their conversation, returned the good nights and decided to leave.

Andrew was concerned about how wobbly Rebecca was and asked if he could drive her home.

"Hey, what if I drive you home and pick you up for work tomorrow. You can leave your car at the store. We're both in at the same time, anyway."

Rebecca replied with a slight slur. "You're not trying to take advantage of a girl who had four too many scotch mists..ss...too many are you?"

"Would I do that?"

"No damn it, I don't really think so." Rebecca was slurring her words just a little more now.

Andrew smiled a broad smile. "Ah, fooled you again."

They left arm in arm for the short one block walk back to the store. The fresh air was enough to help clear their heads, slightly. Rebecca cautiously approached her car door and turned to Andrew. He was stationed right behind her, suddenly stepping back as the car door swung open. Rebecca moved forward with the door between them.

She appeared to be putting an obstacle between them, but in reality she wanted to strike another provocative posture. She looked up at Andrew in her dreamy state. "I guess this is good night," she sighed, resting on the window frame of the car door.

"I guess it is." Andrew answered.
"I guess I'll go home now."
"I guess maybe you should."
They were face to face again, as they had been most of the night. Neither one wanted the other to leave. For five years they had kept their distance, but tonight it would be different. Everything was right, the mood, the place, and the time. They both had enough to drink to lower their defenses and no one was looking over their shoulders. They wanted each other, but were afraid of the complications and hurt that might follow this moment. Down deep they had great respect for one another and that made them more cautious than usual. If this were going to be a one-night stand, they both would lose something.
They stood impervious to sights and sounds around them, not saying a word. Andrew broke the hypnotic silence. "I think I need to kiss you."
"I think maybe you should."
"I think I'll do it right now."
"I think you talk too much."
Andrew touched her lips with his, ever so gently.
Then he backed away a little and opened his eyes. Rebecca still had her eyes tightly sealed. She tilted her head to the side and said.
"More, more" in her softest voice. Andrew tenderly kissed her again, fondling her lower lip with his.
He cradled her head in his hands and stroked her cheeks with his thumbs as he longingly gazed down at her. He moved to her upper lip in the same gentle way.
Intense passion was building in both of them. Andrew continued to touch her lips with delicate caresses. Rebecca murmured a frail acceptance. Andrew moved around the door without releasing the embrace they held. Their mouths yawned wider and what was a gentle teasing by both of them, became a passionate acceptance of mind and body. She tenderly squirmed against him. He in turn pressed hard into her. They kissed and fondled each other without regard for circumstances.
Positioned under a yellow halo security light in the parking lot of Adventures End was not the perfect setting for such a passionate scene. Rebecca broke the spell when she felt Andrew responding to her excite-

ment.

"Wow! I think we need to calm down a little." Rebecca said as she withdrew her head and placed one red-manicured finger gently across Andrew's lips. He slowly opened his mouth and let her finger explore the limits of his mouth. He deliberately and slowly sucked on her finger, and mumbled past her inserted finger. "I think you're absolutely right, but it isn't going to be easy."

Rebecca replied, "Well, hold that thought."

"I'm not worried about holding the thought, only the blood pressure."

"Don't worry about it, I have just what the doctor ordered. Would you like to come to my house for a night cap...and gown?"

"Lead the way, Doctor Livingston."

Andrew couldn't help looking at Rebecca's beautiful long legs, as she slid into the seat of her car. He absentmindedly closed the door and didn't try to hide the fact that he was still focused on her legs. Rebecca gazed down at her legs, then back up at Andrew and said. "Follow me." Andrew rolled his eyes, bowed slightly and replied. "Anywhere, lady, anywhere."

They drove off as a tag team, Andrew following closely behind Rebecca. Half way to her apartment, Andrew pulled up along side of Rebecca's car at a stoplight. He wanted to make sure she was all right. He gave her the scuba divers' 'OK' sign.

She gave him a broad smile and returned the signal that she was doing fine. As the light changed, Rebecca turned to Andrew, kissed her fingertips, and pressed them to the window.

Andrew fell in behind Rebecca again and followed her across town. He thought of what he was about to do and whether he could deal with this evening and its long-term ramifications.

During the twenty-minute drive, he began to question his motives.

Should he make sure she got home, then say good night, and leave? On the other hand, should he press the issue and make love to her.

"What if I go for it and nothing happens? It happened before, remember? But that happens to every guy," he said, looking at himself in the rear view mirror.

Andrew debated with his inner self all the way to Rebecca's apartment. By the time he got there, he was a nervous wreck.

Rebecca pulled into her parking space while Andrew searched for a visitor parking space. He walked with a slow, leisurely gait to the front of the red brick apartment, fully intending to say his goodnight. When he saw Rebecca gracefully positioned on the green slate steps under the two entrance lights he thought, "That woman is stunning. I must be nuts to think about passing on this night."

Rebecca quickly unlocked the door and reached out for Andrew's arm.

"I'm glad you decided to stop. You looked a little hesitant," she said.

"Was it that obvious?"

" It's all in the eyes, my dear. Your eyes give you away every time. They are very expressive."

Andrew blushed slightly. "I didn't think it showed that much."

"I work with you every day remember, I know you."

"I only hesitated, because I'm very fond of you and don't want either of us to get confused."

Rebecca flopped down on the sofa, kicked off her shoes and reached up for Andrew, kissing him as he sat down next to her.

"Andrew you still talk too much and now you're full of bull." She kissed him again, longer and with more feeling. They parted briefly, long enough for Andrew to say. "You're right. I talk too much." He kissed her passionately this time and they slid down the sofa back until they were lying next to each other. Rebecca position her legs around Andrew, and then eased herself atop him. His arms pressed their bodies into one, as his strong hands repeatedly stroked her athletic back and narrow waist.

Beads of perfumed moisture glistened on her skin and transferred to Andrew's body. He passionately pulled her down, holding her firmly by the buttocks.

Their lips were crushed together in wave after wave of excitement, as their muffled breathing was becoming more labored. Both tried to catch their breath, but the moment was too intense. Suddenly, Rebecca leaned back and paused, "Andrew, I"... Andrew interrupted her sentence. "What again?"

"This could be a heart attack in the making. I am very fragile you know."

"Not here, come with me." Rebecca said as she rose up and smoothed her dress. Leading him into the bedroom, she switched on a diminutive, brass night-light on her bed stand.

Andrew stood facing the foot of the bed, fascinated by her graceful move. He was embarrassed at how excited he was, and it showed.

Rebecca smoothly turned back to him and closed the gap between them. She braced her body against his and kissed him as intensely as before.

Andrew lifted her dress from behind and felt the smooth surface of her red satin panties.

Rebecca whispered into Andrew's ear.

"I want you to just stand there."

Andrew was not about to argue. Rebecca moved behind him, running her hands around his chest and settling on the back of his neck. She pulled his shirt out of his pants from behind and slowly reached up under his shirt. Her hands soothed his back until the very tip of her fingernails pressed into the base of his neck. She etched a red path down to his waist. Andrew knew that would leave marks on his back, but he didn't care; besides, he thought, "It's kind a like a badge of honor." A name for the experience at this point didn't matter; he was almost out of control anyway.

Rebecca had pushed his hot button and from here on out it was her show, as far as he was concerned. She wrapped her arms around him and sensuously slashed his chest with her nails, just enough to raise slight welts, but not enough to really hurt.

"Do you like that?", she teased, as she kissed the back of his neck and than breathed a hot breath in his ear.

"Doesn't it show?", he said, straining his neck muscles to speak directly to her. Her warm hands moved around his waist again, but this time she unbuckled his belt and, unzipped his fly, causing his pants to crumple on the floor. They fell to the floor silently, with just the slightest jingle of coins and keys. He stood motionless, not knowing what she would do next. Should he step out of his pants or wait for her advances?

It took only seconds for Rebecca to answer his question. She etched her nails down the outside of his legs; again leaving long strips from thigh to ankle. He lifted his feet at her prompting and stepped out of his pants. She gracefully stood up, creased his pants in perfect folds and laid them across the love seat in the corner. It seemed an eternity waiting for her return, but he was rewarded with a full-length view of her sensuous body when he glanced around.

She commanded, "No peeking."

Andrew snapped his head forward in compliance, wanting to continue the game. He felt uneasy again, just standing there, so he slowly bent down to remove his shoes and socks. It always bothered him when he saw men in movies making love to women with their socks on. If he hated it, he could imagine how much women liked it. Before he removed his footwear, Rebecca said, "I'll do that, you just stand there."

"Well, you're the doctor."

"We'll get to play that later, if there's time", she said, unbuttoning the rest of his shirt and discarding his tie.

She followed the same ritual of folding everything perfectly and placing it in order neatly on the chair. Andrew had the impatient feeling he couldn't hold back from embracing her. He realized now that she must have pondered this moment, because she orchestrated the teasing and backing away in perfect rhythm. He wondered how long he could stay this excited. His heart was beating rapidly and he imagined the worst, an end to his level of excitement.

Or so he thought, until Rebecca bent down in front of him and took off one of his socks, while she rested her head against his belly just above his Jockey shorts.

She turned into his stomach and kissed him along the elastic band, each time she further removed a sock. Her silken hair tickled him as she moved from side to side. After several minutes, she moved upward against the front of his body, delivering dozens of gentle butterfly kisses, until she had her lips pressed against his mouth.

He learned quickly how to kiss her back. Rebecca became more responsive, more then she had been since they came into the bedroom.

"OK, now we're getting somewhere" he thought, as she relaxed her body in his arms. They explored each other with delicate movements, sometimes with outstretched hands, allowing each finger to play over their bodies. Feeling every contour and ripple helped to raise the level of emotion. Occasionally, they would stop the movement, only to preserve the sensation in their hands.

She expertly placed her fingertips inside the rim of his underwear and drove it down against his knees and then to his ankles.

She returned to his lips instantly for more simmering kisses. Their hands became trapped in front of them as they pressed together. Andrew took little steps forward, gently forcing Rebecca backward until the back of her legs touched the bed.

She bit his lip sensuously but firmly enough to let him know she was still running things. She danced out of his grasp and held a wide standing pose near the bed lamp.

Andrew pleaded, "If you don't cut this out, I'm going to have a God damn stroke."

She playfully fired back. "You get a stroke when blood is kept from the brain. It doesn't look like there is anything blocking your blood flow. Your blood is right where it will do the most good."

Andrew looked down at himself. "I guess you're right, but how about a heart attack? Maybe I could have a heart attack. Did you ever think about that?"

"I thought of that, but I do have priorities. Aren't you enjoying yourself?"

"Yes... but." He never finished his sentence as Rebecca began to undress. She slowly peeled one layer of clothing off at a time. She folded and placed each item on the chair, as she did with Andrew's articles. Her graceful movements were choreographed with short breathless hesitations. She took deliberate time to fondle Andrew and then continued to slowly remove the next piece of clothing. Some of her movements were decidedly unsteady, a sign that this dance hadn't been practiced.

Andrew savored her strip tease. He knew Rebecca was trying something new herself, and making this event special for them both. When she finished, she lay on the bed and reached up for him to join her. He kissed her tenderly, starting at her toes and slowly inching his way to her breasts. The aroma of sexual arousal was very powerful. He was no longer concerned about disappointing her. Their lips met and she whispered. "Now, it's your turn."

"Andrew said softly "It's about damn time."
They both smiled and began making love as if they had made love many times before. Andrew explored every erotic dream and fantasy he had imagined. He was responding to his most primitive impulses without indecision. She had allowed him to unleash those desires without fear of recourse. Rebecca knew he had his own built in restraints, so she had little concern that he would be carried away. Nevertheless, she was still taken by surprise when they eventually got around to intercourse.

His strength was something she had not experienced before. It was a delicate balance between loosing control of his inhibitions and Rebecca being handled too roughly. Rebecca needed only to flinch slightly and Andrew would relax. He joked with her; "I pride myself with being a fast learner so it only takes a little pause on your part for me to get the message."

"Don't worry about it. I'll let you know when you have to back up a little."

During the remainder of the evening, Andrew played aggressively, but not too forcefully. He reacted to her pace, responding when she gave him a reason. They made love until sunrise and were surprised to hear the chirping of birds.

The cotton bedding was outlined in perspiration from each in turn taking the dominant role. Andrew was nearly spent and thought he would have to stop, when Rebecca said, "I need to rest." Andrew was relieved. He dropped his arms from around her and they fell to the bed with a thud.

"Thank heaven, I'm really spent too. I don't have an ounce of energy left," Rebecca said as she flattened herself out on Andrew's chest.

"Am I too heavy?"

"No, I love it. Don't move."

She whispered to him, "I knew you would be like that. I felt it a long time ago."

"I had no idea you would be that terrific. I'm glad you asked me to come in."

Rebecca rolled to one side and lay next to Andrew.

"The sheet is all wet and it's freezing," she said with a smile.

Andrew slid one hand under Rebecca's waist and rolled her over his chest to the other side.

"That was impressive. I thought you didn't have any strength left?"

"I don't. I was just showing off."

Rebecca leaned on one elbow and looked into his blue eyes.

"Oh my God, you didn't have a climax, did you? I'm sorry."

"Don't be. I'm the one that fought it off so that I could make love to you longer. I don't feel bad about it, he joked. "I may have one later, but not right now."

Andrew placed his hand behind her head and pressed it gently into his chest.

"Don't worry about it. It was my pleasure not having one. Really!

"Rest now, we only have a few hours." The words barely left his mouth before he was fast asleep. They fell asleep in each other's arms.

Two hours later, Rebecca awoke, reached down for the sheet and pulled it up to her neck. Andrew awoke also and stepped off the bed to reach the blanket that had been tossed to one side. He spread the blanket evenly across the bed. Rebecca opened one eye, smiled and pulled the blanket up to match the sheet.

She made a kissing sound and rolled to one side with her back, positioned against Andrew. He lay there thinking about the evening. He always felt that one-nightstands left a whole bunch to be desired. It takes time to learn the little nuances of your partner's lovemaking. There is also a rhythm in lovemaking, a harmony of spirit when you embrace. All those things require time and shared experience to fully develop. He thought. "So what happened tonight? You can't put that all together in one night. There goes another theory down the tube."

Andrew wondered how it could be better than this. Before he could answer, he was fast asleep.

Five hours later, Andrew awoke and slipped quietly out of bed, hoping not to disturb Rebecca. He paused for a moment, savoring the refreshing feeling of the cool wood floor on his bare feet. He straightened his body upright and stretched his rib cage to full size with a huge inhalation of air. After a generous minute, he finally slumped back to a comfortable level-shouldered posture. He continued his normal routine of stretching by flexing his head from side to side. Many of these loosening exercises were ingrained habits from his short-lived boxing career. If he were in his own apartment, these stretching exercises would have continued for more than a half hour.

Andrew looked back at his beautiful nighttime companion. She was lying on her back, the sheet still pulled modestly up around her neck. Through the sheet he could see the exquisite curves of her body. Gazing at her, he wondered if he would look at her the same way after years of association.

Would she react the same way ten years from now as she had last night?

"Let's not get nuts here," he said to himself, tiptoeing around the room and gathering his clothing. They were on the love seat where they had been neatly piled earlier that morning. He picked up the clothes and sat down, laying them on his lap.

Cradling his head in both hands and resting on his elbows, he gave some thought to making breakfast in the buff. He rejected the idea, pulled on his pants and headed for the kitchen. After looking in several drawers and cabinets for utensils, he began to make breakfast. Rebecca, like most women, had her refrigerator fully stocked. There were enough fixings stuffed in there for a week of seven course meals.

Andrew scrambled four eggs, made bacon, coffee and toast.

He was about to carry her tray into the bedroom, when she appeared in the doorway. She was wearing his shirt with one mid button, buttoned. When he felt her presence, he glanced around and said,

"Hope you don't mind."

"Mind? Are you kidding? No one ever made me breakfast in the morning, except my mother."

"Anyone that looks as good as you in the morning deserves break fast in bed."

Rebecca smiled and stepped forward into his arms. She wrapped herself around his body and said "Mmm, I like that, keep it up."

They kissed each other passionately until Andrew broke the embrace slightly and shifted his eggs to a burner without a flame.

"You know, this is ruining my eggs."

"I don't care. I'm too excited to eat. Besides, I'm not hungry for food anyway."

"Lady, this is some of my best work. This recipe is from an old Czechoslovakian monk. He died at the hands of the Germans rather then reveal its con..."

Rebecca stopped the punch line with a smoldering kiss.

They parted and she jokingly said, looking up into his eyes,

"Hey big boy is that a spatula in your pocket or are you glad to see me?"

"No, it's a very tender, temperamental misfit that has no master."

"In that case, I'll have to have a talk with your friend. Come in here, lie down on my couch and tell the doctor all about your problem. By the way, will your nonconformist friend have any reaction from hand lotion? It will take away some of his tenderness."

"I think his reaction will be quite predictable."

Rebecca and Andrew made love until noon.

Responsive hours of the morning had slipped away so quickly, that neither of them realized the time. They scurried to get dressed and raced to get to work. If they were both late, it might provoke questioning. There would be some speculation anyway, especially after closing the School Yard together. Everyone from the store that stopped for a nightcap knew that they were the last two at the bar.

Rebecca pulled into Adventures End parking lot and Andrew followed a few minutes later.

Andrew hesitated before getting out of his car, wondering why they had been caught up in this secret game.

He leaned forward, with his hands tightly gripping the steering wheel, pressing his lips into the back of his hands. He stared intently at her through the windshield and considered, "Who the hell would care anyway? I sure don't. I'm only going along with it, since Rebecca seems to

want it that way. For my part, I wouldn't mind dating her for a while, just to see how things worked out."
He watched Rebecca saunter through the back door of Adventure's End and waved as she turned to blow him a kiss. Adventure's End was busier than normal, so Rebecca and Andrew had little chance to trade glances. He had to teach a scuba class that afternoon and a second session that evening. Rebecca had already gone home by the time he returned from his afternoon class.

Upon returning to the store after pool lessons, he thought, "She is probably as pleasantly tired as I am and is home snuggled under the covers." He was right! She was fast asleep before his evening class had finished.
Rebecca didn't work the next day and Andrew was off the following day. He considered calling to see how she was doing, but didn't want to appear overly pushy. He sensed that she was the personality type who liked to be in total control, all the time. However, that was part of her defense mechanism. The other night after she quit playing her little games, she surrendered herself to him completely.
The vulnerable little girl she became later was the real Rebecca, he realized. He reflected on the way she laid on his chest, her soft voice and her beautiful smile a compliment to that sensuous body. Still, he hesitated to call, because he wasn't all that secure in how she felt now. Things often change after the evening glow wears off. After all, she didn't make any effort to spike his attention all day. Then again, he didn't attempt to entice her either.

He planned his strategy. "I'll just wait until I see her on Friday. No sense getting overly aggressive and blowing the whole thing. Man, she sure has me hooked. I can't stop thinking about her."

Chapter 17

Canada Outback

Andrew was startled from deep reminiscence when his helmet clock struck the seventh hour. It brought him forward once again to the present time.

"Rebecca, she was really something; I wonder how she is doing. I bet she is still a good-looking woman, after these thirty years. How long has it been now? Wow! It's been almost 35 years. I wonder if today she would still prove to be such a dynamic, sensual female, so capable and strong, yet vulnerable. Or had she mellowed out like the rest of us?"

Andrew automatically reached for the coffeepot.

"Oh God, I can't do another cup." He turned and looked at the elevator doors again, as he crossed the room.

"Stuart should be up to unlock the doors in a little while. I sure hope he read the checkout register in the lobby and saw that I didn't go home last night. If not, he will probably come bounding in here with his hand on his revolver. The spry, sixty-nine year old security guard certainly takes his post seriously. I wonder if he will recognize me from the door, or just start blasting away. Maybe it's safer to turn my chair a little and face my desk instead of the windows. The profile image will help with recognition and the sun's getting too bright anyway."

Andrew settled into his chair, knowing full well that Stuart would interrupt his day dreaming at some point, but he restrained his memories no longer.

"Rebecca, Rebecca. I wonder what went wrong that day so long ago. One night I was her total focus; the next day she and I were seemingly platonic fellow employees, still friendly, but distant. Just once we took the chance to discuss our wild, passionate evening together. I remember she chided me about it, stating that it wasn't all that great an evening. It sounded as if her old defense mechanisms were protecting her delicate ego and she was afraid to let anyone get close.

I was actually hurt that she felt our night was not equally memorable. Was it something I said or did? Maybe it was because I didn't pursue her attentively and didn't call. Who knows? If she didn't enjoy the evening, she sure fooled me. In my mind, it was a fantastic connection of body, mind and spirit. Reflecting back, I thought I held my own when it came to the serious parts. I'm still not sure if some naive remark triggered a distance in our relationship. If it did, it was really an innocent remark, but more than likely, still stupid. It wasn't like I told everyone about us at the store. I kept our relationship under wraps."

They never discussed that evening again. While they still had a friendly association at the store, they never exchanged so much as a peck on the cheek.

Andrew easily settled back on the leather head-cushion of his office chair. Radiant heat from the sun was starting to warm his chair and his heart. He lifted his arm and pulled back the white monogrammed cuff of his shirt to reveal his gold Rolex Submariner diving watch. It was masculine and magnetic, just how a dive watch is supposed to look. It wasn't designed to compliment a tuxedo, and Andrew could never identify with the delicate, wafer thin watches of his business friends. At heart, he was still a field man in a chief operating officer's wardrobe.

"Funny how you get caught up in memories." He thought easing back to that time more than 35 years ago. "I had so little time with Rebecca and yet she totally captivated my thoughts. Just like now."

That night, long ago, he had only stopped in the Old School Yard bar for one drink. He was still agonizing over the planned search for several fishermen in the Canadian wilderness. He was tranquil sitting there an hour later, when Rebecca gracefully wandered in. With a shiver of recognition, he shifted his total attention to her. This could prove a welcome respite from the emotional trauma of his rescue search.

He needed to postpone those concerns for a while, as he struggled with a new emotional predicament.

After Rebecca and he had their torrid twelve-hour romance, he calmed down and was back on track with the search in Canada.

Unfortunately, they were both working that Friday night so there was little time to talk privately. Andrew needed any spare time he had to prepare to leave for the big snow country of Canada.

If there were any chance of a relationship developing further, it would have to wait until he returned. He didn't make the extra effort to let Rebecca know his true feelings before departing.

Andrew drove to the airport alone his thoughts were divided between Rebecca and the immense undertaking he was about to engage in. He had given a finale summary of the search plan and trip specifics to the wives. They wished him well and sent a basket of food for the trip.

At the airport, Andrew and his dive crew unloaded the enormous mass of equipment.

"I'm glad you didn't plan my vacation," Otto quipped after moving his share of gear into the airport lobby. Jokes were passed around the dive group, but Andrew was too preoccupied with seat assignments to respond. The reservations clerk became ridged and fixed for a debate when she saw the mountain of equipment.

"Sir, you are only allowed two checked bags per person," she said.

Andrew asked to speak to a supervisor. With a stern expression, the disgruntled agent picked up the phone and dialed, directing a scowling look at Andrew. She detailed the problem and referred to Andrew as a scofflaw, who was pleading his case in her free ear.

"I know it's unusual to have all these bags, but this is a group of volunteers going to... He didn't finish his sentence before the annoyed reservation clerk cut him off. "I can't help you, but my supervisor will be here in a few minutes." She directed, "Now...would you mind stepping out of line, so I can take care of these other people?"

Andrew stepped over a few dive gear bags, turned, and spoke directly to his dive team. "I knew we might get some static about the tonnage of equipment, but I thought any roadblock would be from one of the smaller airlines."

"Otto suggested, "You can always send the bags as cargo."

"I know, but I don't have enough money in our budget for that. I was hoping to slide all this equipment past the agent, just as when I put tour groups together. If I have a bunch of divers going on a trip, I have them stack all their bags in one big pile. Then I collect all the tickets and blow all the gear through at one time. That way, an overweight bag would be averaged in with the others."

The supervisor primly walked up and stared at the mountain of canvas and nylon bags. Andrew didn't wait for her to ask questions. He just raised his hand and gave her a sheepish smile. She closed the distance between them and pointed out, "It appears that there are more than two pieces per person here!"

"I know, but we need your help."

Andrew reached into his pocket and retrieved the Milwaukee Journal article about the predicament of the missing fishermen. He had taken the time to highlight the part about the divers "volunteering" a search for the men. When she finished scanning the article, he graced his plea for understanding with a winsome smile and a follow-up explanation.

"We have limited resources to pull this search off, and everyone here is just trying to help these families. If you make us pay freight on this equipment, we'll have to cut the search by at least one day." Andrew was stretching the truth a bit, but his heart was in the right place.

"I'd like to help, she stated earnestly, but I don't have the authority. You're asking us to overlook hundreds of pounds of freight. I'll have to speak to my station manager. What time is your flight?"

"About two hours from now. We leave on flight 211 at 3:30 P.M. Gate 4."

"That gives me some time. Meanwhile, I'll instruct our reservations person to check in your personal bags and your divers. If we have to separate these additional bags as freight we will only need to remove the tags assigned to you."

Andrew commented, "At least we'll have them in the storage room, out of the way,"

"I'll be right back. Don't worry, I'll see what I can do." She flashed Andrew a gracious smile as she walked away.

"Thanks! I'll be waiting, right here," Andrew said with some relief. He turned back to the group. "Why don't you fellows go up to the gate and wait for me?"

Andrew knew from the supervisor's tone of voice that she would plead a strong case to management.

Fifteen minutes slowly passed before he saw the grinning supervisor descend the escalator.

"Your story was very persuasive, Mr. Boyd. We'll let you take all your dive equipment on as baggage and give you clearance for the same weight for your return flight."

Andrew excitedly thanked her and pumped her outstretched hand as if he were priming for water.

"You are indeed welcome, Mr. Boyd. Glad to play a role in any rescue effort. However, I can't guarantee what will happen at your other connections. Each airline has their own policy."

Andrew looked confident, as he moved in the direction of the gate.

"We'll just take it one step at a time."

The first leg of the flight went smoothly, and only took a few hours. Everyone in the group was overly excited and it was beginning to show. Men away from home in a group endeavor will lend themselves to instant metamorphosis. Quiet, reserved individuals become wisecracking, 'Gim-me another drink, babe,' mischievous boys. Within a short time they had the majority of other passengers and airline personnel engaged in similar humorous antics. When the plane landed, Andrew and his crew started to disembark when one of the female flight crew asked.

"When are you gentlemen coming back?"

Otto quipped, "Why, do you miss us already?"

"No, I'm due for a vacation next week and it may be something to think about." She smiled coyly and rested her delicate hand on Otto's arm. "I'm just kidding. I hope you have lots of good luck."

Andrew and his team walked the length of the terminal and headed for their new departure gate. Looking across the tarmac, Andrew said.

"Oh no, this is not good, this is going to be a problem." Taxiing up to their gate was a twenty-five-passenger propeller driven airplane. Andrew quickly calculated. "Man, there is no way that plane could possibly hold six cubic feet of dive equipment and all these passengers."

The group hurried up to the check-in counter and strained to look out the windows. They all knew what Andrew was thinking.

Donald said, "Don't worry, we can always stuff some bags in the head."

"Great, I'll remember that when I need a volunteer to fly outside the plane... say on the wing."

Michael added his two cents worth. "Hey, not to fear, we'll help Donnie when he needs to find a place to stand. There is plenty of space against the toilet wall."

Andrew wrinkled his nose as if he were in pain and turned to face the waiting attendant. "Hi, would you mind if I spoke to your supervisor?"

"Is there some kind of a problem, sir?"

"Well ah, yes. Not your problem, but mine."

"Maybe I can help resolve it for you." The pert, 5'3" red head appeared eager to help.

"I'm sure you are very good at problem solving, but I just went through this a few hours ago in Milwaukee. I think this is going to be a little out of your domain."

The attendant suggestively leaned into Andrew and said, "We won't know that until you tell me the problem, will we?"

Andrew paused and then explained his predicament.

"You are right, it is out of my domain. Would you take that phone at the end of the counter? I'll ring Mr. Gimbecky and you can speak with him."

"Thank you so much." Andrew flashed her a playful smile and shrugged his shoulders at his guys.

He went to the end of the counter and picked up the receiver. There was a lot of head nodding and smiling before he hung up. He walked over to his anxious group and said, "They called here from Republic in Milwaukee and had "Special Continuation" marked on your baggage before we left Milwaukee."

Otto broke into the conversation. "Ah, that's great, but where are they going to put all our stuff?"

Donald Graham injected. "In your seat, while you ride outside tied to the wheel well." The attendant smiled and walked away.

Andrew and his crew boarded the plane. Another big hurdle had been cleared. So far, the trip had been without major glitches. The next big challenge was transportation from the small county airport to the base campsite.

Andrew had agonized over each step of the trip and had reviewed details for days with the wives back in Milwaukee. They rechecked the pickup points and the time schedules. He felt fully confident that they would not be left stranded in a field somewhere. However, he had run dive tours all over the world in the past and experience had taught him to be cautiously nervous. A few years earlier, he had a group of divers stranded on an island, due to over-booking. All their baggage and dive gear arrived at the appointed destination on time, but the divers spent two long days on the wrong island. Andrew, while poised on the edge of his seat, again thoroughly checked his notes. He knew that when they landed, there would be little time to review plans. He thumbed through several detailed pages before his long time confidant, Michael Garon said "I think you have it covered Andrew."

"I know, I know, but there are so damn many details."

Michael wore a big grin as he offered, "We're all capable and self sufficient. If things go out of whack a little, no big deal. You just keep pointing us in the right direction. We can adjust."

Andrew was the starter and Michael was the finisher. He was always there to back Andrew up. What Andrew didn't think of, Michael frequently did. There was abiding trust and affection between Andrew and this diver.

Each time Andrew would come up with some hair-brained idea for a promotion, Michael would listen intently, then say,

"Yeah, we can do that."

Michael had a keen visual sense of how Andrew's mind worked. He could interpret what Andrew was trying to convey without needing much in the way of details. Andrew relied heavily on Michael's feedback. There was never a time when Andrew had to wonder if his ideas were a little off the wall. Michael would let him know how bad they were.

Andrew snapped his brief case closed and pushed it under his seat.

"I just want to insure a timely pick up at the airport and an early arrival at the base camp. The last thing I want to do is to arrive at midnight and stumble around in the dark trying to get things organized."

Michael laid his magazine down on his lap and said.

"If for some reason the ride from the airport is delayed, we can rent a van or hire a farmers truck or something. Don't worry, it will all come together. I'm more worried about getting to the dive site and the waters clarity than anything else."

"You're right. The Royal Mounted Police patrol boat was collecting samples in some lake hundreds of miles away. If they don't get back to 'The Pas Lake' I don't know what we can use as a surface support boat."

"Andrew, I'm sure the men up there know what's needed. They are in the law enforcement business."

Andrew disagreed. "When Elaine and I first called up there, they had some local diver who was going to help. He was supposed to have an extensive and diverse diving background. We checked. He had minimal skills and no experience in recovering victims. I spent more then an hour on the phone talking to him. He was a total idiot!"

"Things won't get any easier when we try to collect clues on what happened that eventful day, weeks ago.

"From what I've been told, the local constable has no crime scene experience other than what he learned in some book training."

"He'll be valueless as a consultant. The Mounted Police are supposed to be on site with a boat, but I'm guessing they won't show. I think we might be on our own for the duration. If the trail to the camp is snowbound, snowmobiles with attached sleds will be required. There are no snowplows where we are going."

"Man, you sure do worry a lot."

Andrew looked grime and said, "Worry, I'm not worried I'm petrified. You want to see worried wait until we are at the dive site."

A few hundred yards above the small airfield, the silver plane broke free of the clouds. Visibility was limited to a few short miles. Circling the field, the plane dipped it's wing low enough for Andrew to thoroughly scan the horizon and the airfield. There was no sign of snow anywhere. As the plane finished a ninety-degree turn, Andrew strained to get visually oriented. More commercial buildings dotted the area than he had imagined. A few hundred yards from the airport runway the man-made structures petered out. He could not see a town or even the suggestion of any blacktop road. A two-lane gravel road led southward and disappeared into the tree line. It sure looked like the wrong place to be. "Where the hells the lake," he thought as the plane touched down with a thud. It rolled to a stop directly in front of the building entrance. Seeming to lean against the wind, the mushroom colored wooden building scarcely measured 50 x 20 feet in outside dimensions. A dimly lit main room was barely large enough to hold a planeload of passengers and their luggage.

Six other male passengers disembarked and picked up what looked like hunting gear. Andrew and his dive group clustered around the baggage counter and gathered their bags. All had arrived safely. Ten minutes after their arrival the airport was empty. Only three or four airport personnel could be seen finishing up various tasks. Andrew paced back and forth impatiently, waiting for their truck driver. Thirty minutes dragged by, then fifty minutes, finally a grizzled, fuzzy-faced bullish man wearing dirty coveralls and huge winter snow boots yanked the weather beaten back door open. "You Boyd?" He asked, masticating the words with crooked stained teeth that needed a thorough cleaning.

Andrew held his arms out crucifixion style and said under his breath,

"Who the hell would I be in this airport with dive equipment and diver jackets on display?"

"I'm Howard Duff. I'm supposed to take you to the camp. You ready to go?"

Andrew checked his watch not for the time but to emphasize the time. "Yes we are. Where are you parked?"

"Out'n back."

The tattered edge of a plaid wool sleeve housed the right hand that jerked backward displaying callused hands that carried the debris from a lifetime of hard toil.

"Lead the way McDuff."

"What?"

"Nothing, Just an expression."

Howard Duff easily pushed open the heavy steel door leading to the parking area at the rear of the building. He pointed at two dust-covered trucks at the end of the row.

"Are those your vehicles over there?"

Howard's unkempt, dust covered green truck and a single rusty van were nosed up to the snow fences about 100 feet away. Andrew and his team shoulder carried as many bags as they could manage on the first trip. With giant strides, they hurriedly returned to the main lobby until all eighteen parcels were efficiently stowed in the truck.
Howard remained ensconced in the truck the whole time munching several ham sandwiches, dripping ketchup on his stubble grazed chin.

Andrew thought. "I really hope this doesn't reflect the rest of the trip," as he hiked himself into the front seat.

"How long before we get to the camp?"

"Depends."

"On."

"How fast I drive."

"How fast are you planning on driving?"

"Fast as I can for the conditions."

Andrew was growing weary of the 'Farmer Brown' type of response.

"Excuse me, but could you be more specific? Are we an hour or two hours away from the camp site?"

"You're kind of an impatient fella, aren't yea?"

"Just trying to get an idea of whether we'll get there before dark. I want to see the spot where the fishermen were last seen."

"You won't find 'em tonight."

"Why not?"

"Because there's a real healthy storm coming our way. See them clouds?" Howard pointed out the front window at a dark cloud bank starting to appear on the horizon."

It was so distant; Andrew could not get a feel for how bad it might be.
"How bad is it?"
"Could be bad, could be nothing."
"How long before it hits where we're going?"
"Might be an hour or maybe not at all."
"Thanks for the forecast."
Andrew turned slightly to Michael Garon and raised his eyebrows. Michael smiled and looked straight ahead.

It took more than an hour to travel the fifteen miles from the airport. The rough roads into the backcountry were twisting and full of depressions and jagged troughs. Andrew had heard that the hot new mode of transportation into the camp was by seaplane, and now he knew why. Too bad he had so much equipment. It would have been better to fly in and maybe get an aerial view of the dive site.

At the camp, Jim Longknife Hood met the group. Jim was a Native American fishing guide and hunter from Montana. He wore long beads and colorful Indian garb, but had little spiritual connection to his ancestors. He quietly ushered the dive group to their quarters and helped unload the mountain of heavy equipment. The sparse, drab cabin was not even close to the description related to Andrew over the phone. With a mere ten feet by fifteen feet with three double bunks lining three walls, the dwelling was minimal shelter. The upper bunks had springs that sagged below the sideboards. They bowed another eight inches when any weight was placed on them.

An old pot bellied stove and a metal bucket full of fragrant wood logs dominated the center of the room. Beyond a two-by-four wall partition was what you could laughingly call a "kitchen," which featured an even older wood-burning stove. A few splintered cabinets held an assortment of leftover foodstuffs. The cabinets held few new secrets but displayed mundane staples of tomato sauce and other cooking elements. Place settings for six and a few chipped bowls took up little space in the barren cabinets. Carcasses from a few unidentified insects that had seen better days were drying their nails while in the prone position. The dining area displayed a cracked oak table with four wooden chairs. A worn out plastic red-checkered tablecloth with eight cigarette burns draped lopsided across the top. A set of mismatched salt and peppershakers held up a half dozen limp napkins. Andrew didn't expect much in the way of amenities. Fortunately, he had arranged ahead for adequate food, woolen blankets and other comfort items.

Jim stepped around the partition into the kitchen.

"Jim, did you know about the food and blankets?" Andrew asked.

"Yes, I left all of it in my truck. I didn't know if you would make it in tonight with the storm coming. I was afraid to leave the food in here overnight without someone to tend to the fire. Freezes here, you know."

"What about the storm?"

"Surprised you came up here this time of year. Most people are smart enough to stay home. Storms can be bad, very bad."

Otto Gehrung, who had been remarkably quiet, grumbled. "Why is everyone so damn snippy around here? Doesn't anyone know we came here to help?"

Jim replied. "People here are not snippy. They talk in clipped sentences. It's been our experience that when people come here in bad weather they usually get lost or snowed in. Sometimes we have to go out in the storm and rescue them so they can help save themselves. Makes for a better story that way. Most visitors lack survival skills training or the necessary experience. I never lost anybody in this area until now. The majority of time they are just cold and hungry when we find 'them."

Donald Graham needed to add his sentiments to the conversation.

"What the hell, no one told me about winter storms and survival. I'm here as a volunteer diver, not as an explorer or woodsman. I'll go along with any program that has to do with water. I for one have had no experience in dealing with subzero temperatures.

Andrew raised his hands and made a quieting motion.

"OK, let's not get carried away here. We don't have a storm and we don't have to track in from some remote outpost.
All of us are a little nervous about the weather. If we have to run for cover, we will never be that far from the cabin… I think."

Jim joined in, "That's not exactly right, because the Mounties found that body on the far side of the lake. That's a forty-five minute boat ride from here if you run diagonally across the lake."

"Forty-five minutes?" Andrew said abruptly. "Man, that is a long haul, we better pack it in for tonight.

Jim replied. "A long haul. I will leave now. I might see you in the morning."

Jim walked to the potbellied stove, which was beginning to radiate heat. He rubbed his hands together and said, "You must to be very alert, do not make mistakes. The water now will take your life...it is the silent killer...no one can live long in it. Here, at this time, nature is your worst enemy. If the snows come you must get out. Even the bears will be in danger. The snow will be very deep. The creatures need time to dig out. If you remain here after the snows come there will be little food in the woods. Bears need to eat too."

Chapter 18

Royal Mounted Police

The cabin door was suddenly thrust open, letting in a frigid blast of air. Outside temperature had plummeted over ten degrees in the short time the group had been touring the cabin.

"I'm Edwin Candle with the Royal Mounted Police."

Candle, a lanky middle-aged man with dark brown hair, a slight beard and ordinary clothing didn't remind Andrew of the movie version of the Mounted Police. He was closely dressed in a heavy green, fur-lined parka and wool mitts that came up to his elbows. His voice was deep and resonant, the kind you might expect from an outdoorsman in this environment. He stamped his feet and self-confidently stepped forward into the midst of the group.

Jim shook Edwin's hand and began introducing him to the dive team.

Edwin shook each hand without conviction. It was easy to tell by his body language that he viewed this group as just more problems. Andrew was the last to be introduced. Before Jim could say his name, Andrew shot his hand out and asked for an update on the search for the bodies. He fired in quick succession. "Where was the body found? Have you found anything else in the last day or two?"

The Mountie looked Andrew in the eye and said, "And who might you be," using his baritone voice to project a slightly superior tone.

"Boyd... Andrew Boyd." Andrew said authoritatively.

"Like Bond...James Bond in the movies?" the Mountie quipped back and moved to the table, while unbuttoning his parka.

Andrew thought, "Oh boy," he didn't like the remark but let it slide. Everyone else was surprised there wasn't a retort of some kind.

"The body was found in a small bay on the far end of the lake."

The Mountie pulled a wrinkled map from his inside jacket pocket. It was worn on the edges, yellowed and discolored from years of use.

"We believe he was Sam Preuss, Joanna's husband, not Christina's husband, David. His face was unrecognizable when we found him. There were no identification papers on him. From the description of the clothing, we first thought it was David."

Andrew hesitated and then asked, "Did you call the women and tell them?"

"I didn't; my office did."

"What else can you tell us?"

"Not much, except that the 20-foot cabin cruiser you were promised will not be available. It had motor trouble while taking a lake survey and couldn't return to shore. In fact, it's in Big Bear Lake, over one hundred fifty miles from here. Any transporting to and from your dive area will have to be done with the smaller camp fishing boats."

Andrew said. "Do you have any more inspiring news?"

"Yes, I will not be able to spend any time with you, other than tonight. With the three men stuck at Big Bear, we're far too short-staffed at the station."

"What! We need you with us! What if we find the bodies? You're supposed to take over and protect the evidence."

"I'm sorry, Mr. Boyd, but each one of the men in my command covers hundreds of square miles of territory. We are needed in many places. If you wish, I will show you the accident site now. It will still be light for at least two more hours. That should be enough time to motor over and return. Please choose someone from your group to go with us."

Andrew was still thinking about all the changes when the Mountie repeated his request a second time.

"Mr. Boyd, pick a man to go with us now."

"Yea OK, Michael; grab your snuggies. We are going boating."

Outside the three men walked a short thirty yards down a rock-encrusted path to the lake. Tied to the handcrafted wooden pier were two fourteen-foot fishing boats. Each had a twenty-five horsepower outboard motor and one five-gallon gas can attached.

They were old wooden Boston Whaler types with blunt bows. The stern transoms were gnarled and splintered from one-too-many overpowered engines mounted on them over the years. The side rails were scraped clean down to the bare wood from unskilled operators banging into the pier. In short, they were ready for a long overdue dry-dock session.

"Mr. Boyd, you bail water from that boat, and I'll get a set of life jackets from Jim."

Andrew examined each seasoned boat. Rolling gently from bow to stern were tiny ripples of water. The water looked to be about three inches deep. Either boat would have been a bad call from a safety inspection standpoint.

Michael said under his breath, "Apparently, the locals believe standing water in the boat, keeps the seams swollen and watertight."

Andrew said. "No, I think they believe keeping the water inside the boat the same height as outside will keep the boat from sinking. Let's bail out this one. At least it has an anchor and some dock lines."

Andrew scooped out fifteen cans of frigid, gray-green water. When the last possible scoop of water cascaded over the side, he could see the bare wood floor. It was apparent this wasn't the first time water had been bailed out. Grooves were worn in the floor from the sharp edges of the bailing cans.

Michael asked Andrew, "Are you nervous about riding in this small boat...like without dry suits on?"

"I don't like it either. That thought did cross my mind, but this guy is in such a hurry that if we ask him for time to don our suits, he'll blow a gasket. He probably thinks we're nuts for being here anyway."

"He isn't the only one who thinks we're nuts." Michael said smiling.

The Mountie quickly returned and dropped three faded orange life jackets into the boat. There were large chunks of dried mud stuck to his boot bottoms. He stepped down into the boat and placed his foot onto the middle seat. His size twelve boot ground dirt into the flat bottomed seat in the form of small round patties, one for Andrew and one for Michael. He turned and sat on the clean stern seat facing the front. "Well gentlemen, shall we get started?"

Andrew and Michael stepped into the boat and disgustedly brushed the dirt off the seat onto the floor.

The Mountie turned to face the engine and made several pulls at the starter cord. The engine sputtered and choked several times and started finally after five hard pulls. Making a sharp turn to the starboard, the boat headed out diagonally across the lake. With a shiver of premonition, Andrew checked the compact thermometer he had on his jacket zipper and noted that the temperature had dropped to 20 degrees F. The brisk wind blowing across the bow, combined with the forward momentum resulted in a crisp air of well below zero to lash coarsely at the men. Facing rigidly forward with stern determination, the two divers huddled under down-filled coats. Their woolen hats merged with turned up coat collars but failed to block the wind.

Andrew and Michael were downhill skiers and ice-divers so they had some experience with temperature extremes. They knew a trained mind could better resist a cold and miserable situation. They also knew when the cold could be dangerous and life-threatening. Both men had considerable training in the effects of hypothermia and knew the way it could sneak up on a person.

Andrew reluctantly poked his head out of his jacket and turned to Michael. "You were right. I would feel a lot more comfortable if I had my dry suit on."

Michael, reluctant to let any cold air into his cocoon, merely nodded an assent.

The little boat plodded consistently along, making less than 15 miles per hour. Their forward progress was so slow the bow wake wasn't strong enough to splash into the boat.

Thirty-five minutes dragged on before the Mountie called to the divers, "We are about ten minutes from the spot."

It couldn't come soon enough for the divers. Their fingertips were becoming numb, a sign that their core temperatures was starting to drop. It would have improved their circulation if they could have danced around a little, but they had to remain sedately seated for reasons of safety.

A dull gray, leaden sky cast an ominous mood. The sun had dropped below the horizon, and the reduction of ambient light seemed to make everyone perceptively colder.

The tired Mountie took one last look at his hand-held compass and turned 45 degrees to port. A craggy shoreline dotted with awkward boulders and edged with a heavy forest of pines and cedars came into view a few minutes later.

Michael said, "Man, that is one dense forest."

Straight ahead, a small clearing straight head about 60 feet wide that seemed to be the only approachable landing site. With no hesitation, the Mountie ran the bow right up the muddy embankment.

Andrew leaped out first. He strained to pull the boat up a little higher and securely tied off the bowline to a recently fallen tree.

Michael slowly stepped out of the boat, cautiously pulled off his mittens and stuffed them under his arm hoping to regain circulation in his fingers. He looked around for several minutes, blowing warm breath into his cupped hands. The circulation finally started to return after he vigorously rubbed his palms together. He said through his cupped hands,

"What a hell of a place to drown."

"I guess if you're going to buy the farm, this is as good a spot as any. You're just seeing it on a bad day, that's all," said Andrew.

"No, Andrew, I wouldn't want to die here. It's far too lonely. Even your spirit couldn't find its way from here."

"We can't think of them as people right now. They are just victims remember, no connection, no pain. After we return them to their home, they will become people again."

Michael lowered his eyes. "Right, right... I know. It still doesn't feel good."

The Mountie projected his voice from the farthest point of the clearing. "Hey you guys, want to come over here?"

Andrew and Michael so engrossed in their surroundings didn't notice that Edwin had walked away. They scrambled over a few fallen trees and through wet marshy patches before they were face to face with the Mountie.

"See here, this is where we found the boat." Edwin pointed out into the lake. "It was in line with that small outcropping on the other shore and in about 12 feet of water." He tramped back to the tree line and held up a red rag about two feet long that was tied waist high to a tree. He cupped his hands around his mouth and again yelled back to the divers at the clearing. "There is another marker tied over there. See the tall evergreen tree. Now look just east of it." He pointed again, this time into the bay at the foot of the lake.

Not satisfied that the divers were following his directions Edwin stomped back to the divers.

"Over there is the third marker." He pointed out into the lake.

Andrew followed each finger-point carefully, but lost his way on the last direction.

"I can't find that last marker. Where did you say it was?"

"Look down my arm. See the big 'V' formed by those trees? Now go right down to the base of the tree on the left. Do you see it?"

"No, I can't even see the tree you're pointing at."

"Do you have this much trouble seeing when you're under water too?"

"Look Candle, this is your backyard. You have area recognition; we don't. Either play the game or take us back right now."

"Can you see the red rag tied about five feet up from the base of the tree, left of the 'V'?

Michael strained to see. "Yes I can, but just barely."

The Mountie didn't respond, but looked annoyed. He grabbed Michael by the shoulders from behind and turned him in the direction of the marker. He pointed along Michael's cheek towards the marker.

Andrew felt a little dumb because Michael found the marker so quickly.

Edwin didn't waste any time. As long as one of the divers knew where the markers were that was good enough. He walked away, not saying another word. He had already pushed the bow of the boat into the water before the two divers returned. Andrew stepped up into the boat just as it left the shore. Andrew and the Mountie exchanged resolute stares. There was apparently a personality conflict brewing between the two based on the roles they had to play. On the return trip, Andrew and Michael sat facing the rear of the boat. Thousands of tiny pellets of glassy ice lashed their numb faces as they cowered against the wind.

Halfway back, Andrew commented, "Don't you think we should follow the shoreline back? That sky looks threatening."

The Mountie didn't reply but swaggered a bit as he turned to face the rear of the boat and pushed his hat back on his head. He stared fixedly into the pale gray gloom.

The green-frilled shoreline, which they had left only minutes before, was now completely obscured by what looked like a solid fog bank.

With a hint of concern in his voice, the Mountie turned back to face the two huddling divers and said. "There's a storm coming."

Andrew fired back. "What the hell does that mean?"

"It means there's a storm coming."

"Then I think we should hug the shoreline."

"You should just sit still. I know what I'm doing."

"Hey! I don't give a rat's ass how much you know. I can tell a damn storm when I see one and this one could be a killer! Head for the shore."

"I'm running the boat, not you. You worry..."

"Before Edwin could finish his sentence, a wet curtain of slushy snow swept down in sheets. It fell with such force that all three men had to shelter their faces. A cold front hit at the same time. The harsh combination rapidly burned any exposed skin. Andrew could not continue his argument for the moment since it was difficult to breathe, let alone argue with someone. The three were engulfed in a swirling whirlwind of white snow that began to accumulate on their shoulders and backsides. Andrew looked with amazement downward. In just a few minutes over an inch of snow had gathered in the boat bottom. If it continued to fall at this rate, it would fill the boat long before they could reach the dock.

Andrew knew from experience that no one was dressed to survive that blistering water temperature. Taking the Mounties route put them in danger of joining the missing fishermen. A storm this violent could easily capsize their small boat. If they were to roll over, there was no way they could swim to shore from here. If they were to head for the shoreline, it would take longer to return to camp, but they would get there alive. Three to five minutes in water this cold would render them as helpless as the victims of their search. He had to insist again to put into the shoreline for safety's sake.

Andrew had to yell at the top of his voice for the Mountie to hear him.

"Look, God damn it, I want you to head for the shore, now!" Andrew had leaned squarely forward so his forceful voice could be heard in the howling wind.

The Mountie, anticipating that Andrew was going to try to take over the rudder controls, quickly lifted the side of his jacket and unbuttoned the cover on his pistol.

"Shut up and stay put," he said. He jarred his pistol loose from his holster. Andrew leaned back, but not before Michael grabbed his arm and said.

"Relax, that moron isn't going to shoot anyone; he is just overly impressed with himself. It can't be much further."

Edwin was uneasily beginning to think perhaps Andrew was right after all. "Better to arrive late than not to arrive at all, he thought.

Andrew turned to Michael and said. "When we get to shore, I'm going to tear that guy a new one."

The snow and wind relentlessly pummeled the little boat and its occupants for another arduous half- hour.

Edwin started to turn to port, adding fifteen more degrees to his compass line. His watch-bob compass became harder to read, because the light was almost completely gone now.

It was taking much longer to return to home base because the boat was being blown off course. It was a constant struggle to maintain a straight line. Forty minutes had passed by and still no sign of the pier.

Andrew and Michael took turns bailing water out of the boat. The water and snow were under control, but it was still a fatiguing task. Then, as suddenly as the storm appeared, it moved down the lake. It was dead still except for the sputter of the clanking outboard motor. No one had the energy to talk. Each contemplated the hazards of their recent adrenaline-filled experience and all were relieved to emerge alive.

The storm had passed and only a light wispy snow was falling.

Visibility was still at zero because the lake fog followed the storm. Andrew turned halfway around to face the bow of the boat. Knowing his pent up emotions were still vexed, he did not want to make eye contact with the Mountie. He was still angry with the Mountie for exposing everyone to unnecessary risk just to save time.

As Andrew lifted his second leg over the seat, the engine started to sputter again. This time it would die.

The Mountie pulled the starter cord ten times, but the engine would not restart. They weren't out of gas. Maybe it was a fuel line freeze. Whatever the mechanical problem, they were dead in the water, drifting helplessly in a freezing lake with no land in sight. The only sound was the lapping of water on the side of the boat.

The men sat quietly, wondering how far they were from shore. There was nothing to paddle with anywhere in the boat.
They couldn't use their hands, because the water was too cold.
Five minutes passed before they heard the distant, welcome, rumbling sound of an outboard motor starting. They must be close to shore. All three men were about to call for help, when out of the fog appeared Jim and Otto in the other boat.

"Hey, you guys," yelled Otto through his cupped hands.

"We're over here." Michael yelled back.

The fog parted and out loomed the blue and green backup boat, with Otto awkwardly hanging over the bow.

"You guys OK? What did you guys do... run out of gas?"

"I don't know." Michael answered.

Otto stretched out his arm to Andrew with a shot line for towing.

"We heard you coming; then all of a sudden it went quiet. We thought you guys got lost. It's almost three hours since you left. We were starting to worry."

Michael affectionately patted Otto on the shoulder as the boat drifted by. "We took the scenic route."

Andrew caught a glimpse of the relief on the Mounties face. He was sure that the Mountie detected relief on their faces also. Andrew softened his anger toward the Mountie. He reasoned that if they had taken the long route along the shore and the engine failed they might not have been found as quickly. Either way, he felt they were both right and both wrong. A seven or eight mile trek alone the shore would certainly be easier than a swim in 38 degree water if the storm had overturned the boat.

The two small boats plowed their way back to the pier, and emptied Andrew and the divers. As they trudged back to the cabin, the Mountie shouted to the group. "I'll refill the gas tank and test the engine for tomorrow's trip."

Andrew decided not to press the threat he made, after the Mountie volunteered to fill and check the engine.

He said loud enough for his men to hear as he led the others to the cabin. "I guess if he's willing to check the outboard motor and fill the gas cans, I'll let him live."

Michael reached over Andrew's shoulder and pulled him in close.

"The guy's just a dick."

They all laughed at the inside joke.

Still chuckling, Otto said, "Donnie prepared a gargantuan pot of thick, sweetened coffee, and some town folks delivered homemade vegetable soup and a fragrant loaf of Swedish rye bread.

The log cabin felt warm and inviting as the bone-chilled divers eagerly stepped through the doorway.

"Man, my ass is frozen!", Michael remarked as he peeled off the snow-soaked jacket he was wearing. His sweater and long underwear were also thoroughly soaked.

Andrew reviewed the repercussions of continuing the friction between he and the Mountie and kept the thoughts to himself.

Michael said loud enough for the men to hear, " If that bozo wasn't a cop I'd take him apart." He stepped forward to his bunk, unzipped his navy blue dive bag. "I've got to get into some warm clothes."

Andrew had the same problem, except he had not brought along a spare sweater nor snow boot liners. He pulled off one boot and squeezed water from his sock into the toilet bowl. He had spare socks, but the boot liners would have to be worn tomorrow, whether they were dry or not. After the two divers changed clothes, they wearily sat down at the small dining table. The chairs were the old rickety wooden types with loose rungs deeply scuffed from countless hunting boots. When anyone sat down, the chairs would creak and groan. The table was a close match. It was shaky and unstable and gave Andrew an instant flashback to his childhood home on Brown street in Milwaukee.

Donald Graham served up the hot soup and moist, butter dipped bread. It was a satisfying ending to a day filled with physical stress and keen disappointment.

The conversation remained limited while the divers shoveled in the soup and bread. Finally the pot was empty and the bread was reduced to a nub and a few crumbs. Andrew suggested that they review tomorrow's dive plan.

Before the forum could begin however, the heavy wooden door swung open and the Mountie, Edwin Candle stomped forward.

"Gas tanks are all filled and both motors work fine. Must have been just a frozen line," he said. "You should have no problem tomorrow. I also called into the station. Weather will be breaking, but the skies will stay overcast."

The divers stared attentively at him without muttering a word.

"No snow for a few days, so you should be fine. Take a course heading 140 degrees down the lake and a reciprocal back. Any questions? If not… I'll be on my way."

No one at the table looked up. Andrew marked in his notebook 140 degrees and laid the pen down. Otto said, "Thanks for your help."

"Yeah thanks!" Donald chimed in.

Andrew and Michael were not comfortable with thanking the Mountie for their dire, four-hour experience. Both divers took safety very seriously. When anyone pushed the envelope too far, they were offended. They also didn't appreciate being shortchanged on the manpower they were promised. This operation would be difficult enough without the additional tension of an uncooperative law officer.

Edwin approached the door and then hesitated. He peered over his bony left shoulder and asked, "Mr. Boyd, may I speak with you outside for a moment?"

"Yeah, sure. I'll get my coat."

Andrew threw on his coat and zipped it up fully. He had a surge of adrenaline as he faced his dive group. Edwin was already outside and had an unfiltered cigarette lit by the time Andrew closed the cabin door securely behind him.

The Mountie was perched at the porch end leaning into the railing. He stood looking out into the woods that pressed against the rear of the cabin.

"You think this is an easy job?", he said, without turning around. Andrew thought, "Here it comes. Next the name-calling starts and then the brawl."

Andrew closed the gap between them, figuring if this guy was so gun happy he wouldn't want to be more than an arm's length away.

Edwin didn't turn around. Instead, he said, "You watch too many movies, Mr. Boyd. I'm not going to fight you. I'm going to apologize."

Andrew swayed back on his heels. "That's the second time someone said that to me," he thought. He was so taken aback he didn't answer.

Edwin squeezed off the tip of his cigarette into a snow pile and pulled the remainder apart, he turned to face Andrew, "Are you going to accept my apology?"

"Well... Well I guess we both acted like knobs."

"What is a knob?"

"You know. A jerk, a pain in the ass."

"You mean like a dick?"

Andrew's face blushed beet-red. He felt embarrassed the Mountie had overheard the "dick" comment. Both men stared at each other and then began to laugh.

Edwin put out an un-gloved hand, and they shook hands as they smiled.

Edwin stepped through the small break in the porch railing and walked toward his truck.

"Hey Mountie." Edwin slowed his pace and turned slightly, looking back as he walked.

"I apologize too."

The Mountie grinned and held up a gloved thumb into the air.

That was the last time Andrew would see him. He felt they might have been good friends, given a little time, now that they had dispensed with testing their metal.

Andrew casually walked back to the cabin and glanced through the porch window.

There were three noses pressed against the frosted glass.

Andrew opened the door. "Any of you guys ever hear of privacy."

"We apologize!!!", the three smirking faces said in chorused unison, as they collapsed over each other in laughter.

Andrew snapped back. "He still shouldn't have taken the short route home."

All the divers sat down to resume their conversation. Michael said quietly. "OK, here is where we are, this is where we're going."

Then Andrew pointed to a map he had drawn. "Tomorrow we split up the team into two boats. Everyone takes their own personal gear, plus an equal share of the support equipment. I think we should be on the water by 8 A.M. How do you guys feel?"

Everyone nodded approval.

"After we are setup at the site, we can make up to four full tank dives in the area where the boat was found. We can use 100-foot sweep lines and use one anchored boat for the apex. I would like to see two divers on the lake at a time; one in the boat, the other situated on the line doing the sweep. The other two men will be on shore finishing up our base camp."

Andrew studied the faces of his men as he continued.

"The second team will build campfires, make coffee and set up a drying rack. When the first team finishes their dives, they return and set up the portable pump and fill the scuba cylinders, etc."

Andrew checked his notes. "Let me make a slight change. Because we are limited to four divers, I think that when we have one diver down, he should have a small float attached to him. Anybody have a problem with that?"

Andrew carefully surveyed his divers for a reaction.

"No? OK. Then the diver down will do approximately 360-degree sweeps and then lengthen his search line, half the distance of the prevailing visibility; turn around and sweep the other way for 360 degrees. The diver in the boat will hold the other end of the line. He should be able to feel the movement of the diver, since I'm going to attach a big d' ring to the anchor and pass the line through it to the diver. We will use standard line pull signals."

Andrew pulled his arm back, demonstrating the amount of arm movement he wanted his divers to use.

"We will use three hard pulls to signal the diver to turn around and go the other way. Anyone need to review the line signals?

No? OK. When your pressure gauge reads 800 pounds, I want you under the boat taking a safety stop...Is that clear? No exceptions!"

Andrew continued the briefing for more than an hour. Questions were answered and assignments were given. Each man had a clear view of what was expected of him. There would not be sufficient time to spend on reviewing details at the dive site. There would be plenty to do as it was, and then there was always the unexpected problem.

Andrew wrapped up his lecture at 10 P.M. and asked for any final questions. Everyone seemed comfortable in their role. The four divers quickly undressed and scrambled into bed. There was little conversation after lights were out. Each diver was fast asleep in minutes.

The next morning the divers awoke without an alarm clock. Donald Graham was the first up and had steaming coffee brewing on the stove. Each diver in turn groaned and readied himself to slide out of bed.

"Geszas Christ, this floor's cold," Michael yelped, dancing on the tips of his toes. Otto joined in, tucking the blanket securely under his chin as he sat up. "It's too cold! I want to stay in bed today." Andrew slipped halfway into his hunting boots. "Oh God, these boots are freezing." He shuffled to the bathroom and poured cold water into the washbasin. He yelled into the cracked bathroom mirror. "Somebody crank up that fire. It's freezing in here!" Donald replied, dancing around the kitchen. "I stoked it earlier. It'll be warm in here by the time you finish shaving."

Preparing breakfast for everyone would be an easy task, considering the only items on the menu were eggs, bacon and bread. This morning the bread would come without butter; it was far too hard to spread. Otto peeked over the top of his blanket watching Donald's polished movements as he effortlessly glided around the kitchen. Donald shoveled the eggs into a warming skillet and gracefully began setting the table with easy fluid motion.

The icy temperature of the cabin didn't seem to faze him.

Donald lightened the spirits of the early morning with his best Donald O'Connor " Singing in the rain" routine. It was just the lighthearted fun that was needed. Otto spoke in a muffled voice, talking through his blanket. "You would think that guy was going to a society dance the way he prances around."

"Actually I think he is very pretty." Michael responded in a falsetto voice, as he imitated Donald's mincing movements by gently placing napkins, just so, on the wobbly table. Donald's retort was, "Hey, it's not my fault you guys have no rhythm. You walk around like you have a board in your ass. A little practice and you, too, could be graceful."

In reality Donald had been a dance instructor for a number of years and was very agile and limber as he moved. Under water his movements were just as fluid. He took their joking in stride, just as everyone did. They all knew it would be their turn in the barrel very soon, so the jokes never got too personal or harsh.

Donald continued frying up eggs and bacon, deftly placing them on a heated serving plate. He made a feeble attempt at toasting bread in a skillet, but only met with a minimum of success. Mostly, he dried out the bread and made the crust washboard stiff.

The divers took turns at the tiny washbasin and were soon fully dressed. They sat down at the table and pounded their knives and forks chanting "Food! Food!"

Donald did a quick pivot and laid the platter heaped with a dozen steaming eggs, on the center of the table.

Michael tilted the platter slightly looked underneath and questioned

"Is this an old hub cap or what? Damn, this is a hub cap...he fried our eggs in a hub cap!"

Donald dropped the bacon into the pan saying. "It's not a hub cap. It's just some kind of a round pan. No problem! I washed it with sand from the beach and water from our own well."

"Water from the well to clean the dishes. Oh, that makes me feel a lot better," Andrew, added.

The pangs of hunger overshadowed the need for Andrew to add any additional dialogue. Otto inquired, "Are there any condiments?"

Michael leaned back in his chair and reached into the cabinet above the sink. "We have a shaker of salt and a half pound box of pepper to match the décor of the dining room. Other than that, we could grind up some tree bark if you like. Bark is very good this time of year."

Donald flipped over the last piece of toast and cracked three more eggs. He would have his meal when the dishes were being washed and the cabin was being tidied up. Breakfast time was informal and relaxing where as dinner would be on the verge of becoming a helter-skelter affair.

The tempo in the tiny cabin shifted faster as the hour grew close to eight o'clock. Each diver finished his meal, placed his scraps in the trash, and washed his own dishes. They settled down on their bunks with their large travel bags and began sorting through the contents. There were things that had to be unpacked from their travel bags and transferred to smaller carry-along sacks. Space would be limited in the small boats. Items like extra socks, extra sweatshirts and wool caps were a necessity. Once their dive was completed their primary goal would be to regain the tremendous heat loss they sustained. They grabbed their coats and stepped briskly outside.

Donald polished off his meal by placing his eggs between two pieces of bread, while pulling his arm through the sleeve of his jacket.

Outside, the air felt damp and chilly. A robust wind benumbed any exposed skin. It reminded Andrew of his one and only deer hunt. He never liked the morning cold with its diffused light and dead silence. This was a bum day to start a search. He thoughtfully gazed out over the lake, measuring the wind and wave movement. He thought. "It doesn't really matter, I guess we have to go anyway."

It was customary for Andrew to have his normal anxiety attack just before a major diving event. The first phase of his attack was to observe the behavior of each diver as they loaded and checked their equipment. He would look for signs that might force him to relieve a diver of his role in the day's drama.

He knew the stamina and psychology of these men well. Each would carry out his assigned task without exception, even if he were anxious or questioned the assignment. That drove up Andrew's anxiety even more. He didn't want his men to push themselves beyond their own personal safe limit. Peer pressure, in a dive recovery like this, could force them to exceed a safe effort margin.

After scrutinizing everyone, Andrew felt reasonably comfortable about this dive, as there didn't appear to be any nervous undercurrents here. One factor bothered him, however. No one else had experienced recovering a body. He had spent considerable time explaining the aftermath of this kind of operation and wondered if words were enough to prepare the men emotionally. He defined what happens to the human psyche when it is fatigued and exposed to such severe sadness and finality. He also explained how some rescuers are permanently affected by the experience and how some people cannot live with victim recovery, while others depersonalize the deceased. Still others place the event into a special dwelling in their mind and are able to review the event without remorse or aftershock.

There is a certain satisfaction to finding a body, because it represents a closure for the family and answers many questions of how the tragedy took place.
Failure to locate a body, however, places an enormous emotional burden on the family and the diver.

"Only time will tell if I'm going to lose one of my divers emotionally," he thought, sitting down on the stern seat, ready to pull the starter cord.

Andrew argued with himself. "Get over it. How many times do you have to take this trip? They can handle it. Relax. These guys have been with you long enough to get it done."

Andrew's anxiety phase needed one last part, the transfer of capability.
During this phase, he resigned himself to the fact that these men are, after all, his peers in age and social responsibility. They can, and will, take care of each other. They are skilled divers, logical thinkers and emotionally responsible citizens. Otherwise they wouldn't have volunteered for this mission. There was little glory or recognition for their efforts. Their reward was bathed in empathy and concern for others.

That is very strong motivation for doing the job right. The more he thought about this day's event, the more his anxiety began to wane. He felt he and his men were prepared for whatever challenge lay ahead.

The small talk was limited to reaffirming safety procedures and humorous comments about the weather. There was some tension, but it derived more from being eager to get started, rather than from being nervous. Staying awake from lack of sleep was a bigger problem. Few people can rest comfortably the first night away from home. With the added annoyance of a cold damp bed and a cabin temperature that drops to forty degrees, and you have a formula for sleep deprivation.

The divers were aware of the first day's operation and what it would take to make it successful. They all shouldered an equal role in the loading and securing of supplies. Stowing equipment in these small boats was critical. The weight and bulk of divers and equipment needed special attention. They hadn't planned on such small watercraft. The eight dive cylinders had to be laid in the center bottom of the boat to give it a low center of gravity. The dive bags were packed in the bows, with the miscellaneous equipment stowed under the seats. The portable air compressor had to be laid on its side because it was too unstable standing upright.

Equipment was packed in every nook and cranny, but a few feet of clear space on the bottom of each boat was needed for bailing. Michael made sure each boat had an empty coffee can on board.

Donald pulled two sets of oars out from under an old boat, which was upside down and resting on two sawhorses. Michael brushed off the spider webs and dried leaves before forcing the oars into the packed boats.

"These babies haven't been used in a hell of a long time."
Andrew added. "We could have used them last night."

"For what, to bean your Mountie buddy?"

"No, I just hate to be up a creek without one." Michael groaned.

The boats were loaded and the four divers stood looking down at the humpbacked watercraft they had just created.

Donald questioned, "Do you think they'll stay afloat?"

Otto observed, "Hey, they're floating now."

Michael said, "That's because they're tied to the pier, you boob."

Andrew asked "OK. Everybody got all their stuff? Did we forget anything back at the cabin?"

"No, mother," Otto said, affectionately slapping Andrew on the back.

Andrew suggested they might don their wet suits for the frigid boat ride. All the divers readily agreed. The dive bags popped open and the men pulled out their suits. While seated on the pier, they slipped them on and zipped up the jackets. Under the outer shell the divers wore long-john cotton underwear. The cotton johns would take up any extra space in the suit, reducing the amount of water transfer inside the suit. Andrew requested that each man put on his neoprene gloves and hood. Now if there would be a serious boat problem, it could be managed. Even if the boat sank, they could survive. They might have as much as an hour on the surface before they would be in any serious trouble.

Andrew wanted to make sure that if there were a sinking incident, the waterborne divers would not need to scurry into the remaining boat. That might cause it to capsize. That way they would ensure plenty of time for a rescue. With a few docking lines thrown overboard they could tow the floating divers to shore.

"One last thing, guys. Pull your fins and knives out. Stick them under your seat. And be sure to zip up your suits tight."

Andrew thought to himself, "Wait a minute, there are only two boats that come with the two cabins. The other one hasn't been used in years.

If each cabin sleeps four to six people, then they could be overloaded every time the boats go out. We are way overloaded with two men and the dive bags. In case of a sinking, the second boat would be of little help; if it had to support six or eight big men. How can these people think this is a safe arrangement when the water gets this cold?" Andrew shook his head in shock and disbelief.

The small boats headed out into the lake. The waves pulsed against the bow, making hollow rhythmic thuds. Andrew felt the wave action was far less injurious to his nervous system than the night before. It appeared as if the weather might clear later in the day. The wind had died down and the gray smoky haze draped the lake again, keeping the visibility to a few hundred yards. The ride over seemed shorter to Michael and Andrew. Their thoughts were focused on the dive this time and not on swimming to shore. Donald and Otto however, complained jokingly that the trip was too long and they wanted faster and more comfortable accommodations for tomorrow.

Suddenly, the small boats slid up on a muddy shore and came to a sudden halt. Andrew and Michael hoisted the dive bags on their shoulders and headed to the tree line. If a brisk breeze kicked up again, they would hug the tree line, and it would create a limited windbreak.

The divers unloaded the boats and started setting up their base camp.

Equipment had to be adjusted, fitted and double-checked. They did not have enough people or time to correct a mess up because of some equipment failure. They gathered firewood and large flat stones that they placed around the perimeter of a fire pit. The stones served the double function of containing the fire and providing a warm dry place to sit.

Andrew said. "Be sure to clear a six foot fire break around the pit also. We don't want to burn down this beautiful forest." He checked his watch "Damn," he said. "It's already 9 A.M. Michael and I will make the first dive, while you guys finish preparing camp. Donald, be sure to build a reflector wall from wood and set it up behind the fire. We are going to be damn cold when we emerge from that 'freeze your ass' cold water. Also, let's erect a drying rack for clothing, and anything else you think we might need."

Andrew paused and added. "Otto, be sure to stack these stones at least two feet high."

Michael turned to Andrew, who was collecting his personal dive gear, and gave him a salute saying. "Yes, my captain."

"What? It sounded that bad?"

"Yes boss, that bad."

"OK, pretty please...Michael. You and I will dive together."

Andrew never got an argument from any of his divers about who would dive first or with whom. They had full confidence Andrew would think each dive plan through with great care and competence. It made his job so much easier. However, when Andrew got a little too pushy, someone would cut him down a few pegs. They also knew if he had to explain every decision in detail, or leave it open for debate, he would waste valuable time.

At this point, the four of them had been together for three years. In that time Andrew had always measured the risk and task loading of the assignment. His decisions today would be made on how well that risk and task loading could be managed by each diver.

"Michael, I'll go in first. You keep a close watch on the markers. We have to keep this search area as tight as we can. We have to maximize our bottom time, since the water is so damn cold."

"You bet." Michael said.

Andrew put on his scuba equipment and stepped into the boat. It would be easier to dress on land than to struggle with equipment in the confined space of their small boat. The dive site was only one hundred yards off the shore, and thus the ride out would not be tiring. Once situated over the site, Andrew would simply roll off the stern, directly into the water.

Andrew brought the boat to a stop and checked the D-ring that he attached to the anchor. He fed the loose end of the search line through the D-ring and tossed the anchor over the side. Michael tied the line off at the bow and coiled the remainder under his seat.

"Andrew, it looks like twenty five feet of water. You won't need your decompression tables."

"Good! I'll get more downtime and I won't get so cold."

"Nice try, but it won't work. Hell, I'm cold already."

"Don't worry, Michael, you won't even get a chance to dive. I'll grab those guys and be right up." Andrew said.

"Right. Just in case, don't kick up the bottom anyway."

"Give me almost a full swing. I'll come back and dive the slice after I'm done."

Michael would have control over Andrew's underwater course heading. Andrew would swim an arc of 360 degrees around the anchor, often leaving a small area not searched. They called it the slice. Michael held the search line in the boat. It would run down to the anchor through the D-ring and be wrapped around Andrew's hand. Each time Andrew completed 360 degrees of his arc, Michael would yank on the line several times and pay out a little more line. How much he would pay out would depend on the visibility.

Andrew exhaled and released air from his vest. He settled to the bottom and checked his depth gauge. It measured twenty-four feet at his waist. He tied an eight-inch white disk on the anchor line and backed away from the line. He checked the length of horizontal visibility.

He thought, "Not bad, at about eight feet. Much better than I thought it would be."

He moved back to the anchor and pulled down hard on the line. He rose to the surface without kicking, with four more tugs on the line.

At the surface, he dropped his regulator mouthpiece into the water. A great spout of water sprayed both divers. Andrew grabbed the mouthpiece and forced it underwater, cupping it. The loud hissing stopped instantly. Michael leaned over the side of the boat and reached down to help Andrew. He snickered "That's professional…first time in a big lake?"

Andrew hung onto the stern transom and spat water at Michael, as he responded. "A giant sea monster grabbed my leg and I had to fight it off. That's why I dropped the mouthpiece."

"Oh yeah, that works." Michael said.

Both divers chuckled and got back to business.

Andrew reported, "Water is twenty-seven feet deep. Visibility is about eight feet, so give me a few extra feet on a sweep. And don't look so smug. You're next, Bozo. Give me a tow float and my yellow personal float."

Andrew tied off the tow float to his weight belt and paid out about thirty feet of line. The float drifted away from the boat with the breeze. The tow float would help Michael keep track of Andrew. If Andrew's compass heading had to be followed for some reason, it could be followed easily. Or if he had to signal the surface, a float bobbing up and down is very attention getting. This was one more safety factor to consider when diving alone. Andrew attached an additional yellow personal float to his tank harness at chest level.

He smoothly descended to the bottom again and started his systematic sweep. He kicked slowly with his fins, which were slightly higher than his head. This would keep the thrust of his fins from stirring up the bottom behind him.

The time dragged on as it had on many other dives just like this one. He was nearing the end of his first sweep when he felt forceful tugs on the line. The signal alerted Andrew that he had completed another sweep. He turned and started swimming back in the opposite direction. This time he would be six feet farther away from the boat anchor. Even if the visibility were eight feet, Andrew liked to have that little margin in case there were pockets of water that had a little less visibility.

Sweep after sweep continued. For sixty minutes, he swam and reversed his direction. Andrew checked his pressure gauge. Only 800 pounds of air remained. He surfaced, reached over his head and grabbed the boat rail. His numb fingers provided little grip and his arm flopped back into the water. On his second attempt, he draped his arm over the side and removed his regulator. Fatigued and chilled jaw muscles made Andrew's mouth droop, and steam billowed out as he tried to speak.

"I've got enough air left for the slice," he said with a gasp. He paused to catch his breath.

"Give me a compass heading."

"Figure 240 degrees and about 150 feet out. I've got the length of your last sweep marked on the line. You want to come out?"

"No, no I've got it.... Be sure to warm up my side of the bed."

Michael smiled and reached down to tap Andrew on his diving hood. He got the long standing inside joke.

Andrew grinned and sank beneath the surface. Michael returned to his seat and reflected on his memories of other dives with Andrew. He remembered one of the many times he and Andrew had been on a dive in Door County, Wisconsin. The bed joke started after they had worked all weekend on raising the Alvin Clark. Exhausted and bone weary the duo headed for the Frank's motel.

Sometimes, Frank Norris had more divers than he had beds. That's the way it was with that salvage operation, either feast or famine.

There was lots of bed space or none at all. Andrew and Michael however, were very consistent in their attendance for the dives. As a reward, Frank always had a room and a bed for each of them. A small mix-up one weekend left only one room and one full-sized bed at the motel.

After a full day of diving at 100 feet in freezing water, no one really cared where they slept. On one particular night, Andrew and Michael were stuck with sleeping in the same bed, which was ancient and sagged ten inches in the middle. All night long they had to hug their side of the mattress so they wouldn't roll into the center and collide. Heaven forbid they would touch each other. Every time they thought of how silly they were, they both chuckled.

Michael watched Andrew's tow float and long trail of air bubbles break on the surface. He checked his compass. "Right on the money" he thought to himself. He paid out the search line until the marker came to his hand. He tightened up on the line and gave it the appropriate number of tugs. The line went slack for a moment. Andrew was starting back in a zigzag pattern. The line went taut suddenly and then loosened. A small bright yellow bobber-float popped to the surface. It danced in a flow of upwelling air. The personal float was used to mark a spot on the bottom. It had a one-pound weight and one-hundred feet of thin line attached to it. Andrew had found something. His bubble stream straightened out and came directly back to the boat. Andrew broke the surface with a fishing pole in his hand.

He handed the pole up to Michael and said. "I think I may have found part of the debris field, but I ran out of air. You have to bring them up."

"You mean you found them?"

"No, just some fishing poles. I left my marker float."

"Turn around, so I can help you with your gear". Michael said. Andrew loosened his weight belt first and handed it up to Michael.

"Right, now turn around."

Andrew turned and loosened his tank harness, while Michael reached down and with a huge grunt lifted the scuba gear into the boat. Andrew hooked his thumb in his fin strap and flipped it over his heel.

The exertion of taking off his equipment was a challenge. However, Andrew had been this cold before. In frigid water like this, the back muscles tighten up and it becomes difficult to bend or flex. Every movement requires concentration and an extra surge of energy.

Finally, Andrew had everything back in the boat, except his body. It was a good thing, because Andrew had all he could do to put one foot on the outboard engine stabilizer and lift his shaky body into the boat. As usual, he had stayed in the water too long. His hands were so numb now that he couldn't pull his mitts off by himself. Michael had felt the cold creeping in on him as well, so he fired up a canister of thermal heat. It was just what both men needed. Andrew picked up the canister and rolled it back and forth in his hands. He muttered, with his teeth chattering, "My ass is so cold I'll need a blow torch to thaw it out. Do we still have the blanket in that green cargo bag?"

"We sure do. Your hooded cotton pullover is in there too."

"Give it to me before my teeth fall out. Man, it's been a long time since I've been this cold."

Andrew's shivering was uncontrollable now. His chest muscles were constricting and releasing at a furious rate. His arms and knees danced about in a spasm of muscle contractions. He pulled the wet suit jacket down, took off the cotton underwear top and pulled the sweater over his head. He wrapped the blanket around his shoulders and placed the heat canister under the blanket. The heat felt good on his upper body. It took a full ten minutes for Andrew to stop shaking. As many times as he tore into his divers for pushing the envelope, that is how many times he broke his own rule. "If you start to shake, its time for a break."

Michael dropped new markers overboard to mark the spot they had just searched. He pulled up the boat anchor and motored over to the little yellow personal float Andrew had left bobbing in the water. This would be the new dive search area. Once again, he dropped the boat anchor and busied himself taking apart Andrew's equipment and assembling his own. By the time he was ready to dive, Andrew had recovered his body heat and slipped back into his diver role.

The wind was dead calm now with nary a whisper from any direction. The gray blue haze returned and hung like a valance atop a window. The men were only 50 yards off shore and still they could only make out shadows on the beach. Andrew contemplated a scene on shore, as he scanned the lake, waiting for Michael to lower himself into the water.

"That campfire sure looks good even from here. Another hour of work and we can both hug those flames. I sure could use a cup of coffee."

The earlier plan was to have Michael and Andrew dive first and use up their air supply. Then they would have a lunch break and Otto and Donald would dive. They would extend the dive site out into the lake from the bay.

After finding the fishing rod, plans changed slightly.
The day of the accident, a strong wind was blowing offshore from the opposite side of the bay. If the boat rolled over, but didn't sink immediately, the men may have drifted around. Finding the fishing rod at that location confused things a bit. It was found closer to the base of the bay than they thought it should be. The shoreline where the body was found was further down in the lake. The angle from where the fishing rod and body were found doubled the distance to shore. It was now clear the fishermen either drifted or swam at too great an angle to shore. But, no one knew why.

Another question was; how long had the boat drifted, before it sank deep enough for the fishermen to start swimming to shore. Did the strongest swimmer, using a float make half the distance and then pass out before he drifted? Did they all start out together and then drop out one by one? If any of those actions occurred, then sweeping 180-degree arcs along that trail might turn up the other victims.

Andrew handed the search line overboard to Michael. He descended slowly to the bottom. After locating the boat anchor and checking the D-ring, he swam in the direction of shore. Only ten minutes into the dive, he spotted a fishing tackle box. It lay upright, spilled of its contents. Michael rose to the surface and handed the box up to Andrew.

Andrew said. "I'll hold you to 20-foot-wide sweeps. Keep the line close to the bottom. You may snag something."

"OK, but this is the part I hate. I wouldn't mind swimming over a body, I just don't like swimming into one."

Andrew smiled saying. "Don't worry. It won't bite you."

"I'm not worried about it biting me. I worry about it sitting up, after I bump into it."

Andrew patted Michael on his head saying. "Stop it, you're scaring me."

Before Michael could get in the last word, Otto forcefully called out from the beach. "Hey, you guys, come in here quick. We found something really important."

Andrew cupped his hands and shouted. "We will be done in an hour. Can't it wait?"

Otto yelled back. "We found a marked trail that looks fresh."

Andrew didn't understand the message and asked Otto to repeat it.

Otto rolled up a cardboard megaphone and bellowed again. "We found what looks like a marked trail."

Andrew waved that he understood. He did not intend to stop the search, now that they were over a debris field.

Michael floated out, away from the boat, before he descended. He swam his 180-degree arc for more than an hour, before he too would be vanquished by the cold. He finally surfaced, shivering and spouting an exhaustive cloud of steam. He called up to Andrew breathlessly. "I didn't see anything else... Tow me in. I'm too pooped to climb out... I'll scan the bottom on the way back." Michael hung onto the search line, about thirty feet behind the boat. Andrew started the outboard motor and headed slowly into shore. They felt it was less fatiguing on Michael to tow him the short distance to shore than to struggle with climbing back into the small boat. Michael skimmed along the surface, face down, using his seasoned snorkel. He had hoped that with dumb luck, he might see something in the shallow waters along the way. Andrew shut down the motor and drifted onto the muddy embankment. Michael stood up in waist deep water and took his fins off. He waded in alongside the boat and slogged his way up the sloped bank. His wet-suit boots stuck in the mud with each step.

Michael did not waste any time getting close to the fire. He laid his scuba system down on the canvas tarpaulin and backed into the radiant heat of the fire. The steam rose from his suit in waves and then dispersed at the slightest gust of wind.

"Boy, that feels a lot better," he said as he rubbed his hands furiously together, trying to regain circulation.

Andrew secured the boat and questioned Otto about his big find.

"What about this trail you found?"

"We were gathering those flat rocks over there." Said Otto, as he pointed down the shoreline to a small six-foot rise in the embankment.

The shoreline continued at the higher elevation for three or four miles, then returned to water level, for the remainder of the lake.

"Up that hill about seventy five yards, there's a bunch of rocks standing upright. It looks like someone was marking a trail."

Andrew pressed for more information. "You mean someone took the time to set up rocks, so that they wouldn't get lost while walking around a shoreline?"

"All I know is someone took the time to stand a bunch of rocks on their ends, with the clean beige bottoms facing in the direction they were going. If you follow them for awhile and then turn around and look back, those light colored bottoms really get your attention."

Michael pulled off his dive hood and said, "I can't believe a couple of guys who just swam in freezing-ass water would have enough energy left to work that hard."

Michael's input was brief, because he was still dealing with a case of the overwhelming shakes.

Andrew pulled Michael's arms out of his wet suit and said with a wavering voice, "Hey, maybe they didn't all swim that far. Or maybe a couple of them were left on the shore before the accident."

Otto added, "Remember, the guy that was found was the strongest swimmer. If he didn't make it, no one did."

Donald jumped into the conversation. "It doesn't matter who made it and who didn't. Someone took the time, recently, to mark a trail. It wasn't some kid playing hide and seek. There may be someone out there in that woods who is dead, or almost dead, right now."

"Donald's right," Michael agreed. "The point is, someone was trying to survive. They left this area and headed for the only campsite around here, on the other side of the lake. That means they may still be out there."

Andrew stared at the fire, warming his hands, while the heated discussion continued. Then he broke in and tried to summarize the situation and plan the next course of action. "First we have three guys missing. The strongest guy failed to make it to shore. The other two either tried to swim with him or were left clinging to the boat until they couldn't hold on any longer. On the other hand, they might never have left land in the first place. We found one set of fishing tackle less than 100 yards off shore. So we know where the boat rolled over."

Donald broke in, "The guy the Mounties found may have been the only one in the boat."

Andrew added, "Right, except, if the other guys were on shore, that would mean they just stood there and watched their partner drown. He never sank beneath the surface, because the seat cushion was wrapped around his arm. He must have had enough strength to swim a portion of the way in. Surely, someone would have jumped in to help."

Michael was warm enough now to stop shaking, and he joined in.

"The possibility of anyone else being in this area at that time is remote. We have at this point found an underwater debris trail we can follow. We can burn the rest of the day in hopes of finding the other guys, which is what we were sent here to do. We agreed to find or not find three husbands, but at least we should make the effort. We have the diving equipment and air to carry out that assignment."

Andrew said abruptly, finishing Michael's thought. "The guys in the lake are dead. That's a fact. The guys in the woods may still be alive. That means there is still some hope. People have survived for weeks in this kind of hostile environment. We can follow the trail into the woods in hopes of finding whoever laid the rock pattern. If there are people out there, time is of the essences. We need to make a decision now. Michael and I can't go back in the water until we can warm up and get some carbohydrates back in our system. If you two go into the woods and follow the trail, it may take you the rest of the day or at least several hours. You will have to follow the trail as far as it leads and then some. You need to push as far as your strength can take you. You must make sure that these trail makers are not languishing some distance beyond their last marker."

"Actually, those guys had to be in good shape to even think of walking out of here. Therefore, they are probably a long way into those woods. I don't think it's a good idea to burn yourselves out walking for hours and then trying to make a dive in that damn cold water. It only puts you at risk. I think you should do one or the other, but not both. Speaking about the edge of our security, I have another thought. If there are big brown things with big ugly claws in there, you will stand a much better chance with four guys, than with just two.

"We have no guns, and sharp sticks may not scare off our furry little friends. So either, all go, or no one goes. OK?"

To a man they nodded their agreement to all go.

"Then let's have a vote. Everyone in favor of following the yellow brick road, say 'we're off to see the wizard." All three divers again were in harmony. Andrew however, was bothered by the decision, even if it was the only logical thing to do. It was always the "what ifs" that caused him anguish. What if the people in the woods had nothing to do with the event that took place just off shore? What if they are the fishermen, and they are hanging on to life with only hours of human endurance left?

"This moment in time can't be repeated. God help us." he thought.

Andrew paused while considering the groups next move. Then said,

"That's it then, pack up all the equipment and stow it in the boat. We may not care much about loading it after our little trek in the woods".

Otto led the dive team up the slope to the first marker, where they stopped. It was the size of a hubcap and sticking upright in the ground. The face of the stone was a gray ashen color, while the under side was light beige, almost golden in color. It could be seen 20 yards or more away if not masked by trees in the line of sight. Because the trail left the shoreline and wandered inland, Andrew suggested one diver walk the markers and one diver stay between the shoreline and the markers.

The other two divers walked inland, but always in sight of the diver on his left. They walked for more than two hours. The forest floor was littered with branches, pine needles and fallen trees. Every dozen yards, the divers had to either walk around or climb over huge fallen trees.

Fully-grown and now dead, decaying trees had lain undisturbed for decades in this region. The area had not been clear-cut or thinned out. This was the way it had been for ten thousand years. No trails or firebreaks were here; just leaves, branches and trees. The forest floor was covered with a thick moist carpet of decomposing detritus ready to be recycled into the amazing web of nature. It felt soft and cushioned each footstep. The smell of pure clean air with a hint of mold was noticeable from the start, but now two hours into the walk, it seemed natural to the senses.

The sun broke through the heavy overcast sky for the first and only time in days. It lasted less than 20 minutes, but gave everyone a surge of energy. The timing couldn't have been better.

As the divers approached a small clearing about 60 feet long and 20 feet wide, the sun beamed down and brought the forest to life. Andrew called for the first break and the divers gathered in a clearing. Had there been anyone or any animal within 200 yards of that clearing, they could have heard all the loud chatter, commotion and yelling going on. Andrew felt comfortable and encouraged all the noise; he knew it was caused by their nervous exhaustion. The divers were very pleased to get a rest period, although they knew it would be brief. It didn't take long before they were hard at analyzing their progress, thus far.

Otto sat down Indian-style in the grass and leaves and rested his back on a fallen tree. "Who's idea was this anyway? I want his name and phone number." He pulled a few pinches of grass out of the ground and flicked his wrist sending the grass cluster filtering back to earth.

"And then I'm going to make him pay for my sore feet."

Donald was snuggled down into his jacket against the base of a tree. He lifted his jaw out of his jacket high enough to add.

"I don't get it. We've been walking for hours and I can still see the water's edge from the last marker. What the hell was the sense of setting up stones, if you never lose sight of the water?"

Lying face down in the grass, his left cheek squashed into the back of his hand, Michael said, "I want to know how they made it this far. My ass is really dragging and I was comfortably housed in a wet suit for my little dip in the lake."

"Well," Andrew paused, "I don't think these markers are the work of our people. No one could be in that great a shape. My butt is hanging a little low, too. I think we should follow the markers for one more hour, hang a flag on the shoreline and head back to camp."

It was a welcome relief for the dive team to hear Andrew place a time limit on what they now considered wasted effort. Each in his own mind had decided long ago no one could have survived a boat sinking, a swim in freezing water and a seven-mile hike in the woods.

There were conflicting facts that gnawed at all the divers. If it wasn't the victims, then who had set up these markers? Who would waste that much time? Moreover, when did they do it?"

Andrew called everyone to their feet. "OK' boys, it's time to dance." Everyone groaned or grunted their discontent, but they all eased themselves up.

"I know how you feel. I think we are into the woods as far as anyone could have walked without an extended rest period. Those guys couldn't have been in that much better shape than we are."

No one laughed, but they did manage to break a smile and it helped to ease the fatigue.

Andrew continued. "What bothers me is the dirt on the bottom side of the rocks. How come the rain hasn't washed it off? Look at the ground beneath the rocks. The wormholes are still perfect. No rainfall has washed down the sides of the holes. That tells me one more thing. Whoever placed these rocks did so since the last heavy rain fall."

Otto climbed on top of a fallen tree and began an unanswerable argument.

"What are the odds that someone within this same time period, in this same area, of this remote place, happened to set up rocks for us to see. And all within a last rain fall?"

Michael grabbed Otto by the dangling jacket sleeves he had tied around his waist and pulled him gently forward off the tree.

"All right man, back off. You have us convinced. We were headed in that direction anyway."

Andrew smiled knowing that as much as these guys liked to gripe, they always did what was asked of them. It was a code they had honored among themselves. "If you aren't going to do the job, then don't show up in the first place. Don't wait until someone is relying on you and then quit or give it less than your best effort."

Another hour passed and the divers were still finding a clearly marked trail.

"Hey everybody." Andrew shouted and waved for everyone to gather around him. "Otto, come on in," Michael yelled through cupped hands.

Michael, who was tracking, as the third man inland from the water's edge was the only one who could see Otto. With Michael's urging he made his way back to the group.

Andrew had decided to turn around and head for camp. "It doesn't look like the markers are spreading out any. That means our trailblazers aren't getting tired. If they are that strong this late in the trail, I believe they could have walked the other two thirds of the way back to the cabin. I think we are following the wrong guys. Anyone disagree?"

Michael said, "Oh no, boss, not us. You know your stuff, we just follow." The others murmured in unison, "Ah haw, ah haw, yes, oh yes." Andrew gave the international sign of defiance and said, "Right."

It was approaching dusk by the time they reached the beach site and launched their boats. The ride back to the cabin was quiet and serene, save for the constant hum of the outboards. No one spoke as they each contemplated thoughts of what they did or didn't accomplish during this arduous day. Each man stared out into the lake, looking at everything and seeing nothing. They passed the spot where they had placed the red marker on the shoreline. It was barely visible from their angle of approach. Nevertheless, they all saw it. Everyone was silent. No one made a comment, no one made a wise crack. It was the end of a tough day and still no concrete evidence of where the victims were located.

The lumbering little boats approached the dock slowly, with their engines laboring from all the on-board weight. Michael jumped out of the first boat and ran forward to tie it off at the metal post nearest the shore. The pier shook from the sudden weight thrust upon it. It shuttered and groaned again, when the second boat bumped against it. Still there were no conversations among the men. Sometimes, it would be quiet like this, when the divers were tired and deep in their thoughts.

Most volunteers engaged in this kind of duty never really escape a personal involvement. They are told and reminded from day one to keep it impersonal. Now, just a few days into the operation, they are drifting into the melancholy that sooner or later gets to every rescuer. These men were all competitive in their own personal lives. Today was a failure for them; they did not accept failure well. The fact this was a victim recovery only magnified the emotion.

Andrew looked around at the men who were busying themselves with their gear. They packed the smaller items into their duffel bag and arranged it to be unloaded.

All the effort, planning and the pressure of the time constraints were starting to show on their faces. He had seen it happen before. It doesn't take long. There is the beginning excitement of a rescue or recovery. The overoptimistic feeling that finding the victim is a surety. But then there's the added fatigue of the search and the damping of enthusiasm as the hours wear on. Take away just one night of sleep and you have a person who will have a dramatic shift in personality.

Andrew knew time was running out. As he unloaded his boat, the same question reverberated in his head. "If we don't find anything tomorrow, how do I explain to the wives that we only found a few pieces of fishing gear?" Tomorrow would be their last chance. If they were unsuccessful, then there would be no return trip.

Andrew hesitated to give any directions. He felt this wasn't a good time to review basic off loading. Everyone knew what he was supposed to do. The boats were somewhat unloaded with the exception of the hard dive equipment and a few bags. The suits would be taken back to the cabin to dry out. None of the so-called super wet suits in the 1960s were ever really that warm. The remaining equipment including the portable air pump could stay on the pier. Andrew noted,

"Not much chance of any thieves out here."

In a shortened version of "follow the leader," the men headed up to the cabin. Their heads hung low as they climbed the dirt path. The steps were reinforced with tree limbs that seemed wider and higher on the way up. Two of the men hand-pressed the top of their knees, in an effort to give their legs more lift. The exertion was obvious as they strained against each step upward. It was another sign of fatigue and despair beginning to take hold. They did not want to return home without some positive knowledge of the trucker's plight. Michael was the first one to the cabin. He pushed hard on the door, but it stuck fast at the bottom corner. He shifted his weight to an outside foot, raised his shoulder and thumped the door open. The door flung open and slammed into the wall. No one raised his eyes, let alone his head. They just walked through the opening. Andrew would normally press to review the days accomplishments and the days short comings, but this was not the time. Maybe after everyone regained the body core heat each had been without for more than nine hours. He let it go.

Michael whispered a "sorry about the door," flopped into his bunk and fixated a stare on the mattress above him. The others did various versions of the same thing.

After a few minutes, Andrew swung his feet over the side of the bed and asked. "Anybody feel like a cup of coffee?" Three Yeas', depicting various degrees of interest, were heard. "Otto, it's your turn," Andrew said, slapping upward into the mattress bottom. A hollow voice overhead whined, "I can't. My feet are broken and I don't know how to fix them. I..."

"Save it Anne Warhall; I was only kidding". Andrew planted both feet down and pushed off from his bunk.

"Your coffee leaves something to be desired anyway... Michael. Did we unpack that coffee we got in the Caymans?"

"No, it's in the blue plastic box located in the black duffel bag, right next to my dirty socks".

"Good, that should add some aroma." Andrew poured the coffee grounds into the old style strainer. He had not used one of these percolator style pots since he was a child. He lifted the dented iron cover and placed the blackened pot directly over the flames. They lapped at the sides of the coffee maker and turned the water drops into sizzling ringlets around the base of the pot. The radiant heat from the stove felt good on Andrew's chest and arms. It helped relieve some of the stiffness that had settled in after the long cold boat ride back to the cabin. He realized when he stepped down onto the floor with every bone aching, that he should have had all the guys do some cool down exercises. Just a walk around and a few stretches before the long cold boat ride. He thought, "Oh, damn. I can't think of everything."

Andrew poured four cups of coffee and walked over to the bunk beds. He handed one cup to Michael and one to Otto, who stuttered a little and asked in a still whiney voice, "I can't get up. Can you get me a straw, daddy?"

"Sit up you big baby, before I pour this down your pants."
Everyone was starting to lighten up. The humor began to surface again. It was time for the divers to put regrets aside and look to the next phase. Positive thoughts would counter the huge emotional letdown they were all experiencing.

Not finding any of the decedents can be more depressing then finding them. Every diver knew that if they were to let the seed of depression begin, it would influence their effort from now on. The boat ride back had given each of them time to reflect on what had been accomplished, if anything. This morning they were very optimistic about finding the truckers. Now ten long hours later, the optimism had waned. The disappointment of not finding the truckers weighed heavy on each diver. Any false hope that maybe someone walked away didn't help either. Andrew requested everyone gather around the table. "I think I know how you all feel about today. I feel the same way. We did exactly what we should have done. There is no reason to look at our decision in hindsight. If we hadn't walked the trail, we would be wondering now if the truckers were out there dying in the woods. We need to move forward from here," continued Andrew. "Tomorrow, we will cover the same area as today, but move more to the south, down the length of the lake. We were lucky the snow squall ran right up the center of the lake. Most of it never touched the land. We start tomorrow with Otto and Donald leading off the dive schedule. Be sure to do a complete equipment check first thing in the morning. We can't afford to forget anything that might delay us again. Michael and I will be pumping our cylinders for the next two hours. You guys can sack it or whatever. Anybody got anything else to discuss?"

Donald spoke up, "If we're going to do another all-day trip, we'd better pack more food and water than we did today. I mean, I didn't even dive, and I could eat the east-end of a horse going west right now."

Andrew had to agree. Until Donald mentioned food, Andrew hadn't noticed his growing hungry. Michael added. "Man, I second that. Let's cook up some grub."

Otto opened the box marked canned goods that had been stored by the guide the evening before. He pulled out two cans labeled beef stew.

"Hey, there's a full meal in a can here. Who wants to taste my specialty?"

"Forget the specialty." Michael said. "Just open the can and heat the contents."

"OK, but you don't know what you're missing. I can make a stew taste like sirloin steak." Otto promised.

Donald added. "It is steak, you dope."

Andrew grabbed his jacket and headed for the door. Michael was right behind him. Andrew stopped at the door and turned to Michael. "You don't have to come down to the compressor. I can fill a couple of cylinders."

"That's OK, man. I love the fresh air."

Michael and Andrew walked in tandem down to the pier. They talked about trivia and everything but the dive. Andrew stood the compressor upright and checked the oil level, the filter and the connections.

"Oil's OK, filters OK. I'll crank it up; you can pull the dive cylinders out of the boat."

Andrew lugged the compressor to the start of the pier, close to the water's edge. He pulled hard on the hand-pull starter. The compressor sputtered and puffed a burst of air, but failed to start. He wrapped the rope around the small pulley again and yanked. The engine turned over once, sputtered again and started. He adjusted the throttle, and the tiny gas engine began to smooth out its rhythm.

The sound echoed across the lake and reverberated from the tree line behind them.

Andrew thought, "I really feel guilty making so much noise. It's so peaceful here. Oh well." He connected the filler hose from the compressor to the valve on top of the first dive cylinder and tightened the bleeder valve. The compressor's hum began to deepen as the air pressure started to climb in the cylinder. He laid the cylinder back in the lake water to keep the cylinder cool. During the filling process, compressing the air heats up the cylinder and allows less air capacity in the cylinder. Michael had lined up the empty cylinders at the water's edge. After each cylinder was filled, he would position them on the pier in a tight horizontal row. As Andrew connected the cylinders, he made a mental note of how long the job would take. "It takes approximately 45 minutes to fill the 71.5 cubic foot cylinder to a full capacity of 2,250 pounds per square inch. Well, this will take a few hours anyway."

Andrew pulled his dive bag from the boat and jammed it up against one of the pier posts. He sat down and snuggled his back up to the dive bag. Reaching up to his red-knit watch cap, he pulled out his cigarettes. Andrew was not a heavy smoker, less than five cigarettes a day. Often it was times like this when he thought it was helpful. It never was. Without realizing it, he was actually meditating, if only for a brief moment. Smoking had little to do with sorting out the problems of keeping his men safe. He knew better than to smoke even after a dive, but in those early days there was little peer pressure not to smoke or warnings about the dangers.

This assignment was much more of a challenge than he originally thought. It was the long, grueling flight that set the stage for continuous fatigue. If there had only been more time to rest. The emotions of searching for people who had drown were evident. A diver can't just write off the empathy he feels for the families. Andrew glanced knowingly at Michael, who was packing his equipment.

"Even him, Mr. Detail, Mr. Matter of Fact Michael, couldn't help showing how, in the span of 35 hours, he has become as much a part of this emotional family as everyone else.

Jokes aside, "These were good guys. They were tough and loyal, and most of all willing to give their best effort. How does a guy get such friendship? There was no money involved. They had joined me on many screwball adventures before, but this was different. This time we were searching for lost people. People who loved and laughed, cried and got angry, just like us. Well, I thought this all before. Now, be very cautious from here on out. Don't let anyone push it. Abort the dive, if you think it's unsafe. Take the emotional hit if you abort the dive completely and don't find the bodies. You could live with that, but not if another person got hurt or died out here."

Andrew pensively scanned the wide lake expanse and prayed aloud, "Out there, lonely, alone... please help us take them home."

Michael, meanwhile, was still busy straightening out his dive gear. The "first in, last out" equipment rule had been instilled in all the divers. The last thing you want to do is search for the first piece of dive gear you need when it's stowed at the bottom of your dive bag, especially in cramped boats like these.

"Stow your gear immediately after the dive" was another ingrained rule. However, when you're rigid with cold during a long return boat ride, all you think about is staying warm and motionless.

Andrew and Michael were cold to the bone. The short stay in the cabin had only tricked the mind into thinking the body was warm. They had little conversation. Each diver stopped for a time and stared out into the lake, wondering where their quarries were hidden. "Were they searching too far into the bay? Did the search line just skim over the top of the prone fishermen? Were they even on the right side of the lake?"

Andrew finally broke the silence, "What if the fishermen tipped the boat over on the other side of the lake and the guy's and boat drifted for days? We can't tell on what day of the trip they might have gone down. What if they sank the boat the first day? They could have been floating for several days or even a week."

Michael shrugged his shoulders and said, "What if one guy was left on shore and saw the boat tip and his buddies drown. It would have been insane to swim out that far to try and save them. Then he packed up and did try to walk out. What if he are still out there, waiting?"

Maybe we should walk around the lake from this side to where we tied the flag, just to be sure.

Andrew jumped up and grabbed his wet suit and threw it over his arm. "I don't need any more freaking questions. I can come up with all the freaking questions. I need freaking answers."

Andrew reached out and squeezed the back of Michael's neck: not very hard, just enough so that Michael knew he was frustrated, but not really angry. They walked to the cabin making small talk, trying to restrain their disappointment. As they approached the porch, Andrew slowed Michael with a tug on his arm. "One last thing, I know we only gave this search a limited time. It can't be compared to a full-blown regular recovery. No one could have found them in such a short time with so little to go on, right?"

Michael turned to face Andrew, "Nobody, unless they were unbelievably lucky. Let's just give it our best shot tomorrow and see what happens."

"Yes, you're right. We will see what tomorrow brings."

When they entered the cabin, everyone else was in bed, sound asleep or very close to it. Andrew sat on the edge of his bunk and discarded his shoes. He stood up and automatically removed his pants. He barely remembered sliding his feet into the cold bottom of the bed and curling up as he wrapped himself in the arms of the sleep fairy.

The next morning was a repeat of the same routine. All the divers ate breakfast and were standing at dockside by 8 A.M. It was another cold, damp and dreary day. Clouds covered the lake as far as you could see. No one was looking forward to getting into his still-damp wet suit and sinking below the 40-degree surface water.

The divers continued the underwater patterns all day, except for a small lunch break. The sandwiches they packed were dry and tasteless. The coffee reminded Andrew of his Army days. Drinking out of a canteen cup has its own distinctive aroma. They would call it the 'metal blend' coffee. Still, it was a chance to warm up somewhat by the blazing fire. Each man took his turn at the underwater search. Each time that a diver returned to the surface, he simply shook his head 'no'.

By 4:30 P.M. the search had moved out into the lake a good distance, far beyond the area that was established as the starting point. Andrew planned that as soon as Otto surfaced, they would call it a day. He yelled out to Donald to come in when Otto was finished. Donald waved in agreement. Ten minutes later, Otto came up. Donald towed him into shore, hoping that the one last look might be the lucky one. Otto floated up to the shoreline as he hung onto the boat transom. Face down in the water; he casually floated there for several minutes.

Michael walked out in the waist deep water and turned Otto over to make sure he was all right. Otto rolled over like a seal at play and lay there with the regulator in his mouth. Donald had climbed out of the boat and was now standing on the other side of Otto. He reached down and pulled the regulator out of Otto's mouth. There was a gush of air and steam billowed out. Otto didn't respond, only exhaled long spouting clouds of steam.

"Somebody help me. I have to pee!" Everyone broke up as they helped Otto to his feet and assisted him in removing his fins.

Donald joked. "You got to pee; you got to hold it. My hands are too cold."

The boat ride back was less gloomy than the day before. The divers were fatigued, but they knew their search was approaching an end point. The entire group felt they had given their fair share of effort. Even if the goal had not been achieved, it was likely that no one would have done it more successfully.

The weather was beginning to turn wintry again, as they docked the boat. Another storm was moving up the lake. After the boats were pulled from the water and the equipment was hauled up to the cabin, Andrew went back to his boat for a small camera bag he had brought along. He had shot seven minutes of eight-millimeter movie film, near the site where the fishing gear was found. He gazed up at the cabin where the fishing gear had been placed. He looked down at the two rolls of film. "Not much for 80 hours of labor and a life time of marriage."

He walked to the cabin and joined the dive team. They had finished packing their equipment and had stacked it neatly outside the cabin. There would be time to reflect while they waited for the truck to arrive.

It was quiet in the cabin. The door was kept open slightly while the stove was allowed to burn out. Each diver was lying in his bunk, staring into space, with their booted feet slung over the foot rails. The heavy winter jackets they wore were loosely buttoned. Hands were clasped on their stomachs or tucked under their sides. There was a lot serious thought that late afternoon.

Andrew and his dive team returned home without incident. The airline people kept their word and allowed the team and all dive equipment to travel without a hassle. The rough part for Andrew was about to begin.

Andrew called the wives from his apartment and promised to meet them the same evening. His conversation was brief. Generally, he told them the team had failed to find the men, and all they had recovered was some fishing tackle. After the calls were made, he decided to crash for several hours. Then, he would face the families and tell them the details of the trip.

Andrew met the families at 6:30 P.M. to show his short eight-millimeter movie, and he provided a graphic picture of the dive area. They listened attentively and asked a few direct questions. They had all resigned themselves to the fact no one might find the missing men. They would have to wait until summer of next year with hope evidence of the men might surface.

Andrew kept track of the families for a few years, but to his knowledge, the remaining husbands were not found. The families went their separate ways and somehow created new lives. Andrew still retains the image of their blighted faces in the deep recesses of his mind. He always felt the story was incomplete. A sorrowful mystery that had no real closure; but then, that's how life sometimes deals the hand.

Andrew leaned forward to rise from his office chair. The sun streaming in the window was radiant and reassuring, but the glare forced him to again curtail his reminiscing. He pushed off from the armrests with an audible grunt. "A back, a back." He said. "My kingdom for a back." It didn't help, it seldom did.

As he walked around the chair he stamped his feet, trying to stretch out. He stood with one hand on his chair as if he were posing for a portrait and paused. The office elevator made a ding-dong sound, and the doors opened. Andrew crossed the room and pulled open his office blinds. It was the security guard who reached around the doorframe and turned the elevator key to the all-access position. The security guard waved to Andrew through the glass window and said, "Just turning on the elevator, Mr. Boyd. Folks will be coming up soon. Have a nice day."

Andrew stood in his office door and returned the greeting.

"You too... don't forget to take your heart pill."

Andrew took a step out of his door and looked around the spacious outer office checking to see if someone had come in while he was daydreaming.

"No," he thought. "I'm the only one dumb enough to stay here overnight."

Sometimes his absentminded security guard would bring people up to the office before it officially opened. That would break company policy. File drawers and computers held sensitive business details and some items were government classified. Andrew had never pressed the issue or made a big thing out of the guard's need to be accommodating. So far, only personnel cleared to be there had violated the early arrivals. The elevator, when stopped at ground level, would not move without a scan of a personal ID card. The elevator measured the total weight, based on the ID card information, and would then take a thermograph reading for the indicated number of people. If personnel arrived too early, they waited in the lower lobby. The workday would begin in a matter of minutes. There would be no more time to reflect back to the fall and winter of 1969. Andrew knew full well these times were not like the good old days he has just spent three hours thinking about.

Life in his beloved United States would never be the same. Recently a reporter asked him, "You have been all over the world. In places where there is unrest. Is war the worst thing you have ever dealt with? Andrew thought for a moment and said, "I heard a quote when I was a child. I don't know who said it. It may have been 'Thyestes' of Greek mythology. 'Worse than war is the fear of war.' After 9-11, no matter what happens in the near future we will always have the fear of war on some level. How we deal with it is up to each individual."

Andrew Boyd has struggled with demons created by his surroundings and himself. At this point in his life he has managed to suppress those demons with shear tenacity. Fear of the dark was the demon of his childhood. Fear had taken many shapes, always in substitution of being vulnerable. His answer thus far, is strength of mind to suppress the fear. But pushing the outer limit of the envelope is not the solution; it only disguises the fear, which reappears in another form. As his life passes through each stage of maturity he replaces one fear with another often less dominant. He will in the future find peace in his soul. But, for now, life has a tendency to redefine itself with each passing decade. The fears at age twenty-nine are not the same as the fears of fifty-five or seventy-five.

Andrew turned and sat on the edge of one of the computer desks. He folded his arms and stared at the floor indicator above the elevator. He thought "One of these days, I'm going to revisit my life from 1970 on. The treasure hunt, the salvage operation in the Caymans and..."

Before he could finish the thought, three computer monitors behind him sprang to life. They started to download information from the field offices. The elevator dinged again. Andrew leaned over one of the computer keyboards and said quietly to himself, "and then who knows? Maybe I'll have time tomorrow morning to think about the years 1970 up to, well, when ever."

About The Author

Richard Bennett was born in Milwaukee, Wisconsin. In August of 1954 he ventured into a stone Quarry in Okauchee Wisconsin. From that day on he has spent 3500 working days (nearly 7000 hours) underwater. Bennett has taught scuba for more than 37 years as a certified diving instructor and logged more than 7700 dives in both sport and commercial diving. By 1957, with the purchase of a complete set of diving equipment including a pull over neoprene wet suit he was ready for business. He formed a small diving business named Underwater Salvage Co. with three of his best friends. They salvaged lead rifle shot from Lake Michigan and scrubbed boat bottoms while using scuba. In northern Wisconsin they pulled sunken trees from lakes.

For the next three years they would recover everything from sailboat centerboards, false teeth, jewelry, fishing tackle and a list too long to print. The least desirable task was his volunteer *victims recovery* work for the municipalities. After a dozen or more body recoveries, he decided to train agency divers to handle the sad undertaking. The Milwaukee Medical Examiners Office recruited him as a diving accident consultant in 1986 and is still active at present.

Richard's vocation as a diving instructor began in 1964 at Sea & Ski Inc., a sporting goods store in Milwaukee. He was an accomplished scuba diver for nearly ten years before being hired to run the dive center at the store. The summer of 1966 gave him two international scuba instructor certifications, PADI and NASDS. His first commercial diving assignment to pay over $500.00 came with a Lloyds of London insurance claim in 1967. That same year he directed and filmed the first underwater student training film used to instruct basic divers. The 1968-69 season occupied much of Richard's time as a salvage diver of the wreck of the Alvin Clark. The summer months of 68-69 also required his attention for the deep dive in Big Green Lake. The spring of 1970s found him as general Manager and Chief Diving Office for a Cayman Island treasure corporation named Green Dolphin Ltd. Bennett signed a two-year contract to salvage sunken eighteen-century ships.

About the Author continued

In the spring of 1974 Richard Bennett incorporated Bennett Academy of Ski & Scuba Inc. It grew to a three-store chain by 1980. The store taught scuba, windsurfing, fencing and cross country skiing.
An inaugural part of the store program was international diving tours. Richard conducted more than 90 global trips. Further service included acting as an advisory board member for the Sea Grant program at the University of Wisconsin from 1994 to 2000, and a course in videography for the University of Wisconsin Milwaukee from 1993 to 1998.

He retired from the day-to-day activities of the dive business in 1998 and remains an active master scuba diver trainer instructor. In 1999 he became the founding chairman of the Great Lakes Alliance of Water Safety. At the writing of this book Richard was on the Advisory board of the Great Lake Research Center. He is committed to the dive business by making himself available as a diving consultant and expert witness.

A target date of November 15, 2005 is set for his second book, ***Deep Quest II The Island.*** In the new book by Richard Thomas Bennett he continues the undersea adventures. Searching for the "Treasure of Poverty Island" in Lake Michigan and motors a US Navy LCM6 land ing craft to the Cayman islands in search of more sunken treasure. Share the joy as he brings up the first of several 18th centry cannons. Imagine the fear as Andrew Boyd struggles to free himself from the pull of an underwater suction pump four feet in diameter. Feel the tension as the huge brass blades draw him closer.

Experience the apprehension as Boyd fights to save the landing craft from crashing into a barrier reef on Little Cayman Island.

"Never believe everything you fear"

"Devotion to the protection of our watery planet cannot be a momentary inspiration; it must be a life long obligation."

Richard T. Bennett

Certificate of Appreciation

Manta Publishing Co.

Your name

Address

City

State   Zip Code

E-Mail address

In reconition of becoming a valued customer of Manta Publishing Company we will send you a Free detailed Chronology of the " Treasure of Poverty island." A legendary story featured on NBC's hit television series "Unsolved Mysteries." A saga covered extensively in Richard Bennett next book "Deep Quest II - The Island" due to be published in 2005.
Send this certificate in Now while supplies last.

Send certificate to:
Manta Publishing Company
11609 W. Vliet Street
Wauwatosa Wi. 53226

Web site www.deepquestproductions.com
Phone 414-302-0290

Cut Here